**Praise for the *New York Times* Bestselling
Ghost Hunter Mystery Series**

"Fabulously entertaining.... The setup is marvelous, the pace is quick, and the stakes are high; Laurie wastes no time plunging you straight into the center of the action and doesn't pause to let you catch your breath until she's got you good and hooked." —The Season for Romance

"A series that combines suspenseful tension with humor, romance, and mystery."   —Kings River Life Magazine

"Filled with laugh-out-loud moments and nail-biting, hair-raising tension, this fast-paced, action-packed ghost story will keep readers hooked from beginning to end."
—Fresh Fiction

"Paranormal mystery fans, look no further."
—SciFiChick.com

"Fabulously entertaining.... [Laurie] has a genuine talent for creating unique spirits with compelling origin stories and then using those creations to scare ... her characters and her readers alike." —The Maine Suspect

"Paranormal thrills and chills ... [and] a healthy dose of fun and romance."   —Once Upon a Romance

continued ...

ALSO BY VICTORIA LAURIE

The Ghost Hunter Mystery Series

What's a Ghoul to Do?
Demons Are a Ghoul's Best Friend
Ghouls Just Haunt to Have Fun
Ghouls Gone Wild
Ghouls, Ghouls, Ghouls
Ghoul, Interrupted
What a Ghoul Wants

The Psychic Eye Mystery Series

Abby Cooper, Psychic Eye
Better Read Than Dead
A Vision of Murder
Killer Insight
Crime Seen
Death Perception
Doom with a View
A Glimpse of Evil
Vision Impossible
Lethal Outlook
Deadly Forecast

THE GHOUL
NEXT DOOR

A GHOST HUNTER MYSTERY

Victoria Laurie

AN OBSIDIAN MYSTERY

OBSIDIAN
Published by the Penguin Group
Penguin Group (USA) LLC, 375 Hudson Street,
New York, New York 10014

USA | Canada | UK | Ireland | Australia | New Zealand | India | South Africa | China
penguin.com
A Penguin Random House Company

First published by Obsidian, an imprint of New American Library,
a division of Penguin Group (USA) LLC

First Printing, January 2014

ISBN 978-0-451-24060-6

Printed in the United States of America
10 9 8 7 6 5 4 3 2 1

For Dr. Stephen Pap.

RIP my dear friend.

Acknowledgments

I'm not gonna lie. This is my third pass at writing these. Normally, I look forward to kicking out the acknowledgments—when do you ever get such an awesome chance to tell all the amazing people in your life how much you love them?

But this time it's different. This time . . . it's just hard.

Like most of my characters, Dr. Steven Sable is based on a real guy. Years ago, about the time my agent and I were pitching the idea of a ghostbusting mystery series to my publisher, I slipped off the back porch steps and broke my hand. The break was a bad one, which required surgery, and so the hospital placed me with one of their top guys, Dr. Stephen Pap.

From the minute I met "Pappy," I liked him. He was tall and suave and he had the sexiest accent. I had a serious crush from our first meeting. When he learned that I was a writer on a deadline, he took the greatest care to make sure that I'd be back to typing in no time. He had one of the best bedside manners of any doctor I've ever met.

Initially, I thought a character based on him would make the perfect love match for M.J., and he allowed me the indulgence. I also believe he was secretly pleased by it. At least I hope so.

In the two years following my hand surgery, Stephen

and I kept in touch, and I soon learned that he was head over heels for a beautiful woman named Holly. The two were married shortly thereafter, and by the time I left Boston back in 2006, they were expecting their first child. I remember talking to Pappy on the phone a few days before my move, and I remember thinking how happy and content he sounded. He had the world by the tail.

A year ago last August, Stephen sent me an e-mail. He wanted a psychic reading. I hadn't heard from him in years, and I was insanely busy with a recent move and deadlines, so I told him to wait a few weeks until I could clear my schedule. I wish so much that I'd listened to my gut, which told me to talk to him sooner.

Anyway, the moment I heard his voice on the phone during our session, I knew something was terribly wrong. He sounded eighty years old, his voice so thin that it was barely above a whisper, and he had difficulty forming words. He told me he was sick with some mysterious disease that no one could diagnose. I remember asking him if they'd tested him for ALS—Lou Gehrig's disease. He insisted they had and had ruled it out.

He asked me if there was hope, and when I looked at his energy, I saw something amazing. Sometime in the very early spring, I saw him so healthy and full of life that I could hardly believe the transformation. I told him that I didn't know what he had, but I thought he'd be feeling incredible by March or April. He asked me if he'd be well enough to return to his practice—he'd had to abandon it as he was bed bound—and I told him that I didn't see him doing that, but I did see him doing something else like consulting and helping people in a different way. I couldn't figure out what his new role would be, but I knew he'd love it whatever it was.

But then I saw something odd in the ether. I saw that

he and his wife were going to separate. It felt abrupt and sudden and I couldn't quite account for it. I could only feel her exhaustion, then his amazing transformation, then a separation. I asked him how he was getting on with her, and he replied, "Better than ever. She's my angel. I couldn't do this without her."

I decided not to tell Stephen about the separation—reasoning that I could very well be misinterpreting. Instead I told him to hang in there and continue to look for an accurate diagnosis. I also told him to keep me in the loop about his health.

The following February when I was about halfway through writing this book, Stephen was very much on my mind. I realized I'd never gotten an update from him, so I reached out with an e-mail of my own. His reply was so sweetly simple, it completely and utterly broke my heart. "Sorry to have bad news," he wrote. "I am dying of ALS. I have weeks to live. It was wonderful to enjoy your friendship; take care of yourself and live life to the fullest. My best to you and your family. Stephen."

Stephen died just three weeks later.

Later, when I had a chance to think about it, I realized that all the odd little pieces of his reading could now slide into place. His amazing "recovery" wasn't a physical recovery—it was his crossing over. And the exhaustion of his wife and then their separation also made absolute sense. So much so that it's a wonder I didn't put the pieces together sooner, but I adored Stephen, and I'm quite certain that, because of my fondness for him, I avoided looking too deeply into the ether about his chances for survival. I just assumed that this amazing man, whom I'd only known to have so much vitality and *life*, couldn't be felled by a mere illness. Of course he'd recover.

The moment I got the news of his passing, however,

this book came to a standstill. I was gutted. Just gutted by the loss. I felt a terrible guilt for not penciling him into my schedule sooner, and for not putting the pieces together during his reading. I wanted to wallow in a well of self-pity and sadness and ask all those questions of "WHY?!!" because he wasn't just a good man—he was amazing and it was SO unfair that this young, vibrant, smart, funny, nurturing doctor with three young children, and a beautiful wife, and patients to cure, and a life to live was taken so abruptly from the world.

And then Stephen sent me a sign that I simply couldn't ignore. He sent me several, in fact, each one a little miracle in and of itself, and I realized he was giving me a little kick in the butt to get on with my own life—to live it to the fullest. I owed him that. In fact, that was the least I could do. So I got on with the book, determined to finish the damn thing.

It took a long time. Sometimes I'd write only a paragraph a day. And I worried constantly about his portrayal. Would he be flattered or offended? Would he be amused or insulted? More signs from Stephen on the other side came and I realized that I couldn't worry about it. I'd just have to write the book I wanted and finish it.

And here is the result. Overall, I'm actually quite pleased with it. Especially the final scene. (No peeking!) It took weeks to work up the courage to write those last few pages, but when I did, I felt Stephen so present, peeking over my shoulder, saying, "Good job, Victoria."

I get fewer signs from Stephen these days. I'm sure he's quite busy over there, but sometimes when I'm out for a run, I'll feel him "pop" into my mind to say hello. I've also followed his advice to live life to the fullest— big-time—and I think he's at least proud of me for that.

So these acknowledgments are mostly all about Stephen, who was a lovely, lovely man, and is now a lovely,

lovely soul. If you read these words and you're a Steven Sable fan, send my friend Pappy a wave; I think he'd get a real kick out of it. ☺

While I'm here, allow me to quickly acknowledge all of the amazing people who helped me get through the days when writing about M.J. and Steven felt impossible:

My amazing editor, Sandra Harding, thank you sooooo much for your patience and kindness. You didn't once push me even though I was crazy late with this manuscript. You just let me whittle away at it the best I could until I could pull it together. It means the world to me and I thank you.

Thank you also to my amazing team at New American Library: Elizabeth Bistrow, Kayleigh Clark, Sharon Gamboa, Michele Alpern, Stanley Chow, and Claire Zion.

My agent, Jim McCarthy, who patiently took every weepy phone call and just kept reiterating his belief in me. There's no way I could have gotten to the end without you. It's like Michelle Rowen says, "Jim McCarthy, you is made of *magic*!"

Katie Coppedge . . . can I just write "No words" here? Because there ARE NO WORDS to describe how grateful I am for your friendship, understanding, and sage advice. You da bestest, my BFF. And I luffs you.

Sandy Upham. NO WORDS! Other than I love you, and look forward every day to our chats. Best sister EVER!

Team Lo (Katie Coppedge, Karen Ditmars, Leanne Tierney): ladies, you are—each of you—my personal heroes, and I'm beeeeyond lucky to know you and call you friends.

Brian G., I love you. Thank you for coming to find me in Austin. (And, Stephen, thank you, thank you, thank you for sending him back to me.)

Additional thanks go to: Nicole Gray, Steve McGrory, Matt and Mike Morrill, Hilary Laurie, Nora, Bob, and Mike Brosseau, Silas Hudson, Thomas Robinson, Laurie Proux, Drue Rowean, Suzanne Parsons, Betty and Pippa Stocking, John Kwaitkowski, Matt McDougall, Sally Woods, Anne Kimbol, McKenna Jordan, Jennifer Melkonian, Shannon Anderson, Juan Tamayo, Molly Boyle, Martha Bushko, Juliet Blackwell, Nicole Peeler, and Sophie Littlefield.

You guys remind me every day what living life to the fullest is all about. Love you and I thank you.

Chapter 1

Being a psychic medium definitely has its downers. As a group, we're a pretty haunted lot. (Yes, I went there. . . .) Many, if not most, of us had troubled childhoods that caused us to develop a sixth sense in order to cope. And I'm no exception. My mother died on an autumn morning when I was eleven, and in his subsequent grief, my father turned to the bottle and his work. In many ways I lost both parents that day.

It took years, but Daddy finally let go of the grip he had on his daily half gallon of vodka and sought help. He's been sober for about sixteen years now, but the residual damage to our relationship remains. During my teenage years we fought constantly. In fact, I spent most of my junior and senior years of high school at my best friend Gilley Gillespie's house, being looked after by Gil's wonderful mother, who'd been treating me like one of her own from the moment my own mama passed away.

Things didn't improve even after high school when Gil and I moved from Valdosta, Georgia, to Boston.

Daddy and I just couldn't seem to make peace even with those twelve hundred miles separating us. And every visit back to Valdosta thereafter was torture for me—usually ending with an early flight home to Boston. Recently, however, that's changed, and I can safely say that these days we've never gotten along better. Although that could be because we haven't spoken to each other since I started showcasing my talents on TV.

Daddy was willing to tolerate my rather, as he put it, "disturbing" ability to talk to the dead as long as I didn't make a public spectacle of myself. Nearly two years ago I'd done a cable special on haunted objects, and since then I've landed a nice contract working on my own ghostbusting cable TV series, called *Ghoul Getters*. News of my success on the airwaves spread like wildfire in Valdosta, fueled no doubt by Mrs. Gillespie, who's crazy proud of both Gilley and me. The consequences, however, are that now the only acknowledgments I get from Daddy are a Christmas present (picked out by his secretary) and a birthday card (also picked out by his secretary) with a check inside (probably forged by his secretary).

And as I brought the mail inside my office in Boston, so happy to be home again after a grueling four-month filming schedule, my mood dampened the moment I saw the return address on a small package mixed in with the bills and ads.

"Well, I guess my birthday *is* next week," I said with a sigh, passing through the inner lobby of the little office space I rent out on Mass Avenue, about three blocks away from my condo. After setting the other mail aside, I searched my desk for a pair of scissors.

"Come 'ere!" I heard a squeaky voice cry.

"In a sec, baby," I replied.

"Come 'ere!" the voice insisted.

I ignored the command and fished around the drawer, finally coming up with the scissors, and began to carefully cut through the package.

"Come 'ere! Come 'ere! *Come 'ere!*"

I share my office (and my condo, and my life) with a feathered, red-tailed African gray parrot named Doc—whom I've had since fifth grade. He's adorably sweet, funny, and maybe a teensy bit demanding. "I'm busy, honey," I told him.

Doc climbed along the bars to exit the little door of his cage and make it up to the roof—which houses a nice play stand, and where he could perch and have a better view of what I was fiddling with. "What do you do?" he asked. Doc speaks better English than most toddlers.

"Opening a package." At this point I got the thing opened and managed to pull out a square black box with gold lettering on top, which indicated it'd come from one of the finer jewelry stores in Valdosta—my hometown. Lifting the lid, I sucked in a breath when I took notice of an absolutely beautiful gold charm bracelet with three charms—a golden parrot, a small happy ghost, and a heart. For a moment I just stared at the gift, completely taken by surprise. "What're you up to?" Doc called, trying to get my attention again.

I realized I had my back to him, so I turned and lifted the beautiful bracelet up for him to see. He cocked his head curiously.

"What do you think?" I asked him.

Doc blew me a really good raspberry.

"Everyone's a critic," I laughed. But I went back to staring at the charm with a mixture of bewilderment and delight, while Doc added to the raspberry a long litany of clucks, whistles, and happy chirps.

Doc's been with me since right after Mama died. My

paternal grandmother had given him to me after my mother's passing to help bring me out of the terrible grief I was silently suffering.

The baby parrot was like a beacon of light in a world filled only with heartbreak. My mother had been the kindest, most wonderful and loving person I'd ever known, and her loss devastated me right into muteness. I spoke not one word for many months after her funeral. Even when I fell and broke a finger, I cried silently, unable to free my vocal cords from the crushing weight of my grief. Doc changed all that. Like a phoenix he pulled me from the ashes, and slowly, with his help and love of mimicry, I healed and started talking again. But the chatty, charming bird seemed to have no effect on Daddy. And I'll never understand why, but right from the start Daddy had seemed to resent my delightful pet. In fact, he'd tolerated Doc a lot like he'd tolerated my ability to talk to dead people . . . as in he'd barely tolerated him at all.

So, opening Daddy's gift to reveal something so lovely and thoughtful as a parrot charm and a ghost charm was a real surprise. And the heart was also an out-of-character choice from Daddy. He just wasn't sentimental or outwardly emotive. He was more like a closed door that I'd long since given up knocking on.

For a second I thought that it simply must have been his secretary's choice, but she'd never shown one shred of sensitivity for me. Previous gifts were simplistic items, like a pair of candlesticks, or a paperweight, or a picture frame. I'd long thought of Daddy's secretary of twenty years, Willamina, as a harsh, cold woman who preferred dressing all in black except for the bloodred lipstick she coated her thin lips with.

Her style made her look as if she were perpetually in mourning, and given how my mother's death had turned

Daddy into such a terribly cold and bitter person, I found some irony in that.

At last I tore my eyes away from the charm and fished around inside the envelope it'd come in, finding a card there too. I opened it to read a lovely handwritten note in beautiful cursive, wishing me the happiest of birthdays and hoping to catch up soon. The handwriting wasn't anyone's I recognized, but the signature was clearly Daddy's. And not the forged signature of his secretary, but Daddy's real scraggly scrawl, which added even more mystery to the gift.

I moved to my desk and sat down, because I needed to sit down. Slipping the bracelet on, I stared at it and wondered first what was going on with Daddy, and second, how should I respond to such a lovely, thoughtful gift?

The average normal person would've immediately picked up the phone to call and thank her father for the kindness, but as you may have guessed, I'm not exactly normal. There were too many years of missed opportunities, broken promises, harsh words, and judgmental attitudes to be swept aside by a bit of precious metal.

Still, after taking off the bracelet to set it gently back inside the box, I did reach for the phone. "Sweet baby Jesus, gurl! Why're you calling me so early?" Gilley answered by way of greeting.

"I got a birthday package from Daddy," I said, getting right to the point.

Gilley yawned, and I could imagine him bleary-eyed and mop-headed, tangled in his bedcovers. "Let me guess: This year's check is for two hundred, right?"

"No. It's not a check."

"His secretary just sent a card? Jeez, M.J., why does that man even bother anymore? I'll call Ma. She'll make sure you get a nice present on your birthday."

I smiled. Mrs. Gillespie had been making sure I received lovely gifts on my birthday for twenty-two years now, and she never needed prompting from her son, either. "No, Gil, you don't understand. Daddy sent me a really nice gift."

That won me another yawn. "Black leather gloves?"

"A solid gold charm bracelet with three charms: a parrot, a heart, and a little Casper ghost."

Gilley was silent for about five seconds. "Is your dad sick?"

I leaned back in my chair and threw an arm over my eyes. "I have no idea. We haven't spoken in almost a year and a half."

"Leave it to me," Gil said. "I'll call Ma and get the scoop." Mrs. Gillespie was tied to all the gossip in our hometown.

I hung up with Gilley but kept my arm over my eyes. What if Daddy *was* sick? What if he was *really* sick? I knew that with my abilities I could probably find out the answer, but I was too chicken. There was a part of me that didn't want to know, because I'd already lived through one parent's terminal illness, and it'd nearly been my undoing.

Doc began singing a Village People song and I knew he was trying to coax me out of the distressed state I was in, but my mind was going in circles and I couldn't pay attention to him at the moment. Instead I turned my chair around, propped my feet up on the windowsill, and went back to laying my arm over my eyes. After working for much of the last year in the middle of the night, I find that I think better in the dark.

"M.J.? Are you all right?" a voice asked several minutes later.

With Doc's singing and my whirling mind I hadn't heard the front door open. What's more, as I stiffened and sat up in the chair, I realized I recognized that voice. The day suddenly went from disconcerting to crazy weird. Turning slowly to the front, I took in the tall, dark, and incredibly handsome man standing in my doorway and had to work hard to appear calm and nonchalant. "Hello, Steven," I said. "What brings you by?"

My ex-boyfriend smiled in that way that'd always made my heart quicken . . . okay . . . still makes my heart quicken. Also, the bastard had the gall to smell really good too. "How've you been?" he asked, his voice deep and rich, like a great cup of coffee.

I felt my head bobbing. "Good . . . good. You?"

"Good."

"Good."

There was a bit of an awkward pause and then the door opened again and in walked my current boyfriend, Heath—who also happens to be rather tall, dark, and seriously hunky.

Things went from awkward and weird to *Are you kidding me, universe?*

Heath said nothing; he simply came in wearing a smile, took one look at Steven, darted his eyes to me, back to Steven, then back to me as if to say, *"Seriously?"*

I pretended not to notice. Oh, and I also held in the urge to run out of there as fast as my feet could carry me. "Steven, you remember Heath. Heath—Steven. Steven—Heath."

The two surveyed each other with narrowed eyes and forced smiles. I had a moment to compare the two of them side by side and it occurred to me that as similar as they are in the basics of black hair, dark eyes, and tall stature, they're still strikingly different. Steven's shoulders are broad and his chest is very defined, while his legs are very long. His face is also distinctly European in structure with a wide brow and square features, while

Heath's face is very angled with high cheekbones and deep-set eyes. His frame is also more proportional and corded with lean muscle. In other words, neither was the kind of guy you'd kick out of bed for eating crackers . . . at least not until after you'd had your way with him.

While the men stared each other down, I cleared my throat and shuffled a few things around on my desk, and that's when Heath must've noticed the charm bracelet I'd set back in the box. "What's that?" he demanded, pointing to the box on my desk. "You giving her presents now, Sable?"

Steven's brow furrowed. "Pardon?"

Hastily I put the top of the box back on to cover the gift. "It's from my father, Heath," I explained quickly.

"For your birthday," Steven said with a knowing nod. "That was nice of him."

I noticed Heath paled a little. "Today's your birthday?" he blurted out; then his face flushed red. "I mean, yeah, totally. Happy birthday, honey! I came to take you to a birthday breakfast!" Glancing back at Steven, he said, "My gift's in the car."

Steven smiled (a bit evilly, I thought). "Her birthday is next week, Whitefeather. The eleventh. Might want to mark that down on your calendar."

"What brings you by, Steven?" I nearly screeched, desperate to change the topic before this came to blows, and judging by the furious expression on Heath's face— we weren't far from that.

Steven and Heath glared at each other for a few more seconds before my ex turned back to me and said, "I need your help."

"With what?"

"A haunting."

That took me by surprise . . . much like the entire morning. I waved at a chair and he came forward and took the seat directly across from me. Heath grabbed the other chair and brought it around the desk to park it right next to mine. I held in a sigh, hoping there'd be no suggestion from either of them of lowered zippers and a measuring tape before the conversation was at an end. "Where?" I asked, pulling a pad forward to write on.

"It's not a where," Steven said, and for the first time I could see that his eyes were lined with worry. "It's a who."

I blinked. "Who what?" (I may have been a little off my game from all the testosterone fumes.)

Steven shifted in his seat, and I suddenly noticed how nervous he was. Coming to me hadn't been something he'd done on a whim. He'd had to talk himself into it. "It's not a place that's haunted. It's a person. My fiancée's brother. We think he's possessed."

"Your *fiancée*?" I gasped at the same time that Heath said, "He's possessed?"

Heath turned narrowed eyes on me while the corners of Steven's mouth quirked, and that rather big ego that'd been a part of the reason I'd left him came shining to life again. "Yes. To both of you," he said. (But I thought he looked a bit smugly at me.)

"Well . . . er . . . ," I sputtered, doodling large circles on the notepad while I tried to collect myself. (He was getting married? We'd only been broken up for a few months! What the hell?) "Congratulations!" I said. Perhaps a bit too enthusiastically.

"Why do you think this guy's possessed?" Heath asked.

Steven sighed and rubbed the stubble on his chin. "You have to see it to believe it," he said. "But I'm telling you, there is a ghost haunting this young man. My fiancée, Courtney, can tell you about it better than me. I'd like to introduce you if you're interested in taking on the case."

"Possession isn't exactly our area of expertise," I said. No *way* was I getting involved in this. (Okay, so really, no *way* was I meeting his fiancée!)

"It wouldn't hurt to meet her and talk about it," Heath said, never once turning his face away from Steven. "Is Courtney nearby?"

I felt my posture stiffen. Again the corners of Steven's mouth quirked. "She's at work at the hospital."

Now my smile was forced. "Oh? Is she a candy striper or something?" (Please, oh, please let her job be unimpressive!)

"Surgeon," Steven said.

(Dammit!)

"General surgeon?" I asked. Before a devastating injury to his hand, Steven had once been one of the best heart surgeons in the world. Maybe he'd met another heart surgeon he was attracted to but secretly competitive with. Maybe their competitive nature would eventually escalate to the point that they'd hate each other. . . .

"Neurosurgeon," he said.

(Double-dammit!)

"Ah," Heath said smugly. "A brain surgeon. That's cool."

I was sincerely regretting not having dashed out of the room ten minutes earlier. "Well, I'm sure she's lovely," I said. No one in the room believed me. "And while I'd *really* like to meet her, we're just coming off a crazy intense shooting schedule and I'm not sure we'll have time on this hiatus to take on any new cases."

Steven cocked his head. "That's not what your Facebook page says. Forgive me for keeping tabs on you," he said with a sheepish grin, "but I needed your help and looked online to see where in the world you were. I was surprised to find you back here in Boston, and your status this morning said that you couldn't wait to get back to work on some regular cases."

(A dammit three-peat!)

"We can at least meet her, Em," Heath said agreeably. I wanted to choke him. "How about dinner tonight?"

"That'd be great," Steven said, already standing up. "Say around seven?"

"Seven thirty would be better," Heath said (just to be a pain in the butt, I thought).

Steven smiled tightly. "Of course. Courtney will be coming off a twenty-four-hour shift, but if it's better for you . . ."

Heath wavered and I was still looking for a way out of this. "We can probably make seven," he said.

"Good," Steven said, and with that, he turned and headed to the door. Before exiting, he paused and turned back to look at me. "We can meet at the place I took you to on our first date. Do you remember?"

I felt my posture stiffen again. At this rate I'd need the Jaws of Life to ever get myself to relax again. "I do."

"Excellent," Steven said. "See you." And with that, he was gone.

It took me much of the next hour to get my head around the fact that my ex-boyfriend was engaged. I felt a mix of emotions, all of them small and petty.

I did my best to hide them from Heath, but he was on to me. "Wanna talk about it?" he asked after my eleven-tieth sigh.

I forced a smile. "Nope."

"Wanna go for a run?" he asked next.

I sat up in my chair. A run was exactly what I needed. "Yes," I said. "I think I would."

Heath and I closed up the office and headed to my condo, which was practically next door, to change. I live in a city just outside of Boston called Arlington. I like it because it still has the feel of living in the city but carries a little more greenery. My condo sits in a fairly nondescript building on Mass Avenue, with my unit tucked nicely in the back away from the sounds of traffic. Gilley owns the condo one floor below mine, and often cooks me breakfast. When Heath and I entered my condo, I didn't hear any noises coming from downstairs—no music or the loud clomping of footsteps—and I wondered if he'd gone out. Heath and I changed and hit the trail about a half mile from my home.

My boyfriend is an incredible athlete. He can run for days and barely look winded. He's lean and strong and pushes me to run faster and farther. As we were training for a half marathon in the next few weeks, I appreciated his presence. I also appreciated that he doesn't talk a lot on the trail.

The run was just what I needed. I was able to sort out a lot of my feelings about Steven during the hour run, and put many of those feelings that were hurtful into perspective. I wondered if Steven had felt all of what I was going through when he learned that I was falling for Heath. I hadn't cheated on Steven with Heath—but I'd come close. Steven had been incredibly mature and understanding about it too. I remember seeing the surprise in his eyes when I told him that I didn't think it was working out between us, but I could tell that he wasn't as shocked by the fact that I was breaking up with him as much as he was surprised that my heart had already moved on to someone else.

It made me feel even worse about the way I'd handled the situation, and I knew I couldn't fault Steven for moving on so quickly either.

Still, the truth was that it hurt a little to learn that he hadn't just moved on—he'd committed. A subtle difference maybe, but one that stung.

As Heath and I finished the seven-mile loop, he fiddled with his watch and held his hand high. "Eight-minute mile, girl! Way to go!"

I blinked. The fastest we'd ever done that loop was an eight-fifteen average pace. And although I was winded and sweaty, I hadn't felt the pain of pushing myself to a faster time. "Are you for real?" I asked him.

He showed me the watch. "You did good, babe. You'll be running times in the sevens before you know it." He added a hug and I realized right then that I'd been wasting a lot of time feeling upset about Steven when I'd already landed the best guy ever. Heath was always there for me, in every way. He understood me like Steven never had, and he watched over me without hovering, or being needy. He was also a fellow medium, and that was a whole other side of me that needed no explanation for Heath.

"Love you," I whispered and squeezed him tight.

Heath chuckled and kissed the top of my head. "That's a relief," he said. "I was beginning to worry you might have regrets about us ever since Sable walked through the door."

I sighed. "If I had any, it was only because of the way I handled the breakup." That was a teensy bit of a lie, but Heath didn't need to know that.

Heath let go of me and took my hand. "Come on, let's get some coffee."

Now, I know it sounds weird to go for coffee after a hot, sweaty run, but it was something that both Heath and I really enjoyed. Plus, even though it was late spring, the day was a little chilly. By the time we got to Mama Dell's Coffee Shop, we had both cooled down and were looking forward to the smooth, rich brew that she served.

Mama Dell is a dear friend of mine. Originally from South Carolina, Mama D. is a tiny woman with a bigger-than-life personality. In years past her coffee shop had done quite well in spite of the fact that her coffee tasted only slightly better than tar, and that almost directly across the street from her was a Dunkin' Donuts — a New England staple if ever there was one.

Somewhere along the line when I'd been in Europe hunting down spooks, some brave person had finally posted a review of Mama's coffee on Yelp. It hadn't been kind, but it'd been the truth. That'd sort of sparked a wave of similar reviews, but the funny thing was, almost all the negative reviews had been coupled with four stars, because everyone *loved* Mama Dell. What she lacked in brew know-how she more than made up for in personality.

Still, Mama D. was determined not to let those reviewers have the last Yelp. She flew to South America and took a course in coffee brewing from the best coffee bean growers in the world. Then she flew to Hawaii and cultivated relationships with some Kona Coffee growers. Finally, she even headed to Ethiopia and toured a few coffee plantations there too. She came back with an amalgamation of three signature blends, and now she's got so much business you can almost never get in the door before ten a.m.

It's a little quieter in the afternoons, and Heath and I found the place only modestly packed when we walked through the doors of the cozy café. Mama D.'s shop is full of kitschy touches. There's a large rack to the side of the front door where patrons who plan to have their coffee in can select a mug that matches their mood or personality. Against one wall is a huge bookcase stocked full of dog-eared paperback mysteries that Mama has collected over the years and chooses to share with her patrons. It works on the honor system, and it's a rare thing for a patron to borrow a book and not bring it back. It's far more likely that her customers actually add to the collection. Near the register is a large pastry case chock-full of tasty delights fresh baked that morning, from Mama's famous banana nut bread to fruit tarts created by her husband, known only as "the Captain."

Deeper inside the coffee shop are cozy seating areas, where overstuffed chairs, perfect for taking a load off or sinking into a good book, beckon all who enter. Mama D.'s clientele rarely tap away on computers or phones—that's frowned upon by Mama—and those that continue to resist the unspoken rule soon learn they'd be better suited to hanging out at Starbucks for such activities. Mama Dell's place is for relaxing, chatting with friends, enjoying the ambience, smooth coffee, and delicious pastry. It isn't a substitute workplace, and she makes sure her patrons know the difference.

I think that's the real reason she has such a loyal following. At Mama's you can completely relax, not stress yourself out by reading an e-mail, or seeing that your friends on Facebook are having a better time. Here you can unplug, and it's wonderful.

"Well, there's a sight for sore eyes!" I heard her call as Heath and I picked through the rack of mugs, hunting for just the right ones for our coffee.

I turned and saw her wiping her hands on a towel while she quick-stepped it over to me. "Afternoon, darlin'!" she sang as she wrapped me in a hug before turning to Heath to hug him too. "How y'all doin' today?"

I felt my shoulders relax. Mama D. has the loveliest Southern charm about her. She reminds me of home, and my own mama. "We're good, Mama D. You?"

"Oh, Lord!" she exclaimed. "What a morning it's been! The Captain's been with the architect all morning and I think his head's about to explode. We're going a little over budget, but we need the space."

Mama D. has plans to expand into the office space next door, as the rug dealer that'd previously occupied that space had gone out of business. If they go through with their plans, Mama D.'s will double its square footage.

Our host continued to chat happily at us as she crooked her finger for us to follow her over to the counter, where she ducked behind the pastry case and came up with two slabs of banana nut bread and her delicious honey butter without even waiting for our order. She then filled our cups and waved her hand at Heath when he tried to pay. I saw him put a ten in her tip jar.

And then she said, "Oh, do you know who came into the shop this morning, M.J.? Dr. Sable! And guess what! He's engaged! He showed me a picture of his fiancée, oh! What a pretty girl!"

All that tension that'd fallen away walked right back up my spine. Mama D. had set up my first date with Steven, and even though she knew we'd split up, she still remained a big fan of his. As she chatted on about how well he looked and how good it was to see him, I pushed a big old smile onto my face and nodded like a bobblehead.

"We saw him this morning," Heath said, subtly placing a hand on my lower back. "And we're meeting Steven and his fiancée for dinner."

Mama D. clapped her hands together. "That's wonderful! Oh, I'm so happy y'all are getting along so well."

I was grinding my teeth together so hard that I couldn't really respond, but for Mama D.'s sake I kept that big smile firmly planted on my face, and thankfully, a group of students approached the counter with mugs and hungry expressions. Heath and I managed to move off without looking rude.

We found a love seat near the fireplace and I sat down with a sigh. "Maybe we should cancel," Heath said after a minute of silence.

I'd been staring into the fire and I pulled my eyes away and pushed the smile back up. "It's fine. *I'm* fine, Heath."

He nodded. "Oh, I know you're okay with it. But I'm not so sure about it."

My smile became real and I rolled my eyes a little. Heath was just saying that to make me feel better. I reached out and took his hand. "We'll go to dinner," I told him. "We'll meet the fiancée and see what's up with her brother. It's cool."

Heath arched a skeptical eyebrow.

"I pinkie-swear I'm cool," I insisted. If I said that a few times, maybe it would be true enough soon. "Let's go to dinner, and hear what they have to say."

Heath nodded. "It's just a job, right?" he said.

"Yep. Just a job. And if at any point during dinner you think I'll need reminding that it's just a job, feel free to say something."

"What's just a job?" I heard a voice ask.

Looking up, I saw Gilley standing there nibbling on a puff pastry. "Hey!" I said. "Where've you been?"

"Seeing Michel off," Gil said, adding a pout as he took a seat across from us. Michel was Gilley's new boyfriend, whose mother is French, but his father is a Scot and so is Michel. We'd met him a few months earlier as we were wrapping up our final shoots for our cable show, and he'd proved very good with a handheld camera in some rather dicey situations.

"Seeing him off?" I said, sitting forward. "You didn't break up with him, did you?" I liked Michel, not only because he was a lovely person, but also because he'd taken the annoying right out of Gilley. With Michel, Gil had lost fifteen pounds, smiled more, pouted and complained less, and was just a general delight to be around. Without Michel, Gilley's charming company could be used by the CIA to extract information from terrorists.

"No," Gil said with a sad little sigh. "He's got a job in New York. He won't be back till the weekend after next."

Fourteen days. I wondered if we could all last that long without Michel as a buffer.

"Anyway, I talked to Ma," Gil said next, eyeing his puff pastry with more than a hint of guilt in his eyes. He'd been doing so well on his diet.

Abruptly, I remembered the gold charm bracelet. "Yeah? What'd she say?"

"Well," Gil said, picking away at the pastry, "it seems your dad has a girlfriend."

I choked on my coffee. *"What?"*

He smiled wickedly at me. "It was only a matter of time, M.J.," he said. "Or in your daddy's case, twenty-three years."

I coughed for a bit as Heath patted my back. Mama Dell even rushed over with a glass of water. At last I felt I could breathe without sputtering. "Who is she?"

Gil shrugged. "Ma doesn't know much other than that her name is Christine Bigelow, originally from Jacksonville. She moved to town about three months ago and took up with your daddy soon after that. Ma says she bought the Porters' old place and there's nothing but construction crews up there day and night."

My brow shot up. The Porters had been a prominent family in Valdosta since before the Civil War. Their home was one of those great big plantation estates with Greek columns, grand porches, and lush rolling lawns. Over the years the Porter family had left the area one by one, venturing to more bustling communities like Atlanta, Jacksonville, and the like. I'd heard that the Porter mansion had been all but vacant in recent years, but I was still surprised to learn now that the house had gone up for sale.

I imagined that although the place might be grand,

it'd likely need some major renovation to make it livable. "She bought the Porter place?" I repeated. I was still stunned that my father had taken up with someone. To my knowledge he hadn't so much as looked at a woman since my mother died. I guess I'd taken it for granted that he never would.

Gil nodded. "She's got some bucks apparently."

"What does she do?" I asked next.

Gil smiled slyly. "Do? She doesn't do anything, M.J. Her husband died and left her a boatload of money. Now she spends that and hangs out with your daddy."

"How . . . how did they meet?" I didn't know if I was happy or upset about Daddy dating again. I was bordering on upset because, even though it'd been well over twenty years since Mama died, it still felt a bit like he was cheating on her.

"She went to see him to help set up a trust fund for all the money her husband left her," Gil said easily.

I wasn't surprised Gilley knew all these intimate details. The gossip vines in Valdosta are like kudzu—they're everywhere and cover everything.

"This is good news, right?" Heath asked, peering at me as if he couldn't understand why my eyes might be watering.

I swallowed hard. "It is," I said, already wondering if I could send back the charm bracelet.

"Hey," Gilley said, sitting forward. "Your daddy has been alone for a really long time, honey. It's okay to let him have some company, right?"

"Sure," I said, but my voice sounded flat. "Yeah. It's a good thing."

Gil and Heath exchanged a look, and it irritated me. It said they thought I might be taking all this a little too hard. I cleared my throat and stood up. "It's going on three. I've gotta get showered and changed for tonight."

Gilley and Heath got up too. "What's going on to-night?" Gil asked.

I completely forgot that I hadn't told him yet. Heath beat me to it. "Sable stopped by the office this morning."

Gil's eyes bulged. "Oh. My. God!"

"He asked us to dinner," Heath went on. "With his fiancée . . . the neurosurgeon."

It was Gilley's turn to choke on his coffee. "Whoa," he said when he could speak clearly. Then his gaze shifted to me. "Awkward . . ."

"Steven has a job for us," I said quickly, trying to make light of the fact that my ex had gotten engaged mere months after we'd broken up. Also, I knew I'd have to try to rope Gilley into helping us if we decided to take the job. "The fiancée has a brother who's having some trouble."

Gil cocked his head. "Trouble? What kind of trouble?"

"The spooky kind," I said.

"Yikes. Well, thank God I'm free this evening. What time is dinner?"

"Who said you were coming?" The last thing I needed was a snarky, acerbic-tongued dinner guest when we met Steven's fiancée.

Gilley rolled his eyes. "Honey, I wouldn't miss this for the world."

I glared at him. "No."

Gil gave me an appraising look. "Sugar," he drawled, "you'll need me."

"Ha!" I scoffed. "Like a hole in the head."

Gilley shook his head and *tsk*ed. "So, you're going to rely on Heath to have your back when you meet this gorgeous neurosurgeon with a giant rock on her finger?" Glancing at Heath, Gilley added, "No offense, doll."

Heath narrowed his eyes at Gil. "None more than usual taken, Gil."

But I was more focused on what Gilley had just said. "Who said she was gorgeous?"

"Oh, please, M.J.," Gil said. "Have you ever known Steven to date anyone who wasn't gorgeous?"

"I've only known him to date *me*," I said levelly.

Gil inspected his nails. "I rest my case."

"Em," Heath said, wrapping an arm around my waist. "It's just dinner. You'll be fine no matter who shows up because I'll be there to make sure Sable knows I got the better end of the deal."

I looked up at my sweet, sincere, sensitive boyfriend and caressed his cheek. Then I turned to Gil and said, "Dinner's at seven. At Tango's. Be there on time for once." And then I headed out of the coffee shop to sprint home and get ready.

Chapter 2

Gilley didn't disappoint. He showed up at my condo in the middle of a full-scale wardrobe meltdown. "How's it going?" I heard him ask as I threw one of the last remaining pairs of slacks out the door of my closet.

"How do you think it's going?" I replied. Behind me the bed was a mess of rumpled clothing, hangers, and shoes. I had absolutely nothing suitable to wear because for much of the past ten months, I'd been dressing for demons—not ex-boyfriends and their gorgeous, brainy fiancées.

I heard Gilley clear his throat. "This might work," he said.

I turned and poked my head out to see Gilley standing there with a garment bag and a shoe box. "What'd you do?"

"Took care of you," Gil said lazily. "Just like always."

I grinned and rushed over to take the bag from him. Unzipping it, I peered inside and my breath caught. Inside the garment bag was a gorgeous sheath dress in oh so touchable electric blue suede. Cinched smartly at the waist, it also had a deep V-neck, and a slight slit in the back of the formfitting skirt cut just a few inches above my knee.

I pulled the dress out of the bag and marveled at it. Then I caught sight of the four-hundred-dollar price tag. "Gil!" I yelled.

He rolled his eyes. "Honey, that was before the mark-down."

My brows lifted along with a little hope. "You got a discount?"

"Of course," he said easily.

"How much?"

"Ten percent."

I hung my head. "I can't afford a three-hundred-and-sixty-dollar dress, Gil."

"You can if you'd do a few readings," he reminded me. Now that we were on hiatus, Gil had been pushing me to read for some private clients again. I'd resisted because we were awaiting a big bonus from the network for shooting at a seriously dangerous location, but the network was dragging its heels on the money, and the latest rumor was that we weren't going to see the check until the middle to the end of the summer.

We were also supposed to make a ton of money off the movie that shoot resulted in, but before heading home from Wales, we'd been told that it'd take at least a year or two for that to be released and then another year before we saw any money from it.

And people think that all you have to do is get on television and your money worries are over.

Still, I was reluctant to commit to readings because I'd gotten so burned-out the last time I opened myself up to readings that I was still put off by that exhausting experience. Readings really take it out of me.

"Just a few a month," he coaxed. I used to command two hundred dollars a session. It was really good money, and it'd allowed me to put a sizable chunk down on the condo when I'd bought it. "And just until we go back to work for *Ghoul Getters*," Gilley added.

I made a face at him, but I realized I was still clutching the dress to my chest. I reeeeeeally wanted to wear it, and I'm no longer that girl that tucks the tag in and takes a dress back after only wearing it once. If I wore the dress, I was keeping it. "How many readings a month?" I asked Gilley.

He smiled. "No more than twenty."

I did some more mental calculating. That would be really good money. And it would save Heath and me from having to be so careful about our budget. While I wavered, Gilley added, "I've already got a few booked for Heath."

I blinked. "Heath is doing readings?"

Gil nodded. "He didn't want me to tell you because he wants to buy you something nice for your birthday, and he said that living in Boston for the summer is crazy expensive and he doesn't want you to worry about trying to survive on a tight budget all the time."

I lifted my chin to look out into the hall. I could hear the news broadcast on the TV and I knew Heath was out there lounging on the sofa, waiting for me to figure out my wardrobe for the evening. "He's a good man, isn't he?" I whispered to Gil.

"He's one of the best, honey," Gil replied, handing me the shoe box. "Now, get dressed and do something with your hair. You have half an hour."

The shoes Gil had picked out were black patent leather at the heel with electric blue suede at the toe to match the dress. I got myself together quickly and was relieved to see the dress fit like a glove. And, as long as I didn't breathe too deeply, it was even comfortable.

As for my hair . . . I tried. I tried the curling iron a couple of times and gobs of hair spray, but I have thick chestnut-colored hair that always manages to pull out of the curl. Still, I did manage to at least make it look wavy, and I was happy with the end result.

I walked out of the bedroom after hastily putting most of the clothes on my bed back in the closet, and as both Gilley and Heath jumped to their feet and whistled appreciatively, I think I passed the litmus test.

We arrived at the restaurant, which is just a few blocks down from my place, at only a minute or two past seven. Heath held my hand and I knew he could sense how tense I was—my palm was clearly sweating. He squeezed it and offered me an encouraging smile and I had to marvel at how handsome he was in his black dress slacks and emerald green silk shirt.

On my left Gilley was also smartly dressed in black jeans, matching boots, a charcoal shirt, and snappy vest. On his head he'd even worn his most stylish fedora. He looked like a guy that didn't have to try very hard to look trendy, and I knew that was partly Michel's influence and partly just Gilley's natural taste. It made me feel a little more confident to be buffered by the two men . . . that is, until Steven walked in with a beautiful brunette on his arm.

My ex was dressed in a light tan suede jacket and a white shirt with faded jeans, but his fiancée had on a simple black cocktail dress, which complemented her olive skin tone and set off her hazel eyes.

She had a countenance that wasn't classically beautiful, but lovely all the same, with large doe eyes, a long thin nose, and full lips encased in a heart-shaped face haloed by long curly hair that bounced when she walked. Mostly, she looked kind and approachable, and the minute I saw her and Steven together, I knew they were made for each other. Courtney was tall and lithe, a perfect complement to Steven's six-foot frame.

We had little chance to do more than smile nervously at each other when the host, Estevan, approached us with much enthusiasm. "M.J.! Steven! So good to see you two again!"

I felt my cheeks color. This used to be our favorite hangout, and I didn't think Estevan knew that Steven and I weren't together anymore. In fact, I knew he didn't when he stepped in front of us and glanced at the woman clearly on Steven's arm and my hand clasped in Heath's. Estevan's smile became a little forced and his eyes blinked furiously as I could practically see the wheels turning in his head to put it all together. "Hi, Estevan," Gil said merrily. "There will be five of us for dinner tonight."

Estevan nodded, that forced smile never losing wattage, and turned swiftly to gather menus. "This way, this way," he sang. We followed him to the table and took our seats. Courtney and Steven sat opposite Heath and me, and Gil landed to my right and Steven's left. "I love your dress," Courtney said as I sat in the chair Heath had pulled out for me.

"Thank you!" I replied, with maybe a *little* too much enthusiasm. "Yours is supercute!"

Gil cleared his throat and gave me a look that begged me to chill out. I got busy unrolling my utensils from the napkin. Estevan then rattled off the specials of the day before making haste to hurry off and wipe his now sweaty brow.

The table fell into a bit of uncomfortable silence and it was Gil who broke the tension by introducing himself.

"Hello," he said, offering Courtney his hand. "I'm Gilley. You must be Courtney."

She smiled shyly at him. "Hello," she said. "I've heard all about you, Gilley."

Gil turned his head slightly and prctcndcd to blush. "Oh, my. All good, I hope?"

"All good," she assured him.

"It's good to see you," Steven said to Gilley, and there was genuine warmth in the statement. "I've missed you."

This time Gilley really did blush. He then proceeded to tell Steven all about his new, "devastatingly good-looking" boyfriend and this description and a few of the more humorous tales of Michel and Gilley's adventures since meeting in Wales lasted well into the ordering of our drinks. At last Gil sat back and winked at me. His tactic had worked. We'd all shared a laugh and the tension at the table had eased.

I then felt obliged to make an effort to be nice and asked, "So, where did you two meet?"

"The hospital," Courtney said, smiling brightly at Steven. She reached for her utensils at the same time and I had a chance to see the *enormous* rock on her finger. Gilley hadn't guessed wrong. Steven had gone all out. "We did a consult on a patient who'd suffered a mild heart attack while driving, and he'd had an accident that resulted in a closed head injury."

"Ouch," Heath said. "Did he make it?"

Courtney nodded. "He did. He's had a rough time of it, but he's alive and doing better every day."

The waiter came by to take our orders and we all realized we hadn't looked at the menu. Promising that we'd be ready in just a minute, we all began to skim over the menu. I looked for any vegetarian offerings and found a stuffed ravioli dish with homemade creamy tomato sauce that looked right up my alley. When I placed my order,

Steven looked quizzically at me. "You always go for the filet."

"I've given up meat," I told him. That was a very recent decision, because lately, every time I ate meat, I swore I could feel a hint of the fear and pain the animal had endured before it died. It was something I hadn't known would affect me, and I was learning that many, many psychics ultimately became vegetarians for that very reason.

Next to me Heath ordered the cheese-filled crepes—also meat free—and he nudged me with his shoulder a little. Meanwhile, Steven had rolled his eyes a little at me and ordered the filet for himself and also for his fiancée, and that was more telling to me than anything, I suppose. We really wouldn't have lasted as a couple, even if Heath hadn't entered the picture.

Gilley ordered the salmon and we made small talk until our meal arrived. "So!" Gil said as he tucked into his fish. "When's the wedding?"

Courtney and Steven exchanged a look that suggested they'd had more than a few discussions about that. "We're hoping for sometime in early September," she said.

"First we have to deal with the living situation," Steven said, more to Courtney than to us. I could tell that was also a much talked-about topic between them.

"You're welcome to move in with me," Courtney said, her smile sly.

Steven sighed and focused his attention back on me. "She won't leave her brother alone in that house."

Heath cut off a small section of his crepe dish and set it on his bread plate, then offered it to me without my asking. I realized I'd been staring hungrily at his meal with more than a little buyer's remorse because it looked and smelled amazing—far better than my ravioli. "So, what's going on with your brother exactly?" Heath asked Courtney.

She stopped cutting into her filet and looked up at him, and I was shocked by the tears that began to fill her eyes. "I wish I knew," she whispered.

Steven laid a hand on her back to comfort her. "It's all right," he encouraged. "Tell them what's been going on, *bella*. They can help."

Courtney took a sip of water and shook her head a little, trying to collect herself. "Luke moved in with me about six weeks ago," she began. "He'd been having a lot of trouble at school, and that's not like him. He was top in his class going into his senior year at BU, but then he seemed to have some sort of a breakdown. . . ." Courtney's voice faded away as her eyes misted again.

"What was he studying?" I asked gently, trying to coax the story out of her.

She cleared her throat and took another sip of water. "Nanotechnology," she said, smiling gratefully at me. "Luke is so smart. He always excelled in school, even with all the stuff happening at home."

"What happened at home?" Gil asked.

Courtney shrugged. "Our parents were both alcoholics, and for a time we lived in foster care. It was harder on Luke, I think. He was more sensitive to the erratic and unpredictable nature of my mom and dad. I graduated early and went to college on a scholarship, but Luke is eight years younger, so he was home alone with them for a longer, more troubling period. I finally had him come live with me when he was a freshman in high school, and I was the one that kept him off the streets and focused on school. I managed to get him a job briefly at the hospital and then he got a scholarship to BU and I thought he'd escaped all the hard stuff that comes from having such a dysfunctional home life, but maybe it all caught up to him and he invited this . . . whatever this is."

My brow furrowed. "Whatever what is?" I asked.

Courtney took a deep breath and I could tell that whatever was going on with Luke, it was affecting her deeply. "Something changed," she whispered, almost as if she was afraid that confessing it would bring something bad into the atmosphere. "Luke was living alone in a house he was renting. It was a dump of a house, and I hadn't heard from him in a week or two, so I went over to check on him. I found him alone in the dark, all the blinds closed, the house a complete mess—we're talking garbage on the floor, clothes and bedding tossed everywhere, and my brother sitting on the floor, wrapped in a blanket with a set of headphones on, rocking back and forth maniacally.

"At first I thought Luke had had some sort of psychotic break—I mean, the scene in that house was just so antithetical to his usual neat and highly organized character. But when I bent down to him, he opened his eyes and said, 'Make him go away, sis. Make him go away!'"

I put my elbow on the table and leaned forward. "Make who go away, Courtney?"

She shook her head against the memory, making those long curls bounce. "I didn't know," she whispered. "But I looked into the eyes of my brother and I knew ... I *knew* he hadn't had a psychotic break. He was lucid. His eyes were clear. I'm a neurologist—we're trained to recognize abnormalities of the brain, and this wasn't an abnormality."

"What'd you do?" Gilley asked.

Courtney looked down at the table, still struggling with the memory of that day in the house with her brother. "I wrapped him in my arms and hugged him tightly, promising him that I'd do whatever I could to help him, but he just kept asking me to make 'him' go away. Finally, I sat back and asked him who he meant, and Luke pointed behind me...."

Again Courtney's voice faded away and she struggled to speak. "I . . . ," she said, her voice wavering. "I turned and on the wall of the living room there was this shadow. . . ."

"A shadow," I repeated, trying to help. "Was it in the shape of a person?"

Her eyes lifted to mine. "Yes!"

"A man," I added.

She nodded.

"And the shadow wasn't flat, right? It had dimension, as if the shadow were in three-D."

Courtney put a hand to her mouth, her eyes wide and misty as she nodded.

"Did you hear anything?" Heath asked her.

Her gaze shifted to him. "Yes," she repeated. "I heard . . . I heard . . . laughter, only it wasn't laughter. It was more evil. It was the evilest noise I've ever heard. And it surrounded us in a way that . . ." Courtney seemed to struggle with a way to explain what she'd heard.

"You felt it in your bones, didn't you?" I said.

She gasped. "Yes! That's exactly how it felt."

Gilley set his fork and knife down. I could see the fear and worry on his face. I think when we'd explained to him that Steven had come to us saying that his fiancée had a ghost she needed help with, he'd thought it'd be more like the old days when we dealt with local spooks who just made small bumps in the night. This was already looking to be a much bigger deal. "What'd you do then?" he asked her.

She leaned over a little and hugged Steven's arm. "I grabbed Luke and we bolted out of the house. I took him home to my place and we haven't been back to that house since."

Gilley seemed to relax. "Oh, phew!" he said. "So, you just want us to talk to Luke and let him know that what he encountered is a perfectly natural phenomenon, and that he's not crazy, right?"

"No," Steven said to him. "There's a little more to the story, Gilley." Turning to Courtney, he added, "Tell them the rest, *bella*."

She took another deep breath and continued. "At first, things went back to normal. Well, sort of normal. I put Luke to bed, because he seemed to be exhausted, and the next morning I had an early surgery, so I let him sleep. When I got home, he was still asleep and I became concerned, so I woke him. He told me that before I'd gotten to the house he was renting, he hadn't slept more than an hour or two a night in about a week and a half. I could also tell that he'd lost about ten pounds since the last time I'd seen him.

"He said that it all started a few weeks before winter finals. Walking across campus to his car after one of his night classes, he had the feeling that he was being followed, but he swore that every time he looked over his shoulder, nothing was there. He told me that once he got home, weird stuff began happening. He'd open up the cabinet where he kept his glassware, and instead he'd find plates and bowls. He'd put his clothes in the hamper and find them hanging up in his closet the next morning. Or he'd set something down for a minute only to return and find it in another room. And, he says, the feeling of being followed persisted and got worse.

"Luke swears that every time he left the house, it was like someone was right behind him—he could even hear the footsteps—but nobody was there. He started to wonder if he was going crazy. But then he says that his friends stopped wanting to hang out with him. This happened abruptly. One minute he had a group of buddies to hang out with or study with, and all of a sudden they don't want anything to do with him.

"Finally he couldn't take that feeling of being followed anymore, so he skipped class and stayed home, and that day almost nothing unusual happened. The next day he went out for groceries and the minute he stepped out of the house, he felt that presence again. It was like whatever was following him wanted him to stay put.

"He didn't know what was happening, and he was terrified that he was becoming schizophrenic. He didn't know what to do and he didn't call me because he was afraid I'd tell him that's exactly what was happening. Meanwhile, Luke said that every time he tried to catch some sleep, he would have terrible nightmares of being physically attacked by a shadowy figure wielding a hunting knife. He said he couldn't get away from the shadow person in his dreams and he started to fear going to sleep. At last he started to see the figure of a man out of the corner of his eye, always darting out of sight whenever Luke tried to look. Eventually, he was so sleep deprived he became delirious and he could barely think. That's about the time I found him."

The waiter came by to clear away our plates and offer us dessert. I think he was a little thrown by the somber mood at the table, but we all ordered coffee and Courtney got back to her story. "For the next several days Luke rested, ate, and got better. He'd left all of his belongings back at the other house, but neither of us wanted to think about ever going back there, so I replaced his textbooks, his computer, and his clothes, and took him on walks down by the water to help him try to feel normal again. Luke loves the smell of the bay and I thought that walking along the shore was helping him more than anything, but then one afternoon just a few days into this new routine, as Luke and I were walking, I felt Luke sort of stiffen. When I looked over at him, I could see how pale he'd suddenly become—he looked terrified. I asked him what was wrong and he said that we were being followed. I looked behind us, but there was no one there."

"Could it have been his imagination?" Gilley asked (hopefully, I thought).

Courtney shook her head. "At first, that's what I thought, but then we started walking again and I swear I felt this sort of weird presence behind us too. Luke got so freaked-out that he took off running and it was a minute before I realized what'd happened. I started chasing after him when I saw this black shadow appear out of thin air and keep right on his heels. I think that scared me even more than the encounter at the house. I mean, whatever it was, it was literally chasing my brother all the way down the street. It matched Luke step for step. . . ." Courtney's voice trailed off as she gave in to a shudder and seemed to lose herself in the awful memory. "They were both faster than me, but I did manage to catch up to Luke when he ducked inside a grocery store. When I found him huddled near the produce, I think we both realized that the shadow was gone. Luke said the minute he got into a crowd, the shadow had vanished. It's like it can't pick him out of a crowd or something, but out on the streets and alone in the house, he's fair game."

I glanced sideways at Heath and found him looking at me in return. This sounded bad, and I could tell he thought so too.

"After that," Courtney continued, leaning back so the waiter could set down her coffee, "he begged me not to leave him alone, and so I didn't. I called the hospital and rearranged my shifts, and managed to spend two more days with him. Steven came over and we had a few friends in for a visit, and while the house was full of people during those few days, nothing happened, and I started to hope that maybe we had lost whatever that thing was that had attached itself to my brother. Steven knew something was wrong, however, and after our guests left, he got me to confess what'd been going on, and I was so relieved when he not only believed me, but he told me he might be able to help. Luke and I felt so much better for his company, but then Luke started having those nightmares again."

"The same as before?" I asked.

"Yes. He was always being attacked by a knife-wielding, faceless man who would grab him from behind and put the blade at his throat. He said he couldn't sleep and Steven prescribed him some sleeping pills, which helped for a while."

"He managed to get a few nights' rest," Steven said. "But then the shadows started appearing."

"Shadows?" I repeated.

"Just like Luke had told Courtney," Steven explained. "It was when Courtney's friends left and the house was quiet again. We started to catch small glimpses of a flickering shadow. Sometimes it was like someone passed very quickly just out of view. It was the sense of movement more than actually being able to see anything."

"Meanwhile," Courtney said, taking over the story again, "Luke was having a harder and harder time at night. The sleeping pills weren't working, and I got a little crazy myself from worrying over him. I went out and bought a dozen crucifixes and put them all over the house—I put three in his room alone—but that only seemed to heighten the negative energy in the house. Nobody wants to be alone there, and when I go to work, Luke comes with me and just hangs out in the waiting room. As long as he's around big groups of people, he seems to be okay, but he's exhausted, M.J., and spending all day in the waiting room of a hospital is no life for a twenty-one-year-old man. My brother hasn't had a good night's sleep in weeks and he's had to drop out of school. This is torture for him, and I don't know how to help him. I don't know how to protect him and get this thing away from him. I don't even know what this *thing* is, and I feel like we're all going a little crazy over it."

"I understand," I told her.

She surprised me by reaching out to cover my hand with hers. "I know this is incredibly awkward for you," she said, motioning with her eyes toward her fiancé. "But Steven has told me so much about how amazing you are, and how you, Heath, and Gilley handle stuff like this all the time. . . . Do you think you could find it in your heart to help us?"

Her sincerity and honesty touched me. I had a feeling that as hard as it had been for me to come here and meet her this evening, it might've been even harder for her — especially under these circumstances. I squeezed her hand and said, "Of course, Courtney. Of course we can."

Later, when Heath, Gilley, and I were back at my condo, we tried to decide the best course of action. "I say you two drive several dozen magnetic stakes into the walls of Courtney's house and call it a day," Gil said.

I rolled my eyes. "That might help in the short term, but it's not a long-term solution, buddy."

"Why not?"

"Because Luke is the one being haunted, not Courtney's home. Whatever this thing is, it's decided to make Luke's life a living hell. Which means, every single time he steps outside, he's vulnerable."

"He could wear one of our vests," Heath suggested, referring to one of the magnet-loaded bubble vests that we wear on some of our more dangerous ghostbusts. Spooks can't tolerate big shifts in the electromagnetic frequency of the atmosphere they inhabit. When you bring a bunch of magnets into a space they're haunting, it's like setting off a houseful of fire alarms—it's crazy uncomfortable for them and they'll go anywhere else to escape it.

I considered Heath's suggestion to have Luke wear a vest for a moment before replying, "I don't know how practical that'd be with summer coming on. I mean, you know how hot those things can be. Not to mention how much attention a guy wearing a bubble vest in the middle of summer would attract."

"Good point," Heath said, and we all went back to trying to come up with an idea that might work. Finally, when nothing seemed to be coming to us, I said, "I think where we need to start is by identifying who or what this shadow is and what he wants with Courtney's brother."

Heath nodded. "We need to interview Luke."

I sighed heavily. That troubled me. In fact, in spite of what I'd told Courtney, this case was making me extremely nervous. "I'm worried," I confessed. "This spook attaches itself to people—not objects. If we interview Luke and showcase our psychic abilities, what's to stop this shadow from attaching itself to one of us?"

"Isn't that a risk we'll have to take?" Heath replied.

I fidgeted in my chair. "I think we should be cautious, honey." Heath eyed me curiously and I added, "It's just that we've been sort of forced into too many dangerous encounters in the past year, and I'd like to think that we've learned something about assessing the danger fully before taking any unnecessary risks."

"What're you thinking, then?" Heath asked me.

"I'm thinking that maybe we should start with a conversation with Luke in a nice crowded place."

"He could still bring the spook with him," Gilley said.

"True," I agreed. "But it's unlikely, given what Courtney's already told us about its behavior."

"I think you two should also wear vests," Gil said. Heath eyed him sideways and Gil added, "I'm serious, Heath. M.J.'s right, you two need to be careful with this one, because if it follows you home, we know who it's going to fall in love with." For emphasis Gil pointed to his chest.

Heath and I laughed. "Yeah, yeah, buddy," Heath said. "Okay, for your sake we'll wear the vests."

I called Courtney from my office the next morning and reached her voice mail. I left her a message to call me back; then I went for a run without Heath, who was still back at my place sleeping. Instead of taking the trail, I meandered through the neighborhoods for a while, then made my way over to a small lake in the adjoining town of Medford, which had a nice running path along the water. I noticed a news van over by the lake, and being the curious type, I edged closer. Unfortunately, I might've gotten a little too close, because the female reporter helping to set up the camera called me over. Reluctantly I came to a stop in front of her, very self-conscious of the sweat on my brow and the cadence of my breathing. "Hello, there!" the reporter said with forced enthusiasm as she stuck out her hand. "I'm Kendra Knight from Boston Seven News. Would you like to be on television?"

I smiled. I'd had more than my share of cameras shoved in my face to last a good long time. "No, thanks," I said, preparing to set off again. Kendra quickly shot in front of me and her smile got bigger and her eyes wider. She seemed a bit desperate. "Please?" she said. "There's nobody around and I really need to send my producer an interview."

"What's it about?" I asked, thinking she might want to do an interview about jogging and health.

Kendra said, "Sorry. What's your name?"

I didn't like the fact that she was being so pushy, but I'd been raised in the South, where manners count. "M.J.," I said, and she scribbled that into her notepad. "M. J. Holliday."

Kendra stopped scribbling, and when she stopped scribbling, her grin seemed genuine. "Thanks, M.J. I'd really like to hear your opinion about the trial."

I blinked. "Trial?"

She eyed me curiously, like she couldn't believe I hadn't heard about it. "Yes, the trial of Daniel Foster." I blinked again, and Kendra explained (like I was slow in the head), "The man on trial for the murder of Bethany Sullivan. It's been all over the news for the past four weeks."

I shook my head. "Sorry. I've been out of the country. I have no idea who you're talking about."

Kendra's expression went back to desperate. "Oh," she said, but then shook her head like she didn't care. "That's okay. I can give you a quick overview and you can just give me your opinion."

I sighed. I really wanted to get back to my run, but Kendra wasn't easily put off. "Fine," I said. "What's the case?"

Kendra grabbed her microphone and began to speak to me so rapidly that I had a hard time making out everything that she said. "Bethany Sullivan was a resident of Medford who, last September, while out jogging, was brutally murdered by a man wielding a knife. The police arrested her ex-boyfriend Daniel Foster, found walking erratically a half mile away from the crime scene, covered in the victim's blood. He claimed that he was sleepwalking at the time and has no memory of the actual murder. His trial wrapped up yesterday, and the jury is now deliberating."

I looked around. The courthouse was miles away from

the lake, and I wondered why she'd chosen this spot and, quite frankly, someone like me to ask about what I thought of the trial. "I guess I could express an opinion," I said. "But wouldn't you have more luck finding someone who'd heard of the case closer to the courthouse?"

Kendra nodded. "Coming here was my producer's idea," she said.

"Why would he send you here?"

Kendra pointed to the ground next to us. "This is where Kendra was murdered. She was out running just like you when Daniel allegedly jumped out and stabbed her before slitting her throat."

I felt goose pimples line my arms and the hair on the back of my neck stood up on end. And then I had the very strong sense that a spook was present.

Chapter 3

From the corner of my eye I saw a glimmer of movement and turned my head slightly. About fifteen yards away a small, round, wavy vortex showed up in midair. It looked a little like the shimmering air that comes off pavement on very hot days, but it was round and suspended about five feet off the ground. "She wasn't murdered here," I said, drawn to the energy like a bee to a flower.

"Yes, she . . . hey! Wait! Can I get your comment about the trial?"

But my focus was on the vortex, and I'd already opened up my sixth sense to the hovering energy. I could feel the young woman, sense her pain, and the urgency of her situation. Behind me, I could hear Kendra's footfalls following me. I stopped when I'd reached the orb. "She was murdered here," I said aloud, not caring if Kendra accepted that or not. "On this very spot."

"You look weird," Kendra said, eyeing me closely. "What's happening?"

I ignored her and focused on Bethany. *Hi, Bethany,* I said in my mind. *I'm here to help you.*

Why? I heard her cry in response. *Whywhywhywhy-why?!!!*

I closed my eyes and started to talk to her in the hopes that I might set her spirit at ease. *I'm so sorry that happened to you,* I began. *And I know you're scared, and I know you don't really understand what's happened, but I'm willing to tell you if you want.*

I don't know what I expected, but it certainly wasn't what happened next. Bethany sort of entered my energy, and she filled my senses with her last moments. They unfolded like an awful nightmare, and what I didn't fully realize was that I was narrating the events as they happened in my mind. "She was running because she wanted to lose weight for her best friend's wedding. She worked crazy hours at the law firm, and she didn't get out that day until late. She was hungry and tired, but she figured if she could just get in a few miles, she could have a decent dinner for once, and a glass of wine. She had a special bottle of Zinfandel chilling in an ice bucket at home. She couldn't wait to curl up with her cat, Sprinkles, and relax. It was a little past eight, and it made her nervous to run in the dark, but again, she thought it was just a few miles and she was so close to home."

I turned and stared across the grassy knolls; then I lifted my hand and pointed. "She lived over there. She felt safe if she was within sight of her condo."

Behind me I heard Kendra say something like, "I have no idea, but keep rolling!" It didn't register because my mind was still filled with Bethany.

"She had just one more loop left when she heard footsteps run up behind her. They came so fast they scared her and she jumped, shrieking a little." I turned again and stared behind me. "She looked over her shoulder, but there was no one there. No one. And she couldn't explain it, because she'd heard the footsteps, and then, just when she was facing forward again, Dan came out of nowhere—he appeared like a ghost right in front her. He was just standing there. For just a split second she was almost relieved to see him, only because his was a familiar face, but then in the next instant she saw his eyes. She saw something terrible in them. . . . She saw murder in them, and she knew her worst fears were coming true. And then she saw the knife in his hand. She tried to pivot away from him. . . . Her ankle turned. She started to fall and then something that felt hot and searing like lightning struck her right in the back and with it the most awful pain she'd ever felt. She screamed and then more lightning struck her on the right side."

I clutched my ribs and bent forward. "And then, there was one more slice of lightning. Right across her neck. It was the worst of all. After that, the pain ended abruptly. It was like someone flipped a switch and the pain vanished. But ever since then, she's been trying to go home, to call the police, but she can't seem to get there. She can see it, her condo, from here, but she can't make it home. It's like her feet are made of lead, and they won't work right. And other people just pass her even though she's been asking everyone to stop and help her."

I stood up straight again and squeezed my eyes shut, forcefully pushing Bethany's energy away from me so that I could think for myself again. *Bethany,* I said sternly in my mind. *You have to listen to me. Dan hurt you. He hurt you in a way that your body will never recover from. I know you want to get back to your condo, but the reason you can't go there is because you need to be somewhere else. Do you understand?*

Why? she asked me desperately again.

I answered her truthfully. *Honey, I don't know. But I*

think if you focus on what I'm telling you, that question might eventually get answered.

For a few long seconds Bethany said nothing more to me. She simply hovered close by as if wavering on whether to listen to me or try again to go to her condo. At last I decided to help her make up her mind. "You need to move on to the other side, Bethany. There's nothing for you here. You need to look up, and search for the light, and then you need to let it take you."

Bethany reacted by attempting to enter my energy again, and I knew she was scared and simply wanted to feel what it was like to be alive again, but I resisted her with everything that I had. I couldn't allow her to be tempted into staying in the state she was in. "Honey, it'll be okay," I whispered. "I promise you, it'll be okay."

Finally, as if she'd exhausted herself, she stopped trying to fight me, and she sort of gave in to my suggestion. I had a vision of her lifting her chin slightly, and I realized what a beautiful girl she'd been, with ash-blond hair, light brown eyes, and a beautiful face fit for the cover of a magazine. That face lit up as the light above her approached, and I saw her gasp and her eyes open wide and in the very next instant there was a slight zap in the ether, Bethany disappeared, and behind me I heard, "What the hell?"

"Mike?" Kendra asked. "What's wrong?"

I turned and saw that Kendra was holding up the microphone toward me and her cameraman was eyeing his camera with alarm. "There was a power surge and then the camera died," he said, turning the camera over in his hands. "And the battery's dead even though I just got through charging it."

I realized then that they'd caught my whole encounter with Bethany on film, and feeling a bit overexposed,

I began to edge away from them. Kendra was quick to step forward, and after tucking her microphone under her arm, she said, "What the heck was that?"

I sighed. I was furiously trying to recall what I might have said aloud in front of her, but the truth was that I'd gone into a little bit of a trance and the memory of what I'd actually said was fuzzy. "I gotta go," I told her.

"Wait!"

But I suddenly wanted no part of her interview and turned away to start running again. I heard her call my name several times and beg me to come back, but that only made me run faster. The last thing I wanted was to become some sort of spectacle on the nightly news.

I didn't stop running until I was home again, and as I came through the door, I heard the water running in the shower.

I smiled and felt the tension in my shoulders ease. Slipping out of my sweaty clothes, I headed into the bathroom and slid into the shower. Heath had his head under the spray and I moved in to wrap my arms around him from behind. He jumped a little but then put his hands on mine. "Well, hey, there," he purred.

"Hey, sexy," I whispered. "Feel like getting soapy?"

"Sure. But we should be quick because my girlfriend's going to be home any minute."

I laughed and swatted his butt. His oh so amazing derriere. Heath turned, exposing a few other oh so amazing things, and there wasn't much room for conversation after that. We stepped out of the shower long after the hot water had turned lukewarm and got dressed. Okay, so maybe we went for round two in the bedroom first, but *eventually* we managed to get ourselves together. "Wanna grab lunch?" I asked as I was dabbing on some mascara.

Heath looked at his phone. "Sorry, Em," he said. "I

have an appointment—" He stopped speaking abruptly, like he seemed to catch himself, and I realized why he'd gone suddenly mute.

"It's okay," I said. "Gilley told me you were doing readings again."

Heath scowled. "That guy can't keep anything to himself."

I laughed. "I love that it's taken you this long to figure that out."

My sweetie stepped forward to wrap me in his arms and nuzzle my neck. "You're not mad, are you?"

"Why would I be mad?"

He shrugged. "I know you got really burned out on them, but I miss doing readings. It's fun."

"It can be," I agreed. "But it can also be crazy draining."

"So can chasing spooks."

I sighed and looked at the two of us in the mirror. Heath was so exotically beautiful, with his jet-black hair, high cheekbones, deep-set eyes, and square jaw. He'd acquired a thin streak of white hair at one temple and it made him even more striking. "I think I might start up again," I confessed.

He cocked his head. "Reading for clients?"

I nodded. "We could really use the money."

His arms wrapped tighter around my waist. "Let me take that on," he said. "I can make enough over the hiatus to cover us."

I cocked an eyebrow. "Oh, it's all on you, huh?"

He went back to nuzzling my neck. "I just don't want you to do something that's hard on you," he said sweetly. "I don't mind it, so let me do it."

But I'm not the type to let someone else do all the work. I'm a fifty-fifty sort of gal. "I can take a few clients," I told him. "And if we both work at it, we'll have double the money and we can spend some time in Santa Fe in the fall before the show starts up again."

Heath had agreed to spend the summer with me in Boston even though his mom and family were back in New Mexico. And it hadn't even been my idea—he'd offered. It'd meant the world to me.

He backed up and turned me around to face him. "You'd come to Santa Fe again to hang out?"

The last time we'd been in Heath's neck of the woods, it'd been a wee(*eeeeeee*) bit intense.

"I would," I said, reaching up to pull him in for a kiss. "If I get enough clients, we could relax about our cash flow for a change." We'd been paid well by the network that hosted our ghostbusting show, but living in Boston was superexpensive and I always worried about my long-term finances.

"Okay, babe," Heath said. "But the minute it gets to be too much for you, stop, okay?"

I grinned. "I'll be fine," I assured him.

Heath left and I checked my phone. I had a message from Courtney. Trying her back, I was relieved to reach her. "Have you come up with a plan to help us?" she asked.

"We're working on one," I told her. "But before we jump in, we'll need to know exactly what we're up against. We'd like to sit down with your brother and interview him, if he's open to it."

"He will be," she said quickly, and I could feel her relief vibrating through the phone. "Would you three like to come over to my place tonight? Steven and I are both off in a few hours."

"Actually, we'd prefer to interview Luke in a public setting." Courtney was quiet and I knew she must have been wondering why I didn't want to talk with Luke someplace private, so I explained our concerns. "The three of us have dealt with some of the nastiest, most dangerous spooks on the planet, Courtney," I told her. "And we've learned to be cautious when dealing with something that doesn't act like your run-of-the-mill spook."

"There are run-of-the-mill ghosts?"

I chuckled. "Yes. Most spooks are actually quite harmless. They just get stuck between worlds, and their confusion can sometimes make them disruptive. Usually all it takes to deal with them is some gentle coaxing."

"But you don't think that's what we're dealing with here," she said.

"No," I confessed. "I think we're dealing with something much darker. And because of that, I think that Heath and I could be vulnerable. This spook has attached itself to a person, and these types of spirits can be very fickle. Because Heath and I are mediums, we could be quite appealing to a spook like the one haunting your brother, and until we know more about who or what this shadow man is, neither Heath nor I am willing to risk having the ghost latch onto us."

Courtney was quiet again.

"I know that may seem cold," I said, hearing the words I'd said echo in my mind. "But, Courtney, something like this ghost could really become an issue for us, and we've taken so many risks in the past couple of months with the scariest, most demonic spirits you could ever imagine that Heath and I have to set some clear boundaries. We're no longer willing to put our lives or our sanity on the line."

"I understand," she said, and I felt that she did. "Where and when would you like to meet Luke?"

I turned in a half circle to eye the clock over the stove. "Would five o'clock at the hospital work for you?"

"That'd be perfect," she said. "Luke is here in the waiting room trying to take a nap. I think he'll be thrilled to talk to someone who understands what he's going through."

"Good."

We finalized where to meet and then I called Gilley.

"I've been trying to call you!" he yelled the moment he picked up the line on his end.

That took me by surprise. "Why? What's happened?"

"I've got a reporter calling the office nonstop!"

My eyes widened. Uh-oh. "Which reporter?"

"A Kendra something . . . I don't know," Gil said impatiently. "She was full of questions about who you are and how you could know so many details about some lady who was murdered in the park. Which brings me to my next question: *What* did you say to her, M.J.?"

I covered my eyes with my hand and sighed. "Nothing," I began.

"Oh, this can't be nothing. Seriously, what'd you say?"

"I'm on my way," I told him, avoiding the question, and clicked off without even telling him about the meeting set for later with Luke, Courtney, and Steven. I found Gilley back on the phone when I walked through the door of the office. My inner suite door was shut and I could hear Heath's voice waft faintly from inside. I figured he was still in with his client. "Can you hold, please?" Gilley said tightly before putting the phone to his chest. "It's your new best friend," he said. "Kendra."

I shook my head vigorously.

Gilley nodded his head just as vigorously.

We did that back and forth with each other until we were both dizzy. "I'm *not* talking to her!" I whispered.

"She won't quit calling!" he whispered back.

"Tell her I've left the country again."

Gilley leveled his eyes at me. "I'm *sure* she'll believe *that*."

"I'm not talking to her, Gil."

Gilley put the phone back to his ear. "Kendra? Sorry about that. Listen, M.J.'s feeling a little indisposed at the moment and she can't come to the phone. I'll have her call you back just as soon as she's feeling better, okay?"

I breathed a huge sigh of relief as Gil hung up the phone. "Thanks, honey."

Gil reached into his desk drawer and pulled out a nail file. As he inspected his nails, he said, "Spill it."

I told him about what'd happened at the park and he stopped filing the second I said that I'd made contact with Bethany. His eyes got wider the closer I got to the end. "Did they record everything you said?" he asked me. I couldn't tell whether he seemed panicked or excited.

"I think so."

"This could either be really good for our business or really bad," he told me.

I sat down in one of the wing chairs that made up our lobby's seating area. "They might not even air it," I said.

Gil cocked an eyebrow. "That reporter has called me three times in an hour, M.J. I doubt she'll just let it go."

I tapped my knee thoughtfully for a minute. "You know what bothers me?"

"That you picked that blouse to go with those jeans?" Gil said. "Or that you have no sense of style when it comes to handbags?"

I looked down at my perfectly functional brown pocketbook. "What's wrong with my handbag?"

"You got it at a"—Gil paused while he made a choking sound—"discount retailer six years ago."

I rolled my eyes. "Who died and made you Tim Gunn?"

Gil snapped his fingers. "Make it work!"

"*Any*way, what bothers me is something Bethany said."

"The dead girl?"

I nodded. "She said that on the night she died, she heard footsteps behind her, but when she turned to look, there was no one there."

Gil's brow shot up. "Another ghost?"

"Yeah. But, Gil, when I was connecting with her spirit, I didn't sense anyone else in the ether."

Gil shrugged. "Maybe he or she didn't feel like showing themselves."

I agreed but something else was actually bothering me. "You know what's even weirder?"

"The fact that you won't wear a belt even though *clearly* that's the big thing missing from that outfit and the only way that blouse could possibly work with those jeans?"

"Will you leave off my wardrobe?" I snapped.

"Sugar, now that we're back in the States, you need some help getting your closet in order. I mean, Molly Ringwald called. She'd like her wardrobe from the eighties back."

"Gil," I growled.

"Sorry. Continue. And then let's go shopping."

I inhaled deeply and let it out sloooow. "The weird thing is that Courtney said her brother heard disembodied footsteps following him everywhere he went. And I can't afford a new wardrobe."

"This is New England," Gil replied with a wave of his hands. "The only place more haunted is Europe. There're disembodied footsteps all over the place. And you can afford to go shopping because I've spent all the time I wasn't talking to Kendra booking you appointments."

My eyes bugged. "You've already booked me some appointments?"

Gil leaned over to look at his computer screen.

"Thirty, to be exact. And there're twenty more in my in-box that I haven't had a chance to get to yet."

My mouth fell open. *"Thirty?"*

Gil rolled his eyes. "Chill out, M.J. They're not all on the same day. In fact, I've scheduled you the next ten days off, giving you plenty of time to talk yourself into doing them again."

"How did we already get thirty appointments on the books?"

"I sent out an e-mail to all of your old clients. They're replying in droves."

I blinked furiously for several seconds, crunching some numbers and trying to calculate how much extra cash that'd be.

"Seventy-five hundred bucks, honey," Gil said, as if reading my mind. I squinted at him. I'd come up with a different, lower, figure. "I gave you a fifty-dollar raise," Gilley added. "You're a TV star now. And you can command it."

I groaned. "What's my schedule so far?" I worried that Gil would try to pack them in.

He clicked his mouse and pivoted the screen toward me. "You have twelve a week, honey. Four readings a day, three days a week. A bit like the old days."

I used to read for clients Monday through Thursday, but my maximum then was six a day with a three-day weekend. It was crazy intense and it used to drain the life right out of me. I saw that Gil had set my new schedule up for Monday through Wednesday, with readings scheduled every fifty minutes from noon to four with ten-minute breaks in between. "You'll have to eat lunch before you show up for work, but I thought this would work for you."

I nodded. It'd work well, I thought. "Okay," I said at last. "Just remember, no matter what the response is, don't book me beyond the end of August and no more than twelve readings a week."

Gil saluted. "Now, can we go shopping?"

I eyed my watch. It wasn't even noon. "What about him?" I asked, nodding toward the door to my office, where we could hear laughter. Heath must be having a good time with his client.

"He'll be fine," Gil said, getting up to come around and grab my elbow. "He's got two more clients after this, and lots of time in between. He can handle it."

With that, we were out the door.

Three hours later I was crying uncle. Loaded down with far too many shopping bags and a credit card that was almost too hot to hold, I tried to get Gil to listen to reason. "My feet hurt, I'm hungry, tired, and I still have to go home and change before we meet Luke and Courtney!" (Okay, so maybe my argument wasn't exactly laden with "reason.")

"Just one more stop," Gil called over his shoulder as I shuffled along behind him.

I glared hard at his back. He'd been saying that for the past three stores. "Gil," I whined. "Come on!"

But he wasn't listening. He was scooting into yet another store. I thought about leaving him, but he had the car keys. With a (huge) sigh I trudged into the store and almost came up short. All around me were racks and racks of gorgeous handbags. My eyes darted around until I spotted Gil, already talking the ear off one of the sales associates. As I headed toward him, two other associates saw my shopping bags, and when they blinked, I swear I saw dollar signs in their eyes.

I kept my head down and hurried over to Gil. "Try this on," he said before I could even get a word out. In an instant the shopping bags were pulled out of my grip and a gorgeous black leather handbag with plenty of brass accents was draped over my shoulder. Gil stood back and tapped his finger to his lips. "Maybe," he said.

"I like it," said the salesgirl.

"It might be a little big," Gil replied. "If it hits her too low or too wide, it makes her look hippy."

"I like it," Salesgirl said again.

"Try this one," Gil suggested, plucking the handbag off my shoulder and replacing it with another equally beautiful bag.

"I like it," Salesgirl repeated for the third time. Clearly she was a one-hit wonder.

"The first one was better," Gil said. My opinion had stopped mattering four stores ago. So I just stood there stiffly as bag after bag was draped over my shoulder until finally Gil made the decision to go with the first one. I blinked wearily and lifted the price tag, nearly choking on the gasp that came with it. "Holy freakballs! Gilley! Four hundred and fifty dollars?!"

He stared at me like he couldn't understand why I was so upset.

"Four *hundred* and fifty *dollars*!" I repeated . . . perhaps a little louder than I should've.

The confusion on Gil's face lingered.

"Honey, the bag I came in with only cost me forty dollars!"

Gil pursed his lips and looked at me with disapproval. "Sugar," he drawled. "This is Michael *Kors*, not Michael *Kohl's*."

"Should I ring that up?" Salesgirl asked Gil, even though *I* was the one holding the credit card.

"Yes, please," Gil said, reaching for the card. I held on to it firmly and Gil and I had a tug-of-war in the shop for ten seconds before he poked me in the side and I let go.

Just when I was about to yell at him that I wasn't buying a four-hundred-dollar anything, my cell rang. Looking down, I saw the call was from Heath. "Hey," I said, still glaring furiously at Gil. "Did you get our note?"

"That you went shopping? Yeah, I got it. And Gil's been texting me the whole time."

"He's been texting you?" I repeated. "What's he been saying?"

Heath cleared his throat. "You wouldn't like it."

My narrowed eyes became slits, and I mouthed, "You're dead!" to Gil. He shrugged nonchalantly and turned away.

"So, are you guys heading back soon?"

"Definitely. This is our last stop or I'm going to threaten to return everything we got. Did you want to try and grab dinner after we meet with Luke and Courtney?"

"Uh, sure, but that's not why I'm calling."

Out of the corner of my eye I saw Gilley hand Salesgirl a belt before he twirled in a circle and began to head toward the clothing section. Trying to shift the phone to my shoulder while I picked up the bags, I asked, "Oh? What's up?"

"You're on TV."

I dropped the phone. And the bags. Gil glanced over at me, smirked, then went back to sifting through the clothing. Grabbing the phone off the floor, I said, "Sorry—did you say we're on TV?"

"No. I said *you're* on TV. Did you do a reading for a reporter this afternoon about a girl who'd been murdered?"

I felt the blood drain from my face. "Son of a bitch!" I hissed.

"I take it that's a no?"

I shook my head. "What *exactly* is happening on the broadcast?"

"Well, the reporter, Karen something—"

"Kendra," I corrected, pinching the bridge of my nose with my fingers. "Kendra Knight."

"Yeah, Kendra, she says that she had a, and I quote, 'bizarre' encounter with a woman named Mary Jane Holliday who claims to be a world-renowned psychic."

"I never claimed any such thing!"

By now Gil had left the clothing rack and was making his way toward me—obviously sensing that something was wrong.

"Not my words, babe," Heath said. "Hers."

"Yeah, sorry. Okay, what else?"

"Well, she says that she thought at first that you were trying to pull some stunt on her to promote your show debuting on cable TV in a few weeks, but then she did some checking into your background and also what you said on camera. She replayed the tape a couple of times and says you seemed to have intimate knowledge of the murder of a woman named Bethany something that no one but the police or the girl's family had knowledge of. And by that, she meant that there was a bottle of wine chilling in a bucket at the girl's apartment, and that she had a cat named Sprinkles, but none of that was public knowledge."

I didn't say anything at first, wondering if there might be more, but Heath didn't add anything, so I finally said, "Did it make me look really bad?"

Heath sort of chuckled. "Actually, I think you've converted a skeptical reporter into a believer. She said that at the moment where you started telling Bethany to look for the light, all of the charge was sucked right out of the battery of the camera and both she and her cameraman heard some sort of buzzing sound. She played that part of the audio back a couple of times and you can definitely hear something electric happening."

"I crossed Bethany over," I told Heath.

"I figured. Anyway, Kendra added that she's reached out to you for further comment, but you haven't returned her calls so far, and since this aired ten minutes ago, the office phone's been ringing off the hook."

"Well, that's just great," I grumbled.

"What's happening?" Gilley asked.

I ignored him. "Don't answer the phone," I told Heath.

He chuckled. "Oh, I'm not touching it. But, Em, this could be good for you and the show. It's great publicity at least."

"Yeah, we'll see. Listen, we're heading back now, and all I need is a few minutes to change and we can head to the hospital."

"Cool. I'll be ready."

I hung up with Heath and told Gil what'd happened. "The phone is ringing off the hook?" he asked, his eyes as shiny as Salesgirl's.

"Don't get too excited," I told him. "Remember, you're under strict orders not to overbook me."

"Yeah, yeah," Gil said. "Come on, let's get you changed."

"Thank God!" I said, picking up the bags and preparing to head out the door.

"Where're you going?" Gil asked.

"Aren't we leaving?"

He laughed and held up three blouses and two pairs of jeans. "Oh, honey, how you *do* entertain me! Now, go try these on. If I like any of them, you'll wear them out of the store."

Chapter 4

We met up with Heath at my place a "mere" three hundred additional dollars later. The minute I walked into my condo, I headed to a drawer in my kitchen and pulled out a pair of scissors. Holding up my credit card so Gilley could see, I snipped it in half.

"You act like I don't have the numbers, expiration date, and security code memorized," he mocked.

I threw the two halves at him and stomped off to my room to change. I put on my favorite outfit from the ones Gil had selected for me, and inwardly I had to admit it was quite flattering—although I'd never let Gilley know it.

Heath whistled appreciatively when I came back out of the bedroom, and I couldn't help smiling. Then he turned to Gil and said, "Nice."

Gil rubbed his knuckles on his shirt. "What can I say? It's a gift."

I headed toward the door. "If you two are done bromancing each other, we need to get going."

"Wait a sec," Gil said, trotting over with two handfuls of thin magnets. "Let me put these in your new handbag just to be safe."

As Gil was loading down my shiny new purse, I saw Heath stick a few magnets into his back pockets. And I noticed as Gil bent over that he'd packed a few in the pocket of the shirt he wore under his sweater.

"There," Gilley said once he'd finished. "We can go now."

We made it to the hospital in only twenty minutes, which was a miracle, given Boston's notorious traffic jams. Gil parked the van in the parking structure and we headed down in the elevator and over to the main entrance. The hospital had several waiting rooms, and I realized I hadn't asked Courtney which one to meet in. I texted Steven, and while we waited for him to respond, I grew impatient, and as I was about to call Courtney, I heard Steven's voice call out to us. We turned and saw him wave us over. "We're upstairs," he said, and I couldn't help noticing that he looked me up and down, and his eyes gave away his approval.

Heath took my hand, and I knew he'd seen it too.

Steven's gaze shifted subtly to the move and he turned away and began to walk toward the elevator. We rode up in relative silence, but there was enough tension in the air to do most of the talking. Steven and Heath were silently bristling at each other, while I pretended we were all best buds and Gil seemed to be finding everyone's reaction highly amusing.

Finally we reached the sixth floor and Steven led the way down the corridor to a door marked PRIVATE.

When we got through the door, I saw Courtney sitting with a young man in his early twenties with sandy blond hair and sharp-angled features that were quite handsome, but deep blue circles under his gray eyes.

I smiled to reassure him as Courtney stood and introduced us to her brother. "Hi, Luke," I said, reaching out to shake his hand. "We're here to help."

His lips parted in a weary smile, but he seemed to be so exhausted that I doubted it was all sinking in. We took our seats at the small table set up in the room—which was obviously a lunch or conference room of some type—and I took control of the meeting. "Your sister has told us a little about what's been happening, but we'd like to hear from you about this mysterious spirit that's been giving you trouble," I said to him.

Luke nodded. "Where do you want me to start?"

"At the beginning," I said. "When did you first notice things weren't quite right?"

Luke sighed wearily. His head hung low and his shoulders were slumped. I wondered when was the last time he'd gotten a decent night's rest. "I think it started at the beginning of the semester," he said. "I came home one day from class and the stuff in my house was all out of whack."

"Out of whack?" Heath asked. He was taking notes, but he almost needn't have bothered—Gil was recording the session on his phone.

"Yeah, it was crazy," Luke told him. "I came home and it was like somebody had rearranged all the furniture. The couch was on the opposite wall, and my recliner was next to the kitchen facing away from the TV—totally not the way I'd left it. And the kitchen was off too. All my glasses and plates were in one cabinet together, instead of spread out in different cabinets like I'd had 'em before."

"Anything else out of place?" Heath asked.

Luke was staring at the tabletop, his expression troubled. "Yeah," he said softly, almost as if he didn't want to tell us. "It was so crazy, though. . . ."

"Tell us," I said gently. He pulled his gaze up to mine and I smiled at him encouragingly.

Luke licked his lips and said, "At first I thought somebody had broken in, you know? I mean what the freak, right? So I sort of went around the house real quick looking for all the expensive stuff like my Xbox and my TVs and stuff. They were all still there, but when I went into the bedroom . . . it . . . there . . ." Luke paused. He didn't seem to know what words to use.

"What?" I prodded. "What did you see, Luke?"

He sighed again and rubbed his hand over his short hair. "My bed was on the opposite wall and so was the nightstand—right under the window. The light was off, but it was still pretty light out and the sun was hitting the bedspread, which was the first weird thing I noticed. I used to never make my bed. I mean, I figured that I'd just get right back in it every night, so why make it up, you know?"

I nodded, hoping to draw the rest out of him. I saw that his hands were trembling slightly. Whatever it was he'd seen that day in his bedroom had seriously shaken him.

"Anyway, so I get to the bedroom door and I'm just standing there, trying to figure all this out, and I see the bed is made up, like, the cover is even pulled up over the pillow, but on the bed there's this . . ." Luke paused again to make a motion with his hands to convey that he'd seen something big there. "There's this indentation," he said at last. "Like, if a person were lying on the bed it would make an impression in the mattress, you know?"

Heath and I exchanged a look. That was a new one for us, but not completely unheard-of. "What did you do?" I asked when he didn't go on.

He shook his head. "At first I just stood there. I mean, I couldn't believe I was seeing what I was seeing, and then I sort of freaked out and got out of there. I mean, I swear I *heard* someone on the bed, like, sleeping—you know, how people breathe real deep when they're asleep?"

Heath, Gilley, and I all nodded.

"It sounded like *that*."

"What happened after that?" I asked.

Luke shrugged. "Eventually I went back home and whatever had been in my room was gone, but the furniture and the stuff was still out of whack. I put it back the way I had it, but then a couple of days later when I came home from my study group, it'd been all turned around again. I was starting to freak out, wondering if someone was punking me, you know?"

"You thought someone might be trying to play a trick on you?" I said. I always marveled at how hard people worked to deny what they saw with their own eyes.

"Yeah," Luke said with another shrug. "I didn't know if one of my buddies was playing me or something."

"Did you confront your friends?" Heath asked.

"I did. They all denied it. Then I called the landlord and I asked if he'd had the locks changed before I leased the place. I mean, I couldn't explain how anybody was getting in. All the windows and doors were locked up tight, and as far as I knew, I had the only key."

"How long had you lived there?" I asked him.

Luke rubbed his eyes. "Just a few weeks," he told me.

"Had the landlord changed the locks?" Gil asked.

Luke shrugged. "Dunno," he said. "He wasn't around when I called, so I left him a message and he never got back to me, which made me wonder if maybe he was playing with me or something."

"Tell me when you decided it wasn't anybody trying to trick on you," I said.

Luke shifted in his chair. "I think it was maybe a week

later. I came home from class and my furniture was all out of whack again, and it was really starting to freak me out. I didn't go into the bedroom because I couldn't take seeing that thing on the bed again, so I just grabbed a blanket and went to sleep on the couch. That night I had this really intense dream. More of a nightmare really. I mean, it was one of those dreams that feels so real and so crazy that you just want to wake up, but I couldn't. I was having a hard time moving, too. Like my arms and legs were made of lead. And then there was all this blood. . . ." Luke's voice drifted off.

"Blood?" I said.

"Yeah," he whispered, extending his arms out to look at them like he could still see the blood on them. "I was covered in it."

Heath stopped writing and he looked up at me. His expression seemed to say, "Whoa. That's bad."

"Was there anybody else with you in the dream?" I asked Luke.

At first the young man nodded, but then he shifted to shaking his head. "Yes?" he said. "No? I don't know. It felt like someone else was there, but I couldn't see them because there was just so much blood."

"I'm assuming you eventually woke up and saw that it was just a dream," I said.

Luke shuddered. "I woke up," he said softly. "But what I woke up to totally freaked me out."

"What'd you see?" Gil asked.

Luke opened his mouth to speak, but it was a long moment before he found his voice. "There was this shadow," he said. "It was like . . . on the wall, but not. It was sort of closer to me than the wall. The room was dark, but it wasn't pitch-black, but that shadow was pitch-black. It was like this black hole that light couldn't penetrate."

"Did the shadow have a form?" I asked. I was very familiar with the kinds of shadow ghosts Luke was describing.

He nodded. "It looked like a guy. Like the outline of a guy."

"How tall?" Heath asked.

"I don't know . . . maybe five ten, five eleven?"

"Did it move?" I asked.

Luke shook his head. "No. I mean, it just hung there for about thirty seconds and then it vanished. It freaked me out. I stayed up the whole rest of the night with all the lights on and the TV at full blast."

"What happened after that?" I asked.

Luke closed his eyes and hung his head even lower. Courtney put a gentle hand on his back. She looked pained by her brother's recounting. "It got worse," Luke said. "I started staying later and later at school, but the library closes at midnight and my last semester was crazy hard. I avoided going home and I called the landlord again, telling him I wanted out of the lease."

I wondered if this landlord had had any other tenants complaining about the shadow in the house. "What'd he say?" I asked.

"He wouldn't return my calls, but he did send me a certified letter letting me know that if I broke the lease, he'd sue me for the remainder of the rent."

"Nice," I said.

"Yeah, he's a real asshole. Anyway, that dream with me covered in blood kept coming back and it got to where I couldn't sleep at night. And then I couldn't sleep during the day. And then I couldn't sleep at all. I was like a zombie. I felt like I was going nuts and I was so twisted up I didn't know if I was awake or dreaming. I stopped going to class, I stopped hanging out with my friends, I dropped out of life."

"Then what happened?" Gilley asked, his expression completely captivated.

Luke stared at the tabletop and shook his head. "I don't know. It's all pretty fuzzy. My dreams got weirder and then I woke up at my sister's house."

Luke paused to take a drink of water before continuing. "I think I slept for three straight days and I started to feel like my old self again."

"But it didn't last," Heath said.

Luke shook his head. "Nope. My sister and I were out on a walk down by the water when all of the sudden I felt the shadowman right behind me again. I just wanted to get away from him, you know? I took off and it followed me until I ran into the Stop & Shop. And then, it was like a miracle—he backed off. I realized that as long as I keep myself near a group of people, the shadowman can't get inside my head."

"But that's hardly a solution," his sister said, reaching out to squeeze his hand. "He's been unable to function normally from sleep deprivation. He comes here and sleeps either in the waiting room or, if I can get him a bed, in one of the doctors' lounges, but the sleep he's able to get is never long enough or deep enough for him to become fully rested. I'm worried about the lasting effects from his lack of restorative sleep."

The room fell silent and I felt everyone's gaze land on me. I was deeply troubled by what Luke was telling me. I knew by experience that he was in fact being haunted, and he looked so worn down and exhausted that I felt strongly that the spook in question might be angling for a full-on possession.

Possessions are particularly tricky, because once that door's been opened—once a spook has gotten "in," so to speak—even if it's exorcised, it is most likely to come back again and again until it all but destroys its host's life.

"I'd like to set up an observation," I said to the group.

"An observation?" Steven repeated.

I nodded but focused on Luke. "I want to see what happens when you try to sleep, Luke. With your permission, I'd like to set up some cameras to watch you overnight. And I'd like you to be alone during the time we're observing you."

"If you think it'll help, I'm willing to try anything. I just want this thing to go away and for my life to go back to normal," Luke said.

I pressed my lips together. I thought I owed it to Steven, Courtney, and Luke to be honest with them. "The truth is that I'm not sure we can help. Whatever is haunting Luke is focusing very hard on wearing him down. I don't know yet what the ulterior motive is, but it's trying to take him over. And if it does, then we're not the experts to help him with that."

"You're talking about possession?" Courtney asked, her face turning pale.

"Yes." I let everyone in the room take that in for a good long moment before continuing. Then, I focused on Luke again, who looked scared to death. "The good news is that I don't think we're at the point where you've been taken over, Luke. But I suspect we might be close. I want to observe you, tomorrow night if possible, and hopefully Heath, Gilley, and I will be able to identify what's truly going on. Then we'll consider our options."

"What are the options?" Steven asked.

"I won't know that until I see what kind of spook we're dealing with. If this is just a grounded spirit, then it's not nearly as bad as it could be."

"How bad could it be?" Luke asked, his voice barely above a whisper.

"It could be a demon," Gilley told him.

It was Luke's turn to pale and I wished Gil hadn't

spoken. I reached out and put my hand over Luke's. "Listen," I said, "whatever it is that's haunting you, we'll figure it out, and we'll come up with a plan. Maybe that plan will include reinforcements. Maybe it'll just take the three of us, but I promise you we won't leave you hanging, okay?"

"You promise?" Luke asked, his expression pleading.

I held up my hand. "On my honor, Luke. We'll help you see this thing through."

The next morning Heath and I slept in. We were going to be up all night observing Luke, so I wanted us to be well rested so that we could focus. Around noon we met with Gilley to go over the strategy and formulate a plan. Courtney had given us a key to her row house along with the alarm code so that we could set up our cameras in Luke's room and around her home. She would spend the night at Steven's place. I tried not to think too much about that.

Meanwhile, Heath and I would be situated just down the block from Courtney's place at an all-night diner while Gilley would be staying at his condo, monitoring all the feeds, and coordinating with us. He'd been invited to set up shop at the diner . . . and he'd declined with a firm, "Whatchoo talkin' 'bout, Willis?" Gil wanted to be as far away from this spook as he could get while still being able to help us.

If things took an ugly turn, Heath and I could be at Luke's side in under a minute, armed to the rafters with magnetic spikes and our newest weapon, the Super Spooker Smasher—Gilley's term, I swear—which is basically a tennis racket restrung with magnetized wire. We'd had only one occasion to use it, but it'd come in super-spooker handy.

Once we'd worked out all the details, we left Gilley at

his condo and headed to Courtney's place, arriving at a lovely brownstone on Commonwealth Avenue. I got out of the car and stood at the bottom of the steps looking up at it, trying to feel out the ether of the place.

Heath came up next to me and for several moments we simply stood silently while our collective intuition reached through the walls of the building and poked around, looking for trouble.

Heath was the first to break the silence. "I'm not sensing anything negative," he said.

"Me either."

"Which is weird, right?" he said. "I mean, we should be feeling something, shouldn't we?"

I frowned. "If Luke is telling the truth, yeah, I think there'd at least be something icky hanging around in the ether."

"Should we go in?"

"Oh, please, would you?" Gilley's impatient voice said into my earpiece. I'd forgotten that Gil was connected to us through the Bluetooth Heath and I were both wearing.

Next to me, Heath chuckled softly and put a hand on my shoulder, motioning for me to go in. We climbed the stairs and I unlocked the door before stepping inside to a dim interior. All the blinds downstairs were drawn, but from what I could see, Courtney had lovely taste.

"What's it look like?" Gilley called into my ear. With a sigh I hit the FaceTime option on my iPhone before holding it up so he could see before I began the tour.

Light wood floors spread out from the entryway to a formal dining room on the left, and a small study on the right. The staircase faced us, and to the left of it the hallway looked like it dead-ended at the kitchen.

The walls were painted a beautiful steel blue with bright white crown molding and gold-bronze accents placed just so. Several oil paintings in gilded frames were spaced artfully about the hallway and dining room, and as I followed the corridor back toward the kitchen, I found the entry to the living room just behind the stairs.

The kitchen was to die for: the granite countertops a swirl of teal, white, and yellow perfectly setting off the lightly stained cabinets and stainless steel appliances. The living room (really not more than a parlor) was another delightful surprise, set in a pale yellow only a hint past the shade of parchment. An off-white suede sofa and love seat dominated the space with a pop of color from the tangerine throw pillows and matching cashmere throw. Under our feet was a creamy Berber carpet and on one wall were a marble hearth and a gas log fireplace. It was the sort of space that begged you to come sit a spell.

"Nice," Heath said, coming up from behind me after he'd inspected the kitchen.

"Yep."

"You okay?"

"Perfect."

"Uh . . . okay?"

"She's upset because Courtney has amazing taste," Gil said. I could hear him munching on something that sounded like popcorn. He was enjoying the show . . . the little bastard.

"Why would that make her upset?" Heath asked, like I wasn't standing right in front of him.

"Can we just forget it?" I snapped, and moved around Heath back toward the stairs. Climbing them quickly, I crested the landing and found the upstairs mirrored the downstairs in its elegance.

The master bedroom was a lighter shade of steel blue, but only slightly, and the bed was an elaborate affair with a huge Indian-inspired headboard and silk bedding that looked straight out of a magazine. On the nightstand was a picture of Courtney and Steven, their foreheads pressed together in an intimate and beautiful moment. I want to say that it didn't hurt to look at that photo, but it did. I wondered if Steven and I had ever had a moment as sweet as that, and I suddenly couldn't think of one.

"Hey," I heard Heath call from the doorway. I jumped and turned quickly away from the photo.

"Hey," I said, trying to recover myself. "Should we set up a camera in here?"

Heath eyed the large bedroom suite. "Wouldn't hurt and we've got extras."

"I'm limiting you guys to five cameras," Gilley said into my ear.

"Why five?" Heath asked.

"Beyond that, it gets too hard to monitor," Gil said.

"Okay, so one in here, two in Luke's room, and maybe one in the kitchen facing out into the hallway and one over the front door facing the stairs and the hallway," I suggested.

"That'd be perfect," Gil told me.

"I'll tackle Luke's room," Heath said, walking forward to hand me a camera from the shoulder bag he carried.

"No," I said, taking the camera and holding out my hand for another. "You set up in here. I'll do Luke's room."

Heath eyed me curiously but didn't protest, and quick as I could, I left the room and that photo on the nightstand.

When I got to Luke's room, I was taken a bit aback by the neatness and orderliness of the place. Luke's bed was perfectly made, complete with fluffed-up pillows, and a bedspread you could bounce a quarter off. He'd mentioned that he didn't normally make the bed, and I wondered at the change in habit. Then I realized it was likely because Luke's life must feel out of control, and perhaps this new dedication to neatness was about providing himself with some small sense of control. It also was probably easy to identify right away if any of his things had been messed with. I continued to look around the room noting the arrangement of his things.

On the nightstand was a thriller by Lee Child, but no other clutter. I opened the drawer to the nightstand and there was the remote control for the TV, which sat on the bureau across the room. I turned on the set. It was tuned to ESPN.

Clicking it off, I moved to the closet. Inside I found only five shirts and about as many pairs of jeans, hanging perfectly spaced a few inches apart. Luke's three pairs of shoes were also arranged neatly on the floor.

Stepping back out into the bedroom, which was smaller than the master but still a nice size, I looked around. I knew that Luke was staying with his sister, who must've been responsible for decorating the room in a soft gray with buttercream curtains, but there wasn't much in it to suggest anyone was living here other than the contents of the closet and the book on the nightstand. I wondered where any other personal effects might be. A magazine, or dirty laundry, or loose change, but all of that seemed to be absent, as if Luke was trying hard not to disturb the atmosphere, to linger as quietly as possible in this room and still his energy so as not to leave an imprint.

I felt out the space with my own radar, and found it lacking any presence of malice or wickedness, and again I wondered what the deal was. Why was there nothing residual in the ether to indicate that Luke was telling the truth? Certainly some trace of this spook would get left behind, wouldn't it?

With a sigh I got to work setting up the two cameras. One I placed over the door and the other I put over the entrance to the closet. That would be our main camera as it gave the best view of the bed. I coordinated with Gil to make sure he was getting a good feed and then headed out to see if Heath needed help downstairs.

I found him perched on a chair from the kitchen, struggling with the camera over the front door. "It's not sticking," he said.

"We might have to drill a hole."

"There's a drill in the van," Gil said helpfully. "In the toolbox."

Heath went out to get the drill and Gilley said, "Sooooo, how you doin', honey?"

"I'm fine."

"Really?" he asked skeptically. "In the home of Steven's new fiancée, you're 'fine'?"

"Peachy."

"Even after seeing that little love nest upstairs?" he said, poking the tiger, as only Gilley knew how to do.

"Can we drop this?" I said, digging around in Heath's bag for the remaining camera to put in the kitchen.

"Oh, come on, M.J. I know it's bugging you! Steven's not only found someone new, but the man's engaged. To a neurosurgeon. Doesn't that drive you a little crazy?"

"No," I said, moving toward the kitchen.

"A beautiful neurosurgeon," Gil continued. "Who's, like, super nice too and has ahhh-mazing taste."

I got to the kitchen and slammed the camera on the counter. "Fine, Gil. It drives me crazy! You happy? It hurts, because as much as I've moved on, there's still a part of me that wonders what would've happened if Steven and I had tried a little harder."

"Uh, guys?" I heard Heath's voice say into my earpiece. "You know I can hear you, right?"

I sucked in a breath and slapped my forehead. "Oh, God! Heath . . . I'm . . ."

I heard the front door open and turned to see Heath step through to the entryway. He held up the drill and said, "Found it."

I could see the hurt on his face and I felt a wave of guilt hit me right in the gut. I was about to go to him when he turned away and climbed back onto the chair to begin drilling.

"Well, *that* was awkward," Gil said.

I balled my hands into fists. "Gil."

"Yeah?"

"Shut it before I shut it for you."

"Roger that, M.J."

Heath and I finished placing the cameras and locked up before heading out. He hadn't said another word to me, and every time I'd tried to look at him, he avoided my eyes. Once we were back in the van, I made sure my headset was off before turning to him. "Can I explain?"

Heath started the engine and checked his side mirror. "It's cool, Em."

I put a hand on his arm and waited for him to look at me. "No, it's not. It's not cool at all. And I'm sorry."

Heath sighed and put the van into park again, but stared straight out the windshield. "I can't blame you. I pushed you into taking this case," he said. "I wanted you to get that you'd made the right choice by picking me."

"Of course I made the right choice," I told him. When he still wouldn't look at me, I leaned in and cupped his face, turning it toward me. "I love you. And even more important, I love us. We make an incredible team, and not even Gilley understands and accepts me the way you do. That means everything to me, especially since Steven never quite either understood or accepted me for me. But you do, and I love being with you and only you."

A smile began to tug at the corners of Heath's mouth. "You're only saying that because the sex is so awesome."

I burst out laughing and kissed him sweetly. "Yes, how could I forget about the awesome sex?"

"Don't know," he chuckled. "Next time you apologize, maybe you should lead with that."

"Noted."

"You ready to get out of here?" he asked. "Maybe grab a bite to eat before we head back to the condo?"

I kissed him again, this time passionately as I wound my hand through his silky black hair. When we were both a little breathless, I said, "How about we head back to the condo first and have some awesome makeup sex?"

Heath turned away from me to focus once again on the road in front of him before squealing out of the parking space. We made it home in record time.

Around eleven p.m. Heath and I went to the twenty-four-hour diner to meet Steven, Courtney, and Luke. "You've seen the cameras?" I asked them as we all sat down.

"We have," Steven said. "May I ask why there's one in Courtney's room?"

I saw Courtney shift subtly in her seat, and I knew the question had been prompted by her. I could imagine that as cool as she seemed about the fact that Steven and I used to date, it was a whole other thing to have his ex put a camera in her bedroom.

Thinking it wise to hold my tongue, I let Heath answer. "We can't have an area of the house out of sight," he said. "And Courtney's room is right next door to Luke's. If this spook wants to roam the house before getting at Luke, we want to know where it likes to hang out."

"Did you get a sense of anything when you were there?" Courtney asked, and I noticed that she barely suppressed a shudder. It had to be hard to live with a sibling being haunted by an evil ghost. I gave her props for being brave and opening her home to Luke.

"No," I said.

"Nothing on the meters?" Steven pressed, obviously remembering the old days when he used to come along on my ghostbusts.

"Not a blip," I told him.

"So what's the plan?" Luke asked. "I mean, I'm just supposed to go stay in the house by myself?"

I focused on him and saw that the dark circles under his eyes were a little more pronounced tonight. I'd told him that if he could stay awake today, it might be better. We needed him tired enough to fall asleep quickly so we could see what happened. Judging by his slumped shoulders and exhausted expression, he'd followed instructions. "That's exactly what we'd like you to do. Go home, make yourself comfortable, and try to sleep. We'll be watching you the whole time, Luke, and we're just a few blocks away. If things start to get weird, we can be at your house in a flash with one of these." I pointed to the stack of magnetic spikes I'd put on the table, which was totally for Luke and Courtney's benefit. I wanted to show them that we meant business, and that they could take us seriously.

Luke picked up one of the spikes. "It's heavy."

I lifted my spoon and held it close to the spike in his hand. It flew out of my fingers and attached itself to the spike. "It's magnetized."

Luke took the spoon away from the spike before letting them clink together again. "So, what? If this thing shows up, you're going to come stab it?"

"In a manner of speaking," Heath said. "But it'll probably get the hell out of there when it sees us coming with one of these. Spooks can't stand to be around magnets. It causes them major discomfort and most can't tolerate them. If this spook runs, though, we'll give chase."

"You'll give chase?" Courtney asked.

Heath nodded. "We need to know where this thing comes from. If it's sinister, then it'll have a link to the lower realms, and to float between this plane and that one, it'll need a portal."

Courtney blinked. Then she blinked a second time. "Come again?"

I smiled. To Courtney's ears, Heath probably sounded like he was speaking in code. I decided to step in and explain. "On the spirit plane there are essentially three realms. There's our realm, where our souls are carried around inside our bodies and we can interact easily with each other. Then there's the higher realm, or what most people think of as heaven or the other side, and then there's the lower realm, which is where lots of negative energy lurks. Grounded spirits—like the one we think is currently haunting your brother—for a variety of reasons can become trapped here in our realm. Some become trapped because they don't realize they're dead, and they keep trying to interact with us as if they still had a body. The way they see this realm can remain fixed, and they aren't aware of time. These are your more traditional ghosts, and, usually, they're harmless.

"Other grounded spirits, however, can become trapped because they don't want to cross over into heaven out of fear of what kind of judgment might await them on the other side. They literally carry the fear of God within them, and if they were bad people here, they might feel that God will be harsh on them when they cross. They're here because they're stalling, so to speak. They think God will come down hard on them."

"If they were bad people, wouldn't He?" Courtney asked.

I shrugged. "I don't know. From my experience as a medium I can tell you that most of the souls I've connected with all suggest that the only judgment we face when we cross over is one of our own creation. We judge ourselves and we aren't able to take with us the veil of denial, so we see ourselves as we truly are, warts and all. It can be quite painful for a soul who led a corrupt or selfish life to be stripped bare and really take a good hard look at themselves."

"So is that what this spook is?" Luke asked. "That kind?"

I sighed. "I don't think so, Luke," I whispered.

His brow furrowed. "Then what kind is he?"

"I don't know, but I suspect he may be a third kind of spook. The kind that wouldn't be allowed to cross over even if he were willing."

Luke's mouth fell open. "You mean, the kind that would be sent to hell?"

I nodded again. "And may already have been. That's the lower realm I'm talking about. Some spooks like to float back and forth between the two realms. They create a portal where they can easily come and go."

"Why wouldn't they just stay down there?" Courtney asked me.

"Because it wouldn't be nearly as much fun," Heath said, without a hint of mirth. "Spooks like that want access to the lower realm to learn how to manipulate things in our plane."

"What do you mean, 'manipulate things'?" she pressed.

"Well, they learn how to gain and utilize energy. If they can invoke fear in you, they can raise the electromagnetic current you produce. Your own electromagnetic energy gets a boost, the same way your heart beats faster when you exercise. These spooks can hitch a ride off that energy and use it to their advantage by moving or throwing things like rocks and small stones, by manipulating electrical currents to start fires, or by taking over a person."

Courtney gave in to her shudder this time and Steven wrapped an arm around her and began rubbing her back. "This is so scary," she whispered.

"I know," I told her. "But Heath, Gilley, and I are very good at this type of thing. Hopefully we'll know what we're dealing with after tonight and we'll be able to put a plan into action."

Steven pushed his chair back and held his hand out for his fiancée. "She's right," he told her. "If anybody can help Luke, M.J. and Gilley can."

Next to me I felt Heath bristle.

Steven eyed him sideways, a slight smirk on his face. "I'm sure you're good too, Whitefeather."

I gave Steven a withering look, but he hardly looked contrite. After Courtney gave her brother one final hug, she and Steven were off to his place. I walked Luke to the door. "Think you'll be able to fall asleep?" I asked him as he zipped up his jacket. It'd turned cool that evening.

"Falling asleep is never the problem. It's staying asleep that's hard."

I gave him a light pat on the shoulder and told him we'd keep a watchful eye on him, then went back to the table to hunker down for the long night ahead.

Chapter 5

Around two a.m. my eyelids began to droop and my head started to loll forward. "Take a nap," Heath suggested.

I blinked blearily at him. He looked just as tired. I inhaled deeply and dipped my coffee cup toward me to take a peek at the contents. It was nearly empty, which was a good thing because I'd had so much coffee that my stomach was a little upset. "I'm okay," I said, leaning back to stretch and rub my eyes. Then I got up and tried to shake off the fatigue. We'd been watching the monitors diligently for the past three hours without a hint of trouble. I figured if we got past four a.m., we'd be in the clear, but the question of why this spook hadn't shown up yet was a troubling one. I thought again about my suspicion that Luke might be making some of this up, but for the life of me I couldn't imagine what he had to gain. And then there was what Courtney had said—she'd seen a shadow at Luke's old house. I believed her even if I didn't quite believe him.

"Man, this is dull," Gil said into my ear.

I hadn't heard a peep from him in over an hour. "Where you been?"

"I took a nap."

"Of course you did," I said flatly.

"It's not like I missed anything," Gil replied, without a hint of apology in his voice.

I opened my mouth to say something smart when Heath suddenly put a hand on my arm. "I think we've got something."

Gilley gasped and I sat down quick, my eyes searching the monitor, but at first I didn't see anything. Heath pointed to the lower left-hand side of the screen, which showed the front hallway. It took me a minute, but I finally realized there was a shadow against the far wall. It blended into the background so well at first I didn't see it until it sort of oozed out of the wall and hovered at the base of the stairs.

"Whoa!" Gil said.

The shadow was about six feet tall, maybe a little shorter but not by much. It had the rough shape of a person but wasn't especially defined and it continued to stand there at the base of the stairs for several tense moments as if assessing the situation before deciding what to do next.

"What's it waiting for?" Heath whispered.

And as if on cue, the shadow seemed to turn sideways and what looked like a head tilted up toward the camera. My breath caught and next to me I felt Heath stiffen. In my ear I heard Gilley make a frightened squeaking noise. There was no doubt from any of us that the shadow was aware of not only the camera but the fact that we were watching it.

Several tense seconds went by, none of us daring to breathe, and then the shadow finally turned back toward the stairs and began to ascend them. "Should we head over there?" I whispered.

Heath shook his head. "Let's wait and see what it does. We need to know the full extent of this spook's powers and how it interacts with Luke before we go over there with guns blazing."

I knew he was right, but it was a tough thing to sit by and watch that creepy shadow make its way slowly up those stairs to where Luke was sound asleep and defenseless.

The spook went out of view of the camera about three-quarters of the way up the stairs and we picked it up on the view from the camera located on Courtney's bedroom wall—which faced out toward the hallway. The spook's movement was smooth like liquid, which lent it an eerie inky quality. I'd never seen a ghost move quite like it. In my gut I had the feeling that it could move a whole lot faster, and that it was purposely drawing out the time to both freak us out and assess what we'd do. And I had no doubt that the spook was fully aware of us, because at the top of the stairs it paused again and focused all of its attention on the camera in Courtney's room.

"It keeps staring right into the camera," Gil whispered, and I could tell he was totally creeped out.

We'd had another spook who'd done something similar on a shoot several months before and that'd scared us all witless, but somehow the shadowman in Courtney's house was taking this particular trick up a notch. I shuddered involuntarily and waited for the spook to continue on.

At last it turned toward the hallway and moved with oozy precision toward Luke's room. It entered and we had to switch our attention to the camera over Luke's closet. The spook headed straight to the bed and stood next to it, hovering there for a long time. "What's it doing?" Gil asked.

"I don't know," I said, squinting at the monitor. Luke appeared to be fast asleep, and then I saw his right leg jerk. I jumped at the movement and bit my lip. The urge to run right over to Courtney's with all our magnetic spikes and the racket was strong. But I knew Heath was right; we had to wait and see how this spook would interact with its target first.

Luke jerked again and his arm flew out as if he was trying to fend off an attack. My own hand reached out and curled around a magnetic stake and my body tensed, ready to fly out of the café and head to Courtney's. Heath reached out and held on to my elbow, not to stop me but ready to go with me the second things went bad.

All the while Luke continued to jerk and thrash, as if he was having the most violent nightmare. His arm thrashed out again and again, but then I noticed that it seemed to change direction and his clenched fist swung down in an arc over and over, as if he were stabbing at something.

And then, in an instant, the shadowman next to Luke vanished at the same moment Luke's eyes flew open and he sat bolt upright. His hair was damp and he appeared covered in sweat. His T-shirt clung to him and he was breathing heavily, as if he'd just run a sprint.

"Where'd it go?" Gilley asked.

"Don't know," I said, my eyes darting around the monitor to the other camera views. "Do you see it anywhere, Heath?"

"No," he said. "Gil, click the camera in the kitchen."

We had views of four of the cameras, and the fifth was being monitored by Gilley separately because it wouldn't fit onto our laptop's screen. A second later our monitor was filled with a view of the front hallway, and Heath and I both leaned in, searching for any sign of the spook, but we couldn't find anything out of the ordinary. "Try Courtney's room," I said.

The monitor switched to the master bedroom and Heath and I searched again. "Where the hell did you go?" I wondered aloud.

"Guys?" Gilley said suddenly. "Luke's getting up."

I reached for my cell and dialed his number. Gil switched the monitor back to the camera in Luke's room, and through the computer I could hear Luke's phone ringing. It lit up his nightstand, but Luke, who was now standing, didn't even glance at it. Instead he moved away from his bed, put his feet into his shoes, and walked out of the room.

"Where's he going?" I said as Luke's phone switched over to voice mail.

"Probably to get a glass of water or something," Heath said. Looking at me, he said, "Try him again."

I redialed Luke's phone and it rang but Luke didn't come back into the room to answer it. "Gil," I said while the phone was still ringing, "put up all the other monitors."

He did and we saw immediately that Luke was in the hallway headed for the stairs. "Come on, dude," I whispered. "Answer my call."

Luke paused at the top of the stairs and I thought for sure he was going to do just that, but then he turned and stared right at the camera in Courtney's room in a way that made all of us catch our breath. He looked straight into the lens, his gaze intense and unflinching, and at the corners of his mouth was the most sinister smirk. I felt my blood run cold, and as his phone once again clicked over to voice mail, I didn't hang up—I just sat there frozen staring at Luke as he gazed at us as if he could actually see us looking back at him. His eyes taunted us and his stance was menacing. I don't know how else to describe it, other than the guy I'd first met at the hospital and who had sat with us just a few hours earlier was gone, and in his place was Mr. Hyde.

With what looked like a snicker Luke was in motion again; moving steadily down the stairs, he walked straight to the front door, opened it, and was gone before any of us could react.

Heath slid out of the booth first, grabbing a handful of spikes and the Spooker Smasher before he took off out of the diner. I grabbed the remaining spikes and dashed out the door after him. We'd warned the waitress that we might need to run out of the place quickly, and we'd already paid our tab and left her a sizable tip to watch our stuff, should the need arise for us to bolt. I hoped she'd look after our laptop and personal items, but I couldn't worry about that now.

I ran as fast as I could after Heath, but he had a good lead on me and he was crazy fast in his own right. I lost ground to him quickly, but that didn't stop me from putting my all into the effort. I managed to catch up with him at the foot of the steps leading to Courtney's brownstone. He was looking up and down the street, trying to spot Luke. "There's no sign of which direction he went," Heath said, his breath coming hard.

"Did you check inside?" I asked, hoping Luke had turned back around and gone back inside his sister's place.

Gilley answered me. "He's not there, M.J. I'm watching the monitors and no one's come back inside."

"Any sign of the spook?" I asked Gil, trying to catch my breath.

"Nope."

I looked at Heath. "Now what?"

"Let's run around the block," he suggested, pointing up the street. "You go east. I'll go west."

I nodded and took off again. This time, I ran at a more manageable pace, twisting my head back and forth trying to spot any sign of Luke. But he seemed to have vanished.

I wondered if he'd gotten in his car and driven somewhere, but then I also wondered if he even had a car. I met Heath around the other side of the block. "Any sign of him?" I called when he came into view.

He shook his head. "Where the hell did he go?"

I shrugged. I had no idea. "Should we call Steven and Courtney?"

Heath pressed his lips together. I could see he was beating himself up for not going to Luke's rescue sooner, around the time I'd suggested we should. "No," he said. "Let's give it a little time." Then he pressed his finger against his Bluetooth and said, "Gil? You still with us?"

"I am."

"Anything on the monitors?"

"Nope."

Heath sighed heavily. "Okay. Keep watching for us. M.J. and I are going to go back to the diner and get our stuff and the van. If Luke comes back into the house, let us know right away."

"Roger that," Gil said.

Heath and I trotted back around the block and took one more look up the street before turning away and jogging back to the diner. We found our stuff just as we left it, and our waitress nodded to us as we collected it. "I kept my eye on it," she said.

"Thanks," I told her, and Heath and I left the diner for good. We got in the van then and started to drive around the neighborhood, pausing at every alleyway and side street to peer into the darkness and hopefully spy Luke. But he was nowhere. It was as if he'd vanished into thin air just like the spook.

By three o'clock we had combed the whole neighborhood, so we headed back to Courtney's and parked the van in a spot across the street. We went inside and Gilley said, "Welcome back, kiddies."

"No sign of him?" I asked a bit desperately.

"Nada."

Heath leaned against the door. He looked frustrated and defeated. "We should probably call Courtney."

"She's gonna freak," I said, hauling out my cell to make the call.

Heath stepped forward and put his hand over the cell. "Let me do it, babe. It's my fault he's missing."

I cocked a skeptical eyebrow at him. He wasn't to blame. "How do you figure?"

"I should've listened to you when the spook first showed up down here. We should've been here to protect Luke."

I leaned in and hugged him. "Honey, we had no idea what the spook was going to do. You were right to say that we should hang back and wait."

Heath squeezed me tight and rested his chin on the top of my head. "We knew the spook might try possessing Luke, Em. We should've thought about the consequences of being so far away when that happened."

I closed my eyes and shook my head. "It's not your fault, Heath. And for all we know, Luke could be sleepwalking. I mean, we don't *actually* know he's been taken over by the spook. Maybe the spook's disappearance has nothing to do with Luke getting out of bed and leaving here."

Heath made a derisive sound. "You really believe that?"

I sighed again. "No. But the point is that we don't yet know for certain what's happened. Luke might be fine. And either way, come daylight he's bound to turn up."

Heath kissed the top of my head and continued to hug me tight. "Let's hope so."

Somewhere in the distance the sound of sirens cut into the quiet of the night. "Eesh," I said. "Sirens after midnight. Never a good sign."

And then Heath and I both stiffened, as if we both suddenly knew that the sirens might have something to do with Luke.

"What's happening?" Gilley asked. I didn't think he'd picked up the sound of the sirens just yet.

I didn't answer him. Instead I lifted my phone and searched my contacts list for Courtney's name. Heath's hand covered the screen again and he took it from me. "Let me," he said gently. "And, Gilley, do your hacking thing and see if you can find out why there're sirens in this neighborhood at three a.m., would you?"

"Sirens? You guys hear sirens?"

"Yes," Heath and I said together.

"That's never a good sign," Gil muttered.

I watched Heath nervously as the screen on my phone lit up his worried face and all the while the sirens closed in. At last he put the phone to his ear and I waited anxiously for him to talk to Courtney. Just as Heath opened his mouth to speak, however, the front door burst open and Luke appeared, looking terrified. Heath was so startled that he dropped my phone and we both grabbed on to each other as we stared wide-eyed at Luke, who slammed the door behind him, threw the dead bolt, then sank weakly to the floor.

As I was trying to process his sudden appearance, a scent wafted to my nose that made my stomach muscles clench. The heavy scent of rust filled the hallway and in the dim light I saw that Luke's shirt and hands were covered in something dark and wet. Heath was in motion first. He went to the side table and switched on the light, and as I blinked in the bright light of the room, I realized that Luke was covered in blood. It soaked the front of his T-shirt, and was smeared all over his arms and neck. There was even a long smudge of it along his forehead.

"Ohmigod!" Gilley gasped. "He's hurt!"

I darted forward as Luke's legs spread out in front of him, his ragged breathing never slowing. Heath was quick to take up Luke's other side and together we worked to figure out where his injury was. "Gilley!" I yelled. "Call an ambulance!"

"And the police!" Heath added.

"Help . . . me!" Luke pleaded before a sob overtook him and he sank even lower to the floor.

"Where're you hurt?" I asked him desperately. "Luke, tell us where you're bleeding!"

I was pulling up on his T-shirt as gently as I could, but I couldn't find the wound. His head rolled back and forth and he was sobbing in earnest now. "Please . . . help . . . me!" he cried.

Heath stood up and ran to the kitchen. I heard the sound of the faucet and then he was back with several kitchen towels soaked in water. He handed me one and said, "We have to find his wound!"

"I'm trying!" I said, scooting closer to Luke to hold him up while I searched him up and down, but I couldn't find the source of the bleeding.

Meanwhile my phone began ringing, but Heath and I both ignored it. After it stopped, there was a slight pause; then Luke's phone upstairs started to chime. In the back of my mind I knew it must be Courtney or Steven, but I couldn't focus on them right now.

While I searched Luke's torso, he continued to plead

with us to help him. At last Heath put his hands on either side of Luke's face, looked him directly in the eyes, and said, "Dude! *Where* are you hurt?"

Luke's eyes were huge. He looked as if he'd seen something too terrible to describe and I had a feeling he was sinking into shock. I reached for his hands and sure enough they were cold. I got up and ran into the kitchen and fished around in several drawers, found a pair of scissors, then opened the fridge, took out a Coke, and ran back to Luke's side.

Heath was wiping off the blood and tossing the soiled bloody towels to the side. He was on the last towel by the time I sat down next to Luke again. I opened the Coke and gave it to Luke. "Take a few sips," I ordered. I had no idea if it was a bad thing to give Coca-Cola to an injured man, but I felt I needed to slow down the progression of shock before Luke lost consciousness. He was shaking so bad he couldn't hold the can, so I held it for him as I tilted it toward his mouth and he took a few sips. Then I set the can aside and talked to him as gently as I could while I took up the hem of his T-shirt and began to cut. The smell of the blood was making me nauseous, but I refused to give in to the urge to move away. At last I had the T-shirt cut in half up the middle, and as gently as I could, I eased it off Luke's shoulders.

Heath got up and took the bloody towels back to the kitchen, where he ran them under the faucet again. Luke's breathing was beginning to calm a bit and he sniffled and wiped at his eyes with the backs of his hands. Using my fingertips, I pressed along his abdomen, chest, and collarbone looking for the source of all that blood. Heath came back and I looked up at him. He seemed to be asking me the silent question, had I found the wound? I could only shake my head. He then handed me a towel and I wiped down Luke's arm, thinking maybe he'd opened up an artery or something, but upon closer inspection I couldn't even find a bruise.

At last Heath and I sat back and exchanged another look. Luke wasn't hurt anywhere that we could tell. And the minute we stopped probing him, he lay down on his side, curled himself into the fetal position, and began to sob in earnest again.

Meanwhile, outside there was the screeching of brakes and then a red strobe light pierced the small window to the right of the door and began to bounce against the walls of the entryway. A few seconds later there was a hard knock on the door. Luke shrieked, covered his head, then got to his feet and bolted up the stairs. Heath and I sat stunned on the floor, each of us trying to make sense of it, and in the pit of my stomach I had such a sense of dread.

"Hey, guys?" Gilley said into my ear. Before I could answer, there was another round of hard knocks on the outside and someone called out from the steps, but it was muffled and I couldn't quite catch what they said. "I found out why the sirens were in the neighborhood," Gil continued, his voice shaking with fear or nerves or maybe even alarm. "A woman was found stabbed about a block away from Courtney's place."

Heath's shoulders sagged as if the news was too heavy to bear. My own eyes misted and I felt dizzy because the truth of all the discordant parts of the evening was suddenly coming together.

A third round of knocks on the door finally motivated both Heath and me to stand and walk forward, but both of us stopped just short of opening the door. Instead we looked around at the bloody mess on the floor—the soiled towels, the shredded T-shirt, Luke's bloody footprints—and for a long moment I knew what Heath was thinking because I was thinking the same thing. . . .

Maybe we should bolt out the back and book a flight for someplace very far away.

A pounding on the door brought us to our senses, and Heath reached for the dead bolt, and then the handle. Pulling the door open, he revealed two paramedics and behind them a police officer was just coming up the steps. The paramedics took one look at Heath and me smeared with blood and the mess on the floor, and as one they stepped to the side, allowing the officer to come up through the middle. I knew they wouldn't enter until the police officer said it was okay.

The officer also took a long look at us and the floor of the entryway before reaching for his walkie-talkie. "This is unit eighteen," he said crisply. "We got another situation here at seven-five-seven-five Commonwealth. Over."

There was a garbled response and I couldn't quite understand it, but then the officer clicked his mic again and said, "Either it's another murder or I just found our suspects."

Then he withdrew his gun and pointed it at us. "On the ground, hands behind your heads. Now."

Heath and I locked eyes and I heard Gilley squeak nervously in my ear. Heath then sighed, raised his hands, and dropped to his knees. I followed suit and before long I felt the officer's knee on my back and the air whooshed out of my lungs as he pressed down and quickly put a zip tie around my hands. "Is there anyone else in the house?" the cop asked as I heard footsteps come up the steps from outside.

Craning my neck, I saw two more police officers step into the foyer, careful to avoid the blood on the floor. "The young man who lives here is upstairs," I answered without hesitation. I didn't know what kind of trouble Luke had gotten himself into, but I knew it was bad, and I wanted no part of it.

"Is he armed?" asked the cop.

"No," Heath and I said together.

"I just texted Steven," Gilley whispered through the Bluetooth in my ear. "He's calling me now. Back in a sec."

The cop who'd been bending over me stood up and I saw one of the other police officers follow him toward the stairs, while the remaining officer stood by the door to guard us. Heath turned his head to look back at me. He mouthed, "You okay?"

I nodded.

Gil came back on the line and said, "Steven and Courtney are on their way there now. Should I call anyone else?"

"Mack Savage," I said softly, but not softly enough. I saw the cop's eyes narrow suspiciously and I knew he'd just detected the little blue light on the earpiece I was wearing.

"What?" Heath asked me.

"Mack Savage is a lawyer friend of mine," I told him. "His family was killed in a house fire when he was still in high school. He was the only one who got out. Over the years I've done quite a few readings for him and it's helped him cope. In return he helps me out whenever I need legal advice."

"Like now?" Heath said with the hint of a smile.

"Yep."

"Calling him right now, M.J.," Gilley said.

Heavy footsteps on the stairs next to me made me turn my head away from Heath to look up. Luke was sandwiched between the two cops as they marched him down the stairs. His head hung low and he didn't look up. I still didn't know what'd happened, but I did try to extend my intuition out to him, just to see if there was any sign of the spook haunting him. Nothing in the ether floated back to me, which was eerie. I felt there should've been some sort of presence around him—a parent, a grandparent, or someone from the other side present in his energy—but the space around him was just blank, as if no one wanted anything to do with him. That unsettled me more than I can say.

"Mack's going to meet you downtown," Gilley said into my ear. "I'm on my way too."

"Gil?" I whispered as Luke was marched right past me and the other cop reached down to pull me awkwardly to my feet.

"Yeah?"

"Thanks."

Heath and I shared a ride downtown in one squad car while Luke rode in the other. We'd been read our rights before being placed in the vehicle, and when Heath asked why we were under arrest, the officer replied, "On suspicion of murder."

That sent a cold shiver up my spine, and my mind raced with questions about who'd been killed and if Luke had had anything to do with it. I found it impossible to think that he might not have—the man had shown up covered in enough blood to either be gravely injured or have had contact with someone who was. Something terrible had happened in the time between Luke's disappearance from his sister's house and his showing up again. And if he had in fact done something unspeakable—what was going to happen to Heath and me? Would we be held as accomplices? We'd had nothing to do with the crime, but I wasn't exactly confident that we'd be left out of it.

As we rode downtown in silence, Heath leaned sideways slightly to touch me shoulder to shoulder, and I was so grateful for his presence. "You okay?" he whispered.

"Scared," I mouthed back.

He nodded. "We'll be okay," he insisted, nudging me with his shoulder again. "I promise."

But his eyes were hardly confident and that worried me.

Once we arrived at the police substation, we were escorted inside through a back door and marched upstairs to the third floor, where we came out into a gloomy open office area with both uniformed and plainclothes cops. The three of us were then separated and placed into individual rooms with a two-way mirror and a metal chair tucked under a table with a loop for the handcuffs. Thankfully I was allowed out of my cuffs but then made to wait alone in the room for what felt like several hours. At last the door opened and in walked a tall, gray-haired woman with a lined face and a look that could've frozen water. Behind her Mack also walked in, looking a little haggard but determined. Mack came to stand next to me as the woman—who was also wearing a badge—took up the seat across from me.

"How you doin', M.J.?" Mack asked softly.

I looked up at him gratefully. "I've had better nights, Mack. Thanks for coming."

Mack squeezed my shoulder as the woman introduced herself. "Miss Holliday, I'm Detective Souter. Your attorney has asked to be present as you give your statement—"

"Actually," Mack interrupted. "I'd like a word with my client before we begin, Detective."

Souter frowned and added a sigh, but I thought it was mostly for show. "Very well," she said, getting to her feet again, but before she left, her eyes locked with mine, and I didn't like what I saw in them. She clearly thought I was guilty of something, and I didn't think that anything I could say to her when Mack finally let me talk was going to persuade her otherwise. So I held her stare and tried my best to keep my expression neutral.

After she left, Mack took up her seat and put his legal pad on the table. "What happened?" he asked.

I told him everything as quickly and efficiently as I could. He nodded and took notes, and I was so grateful that Mack was unaffected by much of what I told him about why Heath and I came to be at Courtney's house, attempting to rid Luke of some spook he claimed was haunting him.

When I was finished, Mack set his pen down, sat back in the chair, and rubbed his eyes tiredly. "Gilley told me a lot of this while we were waiting to see you," he said. "He's also got all the visual and all the audio on tape, thank God."

"He recorded it?" I asked. I don't know why that surprised me, but I was so relieved that Gil had had the foresight to record the events of that evening, so that at least Heath and I had some kind of an alibi.

Mack nodded. "The timing is a little tricky, because you're out of view of the cameras until shortly before Luke shows up covered in blood. But Gilley has been able to sync it to the recording of the audio off your Bluetooth, so we know that you weren't anywhere near the woman when she started screaming."

I felt the color drain from my face and a small wave of dizziness came over me. "Screams?"

Mack crossed his arms and studied me. "How much do you know about the murder?"

I shook my head. "I know very little other than that, after disappearing on us for a couple of hours, Luke showed up at his sister's house again covered in blood, and Gilley told us later just as the cops showed up that there'd been a murder down the street."

"Did Luke say anything to you?"

I shook my head again. "Nothing. Well, nothing other than begging us to help him. I think he went into shock, actually, and Heath and I thought something had happened to him."

"Like what?"

I shrugged. "I don't know. I guess I thought maybe he'd been hit by a car, or that somebody had stabbed him. I mean his clothes were covered in blood. . . ." My voice trailed off as I realized that there were traces of that very same blood on my hands from when I'd been searching Luke for a wound. It lined my fingernails and there were smudges of it on my cuffs. My stomach lurched suddenly and it was all I could do not to turn my head and retch.

"M.J.?" Mack asked.

I opened my mouth and took several deep breaths. "Gimme a minute, Mack," I said, swallowing hard several times to try to tamp down the sickly feeling. At last I felt the nausea ebb and was able to focus on Mack again. "Who was she?" I asked.

Mack didn't answer right away. He studied me for a few beats, probably wondering if I was well enough to continue, before he said, "A woman with an address in Cambridge. I don't have a name, just that she was a twenty-nine-year-old woman out alone for some reason. Her car was parked about a block away. She had ID and keys but no cell phone. It's either missing or she left it at home. The police are trying to figure out what she was doing there at that time of night."

"What happened? I mean, there was so much blood, Mack."

"Don't know much about that either, M.J. The news is reporting that she was stabbed multiple times and her throat was cut. Someone inside the brownstone near where she was murdered heard a woman scream, and they called the police. The cops found the girl dead and a blood trail leading in the direction of the house they found you three in."

I had to swallow hard again. This was all getting a little too real for me. "What do you want me to say to the detective?"

Mack smiled crookedly at me. "I want you to tell Souter the truth. But only answer the questions she asks you. Don't elaborate, but don't lie. Whatever you do, don't lie."

"Got it."

Mack stood. "I'll call her in," he said.

"Mack?" I asked, stopping him.

"Yeah?"

"My boyfriend, Heath, is here too. Did Gilley tell you that we both need your help?"

"It's covered, M.J. I've already signed Heath on as a client and he's given his statement to Souter in my presence. As long as your stories match, I think we'll be out of here in an hour or two."

"How's Heath holding up?"

"He's fine," Mack assured me. "He seems like a good fit for you too, if I might add."

That got me to smile. "How can you tell?"

"I'm a good judge of character," he said.

His reassuring smile did a whole lot to settle me. Then I asked, "And Luke Decker? Will you help him out too?"

Mack shook his head. "Your ex, Dr. Sable, called in a lawyer for him. He's got representation and it's pricey. My guess is that Luke won't speak a word to anybody between now and the end of his trial."

I gulped. "You think we'll go to trial?"

"Not if I have anything to say about it. Gilley's recordings should provide you with the alibi, but they'll also point the finger more firmly at Decker. I know the lawyer Sable hired, went to law school with him actually. Name's Caldwell Fischer, and he's a son of a bitch who'll throw anyone he can under the bus to make a play for reasonable doubt. You've got to be prepared for Fischer to point the finger at you and Heath, M.J. He'll try and make it look like you two might've set Luke up. That's why I want you to have nothing to do with Luke from here on out. No contact. *Capisce?*"

"Understood," I said, more nervous than ever to talk to Souter.

"Good," Mack said. "Now, let's get this over with so we can get you out of here, okay?"

I nodded and Mack went to the door to let Detective Souter in. She surprised both of us by bringing in Gilley's laptop, which was easily identifiable, given the large sticker of the *Ghostbusters* ghost on it. "How'd you get that?" Mack barked as the detective set the computer on the table.

She handed him a piece of paper. "Gillespie surrendered it when I handed him this warrant."

Mack snatched the warrant and skimmed it. He scowled hard but didn't protest more than he already had. The door opened again and another detective appeared with a chair. This he handed off to Mack, who took it and parked it right next to me. Once we were all settled, Souter began. "We've had a chance to review the footage of you and Mr. Whitefeather on here," she said. "Mr. Gillespie has also given us a statement."

Out of the corner of my eye I saw Mack's face flush with anger. I had a feeling he hadn't told Gilley to zip it, and knowing my best friend, he'd done his level best to cooperate with the police in order to help clear us. I wasn't sure if Gilley had just saved us or sunk us.

"I'd like to hear your version of events, Miss Holliday," Souter said.

I could tell Souter was purposely being broad. I glanced

at Mack. He was eyeing the computer moodily. Finally he looked over at me and said, "Start with how you came to meet Luke."

Taking a deep breath, I recited for the detectives exactly what'd gone on, beginning with the day when Steven had first entered my office. The detectives both took notes and asked me some pointed follow-up questions, and by the end, it felt like I'd been talking forever. At last Souter leaned back and said, "Something still confuses me, Miss Holliday." When I offered her only a blank stare, she continued. "Yesterday, I got an e-mail from Kendra Knight at channel seven news. She had some pretty interesting questions for me about the Bethany Sullivan murder case. She wanted to verify that Bethany had a cat and on the night of her murder that there'd been a bottle of wine chilling on her kitchen counter. And not just any wine—Zinfandel. Knight said these were facts she couldn't find in the official report released to the media, but they were given to her by someone claiming to be a psychic whom she'd interviewed earlier in the day. I caught the news story last night, and I made a note to myself to call you sometime later this morning. Kind of a freaky coincidence that I'd be questioning you on a completely separate murder investigation, isn't it?"

I squirmed in my seat. I could see the distrust in Souter's eyes. She was trying to put the pieces of a puzzle together, linking separate events and trying to see the bigger picture, which probably included a scenario where I was somehow guilty of something. "At the time Bethany Sullivan was murdered, I was out of the country. In fact, I've been out of the country for much of the past year. You can check my passport, Detective," I added, feeling confident of that alibi at least.

Souter nodded. "Oh, I'd appreciate that, Miss Holliday. We'd definitely like to verify your whereabouts for the evening Bethany was murdered."

The detective and I then had a little stare down between us and tired as I was, I forced myself not to blink. Finally, Mack said, "Are you going to charge my client, Detective?"

Souter drummed her fingers on the table for a little while before answering. "No. You're free to go, Miss Holliday. But stick close to town and get me that passport, or I'll have to get a warrant for it."

I stood up wearily. "I'll get it to you later today after I've had some sleep."

With that, Mack and I left the room. We found Gilley pacing and biting his nails outside in the hallway, and just as he looked up, I spotted Heath coming out of a corridor on the other side of the room. He looked relieved to see me and I felt my heart flutter with affection and relief of my own. I realized how much I was coming to count on him being nearby when things got dicey. Mack, Heath, and I reached Gilley at almost the exact same time. He greeted us by saying, "Where's my laptop?"

"Souter will probably keep it until she's had the tech guys look at it," Mack told him. "She'll want them to confirm there was no monkey business with the audio and the video taking place at the time of the murder."

Gilley looked ready to start yelling, so I took him firmly by the arm and pulled him toward the door. "Come on, Gil. You've got three other computers at home."

He squawked all the way out of the police station, but at least we got out of there without further incident. Gil drove us home, grumbling the whole way while Heath and I exchanged weary looks and eye rolls. At last we made it back to my condo and Heath opened the door for me. As I passed him on the way inside, I said, "Are you hungry? I can fix you something to eat if you are."

He smiled. "Later. Right now the thing you and I need most is sleep."

I tried to smile but I was too tired to put much into it. Heath and I headed straight to the shower for a quick scrub down to get the blood off us, then right to bed, and I was out like a light the minute my head hit the pillow.

Chapter 6

I woke up freezing. There was a dampness to the air and a chill so sharp it crawled through my skin, into my bones, and rippled along the marrow. I could only suck in a small breath of air before I felt frozen and suffocating, as if the chill were absorbing oxygen while it moved over and through me. Alarmed and afraid, I attempted to move, but it was as if my limbs were struck with sudden paralysis. Even opening my lids took tremendous effort. At last I managed to lift my lids, and discovered that I was lying in what looked to be an old house, with yellowed paint and a dingy feel. It wasn't anywhere I recognized or wanted to be.

I would have shivered, but my limbs were still locked in place and I felt a mounting panic over not being able to breathe. I closed my eyes and fought against the cold as if it was emanating from a force with evil intent, attacking and paralyzing me—and by this time I knew that it was *exactly* that. With extreme effort I managed to inhale. It wasn't a deep breath, but it was enough to reclaim my lungs. I took another breath, and another, and another, and soon I could feel the cold ebbing ever so slightly.

My limbs still wouldn't cooperate, so I focused on them next. I tried wiggling my toe. Nothing. I tried again, and again, and again, until finally I could feel my toe wiggle ever so slightly, and encouraged by that, I focused on moving my foot, then my other foot, then my hands. At last I felt myself lifting out of the paralysis and I opened my eyes again.

I gasped when I stared into the face of a man standing over me, who looked so menacing and angry that it chilled me right to the bone again. There was something else about him too . . . something evil and dark that'd definitely left its mark on him.

"Why have you come?" he asked me, his expression darkening even more and his voice sharp and jagged, like broken glass.

I tried to wiggle back away from him along the floor, but my arms and legs were still slow to cooperate. He picked up his foot and set it down in the center of my chest, and a jolt of cold that was so sharp and painful it was like being stabbed shot through me.

Again I couldn't breathe, and while my mind reeled, he leaned down and said again, "Why have you come?"

I closed my eyes. This wasn't real! I knew it wasn't real. I knew I was having an out-of-body experience, something I had quite often, but everything felt sharply real. I was really cold. I really couldn't breathe. His foot really felt heavy on my chest. And, most important of all, I really couldn't seem to wake up out of this nightmare.

The man's foot pressed down harder on my chest and the sharp bite of the cold cut into me again. "Stop!" I mouthed. "Stop!"

But he didn't. He continued to stand there and press

down on top of me. I grew dizzy from lack of oxygen. I wondered if my physical body had also stopped breathing. And then I had a most frightening thought—could this man kill me here and sever the connection between my soul and my body, effectively killing me in the physical plane too?

Fueled by panic, I managed to reach up one hand and slap it against his boot. It had no effect other than to encourage this cruel stranger to press down even harder. I opened my eyes, feeling as if my soul were sinking into the cold floor, and my limbs began to go numb again and I realized he held a knife in his hand. A knife that appeared rusty with dried blood. I swiped at his boot again, but my arm fell back to the ground with a loud slap, and the hurt barely registered—I was so filled with adrenaline and fear.

My vision clouded with pinpricks of light. He was killing me and I didn't know where my soul would go from here.

And then, like a small miracle I heard Heath's voice loud and clear, as if he'd just come into the room. "Get off her!" he commanded. The weight on my chest lifted a fraction and the cold also receded a tiny bit, but I still couldn't take in much air. The pinpricks of light in my vision winked out, and blackness began to close off my sight.

"He-He-He-Heeeeeath!" I gasped. It came out barely a whisper.

Quick footsteps to my left sounded and then the weight on my chest vanished and a loud crash erupted from the corner of the room. My vision cleared, and there was Heath, standing strong over me, his hands curled into fists and the white streak in his hair glowing brightly as he glared hard at something across the room. "Leave this place!" he yelled.

With effort I turned my head slightly, realizing I could move again at the same time that I saw the cruel stranger trying to right himself after crashing into a few rickety-looking chairs across the room. He got up snarling and kicking the chairs aside, and Heath stepped over me, putting himself between me and my attacker. "I'm warning you," he growled.

The stranger's eyes darkened and he flew at Heath, the hand wielding the knife arcing up. Reflexively, I rolled to my side, curling into a ball and covering my head with my arms. I heard the impact between Heath and the man more than I saw it. There was a loud *whump* and I braced myself, fully expecting them to crash on top of me, but instead out of the corner of my eye, I saw Heath block the hand with the knife, twisting the man's wrist sharply before he embraced the attacker, turned him in a half circle, lifted him right off the ground and threw him over and away from me. It was a spectacular move of grace and athleticism that stunned me.

In the next instant, Heath was bending down low and scooping me up. He held me cradled me in his arms and I could feel his warmth seep into me, repelling the bitter cold that had me racked with shivers. "Close your eyes," he whispered, "and think of us, in our bed, me holding you just like this. Focus on it, Em. Feel yourself wrapped in my arms in the condo. Smell the sheets. Hear the furnace kick on. Listen for the sound of traffic outside your bedroom window. . . ."

And just like that, I felt and smelled and heard all of those things. With a gasp I opened my eyes and realized that I was still cradled in Heath's arms, but he was sitting up with me in bed, holding on as if for dear life. "What the freak just happened?"

In the dim light I saw Heath's lips quirk. "We're back," he said, then opened his own eyes.

I shuddered, feeling spooked and still cold from whatever encounter I'd just had. I wound my arms tighter around Heath and squeezed. "Honey, what the hell was that?"

Heath put a hand on the back of my head and pressed me close. I could feel his heartbeat against my skin. The steady rhythm helped to reassure me. "I was sound asleep and I heard you scream, but I couldn't seem to wake up. My arms and legs were paralyzed and I couldn't get to you."

"That's exactly what happened to me!"

Heath nodded, the stubble on his chin prickling my scalp a little. "I knew I was having an out-of-body, so I waited for what might happen next. And that's when my grandfather suddenly appeared next to me and he pulled me out of bed. He said I had to get to you quick. I asked him where you were, and he told me to run through this door, which I swear appeared right in front of us. I did, and that's when I found you on the floor with that bastard standing on you, ready to stab you."

I breathed out a long sigh. "Thank God for Sam Whitefeather."

Heath chuckled. "Yeah, Gramps is pretty fond of you too."

We were both quiet for a bit before I said, "What I really want to know is, who the heck *was* that creepy son of a bitch?"

Heath squeezed me tight again. "Don't know. Don't want to know."

And then a terrible thought occurred to me. "Do you think it might have something to do with this case?"

I felt Heath stiffen and his arms wrapped a little tighter around me. "Naw," he said, but I could tell he was trying hard not to own that very real possibility. "I think you had an OBE and got pulled down to the lower plane and some random crazy spirit was just trying to freak you out."

I nodded and didn't try to argue the point because I was definitely still a little freaked-out and needed the comfort of Heath's denial more than I wanted to admit.

OBEs—out-of-body experiences—aren't an unusual occurrence for me, but where I'd gone specifically, and who that evil man in the room was, was a mystery. I wasn't in the mood to think about it overly much—hell, what I really wanted was to forget it, and luckily, the heat coming off Heath and his half-naked body pressed up against me was starting to pull my thoughts in other directions. He was such a sexy beast of a man. Lean and corded with muscles, Heath possessed an inner, incredibly masculine power—it simply turned me on. I didn't just feel safe in his arms; I felt free to be who I really was, and after a lifetime of feeling the rejections of my father and other people who didn't fully understand me, it was a wonderful thing to know that someone in the world got me in ways no one else could ever possibly understand. It was an aphrodisiac like no other, and I was starting to feel the full force of it as I sat with him. "You're beautiful—you know that?" he said softly to me.

I smiled slyly. Apparently he was feeling a little frisky too. Lifting my chin, I looked into his dark brown eyes and drank in the sight of him. A smile spread to his own lips a half second before they dipped down to mine. He kissed me sweetly at first and I relished the feel of those velvety lips before he moaned and the kiss deepened, sending a flutter through my chest. We spent the next hour naked and entwined, our need for reassurance that we were okay as strong as our passion.

At last we lay next to each other, holding hands and sated. Well, I was sated; Heath was looking like he could go for round three. I chuckled and gave him a pat on his six-pack. "I'm headed into the shower. At some point we've got to get up and deal with Luke and what happened last night."

Heath groaned. "Can't we just pretend it never happened?"

I sat up and looked at my phone on the nightstand. I'd turned it to silent, but one swipe of the screen showed me that I had missed six calls and Gilley had texted me a dozen times. With a frown I held the phone up so Heath could see. "I'll bet your phone looks the same."

Heath rolled his eyes, then reached for my phone. "Go take your shower and I'll deal with this."

I kissed him and hurried to the bathroom before he changed his mind. Once I was clean and dressed again, I came out to find Heath in the wing chair in the corner of my bedroom leaning forward, staring down at the ground with the phone pressed to his ear. "Oh, come off it!" he snapped. "What else did you want us to do? Luke showed up covered in blood. We thought he was hurt and he wasn't talking! What the hell would you have done?"

Immediately I knew Heath was arguing with Steven, and I felt my own temper flare. It sounded as if my ex was blaming my current S.O. for Luke's arrest. As I moved across the room prepared to talk some sense into Steven, Heath yelled, "Well, I'm no doctor, Sable! And maybe I'm not the guy you should be yelling at! Luke's the one accused of murder here! Why don't you ask him what the hell happened last night!" With that, my sweetheart pulled the phone away from his ear and hung up. I stopped when he looked up and he seemed surprised to see me standing there. "Sorry," he said sheepishly, holding out the phone. "I can't talk to that asshole."

I took the phone. "It's okay."

But Heath was irritated. "How the hell could you date that egomaniac anyway?"

Uh-oh. This was about to take a bad turn. "I'm not dating him now, honey. I'm dating you, remember?"

But Heath seemed rattled and upset by whatever Steven had said. "Are you sure you want to be?"

I bit my lip and felt the sting of that even though I knew Heath didn't mean it. Immediately he tried to take it back. "Hey," he said, holding up his hands in surrender. "Sorry. That was a shitty thing to say. I didn't mean it. I guess what you said to Gilley yesterday about missing Steven is still bugging me."

I swallowed hard, and felt my eyes glisten. "How long are you gonna make me pay for that?"

Heath sighed and stared at the floor, shaking his head. When he looked up at me again, I made a point of moving my gaze to the bed, where we'd just had such a lovely time. Heath's face flushed and he stood up to step forward and wrap me in his arms. "I'm sorry, Em," he said. "Sable can just get under my skin, you know?"

"I do know," I said, already forgiving him. "But I'm with you because I want to be with you, honey. Every day that feeling gets stronger and I get more committed, so please don't read into a stupid comment I made yesterday, okay?"

Heath kissed my temple and cradled my head against his chest. "Deal," he said. Then he stepped back. "My turn for the shower. Maybe you can talk to Sable and calm him the hell down. I didn't get a chance to talk to Gilley yet."

"Go," I told him, pointing toward the bathroom. "I'll deal with Steven and Gil."

Once I'd heard the shower turn on, I called Steven. "What?" I said bluntly when he answered.

"What do you mean, what?" he replied. I could hear the barely veiled anger in his voice.

"I'm assuming that, by what I overheard you say to

my boyfriend, you're blaming us for Luke's arrest?" I made sure to emphasize the words "my boyfriend" just to let Steven know where my allegiance stood.

"I'm not blaming you for the arrest," Steven growled. "I'm blaming you for not calling me and *my fiancée* first."

Apparently two could play at that game. "Steven," I said levelly. "Luke showed up at the house covered in blood. We thought he'd been stabbed, or shot, or hit by a car. We had no idea what'd happened to him, and our first thought was to help him. So, yes, we dialed nine-one-one before we called you. And I'm not sorry for that. I know you want me to be, but I'm not. I reacted like anybody else would've in that situation."

Steven was quiet for a few beats before he said, "If you hadn't lost Luke in the first place, none of this would've happened."

I took a deep breath and counted to ten. I wanted to yell my reply, but I knew that I couldn't, so I took a few beats of my own to collect myself. Then I said in a low and even tone, "For the record, Dr. Sable, we did not *lose* Luke. He got up and walked out of the house before we could even make it out of the diner. And at no time during our discussions with you or him did we agree to be responsible for his actions. Pinning what happened last night on us is bullshit. And you know it."

Again, Steven took his time answering. At last he said, "You're probably right. But we still need to know what happened, M.J. A girl is dead and my fiancée's brother is accused of the crime. How is that possible?"

I sat down in the chair and pinched the bridge of my nose. As much as I wanted to tell Steven that I didn't know and didn't want to get further involved, I knew that even if I tried, I couldn't walk away from this now. Heath, Gilley, and I were involved. Like it or not. So the only recourse I had left was to try to figure out what'd happened. My sneaking suspicion was that either the spook we were trying to identify had taken possession of Luke and caused him to commit this random murder, or there was a dark side to Luke that no one really knew about, and the spook was just an excuse to carry out some sickly weird agenda.

Of course, there was a third possibility, but it seemed highly unlikely. Luke may not have had anything to do with the crime. He could've been in the wrong place at the wrong time and somehow gotten blood all over himself. That was the leap I figured his attorney was going to take. But I'd been there when Luke had entered that house, covered in blood. No way had he just been an innocent bystander. "Steven," I said, with that in mind, "has anyone managed to get Luke's side of the story?"

"No. He's in custody and the attorney I've retained for him won't allow anyone to speak to him. He says that all of the conversations Luke may have with visitors can be recorded. Except those between Luke and the attorney. Those are bound by attorney-client privilege. But everyone else isn't allowed to speak a word to him or to take phone calls from him. The attorney doesn't want Luke to say anything that could be used against him later."

"Well, then, we're stuck, aren't we?"

"No, we're not stuck," Steven insisted. "Gilley said that Luke was possessed last night when he walked out of the house. I think that ghost took over Luke's body and was responsible for the murdered girl."

I wasn't shocked that Gilley had been running his mouth without knowing for certain that was the case, but it irritated me no end that Gil had made a bad situation worse by saying such things to Steven. "We don't know for sure that Luke was possessed last night, Steven. We only know that he was acting weird, got up, walked downstairs and out of the door. The next time we saw him, he was clearly in distress and covered in blood. Only Luke knows what happened."

"But what if he doesn't?"

"What does that mean?"

"I overheard one of the policemen at the scene say that when he put Luke in the car, he told the cop that he couldn't remember anything about what'd happened."

I sighed and went back to pinching the bridge of my nose. "Steven, I don't know how we can help. This is way outside of anything we've ever dealt with—"

"That's not true and you know it, M.J. I've seen the things you've dealt with firsthand. If anyone is going to get to the bottom of this, it's you."

"I'm not a detective, Steven!" I said a bit too loudly. "I wasn't there! I didn't see what happened! I only saw Luke get up and leave the house. The next thing we know, a girl is dead and Luke is covered in blood that, quite likely, came from her."

"M.J.," Steven said calmly, "please. You have to try to figure out what happened. I know this young man. He's not capable of doing something like this."

I tapped the arm of the chair with my fingertips. I felt trapped and cornered and I didn't like it. "Let me talk to Gilley and Heath," I said at last. "If they agree to look into this, then we will. But if either of them doesn't want to do it, then we're out, Steven."

"Did I really mean that little to you?"

The comment caught me off guard. "What?"

"You heard me," he said softly. "A year ago you would've dropped everything if I'd needed you. Now it's like we're strangers. Like there was never anything special between us, when you know there was. I know you do."

I nearly took the bait, but with effort I managed to keep my wits about me. "This has nothing to do with how

I felt about you in the past, Steven. Nothing. This has everything to do with this being a matter for the police to figure out. If we get involved, we risk everything from obstruction charges to being implicated in the murder. It's risky, is all I'm saying, and while I might be willing to get involved to help you, I won't commit either Gilley or Heath to that without their buy-in."

Steven seemed to think that over. "Fine," he said at last. "But if the situation were reversed, M.J., I wouldn't hesitate to help you."

I clenched my jaw—that was an exaggeration and completely unfair. Steven wasn't in my position, and I *knew* he'd never commit Courtney to such risks if the situation were reversed. I understood him far better than that. Still, I decided not to call him on it. I wanted off the phone and away from the guilt trip, so I simply said, "We'll be in touch," and hung up.

"That sounded like it went well," Heath said from the doorway of the bathroom.

I started. I hadn't realized he'd been standing there. "How much did you overhear?"

"Enough. He wants us to investigate this?"

I nodded. "He's convinced Luke was possessed and that the spook made him do it."

"Wait a sec. We haven't had a chance to talk to Luke to see what the hell was going on inside his head, so how does Steven know that's what happened?"

I sighed. "He had a little help arriving at that conclusion." When Heath's brow furrowed, I added, "Gilley told him Luke was possessed when he walked out of the house last night."

Heath shook his head and scratched the back of his neck. He wore a towel around his waist and droplets of water glistened off his bare chest and shoulders. "Leave it to Gil," he said.

"Hmm?" I asked, distracted by the sexy sight of him. "Oh, yeah. Gil."

"You rang?" said a voice from the hallway. Heath and I both jumped just as Gil appeared in my bedroom doorway. "Why, hello, gorgeous," my BFF said the moment he laid eyes on a half-naked Heath.

Heath blushed, which I thought was incredibly cute, before he recovered himself. "Keep it in your pants, Gillespie. You know I only have eyes for Em."

Gil sighed sadly. "Yes, I know. Such a shame."

I laughed in spite of myself. Then I remembered the conversation I'd just been having with Heath. "Gil, why the hell did you tell Steven that Luke was possessed last night?"

Gilley made a face like he didn't quite understand my question. "Because he was."

"We don't know that," I insisted.

Gil blinked. "Wait. Didn't you see what I saw? That boy had possession written all over his face. I mean, did his head spin around? No. Did he projectile vomit? No. But did I expect both of those things to happen the minute he sat up and stared at us like he did through the camera? Yes, yes, I did. That boy was *full-on* Linda Blair last night and you know it."

"No, Gil," I repeated. "I don't know it. I only know that Luke got up, looked a bit off, and left the house. What happened between the time he walked out and showed up again covered in blood is a complete mystery."

"A mystery that Sable wants us to figure out," Heath said, looking to me to confirm.

I sat back in the chair. "Yes."

"Has anyone asked Luke what the hell happened?" Gil said.

"No," I told him. "His lawyer won't let him say a word

to anyone. Whatever went down, we won't know about it through Luke."

"Why won't he let us talk to him if we might be able to help?" Gilley asked.

"Because we could be called to testify about what Luke said to us in relation to last night."

"Ahhh," Gil said. "So, Steven wants us to figure out what happened last night without being able to ask Luke?"

"Yes."

"Why doesn't he just hire a private detective?" Gil asked next.

"I don't think a PI is going to understand the whole 'possession' angle," I replied, using air quotes.

"Even if we can prove that Luke was possessed, how does that help him?" Heath said. "I mean, what jury has ever bought the whole the-devil-made-me-do-it argument?"

I shrugged. "I don't know, honey. But the one thing that's bugging me is that if this spook can possess someone like Luke and get him to commit such a heinous crime, what's to stop it from trying that again on somebody else?"

Heath and Gilley were silent for a long moment, and the room felt heavy, like it was loaded with bad options. "We have to find out what this spook is really capable of, don't we?" Heath said at last.

"I think we do," I replied.

Gilley walked over to the bed, turned, and fell backward onto it. "How do we always get mixed up in crazy shit like this?"

"Dunno, buddy. Maybe we're just lucky."

Gil lifted his head and looked around at the bedcovers, his eyebrows bouncing. "Speaking of getting lucky . . ."

I bolted out of my chair. "Don't even think about going there," I told him, heading out to the living room. Gilley followed me while I suspected Heath was getting dressed. I walked right over to Doc's cage, where he lived when I wasn't at the office, and opened the door so he could come out and climb onto the play stand on top. He blew kisses at me and whistled. I thought Doc had it pretty good, free of worry from spooks and demons and such.

Gil took up the barstool in front of my kitchen counter. "Where do we even start with this, M.J.? Our only link to the demon is currently sitting in a jail cell waiting to be arraigned."

I moved to the kitchen and opened up a cupboard to take down some Rice Chex cereal. I held the box up and shook it a little. Gil shook his head. Pouring the Chex into a bowl, I then rooted around in the fridge for some almond milk. Behind me I heard Doc say, "Cuckoo for Cocoa Puffs!"

After drenching my cereal, I put some into a much smaller bowl and walked it over to my sweet bird, who happily squeaked and got down to breakfast. "I think we should start with the woman who was murdered," I said, as much to myself as to Gilley.

"What's that?" Heath asked, coming out of the bedroom.

I looked up. "The woman who died last night," I told him. "If her spirit has been grounded, then she's the only other person besides Luke who might be able to tell us what the hell happened last night."

Gilley shuddered in his seat. "This whole business is so macabre."

I ignored him and moved back to the counter to take up the seat next to him and dive into my breakfast. "What if she's not around?" Heath asked after moving over to the cereal box to pick from the package.

I sighed, thinking that through. I felt blind on this one. "The only other idea I have is to go back to the house where Luke was living when he claimed all of this started to happen."

Heath and Gilley were silent for a moment as they considered that, until Gil said, "I have a question."

I turned to him. "Which is?"

"What if the spook is still controlling Luke?"

"Then at least they're both locked up for the moment," I said.

Gil shook his head. "No, you're missing my point. What if the spook has control of Luke and won't let go? He's in jail. It's not like we'll be allowed to pass him some magnetic spikes and lock down whatever's gotten hold of him."

"True. But if we can find the portal of this spook and shove a few magnets into it, then maybe we can cut him off from his power source and he'll eventually weaken."

Heath's brow rose. "That's a really good idea, Em."

"First I think we should focus all our efforts on trying to figure out who this spook is. If we can learn something about him, maybe it'll help us understand why it's been targeting Luke. I mean, these spooks usually go for kindred spirits, don't they? Do we really think after meeting Luke only once that he's this great guy who couldn't hurt a fly?"

"I guess it couldn't hurt to check him out," Gil said.

I polished off the last of my cereal and pushed the bowl aside. "I agree. Let's try and look into Luke's background a little. See if he's really as innocent as his sister claims."

"Shouldn't we also get some background on the woman who was murdered?" Heath said.

I blinked. Why hadn't I thought of that first? "Yes, definitely. But, Gil, if you'd hold off telling us anything about her until after Heath and I try to make contact, that'd be good. That way we know what we're getting is genuine and not influenced by anything we know."

Gil was taking notes on his iPhone. "Got it," he said. Then he pushed back from the counter and added, "You two do what you do, and I'll be digging up dirt."

With that, he left us. Heath and I headed out the door just a few minutes later, stopping by Mack's office to drop off both of our passports, as Mack had asked us to let him take them to the police. My thinking was that he wanted to be absolutely certain Heath and I hadn't been in the U.S. at the time of Bethany's murder. The stamps in both of our passports from Scotland were undeniable, so I wasn't at all nervous about turning them over. And if Heath and I handed over our passports and the police kept them for a while, then we couldn't very well leave the country to face more demons and evil spooks for our cable show. Given what I suspected we were up against here, that was sounding like the one bright spot in a pretty cloudy future.

Chapter 7

After leaving both passports with Mack's secretary, Heath and I drove over to the scene of the crime, so to speak. We parked just down the street from Courtney's place and saw the yellow tape looped across the span of the steps leading up to the front door. There was additional tape across the door in the form of a large X, and a big yellow sticker was stuck between the door and the frame to seal it. Heath and I approached cautiously, both of us looking up and down the street—not for spooks, but for cops. We'd had a brief discussion in the car about the danger of showing up at the crime scene while under the suspicion of the police. The last thing we needed was to be seen poking our noses in places Detective Souter didn't think they belonged, and I was absolutely convinced that if she knew we were here, she'd suspect that we were up to something like hiding evidence.

There was no sign of the police or CSI, but I stiffened when I heard a siren in the distance. Heath moved close to me to take up my hand and walked right beside me as we crossed the street. Once on the sidewalk we both gazed up silently at Courtney's front door. I pressed my lips together when I noticed a rusty stain on the door handle, and an additional faint rust-colored handprint on the door itself. There were also the familiar smudges of dark gray powder all along the door's edge.

I knew I'd need to open up my sixth sense to get a feel for the murdered girl, but I was hesitant in that way one is about diving into a cold pool. Heath seemed to have no such reservations. He lifted his chin a little and looked down the street, his eyes unfocused and that familiar expression I knew too well. "You've got something?"

He nodded and began to move past me, taking up my hand again to bring me along. As I walked beside him, I opened up my own senses and felt the energy around us expand.

It's a little bit of a neat trick I discovered about working with Heath that when he and I are together, if we're both using our sixth senses, our ability to pick up information and the presence of spirits expands exponentially. It's a bit like putting a big antenna on a radio—the range is broader and the information coming in much clearer. It's a sum-of-the-parts-being-greater-than-the-whole type of thing, and it's one of the reasons I really love working with Heath.

"She's this way," he said softly as we walked.

I tried to detect the energy he was talking about, and I had only the slightest sense of her, but I knew that by keeping my intuition open I was helping him make his connection to the spirit of the dead girl stronger.

"Is it the woman who was murdered?" I asked him.

"Amy," he said. "I think her name was Amy."

At that moment Heath stopped abruptly, and because he was leading me, I did too. I looked at him closely and saw his brow furrow. "Weird," he said.

"What's weird?"

Heath was turning his head this way and that, as if he was listening to more than one person in a conversation. "This girl feels young," he said. "Didn't Mack tell you that she was in her late twenties?"

"He did."

Heath shook his head. "She feels about ten years younger. But it's gotta be the same girl because her throat was cut." I watched as Heath's hand lifted to his own throat and he seemed to grimace a little.

At that moment my own radar kicked into full swing and I felt a tug from just down the street. The smell of blood wafted under my nose, and I nearly gagged. I put my free hand over my nose—the scent was so powerful and nauseating—and sure enough as I looked farther down the street, I saw a door with the familiar yellow X across the door.

I couldn't feel the girl—she seemed to be communicating only with Heath—but I could sense the violence that'd occurred in the spot we were standing in. It was awful. The assault had been intense, and unrelenting. I felt myself cringing and stepping closer to Heath. Looking up at him, I saw that he'd closed his eyes and he was standing so stiffly I didn't think he was even aware of the fact that I'd moved closer to him. He'd also gone a little pale, and I had a feeling he was getting details that were far too grim to witness.

I squeezed his hand, which had gone cold in my palm. "Babe," I whispered, but he didn't acknowledge me. "Heath," I tried again, a little louder. I felt a shudder go through him and he opened his eyes, staring at me with such a haunted expression that I reached up to cup his face. "You okay?" I asked.

"No," he said, his eyes misting slightly. "Em, let's get out of here, okay?"

I nodded and took him by the hand again, leading him back across the street and to my car. Heath paused to fish out the car keys from his pocket, but his hand was shaking so bad that he dropped the keys. I ducked to pick them up first and said, "How about I drive?"

He nodded and moved stiffly around to the passenger side. Once we were inside, I started the engine and cranked up the heat. Heath was pale and shaking and I couldn't imagine what he'd gotten from the ether to affect him so much. I didn't press him for details; instead I drove straight to Mama Dell's. The minute we were through the door, Mama appeared, as if she knew someone was troubled and needed a good dose of Southern charm.

"Well, good afternoon, y'all!" she said, sweeping toward us all smiles and open arms. She aimed those open arms toward Heath first and I was so grateful. "Darlin', you feel cold!" she said to him, squeezing him tighter. I stood back and let Mama's warmth funnel its way into Heath, and before my eyes some color returned to his cheeks and I sighed with relief.

Mama let go of him after a bit and graced me with a hug too, but I could tell her mind was still on Heath. "Come in, y'all, and take a seat. I'll bring you some coffee and some fresh buttermilk biscuits to warm your bones."

"Mama, can we trouble you for some hot cocoa instead of coffee?" I asked. I was worried that Heath might be suffering a mild form of shock, and as he'd pretty much skipped breakfast, save for a few handfuls of cereal, I thought the sugar might be what he needed.

"Of course!" she said, already turning to fetch us the order.

I guided Heath to a cozy corner where we weren't likely to be overheard and sat down across from him without saying a word. He sat there numbly, his eyes troubled and his hands still shaking slightly. I waited until Mama had delivered our cocoa and biscuits. I had to encourage Heath to take up the cup and sip his drink, but after a few swallows he seemed better still. "What did you see?" I asked him after he'd set his cup back down.

He closed his eyes and shook his head. "Her name was Amy. She was sweet, you know? I had the sense that she was pretty naive and innocent, just out for a walk in the warm night when out of nowhere she was grabbed from behind and stabbed. I could feel her shock and her pain. It'd been quick, but not quick enough. Her throat was slashed too, but it wasn't deep enough to kill her quickly. It took a few minutes. . . ."

Heath's voice trailed off as he put his fingers up to his neck again and swallowed hard. I winced and reached out to squeeze his free hand.

"Did she know who grabbed her?" I asked when it looked like he could talk again.

Heath shook his head. "No. She just kept saying 'Why?' to me. She knew she was dying. She knew she was being murdered, but she didn't understand why. It felt so random."

"Did you get her to cross over?" I asked, knowing that if Amy was still grounded, as I suspected she was, Heath would've worked telepathically to talk her into crossing to the other side.

He leaned forward in his seat and rubbed his hands together as if they'd gone cold again. "I didn't have a chance to talk to her beyond what'd happened during her murder, Em. Something else came into the ether."

My brow furrowed. I hadn't sensed anything else. "Something else?"

He nodded but stared at the ground while he tried to explain. "I was trying to help Amy, waiting for her to settle down a little, when something sort of entered my energy."

"I didn't feel anything," I said to him, thoroughly puzzled. I'd felt the violence surrounding us, and a hint of the girl Heath was connecting with, but nothing more.

"I know," Heath said, finally looking up at me. "It's hard to explain, but I felt this energy try to connect directly to me and only me. For a few seconds it seemed to enter my thoughts and try to take them over. And it let me see what it was about, and it was bad. Like evil bad."

"What did it show you?"

Heath shut his eyes again. "Blood. Whatever it was, it lusted for blood. The smell, the taste, the texture of it. Like . . . a blood addict, and I know that sounds crazy, but that's what it felt like."

I remembered the overwhelming scent of blood that'd wafted under my nose while I stood next to Heath on the sidewalk. "I felt a tinge of that," I admitted.

"You felt it?" he asked me.

"Sort of. While I thought you were communicating with Amy, I smelled this overpowering scent of blood just under my nose. It was so potent I nearly gagged."

Heath nodded like he understood perfectly. "The thing of it is, Em, that I didn't get the sense that all that blood filling my thoughts came only from Amy. It felt like there were others."

"Others?" I asked.

Heath nodded.

I shook my head. "That could be bad."

"Yep."

"What else did you get from this energy?" I asked.

"It's hard to describe," Heath said. "I don't even know if it was human, Em."

"You said that it tried to take over your thoughts. What'd you mean by that?"

Heath lifted the cup of cocoa and held it between his hands. "For a few seconds after I became aware of this thing, it crept into my mind and I couldn't think straight. I mean, Em, I couldn't even remember my name for a tick or two."

"How long did it last?" I tried to hide the alarm I felt because I'd never seen any hint of an assault on Heath's energy the whole time I'd been standing next to him.

"A few seconds," he said. "I heard you call my name, but I didn't make the connection until you touched my face and I could focus on you. And even after that, I had a hard time thinking straight. I know you drove me here, but I don't remember much beyond you leading me back across the street."

I stared at Heath for several seconds. I wondered worriedly if perhaps there was something to Luke's story after all. There was a spook I couldn't sense that had tried to take over Heath, and I'd been oblivious other than smelling blood. "Did it say anything while it was trying to take you over, honey?" I desperately wanted to figure this thing out.

"No. But . . ." Heath's voice trailed off and he seemed to be struggling with what he wanted to say next. "There was a moment, Em, just a second really, when I felt like killing somebody. Like . . . I was thirsty for it."

I shuddered and sat back in my chair. "Whoa."

Heath nodded. "We've been under assault from spooks before where they've taken us over, but this was different. This was so fast and without any warning. One minute I'm trying to help Amy and the next my mind's being taken over by something made of pure evil."

Heath and I stared at each other for the next several seconds without saying a word. We didn't need to. At last I said, "I hate this case."

"Me too. Wanna quit?"

"Yes. But I know we won't."

Heath broke into a lopsided grin. "Sucks being a woman of your word, doesn't it?"

I nodded. "Some days it sucks more than others."

Heath got up and pulled out his wallet. After leaving a twenty underneath his coffee cup, he reached for my hand. "Come on, beautiful. Let's go find Gil and tell him we made contact with the murdered girl. Maybe we can find a different place to connect to her energy, away from that thing, whatever it was."

We found Gil hunched over his old laptop in my condo. Doc was sitting on his shoulder, preening himself and fluffing his feathers. Doc has a serious crush on Gilley, and every time Gil is nearby, my sweet birdie makes a point of getting himself to look as pretty as possible. The scene was doubly sweet because I noticed that Doc would periodically tilt his head to the side and make kissing noises in Gil's ear. Gil would respond absently by making the same kissing noises back. It was a lovefest.

"Hey," Gil said when he finally looked up at us. "How'd it go?"

"It went," I told him, heading straight to the couch. Heath sat down next to me and I let him take the lead. "We made contact with the victim."

Gil paused his typing to lower the lid of the laptop. "Was it rough?" he asked, probably taking note of Heath's reserved countenance.

"It was, actually. Her name was Amy, and I got the initial *M* attached to her last name. She felt young too. In my mind she was in her late teens, but maybe she was just immature. I got a sense of light hair color too—blond, I think—and the night she died, she'd been wearing a new white dress. She made a point of telling me that; I think because she was preoccupied with it when she was attacked. Another detail she gave me was that she's related to an Ellen or a Helen. Might be a sister or a mother figure. She asked me to find them for her because she was having a hard time getting to them. On the night she was murdered, she was stabbed multiple times and her throat was cut, but it took her a little while to die. Whoever killed her came from behind and she never saw his face. Hard to tell if it was Luke or not because I don't think she knows."

As Heath spoke, my attention went between him and Gilley, but it quickly settled on Gil, because he was wearing the most confused look on his face. After Heath had finished talking, Gil said, "Buddy, I have no idea who you made contact with, but whoever this Amy person is, she wasn't last night's victim."

I sat forward. "Wait . . . what?"

Gil opened his laptop and peered down at the screen. "The woman murdered last night was named Brook Astor. She was twenty-nine. A pretty brunette who didn't die slow. She was stabbed a dozen times, three times directly into the heart before her throat was cut. The coroner says Brook was dead before she even hit the ground. Oh, and one more little tidbit. Brook was eight weeks pregnant when she was murdered."

I sucked in a breath. "She was pregnant and stabbed *twelve* times?" I was repulsed by the idea.

"Yes. The coroner's report with photos was released to the cops this morning. I obtained a copy through back channels."

By back channels, Gilley meant he'd hacked into the PD's computer network, but I wasn't about to call him on it. Besides, I was way more concerned with the fact that Heath had apparently bumped into a completely different murdered woman on the same street. "So who did we make contact with?" I asked out loud.

"Got me," Gil said.

Heath shifted in his seat, and I could see him mentally going over the information he'd gotten from Amy. I could tell he might be doubting himself, but I knew better. "That could explain the scent of blood," I told him, trying to put the pieces together.

Heath nodded absently. "Two woman stabbed to death on the same street, though?"

"It's Boston," I told him. "Not the safest city in the world. Besides, there's no telling how long poor Amy has been haunting that spot. Her ghost could be a hundred years old."

Heath ran a hand through his hair. "I didn't get that feeling, though, Em. I mean, maybe her ghost could've been a few decades old, but you know how spooks from centuries past feel different?"

I did know. It's tough to put into words, but a ghost from the eighteen hundreds feels very different from a ghost from the late nineteen hundreds. It's sort of in the way they communicate. The older the ghosts, the more formal and reserved they tend to be.

"Are you sure you got the name right?" Gil asked. "Maybe it was Brook and you just missed the name and the age." I knew he was trying to be helpful, but he came across as a little too doubtful for my taste.

"I know what she told me, Gil," Heath said, his voice a bit hard.

"Sorry," Gil said quickly.

Heath sighed. "It's cool, dude. What can I say? I only tuned in to one dead girl today, and it wasn't the murdered girl from last night."

Gil began typing on his laptop as if he had a sudden thought. A moment later he said, "Whoa!"

I leaned forward. "What's 'whoa'?"

"I put a search into the *Boston Globe*, and guess what I pulled up."

"Do we have to guess?" I asked wearily. "Or can you just tell us?"

Gil made a face and swiveled the laptop around so that we could see the screen. Heath and I both squinted at a headline that read, MURDER ON COMM AVE. The tagline underneath read, *Young woman's throat slit in brutal stabbing attack.*

"When was that?" I asked. I couldn't quite make out the date.

Gil swiveled the laptop back around. "April sixteenth, nineteen seventy-five."

My brow shot up and Heath looked equally surprised. "I knew I wasn't wrong," he said.

"The victim's name was Amy?" I asked Gil, who appeared to be skimming the article.

He nodded absently. "Amy Montgomery. She was eighteen. According to her roommate, she went out for a late-night walk because she couldn't sleep. When she didn't come home, the roommate went looking for her and found her body a few doors down."

"Did they catch the killer?" Heath asked.

Gil typed something and skimmed more of the screen before he answered. "Yes. The brother of her best friend was charged six years later and convicted. He got life."

I turned to Heath. "Think whoever tried to get into your head was Amy's killer?"

Heath shrugged. "Don't know. Could've been."

"I'm lost," Gil said.

Turning to him, I explained that a spook had tried to take Heath over while he was communicating with Amy. "If Amy's killer is dead, then his ghost could've come back to the scene of the crime and tried to get inside Heath's mind."

Gil frowned and typed some more on his computer. "Couldn't have been the same guy," he said after a bit.

"How do you know?" I asked.

"Because Amy's killer—Guy Walker—is still alive. At least he was alive as of six months ago. He gave an interview to the *Globe* last November and you're not gonna believe what he says happened on the day he killed Amy."

"Try us," Heath said to hurry Gil along.

"He claims that a demon made him do it."

I shuddered, but then I wondered how common that excuse was. Certainly that was a common theme with schizophrenic sociopaths. "Any hint in Walker's record of schizophrenia?"

Gil scanned his computer screen. "None that I can find, but I think most people would read the article and think it a foregone conclusion."

I lay back against the cushions, thinking about the creepy coincidence of Guy Walker murdering a woman on Comm Ave in exactly the same manner that Brook Astor had been murdered. And this whole "demon made me do it" excuse was a bit too close to home to ignore.

"Think Walker's demon could be connected to Luke's demon?" Heath asked me.

I nodded. "It's too much of a coincidence to ignore. What do you think?"

Heath raised his arm toward me as if to show it to me, and when I looked, I saw that it was covered in goose bumps. "The goose bumps never lie," he said. "There's a link."

I reached out and gripped his hand, rubbing away the goose bumps. "What do you want to do?" I said to him. I was ready to quit this gig. It felt creepy and dangerous on a level that we'd experienced too often before, and had been frustratingly helpless to quit. But this time was different. We could walk away without fear of getting sued into the ground by a network hungry for ratings. The worst that would happen to us if we walked this time was that we might be accused of being accomplices in a murder, but I had faith in Mack as my attorney, and also the solid alibi that the recordings gave us. I also considered that if we walked, we'd feel pretty guilty about it, but I was willing to shoulder that if Heath wanted out.

So it was with some surprise when he replied, "I think we need to stick with this case for now. This could be bigger than we originally thought. More lives could be at stake if we don't keep digging."

I nodded, knowing what I had to do next. "I have to go back to Comm Ave."

Heath's brow furrowed. "Why?"

"One of us has to try and make contact with the girl who was murdered yesterday, sweetie. And after what happened to you today, I don't think it's safe for you. That leaves me to try."

Heath gave me a look that clearly said he was not about to be left behind. "We're going together," he said firmly.

"Okay." I relented. "But you're wearing magnets. And I want you to wait on the other side of the street."

"No."

"Heath . . . ," I said with a sigh.

"I'll wear the vest, but I'm not going to be that far away from you, Em. If you get in trouble, it'll come on fast and furious."

"I'll be fine," I told him. "Whatever this spook is, it apparently likes to haunt men, not women."

Heath scowled. "Yeah, it doesn't like to haunt women. It likes to kill them. I'm going with you. I'm wearing a vest. And I *will* be on the same side of the street."

"Okay," I said, giving in with another weary sigh. "How about we get some subs and map out a plan?"

Heath's hard expression softened. "I could eat."

"Me too!" Gil said enthusiastically. Of course, Gil could always eat.

I stood up, stretching. "I'll go this time," I told them. "It's my turn anyway. Write down your orders, boys."

Gil reached for his phone and tapped at the screen. A few seconds later I had an incoming text from him. "Turkey BLT on wheat," I read.

Heath followed Gil's order by texting it to me, and after kissing him on the lips, I grabbed the keys from the dish on the counter and headed out. As I got into the car, I smiled wickedly. That'd been a little too easy.

I drove straight to Comm Ave and had to circle the block twice before I found a parking spot. Getting out of the car, I turned my phone to silent and jogged down toward Courtney's place. I slowed when I was in sight of the door. I then walked on the outside edge of the sidewalk, wary of the spot where Heath had encountered Amy. Hastening my pace, I continued down the sidewalk to the second door marked with the big yellow *X*. Once I was there, I paused to take a few deep breaths. The stairs leading up to the door were crisscrossed with more yellow tape, and the stains on the steps indicated why. There were rust-colored blotches that turned my stomach. Backing up slightly so that I stood on the very edge of the curb, I eyed the sidewalk up and down the block. A makeshift memorial had been set up at the base of the steps and two bouquets of wilting flowers leaned against the stone column to the side of the stairs. Briefly I wondered whom they might have been from, but I knew I couldn't spend time speculating. I stood still and closed my eyes, reaching out with my sixth sense. A series of sensations assaulted me. I felt the dramatic violence of the area. I felt the fear and panic of the victim, and then I also felt her pain. Involuntarily, I put a hand over my chest. It wasn't quite like I could feel the knife going into the poor woman, but it was close to that sensation. She'd felt many of those stab wounds before one had pierced her heart to end her life and I shuddered against the sensation of that coup de grâce, because it felt the most pronounced. I could also smell that familiar scent of blood wafting under my nose, and I had to fight hard against the ensuing nausea it caused. And through this sort of chaos of sensations I attempted to find and talk to the spirit of the murdered woman, but it was like flailing around in a smoke-filled room. She didn't seem to be within easy reach of me.

So, I backed off trying to find her and concentrated on the imprint that her attack had left on the ether. There was a clue there. I could feel it in my gut. I sifted through the attack, going back over it a few times, using my intuition to pick it apart, and at last I had the clue I'd been looking for. It was a eureka moment for me and I opened my eyes only to come face-to-face with Detective Souter.

"Miss Holliday," she said with a slight sneer.

"Detective!" I replied, shocked to be caught in front of the crime scene.

"Want to explain what you're doing here?"

My palms started to sweat. Should I answer that? Would Mack want me to take the fifth and call him? Would getting caught here make me look even more suspicious?

I felt flustered but also a bit excited by what I'd discovered in the ether, and I decided to take a chance. "She was grabbed from behind," I said.

Souter's furrowed brow rose in surprise. "Excuse me?"

I moved closer toward the stairs. "She was coming down the street from this direction," I explained, feeling the ether out as I went. "And someone came up behind her. They put her in a choke hold and twisted her slightly toward the stairs. . . ." My voice trailed off as I demonstrated, but the minute I lifted my right arm up high, as if I was about to wrap it around someone's neck, I hesitated, then lowered my arm and reached up with my left arm instead. "He grabbed her with his left arm," I continued, talking it out. "And he used his right hand to stab her."

Souter came up next to me, her mouth slightly agape. "You saw this?" she asked me incredulously. "You're telling me you witnessed the murder?"

I shook my head. "No. I'm telling you what happened. The attack left an imprint on the ether."

She squinted at me. "Come again?"

But I was still working my way through it. "His first attempt was a little shaky," I said. "The knife hit her dead center on the breastbone." I shivered as that thought really sank home. "She screamed. He was really fast. He tried again and again. It took"—I closed my eyes, slowing down the event in my mind like slowing down the reel of a movie—"four, no, five stabs before the one that killed her. She died instantly from that blow, but I know he kept going."

I moved back from the steps and caught Souter's eye. She was staring at me, her expression hard and suspicious. Still, I decided to go ahead with the recounting because the tape of Heath and me at Courtney's house during the time of the murder was a solid alibi and I was hoping to pull out clues for Souter to chase . . . ones that would lead her away from Heath and me and also maybe even away from Luke.

"Did Decker confess this to you?" Souter asked me.

I shook my head. "I told you in the interrogation, Luke didn't say a thing to me when he came through the door, and I believe you also saw that for yourself on the tape that Gilley recorded of the events inside the house that night. Still, I know how it looks—Luke was covered in the victim's blood, but don't you see? *That* proves he couldn't have done it, Detective."

"What're you even talking about?" she all but yelled.

I turned to face her and looked her squarely in the eye. "Luke didn't murder anybody. The fact that he was covered in blood proves it." I pulled out my phone, prepared to dial, when Souter's hand landed on my arm.

"Color me curious, Holliday," she said. "How does *that* prove he didn't murder the vic?"

I pointed to the stairs. "See all that blood?" I asked. She nodded. "The murderer grabbed Brook Astor from behind. The blood splatter was away from her attacker. I doubt he got much on him at all. But Luke was covered in it. No, I have an alternative theory, Detective. I think Luke came by shortly after the attack and found the victim bleeding on the stairs. I think his immediate instinct was to try and help her. Hell, I bet he probably tried to revive her, but when he realized she was too far gone, and saw himself covered in her blood from his efforts to try and save her, he must've panicked and bolted down the street to his sister's house, looking for anybody who could help."

Souter let go of me and crossed her arms like she thought my theory was pretty far-fetched. "Or," she said, "he could've been struggling with her while he was stabbing her, and she turned in his arms and he got the blood on him that way."

I rolled my eyes and pointed down at our feet. "Then show me the evidence of that, Detective. The stairs are where she bled out. Not the sidewalk."

"It's still a pretty flimsy theory, Holliday."

I shook my head and muttered, "It's not flimsy, Detective. It's actually a solid theory that I'm positive Luke's lawyer will offer the jury, and I'll bet it'll be good enough to get at least a few jurors thinking reasonable doubt." I then focused on my phone, and finding Heath's name in the contacts list, I pressed the call button and put the phone to my ear. "There's one other thing you're forgetting," I said as Heath's phone began ringing.

"What's that?"

"Luke Decker is left-handed." I knew that for certain because I'd watched him pick up the magnetic spike at the diner and toy with it using his left hand.

Souter's brow furrowed again. "That doesn't prove anything," she snapped.

Heath's voice mail began playing in my ear.

"Oh, I believe it proves reasonable doubt," I said softly, turning away from her to walk down the block toward my car. "Hey, sweetie," I said quickly. "It's me. Sorry I'm taking a while. The line here is crazy long. I'll be home in the next twenty minutes or so."

After leaving the message, I got into my car and reached to start the engine . . . which was when I saw our van roll up alongside me. The window rolled down and Heath's angry eyes pinned me to the seat.

"Why?" he demanded.

"Had to be done," I told him, turning the ignition key. "I'll meet you at home and explain there."

And then I pulled out as fast as I could get away with.

Chapter 8

Heath took a shortcut and beat me home. He met me at the door of my condo with arms crossed and eyes narrowed. I flashed him a winning smile. It worked about as well as you'd expect. "Why?" he demanded again.

I dropped the smile and sighed. "I couldn't risk you opening yourself back up to whatever had you on the sidewalk this morning."

His brow furrowed a little more. "And having you open yourself up to the same thing seemed like a better idea?"

"At the time, yes."

It was Heath's turn to sigh.

"She's been like that since she was little," Gilley said from somewhere inside my kitchen. "M.J. used to drive her daddy crazy. He could tell you stories for days about her stubborn streak."

It was my turn to scowl. "Leave me and Daddy out of this, Gil."

"And it's not just her daddy," Gil continued, as if I

hadn't spoken. "I think M.J. has a problem with men in general. Ask any of her ex-boyfriends. Ask Steven. He'll tell you."

"Gilley!"

"You're only mad 'cause it's true," Gil said as I tried to push past Heath into the kitchen to take a swipe at Gil. Fortunately (for Gil), Heath had a pretty firm grip on my middle. "Easy there, woman," Heath said while I glared hard at Gil. "Why don't we all have a seat and talk it out?"

I continued to look meanly at Gilley. "Fine," I said levelly when he simply stared back like he wasn't sorry at all for what he'd said.

Heath let me go and I moved toward the barstools on the opposite side of the kitchen counter. Gil made sure to give me a wide berth as I passed him.

Wise.

"I was able to feel the imprint of the murder from last night," I said after we'd all taken our seats.

Heath's brow shot up. "Did you connect with Brook?"

"No. I felt the imprint of her emotions and the attack and her murder, but not a direct connection with her spirit."

Heath's brow lowered and he frowned. "Damn. I was hoping we could link up with her to see if she could tell us if it was Luke who murdered her."

"It wasn't," I said.

"What?" Gil said. "How do you know?"

I explained what I'd felt on the sidewalk, and also what I'd relayed to Detective Souter. Neither Gil nor Heath looked happy to hear that I'd given my impressions to the detective. "I think we should call Mack and tell him what you said to Souter," Gilley said.

I stiffened. I knew that was the right move, but I still couldn't help asking, "Why?"

"Because you just gave details to a detective about a murder you claim you didn't witness and had nothing to do with. Don't you think you might've put yourself a little more firmly under the suspicion spotlight?"

I bit my lip. "I guess I didn't think it through before I talked to her. Souter just appeared next to me when I was fishing through the ether."

"That's what happens when you try to go it alone," Heath said. "I'm not there to have your back."

I let my gaze fall to my lap. I saw his point, but I still wouldn't have done it differently. I didn't want to argue about it either. I wanted to talk to Steven and Courtney and let them know that I believed Luke didn't have anything to do with the murder. Gil, however, had other plans. He started whining about lunch—which I'd failed to pick up—and as Heath didn't want to leave me alone again, we decided to all go out to eat and discuss our next move.

I called Mack on the way, and he was not happy with me. At. All. By the end of the conversation he had me feeling like I might be lucky to avoid an arrest. "Do not talk to *anyone* about your impressions of that murder scene!" he yelled at me.

"But I have to tell Steven and Courtney!" I protested.

"No. Hell no, M.J.!"

"Mack," I tried, "they've gotta be going crazy right now, not knowing if Luke might be a killer."

"No!" Mack snapped. "Listen to me, okay? Luke's attorney, Caldwell Fischer, isn't somebody to mess with. That man's not just a shark; he's the shark that ate all the other sharks for breakfast. He hates to lose, and with a case like this where there's plenty of incriminating evidence against his client, he'll try to use any means possible to discredit the video on Gilley's computer. And that means he'll work to discredit *you*. If you start talking about how the murder went down, he'll find a way to point the finger at you three. You *cannot* talk to Dr. Sable or his fiancée about this! Do you understand?"

I ground my teeth together. I hated all this legal crap.

"M.J.?" Mack said. "Tell me you understand."

"I get it, Mack," I grumbled. "But it sucks."

I heard Mack let out a long, relieved breath. "I've never had a case that didn't suck. It comes with the territory."

Heath parked the car at that point and looked at me expectantly. I got off the line with Mack and waited until we were inside and seated to talk about what Mack had asked us to do. Or, rather, asked us not to do.

"But, M.J., it's *Steven*," Gil said to me after I told him we couldn't say a word to anybody about my impressions at the murder scene.

"I don't like it any more than you do, Gil," I said. "But we're too vulnerable here. We just can't talk to him right now."

As if on cue my phone went off, and looking at the caller ID, I saw that it was Steven. "Speak of the devil," I heard Heath mutter as he leaned over my shoulder. "You gonna answer?"

I nearly did, but I didn't trust myself to talk directly to Steven, even to tell him that I couldn't talk to him. My ex was wily. He'd pick up on my evasiveness in a heartbeat and demand answers. I'd be hard-pressed to put him off. I pushed the call to voice mail, but I knew I couldn't avoid Dr. Steven Sable forever. So I looked at Heath and Gilley and said, "We have to solve this."

Gilley cocked his head. "We have to solve what?"

"This case. It's not just enough to prove that Luke didn't do it. We've got to find the murderer."

"Isn't that a job for the police?" he said, his expression a bit alarmed.

"Normally, yes. But as we're looking pretty suspicious to them right now, and as I'd like to avoid having an innocent man go to jail, or having the three of us roped in as accomplices, I think we need to put some serious effort into helping the police with the investigation."

Heath and Gilley exchanged a look. The look said that they thought I done just lost my mind. "Em . . . ," Heath began.

"I'm going to work on it," I told him flatly. "You're either with me in this or you're not."

"But how would we even *do* that, M.J.?" Gilley protested. "I mean, we're not law enforcement. We're not even private eyes. We have no skills where that's concerned!"

I crossed my arms stubbornly. "We got plenty of skills, Gil. We investigate ghosts for a living, remember?"

"Yeah, but there's a difference between investigating dead people and looking for a live, murderous person! A live, murderous person who might like to murder someone like . . . oh, let's say *me* next!"

"Gil," I said, "no one's going to murder you."

"You always say that and then it's 'Oh, Gilley! Look out! Run for your life! You're about to be *murdered*!'"

I sighed wearily. "Honey, if you want out of this investigation, then fine. I understand. But I'm going to pursue it. My ass is on the line and I'm not gonna sit around and wait to be arrested simply because the detective assigned to the case is a skeptic. And if we don't do something, then this spook will move on to another target and another girl will get killed. I can't have that on my conscience."

Heath shifted in his seat as if I'd struck a chord with that argument. "I'm in," he said after a minute.

Gilley gave him the most disgusted look, and he turned those eyes on me and seemed really mad about something. "You always do this," he spat.

"I always do what?" I asked.

"Not just you." Gil wagged his finger at Heath and me. "The two of you. You gang up and go all, 'Gil, you can stay out of this if you want—it's totally fine—but we two fools are proceeding with this idiotic plan,' and then I cave because I worry, and then in no time I'm running for my life, about to be *murdered*!"

I shook my head and felt a little mirth tug at my lips. "Yes, it's part of our master diabolical plan, Gil. We've been trying to do away with you forever, but somehow you always manage to escape being *murdered*."

"Har, har," he said with a glare. "I'm serious, M.J."

I feigned surprise. "And I'm not?"

Gilley glared at me and I was willing to wait him out, but Heath had less patience. "You in or you out, buddy?"

"Oh, I'm in," he groused. "Because I'm *always* in, aren't I?"

I gave him a winning smile. "Good. Now let's talk about how to proceed."

Heath nodded but covered my hand with his. "Before we talk plan of action, I want to make it clear that whatever we decide to do, we do it together. No one goes off alone and does something stupid without backup."

I bristled at being told I'd done something stupid, but then I had to admit to myself that Heath had a pretty good point. "Fine. We stick together."

"I'll be in the van," Gil said, just to make it clear that the sticking-together part belonged to Heath and me. "Or in the condo doing research."

I nodded. "Fine, Gil. Can the three of us talk about strategy now?"

Heath waved a hand for me to proceed. "Where do you want to start?"

"With the house Luke was staying in when our spook arrived on scene."

"You think that's where the portal is?" Gil asked.

I shrugged. "Don't know. Which brings me to my next point—I don't even know the address. Gil. Is there any way you could get that for us without us having to ask Steven or Courtney? I want to try and keep a low profile with them if I can."

"Child's play," Gil said, making a note in his phone.

"Awesome. And we also need a way into the house. If it's a rental, then we might be able to contact the landlord and tell him we're interested in renting it—assuming it's available for rent."

"I'll look that up too," Gil promised.

"Cool. And while you're at it, maybe you can get something on the landlord. I mean, he has to know what's happening there, right? He might even have lived there once. Let's see who he is and what kind of a guy he is."

"This sounds like a lot of work for me and not a lot of work for you two," Gil said, wagging that finger at Heath and me again.

"We'll be plenty busy," I assured him. "Just get us started by getting us into that rental house. Meanwhile I want to take Heath to Brook's murder scene again, only this time, I want him to approach it from the opposite direction."

"Why?" Heath and Gilley said together.

"Because I know what I felt in the ether, but I'm not sure what Heath encountered. I want him to go to the crime scene from last night and see if he senses the same thing he did from further up the street. I have a weak but nagging theory that there could be a connection between Brook Astor's murder and Amy Montgomery's, and if I'm right, then this spook may have been responsible for more than just one dead girl."

Gilley and Heath both paled. "But those two murders were decades apart," Gil said.

"Doesn't matter," Heath told him, a slight shudder traveling through his shoulders. "You know that, Gil. Spooks aren't aware of time. And evil spooks don't care about anything but opportunity."

I played with my straw nervously. The thing Heath hadn't mentioned was how risky my plan of taking him to Brook's murder scene was. "I'll be standing nearby with a vest just in case things get sticky," I told him.

"Thanks," he said. "If you're right, I may need it."

"We should have a code word or something," I told him, suddenly thinking of the idea.

"A code word? For what?"

"If you start to sense that this thing is trying to take over your mind, you should say something like . . ." I paused, trying to think up a word.

"How about, 'Run for your life. You're about to be murdered!'" Gil suggested.

I leveled my gaze at him. "Not helping."

"How about something simple like . . ." Heath paused, trying to come up with one himself.

"Not as easy as it sounds, huh?"

"Oh, you two!" Gil said. "If you need a safe word, use mine: banana."

Heath and I both turned wide eyes on Gil.

"What?" he said. "Michel and I use it all the time."

I made a face. "TMI, buddy. TMI."

Gil rolled his eyes dramatically. "Yes, and you two are pure as the driven snow."

I felt a blush touch my cheeks. "We'll come up with something," I said quietly to Heath, who was grinning at me. "Anyway, let's get a move on. I want to find this spook and shut it down before it has a chance to use someone to kill again."

With that, we paid the bill and were on our way.

After dropping Gilley off at the condo, Heath and I

headed back to Commonwealth Avenue. I was really nervous the closer we got to Courtney's place. I had a feeling it'd be a pretty bad idea to get caught sniffing around the crime scene for the second time that day. What if Souter thought we were trying to retrieve a key piece of evidence or something? I mean, I've watched enough crime shows to know that snooping around a crime scene is highly suspicious behavior.

Just as I'd suspected, as we turned onto Comm Ave and started looking for a parking spot, Heath pointed ahead and said, "Guess we're not going back there today."

A patrol car with a cop inside was parked right in front of Brook Astor's murder scene. "Dammit!" I swore. Fishing out my cell, I called Gil. "We won't be getting close to Brook's murder scene today," I told him.

"Is the place swarming with cops?" he asked, probably guessing we'd encountered an official roadblock.

"Not so much swarming as one guy in a patrol car, but, yeah, it's a deterrent."

"Well, I have another lead you can scope out. I found Luke's old address. Got a pen?"

I rummaged around in my messenger bag and retrieved a small notepad and pen before I scribbled down the address. "Did you talk to the landlord?"

"I have a call in to him," Gil told me. "I'm hoping he calls me back in a bit. You guys head over there and sit tight until I hear back from him, okay?"

I showed the slip of paper to Heath, who plugged it into his phone's navigation app and said, "Thanks, Gil. It should take us about twenty minutes or so to get there."

We drove our way through Boston's winding streets, and I could see Heath focusing hard on the navigation app on his phone. Boston's roadways can be confusing even to the locals. I managed to point him in the right direction a couple of times when he almost took a wrong turn at a rotary, but eventually we found our way to a street called Stoughton, and about midway down we found Luke's old home.

Even from our spot across the street the place looked creepy. "Yikes," Heath said as he put my car into park. "Why would anybody want to rent that place?"

The exterior of the home was wooden shingles stained so dark they were almost black. The shutters were an ugly muddy color and the front door was once red, but was now faded to an ugly pink. The windows were coated in grime and probably full of drafts, while the lawn was still brown and scrubby, and some bushes along the front appeared to be hanging on to life by a thread. Nothing about the place was either inviting or appealing.

"Maybe it was cheap," I said, squinting at the place with distaste.

"It'd have to be," Heath said. "And even if it was free, I wouldn't live there."

I knew what he meant. The house gave off a bad vibe. As Heath and I were waiting on Gil to call back, we saw a silver Honda pull up and park right in front of the house. About ten seconds later, a white pickup parked behind the Honda and the occupants of both vehicles got out together.

Exiting the pickup was a reedy-looking man I put in his late sixties to early seventies. He had silver hair and nondescript features. The owner of the Honda was a woman I recognized. Immediately I scrunched down in my seat. "You know her?" Heath asked me, noticing right away that I was afraid of being spotted.

"Yep. And you know her too."

Heath peered out the window. "Hey, isn't that the reporter from the news?"

"Kendra Knight," I told him.

"What's she doing here?" Heath wondered, just as Kendra and the man from the pickup truck shook hands.

"Don't know," I said, feeling nervous about how close we were to them. The last thing I needed was for Kendra to do another feature story on me. "Maybe she's investigating Brook's murder now."

Heath started the car and put a hand on my shoulder. "Duck down," he said, easing the car out from the curb. "We're a little too conspicuous here."

We drove around the block and cruised slowly back down the street, tucking in behind a minivan, which we hoped would block the view back to us from the house. Then we watched Kendra and the man in front of the house; it appeared she was interviewing him, as she had her notepad out and she was scribbling in it as the man talked and gestured toward the house. This went on for a good ten minutes until Kendra shook the man's hand again and turned to go back to her car. I saw her head lift in our direction and Heath and I both ducked low in our seats, peeking up over the dash.

I let out a breath when Kendra got into her car and drove off. Meanwhile the man appeared to have gotten a phone call because he was on his cell pacing in front of his truck.

"Think that's the landlord?" Heath asked me.

I sat up a little straighter in my seat. "Could be."

"Only one way to find out," he said, hopping out of the car before I had a chance to tell him to hold on. I followed and caught up to him just as he began waving at the man to catch his attention.

I heard the guy on the phone say, "The rent's twelve hundred a month. If you want to see it, you can come by now, but I got places to be, so I can't wait for you too long."

It was then that I noticed on the other side of the

truck he'd leaned a FOR RENT sign, which he clearly planned on putting in the front lawn.

Heath waved again and the guy said, "Look, I got someone here who seems to be interested, so I gotta go. Come by or don't. I'll be here for fifteen minutes or so."

"Is this the place that's for rent?" Heath said the second the guy hung up.

"Yep," he said.

"Mind if we take a look?"

"Don't rent the place to couples," he said. "Too much of a headache when they find out they can't live together and both of them skip out on the rent."

I laughed like he'd just said something funny. "I'm his sister," I told the man. "We're not a couple."

I saw the guy's eyes shift from me to Heath and back again. "You don't look alike," he said, clearly suspicious.

"Stepbrother and -sister," Heath said, thinking quick.

The guy rolled his eyes a little but waved us toward the house. "Come on, then," he said. "But make it quick. I got another guy coming over in about fifteen minutes."

My phone rang at that moment and after a quick glance at the caller ID I sent it to voice mail. Heath looked back at me and I mouthed, "Gilley."

I had no doubt that Gil had been the one to call the landlord as we approached and he was calling me to let me know we could meet the landlord.

"I'm John," Heath said when the guy began fumbling with his keys.

"Ray," the guy said by way of introduction.

"Nice to meet you," Heath told him.

Ray didn't reply; instead he simply unlocked the door and walked inside, holding it open for us. Heath went through first and I followed. We entered into a living room and Heath came up short, causing me to bump into him a little. I moved to the side instinctively, wondering why he'd stopped so abruptly, and looked up to see him slack-jawed.

Immediately I focused on the room and couldn't believe what I was seeing.

"All this will be cleared out," Ray said from behind us as he also moved to the side. I had a feeling he was mistaking our shock for simply not liking the furniture strewn about on the floor. "The last tenant was a piece of work," he told us. "Tossed the place. Then he cut out on the rent."

I nodded but I was barely listening to him. The interior of the house was exactly like the one in my out-of-body nightmare from earlier. Even the chairs where Heath had tossed the creepy man who'd pinned me down were wrecked in exactly the same way. As if the whole thing had *actually* taken place. "What the hell?" I heard Heath whisper as he moved close to me and took up my hand.

"It doesn't look like much, but it cleans up okay," Ray was saying, making small attempts to pick up a few sticks of furniture.

I squeezed Heath's hand. Just being in the exact same setting from my OBE was really unnerving. Out of the corner of my eye I saw Heath's head turn from side to side, and I wondered if he was looking for the creepy dude who'd attacked me to appear in the flesh.

"The rent's twelve hundred a month," Ray said, and I saw that he was watching us closely. I knew we were acting weird.

Taking a deep breath, I let go of Heath's hand and said, "Let's look around."

He got the hint and we moved deeper into the house.

It was a small place, probably only about seven hundred square feet. The living room was narrow and not very long. There was a sofa parked up against one wall, but no TV or other electronics were in evidence. I had a feeling maybe Ray had taken those out when it was clear Luke wasn't coming back.

The area with the toppled table and chairs was closer to the door, and it'd served as the dining room. Behind that was a doorway, which led to the kitchen. I moved there and looked around. The place had the feeling of violence in it, but I couldn't pinpoint anything specific. It gave me the serious creeps too, and I couldn't understand how anybody would want to live here.

What I didn't pick up—and was a little surprised not to—was any sense of a spook. The house had definitely seen spectral energy; there were remnants of it in the ether, but nothing that I could pinpoint specifically as a ghost in the room.

Still, I walked through the kitchen to another door and flipped the switch. An overhead light came on, illuminating a bedroom, which looked like it'd been tossed by a professional robber. The bed had no linens, just the mattress, which was slightly askew. There was trash on the floor and all the drawers had been pulled out of the dresser.

I stepped carefully around the mess to the closet, pulled there by my own intuition. The door opened with a squeak and I peered inside. It was a small closet, not much room for more than a few clothes, but most of what'd been on the wire hangers dangling from the bar had been removed, whether by Luke or Ray I couldn't tell. I reached for the string to the overhead light and heard Heath call my name. I tugged on the string and the dingy walls of the closet lit up with graffiti. I felt my brow furrow as my eyes scanned the walls. *Deadly Dan was here,* read one blotch of black ink. *Slayer Sy was here,* read another. *Butcher Bill was here,* read another block, and a knife with dripping blood was drawn next to yet another name, *Gut-you-Guy was here.*

My gaze darted around the closet, and the hair on the back of my neck stood up on end. Each autograph was distinct enough to have been drawn by a different hand. There were at least a half-dozen autographs, and the one that my gaze finally came to rest on was one that sent a cold shiver down my spine.

"Heath!" I called, riveted by the walls of the closet.

"Yeah?"

"Come here, please!"

I heard his footsteps come up behind me, his cowboy boots striking the wood floors, and for just a fraction of a moment I felt a terrible foreboding at his approach. I shoved that thought out of my head as his hand came to rest on the small of my back. "Look," I told him.

I watched him squint at the interior of the closet and take in all the names. Some with pictures of knives next to them, and others with a few added lines of macabre poetry.

And then I pointed to the back wall, midway down, to where it read, *Lethal Luke was here. . . .*

Chapter 9

"Whoa," Heath whispered right before I heard another set of footsteps coming toward the bedroom. Thinking fast, I snapped a photo of the inside of the closet with my phone and quickly shut the door. We turned around just as Ray came into the bedroom. He eyed us suspiciously again. "Seen enough?" he asked.

"Yeah," Heath told him. "And I think I'll keep looking."

"Suit yourself."

"We should go," I said, taking hold of Heath's arm and moving toward the door. Ray shifted his stance and I was starting to get uncomfortable around him.

"I would've cleared all this junk out before you moved in," he said, waving his hand around at the clutter.

Heath shrugged as we passed Ray by, and I was glad he didn't try to offer more of an explanation.

Still, the landlord kept right on our heels and I was never happier to get out into the sun again. Heath and I didn't say a word as we left, not even a good-bye or a thank-you, which was probably pretty rude, but we both just wanted to get away from that place and talk about the closet.

Heath took up my hand as we crossed the street and we heard Ray's truck start up. We kept our eyes on the prize and at last reached the safety of my car. Heath undid the locks and I jumped in, already fiddling with my phone to pull up the image. Heath leaned in so we could both have a look and that's when three loud raps on his window made both of us jump.

A woman waved at us through the window. "Hi, M.J.," she said, a Cheshire grin on her face.

My breath caught. "Shit," I muttered.

"No comment?" Heath whispered to me.

"Oh, come on!" Kendra Knight called to us. "Talk to me, M.J. Please?"

I was tempted to have Heath drive off, but I doubted she'd let us get away. She seemed a bit on the tenacious side, as all good reporters are. I looked at Heath to see what he thought. "Your call," he said to me. "Say the word and I can get us out of here before she can even make it back to her car."

I squeezed his hand. "You're pretty awesome, you know?"

He grinned at me. "I memorized the awesome-boyfriend handbook."

That made me chuckle. Kendra tapped on the window again. "I'm not gonna go away, you know," she told us.

I sighed. "Better roll down the window," I told Heath, clicking my phone off and tucking it into my pocket.

"We have no comment," Heath said the second the window was down.

Kendra frowned. "I understand you may not want to talk to me," she began, and I could tell she had a pretty good argument lined up for why we should reconsider.

"But when I saw you two across from this house, I got curious, and I'm wondering if you're starting to put two and two together as well."

Okay, she'd piqued my curiosity. "Two and two?" I asked.

"I thought you weren't commenting," she said with a sly grin. I leveled a look at her and she added, "If I share what I know, you two have to share what you know."

"We can't share anything," I told her, thinking she was fishing for an inside scoop on the murder on Comm Ave. "But you may speak to my attorney if you'd like."

Kendra blinked. "Your attorney? Why'd you retain a lawyer?"

It was my turn to blink. Was she playing coy? "You know why we did," I said, telling it straight without giving her anything to quote me on.

"No, I really don't," she insisted. Then she squinted at me. "Why are you here?"

"Probably the same reason you're here, Kendra, but just for kicks, how about you tell us why you came by, and if it's the same reason, then we'll tell you?"

There was no way in hell it was going to be the same reason.

Kendra seemed to think that over. At last she said, "I'm here because this house was the former residence of three men charged with the brutal stabbing and throat slashing of innocent young women: Dan Foster, who murdered Bethany Sullivan, and Guy Walker, who murdered a young woman named Amy Montgomery in the nineteen seventies, and also, as I discovered this morning, Luke Decker, who right now is being held on suspicion of murder in the brutal slaying of Brook Astor last night. I'm thinking three murderers sharing a former residence is a pretty *big* coincidence, and I'm here trying to find the connection between the three."

I was stunned to realize that the very ghost Heath had connected with earlier on Comm Ave was murdered by a man who'd lived in this house, and my mind flashed back to the closet and the names on the wall: *Gut-you-Guy was here. . . .*

I was also stunned to hear that Dan Foster had once lived here too.

"Now how about you tell me what you're doing here and why you've retained an attorney."

It surprised me that she hadn't heard that we'd been brought in for questioning by the police on Brook Astor's murder, but then, we hadn't been charged with anything, so maybe our presence just down the street hadn't been reported to the media. Still, Kendra was like a dog with a bone, and I knew she'd find the connection sooner or later. "We were just down the street from Brook Astor's crime scene on the night she was murdered," I confessed. Out of the corner of my eye I saw Heath look sharply at me.

Kendra's expression told me she was pretty shocked too. "Whoa," she said, and I could see a thousand questions start to form in her eyes.

"We can't discuss what happened of course," I said quickly, wanting to shut her down before she began pestering me for details I knew we couldn't give her.

"Oh, come on!" she said. "Are you kidding me?"

I shook my head. "Sorry, Kendra. And we've got to go. Thanks for sharing, though. We appreciate it."

Kendra put a hand on the window frame. "I can make you a confidential source," she said desperately.

I motioned to Heath, and he edged the car ever so slightly away from the curb. Kendra continued to cling to the window frame. "Hey!" she said, attempting to keep us there. "I think there may be more murderers connected to this house. I had to sift through thirty years of records to find Guy's old address, but I think there may be more men who've lived here who've committed murder. What I can't figure out is how this house plays into it. But I think you know," she said as Heath put the car into drive. "I think you're here fishing around for the same answers."

"Please let go," Heath said to her.

But Kendra wouldn't. She continued to hold on to the car door even as Heath eased us forward a fraction. "Kendra," I said to her, "please let go. We have nothing to offer you."

She did let go then, but she started trotting next to the car, and then a bit of paper fluttered into the car and onto Heath's lap. I realized it was her business card. "I have tons of notes," she said, panting now to try to keep up with us. "We could pool our information! This could be an amazing story, M.J.! I could make you famous! Think about it!"

Heath cleared the curb and pressed the accelerator, pulling away from Kendra. He didn't let off until he was well away from her.

I turned to look back and I watched Kendra stand in the street watching us drive away. I had the most unsettling feeling about her probing into this case. I was having a hard enough time trying to figure out the spectral energy of that house and the men involved in what appeared to be a string of murders. It was eerie and creepy and way too much for a layperson to handle. This was the stuff of horror movies and I started to worry about Kendra.

"What?" Heath asked, reading my expression.

"I don't like her poking her nose into this."

"*This* or *you*?"

"This," I said. "Okay and me, but I'm more worried about her. If there really is some sort of occult connection to all these murders, then she could be in real danger. We know how to protect ourselves. She's too naive to get it."

"Should we set up a meeting with her?" Heath asked. "Just to warn her?"

I lifted the card out of the cup holder where Heath had put it while he pulled away. "No," I said. "Not yet. Let's go back to my place and look at the names on the wall. Gil might be able to match them to other murders."

Heath's mouth pressed into a thin line. "There were a lot of names in that closet, Em."

I nodded. "Including Luke's."

"Maybe we're wrong about him. Maybe he really did kill Brook."

I was so confused by my own impressions and the evidence that kept presenting itself to point the finger at Luke that I didn't know what to think.

We got home a bit later and found Gil in my kitchen raiding the fridge. "You just had lunch," I said, passing him on my way to the living room.

"That was hours ago," Gil said, coming up from the fridge with a cupcake I'd been saving for after a really good run.

Before I could stop him, Gil took a huge bite. "Hey!" I shouted. "I was saving that!"

Gil paused his consumption of my cupcake long enough to grin at me. "I'm saving *you* from all these extra calories. Junk in that trunk ain't gonna help you across the finish line, honey."

Between the two of us, Gil had far more to worry about. He'd put on some considerable weight while we were in Europe, but since he'd been dating Michel, he'd done a good job of trimming down. Now that Michel was in New York on a shoot, I could tell Gil was starting to really miss him, and was binge eating to deal with it.

"When you're finished stuffing your piehole, come over and help us with something," I said, giving up because Gil could devour a sweet treat faster than anyone I knew. I'd get another cupcake.

Heath came to sit next to me while I uploaded the photo from my phone onto my laptop, where I could expand the image to see if I'd gotten all the names.

"There they are," Heath said with a whistle. "There're at least a half dozen, Em."

"Half-dozen what?" Gil said from over Heath's shoulder as he peered at the computer screen. "Hey, why'd you take a picture of a marked-up closet? Which reminds me, did you get over to the rental house?"

Heath and I both took our gazes off the computer screen to stare at Gil. He'd asked three separate questions in under ten seconds. "Have a seat," I told him. It was just easier to start at the beginning with him. Once I'd filled him in on our little visit to Luke's last residence and the conversation we'd had with Kendra and her theory that there were other murderers connected to the house, Gil looked properly intrigued. "Lemme see that photo," he said.

I tapped the mouse pad and the photo came up. I enhanced it so that we could read the names better, and Gil's expression changed to a frown. "How the hell are we supposed to identify any more murderers with this?" he said. "Deadly Dan? Gut-you-Guy? What kind of a list is that?"

"Dan is Dan Foster—he killed Bethany Sullivan—and Guy is Guy Walker, who murdered Amy Montgomery, the ghost on Comm Ave that I bumped into this morning," Heath said.

Gilley blinked. "Wait," he said. "Two guys on this list are the same men who murdered the two women on Comm Ave whose spirits you two fools bumped into today?"

I nodded. "Apparently. Freaky coincidence, huh?"

"Gurl," Gil said with a tisk and a shake of his head. "Freaky doesn't even half cover it. Okay, so we know who two of these guys are—"

"Three," Heath corrected, pointing to the name on the bottom. "That's Luke."

Gil's eyes widened. "Whoa!"

"Yep," I said.

"But I thought we were going with the he's-left-handed-so-he-must-be-innocent theory?"

"Yeah, well my jury's still out. I'll admit that I'm still a little back and forth on his innocence or guilt."

"But what about your impressions at the crime scene this morning?" Gil said.

I shook my head and sighed. "I know. I can't figure out how to reconcile it. I mean, look . . ." I pointed to the screen where the words *Lethal Luke* were scrawled against the back wall of the closet. "I was all set to paint him as an innocent bystander, but his name in that closet is tough to ignore, you know?"

Next to me, Heath scratched at the stubble on his chin. "I just don't see Luke capable of being a killer, Em. Even if he was possessed by this spook. The kid's strong. If that evil entity—whatever it is—really did get inside his head, he would've fought."

I looked Heath in the eye and said, "That'd be assuming he didn't want to commit murder, though. And we don't know him, honey. We don't know what's really going on inside that head of his."

"You guys also don't know this spook either," Gil pointed out.

Heath and I both looked at him. "What do you mean?" I asked.

Gil shrugged. "Well," he said, pointing to the image on the screen, "it looks like Luke was at least telling the truth about one thing. There is a spook that seems to be possessing the men who live inside that house. And either that thing is turning these men into killers, or they were already flawed to begin with and he's helping them along with their evil deeds. I think the next place to look for clues is to find out more about this spook."

"We were in that house today, and we didn't feel any kind of spectral presence," Heath said.

"Which reminds me," I said, suddenly thinking of something. "What'd you get on the landlord, Ray?"

Gil shook his head. "Nada. I found his name on the rental listing posted to Craigslist, but nobody named Ray ever lived at that address on Stoughton. I'm gonna keep looking, though. I mean, Ray could be a nickname or a middle name. I'll find out who owns the place and for how long, not to worry."

I rubbed my eyes. I was suddenly very tired. "The hard part of this is finding that spook. He wasn't at the rental house and when we were in Courtney's place, we didn't feel it there either. Where else is there to look?"

Gil shrugged and said, "You guys said it yourself yesterday that this isn't a spook that haunts locations. It haunts people. If you want to find this thing, you gotta go look for a person it haunts."

"We're not allowed to talk to Luke," I reminded him.

Gil pointed to the screen again, but this time to the name of Deadly Dan. "No one said you couldn't talk to one of the other killers."

My breath caught. I understood immediately. Still, I could see more roadblocks in front of us. "I don't think we'll be able to get in to see Foster," I said. "Not with all the media scrutiny around his trial."

"But you could go see Guy Walker," Gil said. "He's still alive, at least according to the prison record I pulled up this morning."

I looked at Heath. "What do you think?"

He tapped his knee with his fingertips. "I think it might be the only way to figure out who or what this spook is."

"I agree." Turning back to Gil, I said, "How do we get in to see Walker?"

Gil pulled the laptop toward him and began to type. "You simply send a request to the prison. They'll inform Walker, and if he's not in solitary or otherwise banned from visitations, they'll let you come up. Visitors are allowed on Mondays, Wednesdays, and Fridays. With luck we can have you talking to him the day after tomorrow."

"Do you think he'll agree to see us?" Heath asked. "I mean, he doesn't even know us."

Gil smirked. "Walker's been in prison for over thirty years. I doubt there's anybody left on the outside who comes to see him anymore. He'll agree to see you out of sheer curiosity."

"Do you think we'll be safe?" I asked, nervous about going into a prison, even for a visit.

"Sure," Gil said, like he visited them all the time. "Just don't make eye contact with any of the other prisoners, and if Walker asks you anything personal, like where you live or what you do, try to keep it really vague."

"That's a given," I said as a small shudder went up my spine.

"I can go alone," Heath said, reading me well.

Gil stopped typing and looked up. "Actually, it really should be just M.J. who goes to see Walker."

I blinked. "What? Why?"

"If you're not a relative, they only allow one visitor at a time. And Walker's not going to turn down a visit from a girl. Trust me."

"Unless he plays for your team," I told him with a wink.

"Oh, please," he said, swiveling the laptop around. "Does that look like a face pretty enough to be gay?"

On the computer screen was the image of an old man with mean beady eyes, bushy white eyebrows, and thick silver hair. His face was turned down in a lethal-looking frown, and he definitely looked like someone you'd want to avoid in a dark alley.

Heath took up my hand. "Isn't there a way to get us both in?" he asked.

"I can try," Gil said, swiveling the laptop back toward himself and fluttering his fingers above the keyboard. "I'll have to get creative, though. Maybe I'll go the route of calling you two documentary filmmakers. That may work."

As it happened, that did work. We got the e-mail the following morning that Walker had agreed to see us, and the prison was allowing us to come together. We had to be there at ten a.m. sharp and the prison was in New Hampshire—Walker had been transferred there years earlier, as it was a prison that specialized in housing older inmates, many of whom had health issues. Heath and I were up early and on the road to beat the rush hour traffic, but it still took us a little longer than we'd estimated. Still, we'd packed in a little extra time just in case, so it turned out okay.

At the prison, Heath and I were put through a full pat down and told to empty our pockets. We then had to turn over our phones and keys and other personal items, but Heath was allowed to keep the camera he'd brought along to record our interview with Walker and also to help keep up the "documentary filmmaker" facade.

We were then escorted into a windowless room and told to wait to be called in with the other visitors. Heath and I looked around the room—it was empty, and we shared a smirk.

We waited for about twenty minutes and at last the door opened and we were told to follow the guard down another hallway, through a locked door, and into a narrow cement block room with a row of cubicles that were really just desks with a chair. A window of Plexiglas separated us from an adjoining room that was the mirror of the one we were in. After we had a chance to look around at our surroundings, Heath pulled a chair from one of the other cubicles and we sat in silence while we waited.

At last a door in the other room opened and in shuffled an old man, bent with age, followed by an armed guard with a set of keys. The old man wore a muddy-looking jumpsuit and plastic sandals and pretty much nothing else. I recognized him from the photo that Gil had shown us only by his beady eyes. Guy Walker from the photo had been at least thirty pounds heavier and about fifteen years younger. This man just looked like a crotchety old dude shuffling to the café for a cheap cup of coffee and the morning special.

Guy stopped in front of the chair on his side and regarded us for a very long moment before he finally pulled it out and took a seat. "What?" he said, his voice sharp and jagged like rusty scrap metal.

I took out a photo that Heath and I had taken the day before of the rental house where Luke had lived. "Recognize this?" I asked.

Walker's eyes held mine for another long pause before they moved to the photo. I could tell he recognized it, but he didn't comment.

I put the photo down and took out the one of the closet. I'd had it printed out and blown up. "That's you, right?" I said pointing to his name in the closet.

Walker's eyes again flickered to the photo, then back up to me. His expression was unreadable. I searched the ether around him. I felt only one spirit connected to him. A female who felt distant and weak. Most likely it was Walker's mother, and her connection to her son was tenuous because he wasn't a good person. I see this sometimes with people who are inherently bad. They have very few spirits around them. I think it's because they lose any semblance of spirituality, and so it becomes hard for the spirit world to connect to them.

"My name is Mary," I said to him. "The same as your mother."

Walker cocked an eyebrow.

"Mary died in the month of November," I told him, seeing in my mind's eye the image of a calendar page marked with the word "November," and also the image of a gravestone. "She had diabetes and she lost part of her leg to it." I waved my hand down around my own right leg. "She says it was very cold the month she died. It felt more like winter. I sense that the weather contributed to her death in some way."

"What're you doing?" Walker snapped. He couldn't figure me out and it was irritating him.

"I'm a spirit medium," I said, matter-of-factly. "And I'm connecting with your mom right now."

"Bullshit."

I smiled tightly. "She's not surprised you don't believe me. But she said to tell you that she's glad you keep her picture on the wall of your cell. You've tucked it behind something else, but you know it's there and it brings you comfort. It brings her comfort too."

Walker's fist banged on his side of the desk. "What the hell is this?" he yelled.

The guard at the other end of the room took a step toward him and I held up my hand to show him everything was okay. "Mr. Walker, I need to talk to you about something that most people don't believe in. But I think you do. And in order to convince you that I know what I'm talking about, I needed to prove to you what I can do. Your mom really is talking to me about you. You can believe that or not. I don't really care—it's not the real reason I'm here."

"You're talking in circles," he said, starting to push away from the table.

I decided to speak quickly and play a little fast and loose with the truth. "The other day I was walking along Comm Ave in downtown Boston and I came across the spirit of Amy Montgomery. The girl you murdered. She'd been wearing a white dress that night. That's what drew you to her. You saw it even though it was dark outside. She was like a moth and you were the flame. But it wasn't you that wanted to kill her, was it, Guy? It was the shadowman from the house on Stoughton. The one that followed you day and night and filled your head with dark thoughts and turned your dreams to nightmares. You heard his footsteps behind you everywhere you went, and you felt his presence in that house. You couldn't get away from him. You couldn't eat or sleep because he haunted you morning, noon, and night."

Guy Walker's face drained of color. He'd stood all the way up by the end of my speech, and as I finished speaking, he sat down heavily and just stared at me. "How do you know about him?" he whispered.

"Because he's been following others, Guy. He's been following a friend of mine, in fact. And that friend now stands accused of murder. But I'm hard-pressed to believe he's responsible. I think it was this shadow. The same one that followed you, and pushed you to kill Amy."

Guy looked around the room nervously, the flinty expression he'd worn into the room now a distant memory. This murderer, this mean, awful man, was visibly scared. "Don't talk about him!" he whispered.

Heath and I exchanged a surprised look. "Why?" Heath asked him.

Guy swallowed hard. "You'll call him," he said softly.

"Who is he, Guy?" I asked.

He shook his head. "Stop it," he said. "Let it be!"

But I couldn't. Too much was at stake. "Guy," I said, waiting for him to look at me before continuing. "I'm not just a medium. I'm someone who deals with the worst the spirit world has to offer. My partner and I"—I pointed to Heath and back to me—"we shut these spooks down for a living. It's our specialty. If you'll tell us what you know about this spook, even if it's just a name or where we can find him, we will figure out how to stop him before he gets inside the mind of someone else."

Guy shook his head adamantly. Then he put his hands over his ears and hunched down low, as if he was covering himself for some sort of attack. "He finally stopped coming to me and now you want to call him back? Don't. Don't do it!"

"Walker," the guard barked. "You okay?"

Guy shook his head, then nodded, then took his hands off his ears, but he continued to crouch in his seat. "I don't want him to come back," he said.

"Who, Guy?" I asked, leaning forward and trying to coax a name out of him. "Just tell me if you know his name."

Walker shook his head again and let it drop down to the desk with a loud thunk. The guard looked at us and took another step forward, his hand on his utility belt. Suddenly, Guy's head lifted and he sat up straight. I held my hand up again to show the guard that everything was fine, but he seemed to hesitate, his gaze firmly on Walker.

That's when I felt Heath's hand on my arm. I looked down, then over at him, but he was staring straight ahead at the prisoner. I turned my head slowly and stiffened. Guy was staring at me in a way that made my skin crawl. "Hello, Mary, Mary, quite contrary," he sang. Then he laughed, as if he delighted in making me uncomfortable.

I looked at him closely, even while goose pimples prickled my arms. Something about Guy Walker was definitely different. His eyes—mean before—were downright sinister now. And there was something in his expression that went beyond mean. It was even beyond cruel. I can only describe it as an evil so intense it sent my heart racing, and I was suddenly very glad for the Plexiglas between us. Guy snickered again. "Cat gut your tongue?" he asked me, playing on the words with a wicked grin.

"Who are you?" I asked, but my voice came out hoarse.

Walker smiled. But this wasn't Guy Walker anymore. This was someone—or some*thing*—else. "Who am I?" he repeated. "I'm Gut-you-Guy and Killer Ken. I'm Butcher Bill and Murdering Mike. I'm Deadly Dan, Mary, and Lethal Luke. But always, I'm Sly Sy the Slayer. I'm six for the price of one. But soon I'll be seven. Then eight. Then nine and ten. Which will you be, Mary? Will you be a friend of seven? Or did we already take you? Weren't you one of the first, Mary? Or will we pick you next?" Guy leaned forward to exhale on the Plexiglas, fogging it, and then he lifted a finger and drew a heart with the name Mary in the middle and then he added what looked like a knife going through it. "Like my artwork?" he asked me, snickering again.

Heath stood up and reached for me. Guy's chin came up and he studied Heath as if he'd just realized he was in the room with me. "I know you," he said, that evil grin returning. "I've been in your head. Once I'm in, I'm never out. Want to play again, Indian boy?"

I realized that Heath was in immediate danger and I pulled out of his grasp and bent forward with my fist clenched. I pounded on the Plexiglas as hard as I could. It worked—Guy's attention came off Heath and he focused on me. Ignoring the guard's shout, I pounded on the glass again. "Hey!" I yelled. "Focus on me, you son of a bitch!"

Walker's eyes homed in on me and I realized his pupils had dilated to the point where his irises looked black. That same sick smile continued to play across his face and he licked his lips as if he were about to be served a juicy steak.

Despite the cold fear traveling up and down my spine, I leaned in close. "I will *end* you, spook! Do you hear me? I'll find a way to end you!"

And that's when Walker's face changed to one right out of a horror movie. He bared his teeth and lunged at me from the other side of glass, toppling his chair and sending me back several quick steps. The guard on the other side shot forward to grab Walker's arm and in a move that should not have been possible for a guy so old and withered, he spun around and attacked the guard with hands that looked like claws and the bared teeth of a wild animal.

Heath grabbed me around the waist and literally lifted me off the ground in his haste to rush toward the door. Behind us I heard screams, and I knew they were the guard's, and then an alarm went off and there was some sort of other commotion. Twisting in Heath's arms a little as he pulled the door open, all I saw was a mass of armed guards pouring into the room behind us and the swing of billy clubs just visible above the desk. Through the din of noise I swear I heard the whump of the blows, and a small piece of me hoped that whatever spook was inside Guy Walker felt the brunt of them.

Heath carried me quickly out to into the hallway and he didn't stop until we were met by a guard who was coming toward us looking angry enough to use his own billy club. "What the hell did you say to him?" he shouted at me.

Heath set me down. I was trembling and clenched my fists to try to still the tremors. "Nothing," I told the guard, who was now in front of us breathing so heavily through his nostrils he sounded like a bull. "I just asked him about Amy Montgomery's murder."

The guard's eyes narrowed. "Bullshit," he said. "Walker's been tame for years, and plenty of people have come here to ask him about that night. What'd you say to him?"

I shook my head, sticking to my story.

The guard glowered down at me, but he stepped aside and pointed to the door leading out. "Go!"

We didn't wait for him to change his mind, dashing out as it buzzed. The angry guard escorted us all the way back to where we'd come in and we collected our personal items as quickly as we could.

I shook the whole time, and just wanted to get out of there. Around us we could hear bits of excited conversation from the other guards. ". . . almost bit Gary's nose off!"

". . . four guys to pull him off!"

". . . Tased him three times and he *still* got up!"

Heath grabbed my hand after I'd gotten all my things and he held tight until we had walked all the way back to the car. Once we were inside, Heath started the motor and turned on the heat even though the temp inside the car wasn't that far off from comfortable. I continued to shake for a bit, and he rubbed my back. "Hey," he said. "You okay?"

"What the hell *was* that?" I said in reply.

"One of the creepiest spooks we've ever seen," Heath said. "Which is saying a lot, considering what we've encountered in just the last nine months."

I looked up at the prison nervously. It was as if I could feel the malice of that awful, evil energy wafting out of the walls; like some horrible odor it seeped through the cement blocks toward us. "We should go," I said. "Now."

Heath put the car into drive and backed up out of the space. We didn't say another word until we were back on the freeway. "You okay?" Heath asked again, fiddling with the heat once more to turn it down.

"Yeah," I said. But that was a lie. I'd never seen anything like the change that'd happened when Walker had lunged at me. He'd looked like a zombie, all teeth and nails directed at me. It'd been terrifying.

"I think we should believe Luke," Heath said. "At least the part about a spook haunting him."

I nodded but my thoughts were someplace else. I kept replaying the whole interview with Walker over and over in my mind. Something was bothering me about it—beyond just the freak show aspect of it. There'd been something in the switch between Walker and the spook possessing him that was niggling away at me, but what it was I couldn't quite pinpoint.

"Where's your camera?" I asked suddenly.

"Uh . . . in the backseat. Why?"

I didn't answer. Instead I unclipped the seat belt and turned around to look for the camera. Finding it on the passenger side of the car, I hauled it forward and replayed the video from the interview, praying that the spook's presence hadn't drained the battery or otherwise distorted the image, which often happened with video.

Luckily the video was clear, but the battery was low. I was only able to view the first minute or two before the camera died. Frustrated, I closed my eyes and thought about what I'd seen. There was something. . . .

"Did the camera record?" Heath asked.

The sound of his voice made me jump. "Yeah. But the battery died. We'll have to wait to get home to view it."

Heath and I drove in silence for the next half hour or so before he said, "Kendra said that she only found three murderers connected to that house."

"Which means, in addition to Luke, there're at least three other killers," I said, knowing exactly where he was going with that comment.

"Do you think they've all been caught?"

"God, I hope so. I'd hate to think that only three out of six are behind bars."

"That's assuming that Luke really did murder Brook Astor."

I sighed and turned to stare out the window. I'd really wanted him to be innocent, but if that spook had gotten inside his head, then of course he could've been responsible for Brook's murder. Still, something about the tape was bugging me. Something that didn't fit, and I was anxious to get home and download it to Gil's computer so that I could figure out what it was.

It took us another hour, but eventually we made it back to the condo. We came through the door to find Gilley on the phone to his sweetheart. He all but ignored us when we came in.

"Hey, baby!" Doc sang from his perch by the window. "What you doin'?"

I went straight to him and lifted him off his perch. I needed some feathered love. Doc gave me a sweet kiss and made smoochy noises. When I held him close in a gentle hug, he said, "Love you," in my ear, and that put a smile on my face.

"No, I miss you more," Gil said. "I do! I miss the

sound of your voice. I miss the brown of your eyes. I miss the feel of your lips. And I definitely miss your—"

"Gil!" I said quickly, knowing he was about to get inappropriate for mixed company.

"Sorry, Michel. Gotta go. The prude police have arrived and are probably waiting to put me to work."

Right on cue Heath handed Gil the camera. Gil rolled his eyes but took the camera and got off the phone with Michel. "Did you break it?"

"No, the battery's dead. And M.J. really wants to watch the video."

Gil set down his phone and moved over to his laptop. Taking up a plug, he got the camera hooked up and juiced it enough to download the video. "Anything good on the tape?"

Heath smirked. "Good wouldn't be how I'd describe it. More like useful. Probably."

I gave Doc one more kiss on the beak and set him back on his perch. He whistled at me as I turned away, and thought that as soon as we resolved this case, I was gonna take a few days off from chasing ghosts and hang out with my bird for a spell.

Gilley got the video powered up and we all sat on the couch to watch it. I expected that watching the video would make the experience of meeting Walker less creepy. I was wrong. As we reviewed the video, right around the time when I began to talk to Walker about the spook, a dark shadow appeared against the wall directly behind him. What was even freakier was that neither Heath nor I remembered seeing a shadow in the room with Walker and the guard. But it was clearly there on film, lurking against the wall. And when Guy's head hit the table, the shadow disappeared, and immediately following that, when Walker lifted his chin, we could all see the shift in him clear as day.

"That is freaking creepy!" Gil said, his eyes wide as he stared at the screen.

"It gets worse," I said, studying the footage.

Even with my warning, Gil still managed to shriek when Walker leaped forward at the glass, his teeth bared and his hands trying to grab at me through the Plexiglas. The video jumped around a lot after that as the guard became Walker's next victim and Heath grabbed me around the waist to take me out of there.

I paused the playback and turned to the two of them. "Did you two catch that little bit with the heart?"

"The one he drew of your heart with a knife going through it?" Gil asked, hugging my throw pillow.

"Yeah," I said, my mind going back to it. There was something around that that was bugging me. "Gil, can you rewind to that part again?"

Gil made a distasteful sound but did as I asked. "What is it, Em?" Heath asked.

"Don't know," I said, focusing again on the footage. "But there's something I'm missing and I'm waiting to figure it out."

We watched in silence as Walker leaned forward to fog the glass, his black eyes watching me through the Plexiglas the whole time. "Yeah, he's a freak," Heath said when we reached the end of that sequence again.

"Gil?"

"Yeah?"

"Rewind a little more, would you? I want to start from the beginning again."

Gil hit the rewind button and began to play the footage again. I watched Walker come in, stare at us with little interest, and pull out the chair to take his seat. "Ohmigod!" I gasped, pointing urgently to the screen. "There!"

"Where?" Gil said.

I leaned forward and hit the pause button; then I rewound it to the moment when Walker reached for the chair. "See that?" I asked. "He pulled the chair out with his right hand!"

"So?" Gil and Heath said together.

I pressed the FORWARD button and wound the footage forward to where Walker was drawing on the Plexiglas. "And now he's left-handed. See? He's drawing with his left index finger."

"So?" Gil said again, but Heath seemed to know where I was going. "The spook is left-handed?"

I nodded. "Looks that way, doesn't it?"

I rewound the tape again all the way to the beginning and pointed out every instance when Walker gestured or used his right hand as the dominant hand. "There!" I said, pointing when Walker scratched the stubble on his chin. "He's using his right hand. I'm telling you, Guy Walker is right-handed."

"And Luke is left-handed, right?" Heath said. I could tell he was putting it together too.

"Yep. But whoever killed Brook Astor was right-handed."

"I'm lost," Gil complained.

I got up to pace the room while I worked it out for myself. "If this spook really is getting inside the minds of these men and taking over in order to murder women, then why would Luke—who's already left-handed—kill with his right hand when the spook is left-handed?"

"Makes no sense," Gil said, but more to me than to the line of my argument.

"I'm leaning toward the theory that Luke didn't murder Brook Astor. I think he may have been headed home after doing God-knows-what with that spook inside his mind, and he stumbled on Brook, who was either already dead or dying when Luke found her. He may have stopped to try to help her, and that's how he got blood on his hands."

"But why wasn't he the one to call the police?" Gil asked. "I mean, he finds a bloody woman on the stairs a few doors down from his house and he doesn't call nine-one-one?"

"Honey," I said, "you saw him get right out of bed and head out the door that night and leave his cell on the nightstand. He had nothing to call them with."

"There's another possibility," Heath said.

"What?" I asked.

"Luke could've been possessed by that thing and completely unaware of anything until he was finally released by the spook. And that could've been right at the moment when he found Brook's body."

My brow rose. "Yes," I said, nodding. "That makes sense! That's why Luke isn't talking to anyone. He thinks he might've actually killed Brook while he was possessed by the spook!"

"It'd be good to get that confirmed by Luke himself," Gilley said.

I sat back down in a chair across from the boys. "I know, but that's not likely to happen anytime soon."

"There's one fly in the ointment still," Heath said.

I smiled crookedly at him. "Only one?"

"Maybe a few more than one, but the one that's still jumping out at me is, why is Luke's name in that closet?"

"Lethal Luke," Gil mused. "Wait till the cops get a load of that."

"We can't tell them anything about it," I warned him. "We can't tell *anyone* about it. If they get wind of that, Luke's sunk."

"They're bound to find out, M.J.," Gil pointed out. "I mean, I got a look at the police report that went along-side the coroner's report, and the murder weapon is missing. The police can't find it, and I'll bet they're tearing the city apart looking for it."

That shocked me. "The murder weapon's missing?"

Gil nodded. "And you know what else is weird? In the murders of both Bethany Sullivan and Amy Montgomery, the knife used to kill them was also never found."

"Whoa," I said. Then I had another thought. "Does anyone think it might've been the same weapon?"

"That'd be a little bit of a leap," Heath said, but I could tell the idea had intrigued him.

"The more pressing thing is that at some point the police are gonna search out Luke's former residence, looking for it. The minute they open up that closet door, Luke will be toast."

"He's already toast," I grumbled. But then something else occurred to me. "Still, when they do open up that closet, they'll find five other names. Names that could all cast doubt on Luke's guilt."

"Six other names," Gil said, swiveling the screen of his computer around to show us the paused image of Walker talking to me with those sinister eyes. "Walker gave you a total of seven possible killers."

"Wait . . . what?" I asked, getting out of the chair to go sit by Gilley again.

We listened to the tape again and Gil turned up the sound while he counted off the names on his fingers. "I'm Gut-you-Guy and Killer Ken. I'm Butcher Bill and Murdering Mike. I'm Deadly Dan, Mary, and Lethal Luke. But always, I'm Sly Sy the Slayer," Guy Walker said, or rather the spook controlling Guy said.

"That last line," I said. "'But always, I'm Sly Sy the Slayer,' could that actually be part of the name of our spook?"

Gil jotted some notes on a pad by his computer. "I'll

plug a few searches into the Interwebs and see what comes up for Sly Sy the Slayer. Maybe we'll get lucky."

"And what about these other names?" I asked. "Killer Ken, Butcher Bill, Murdering Mike. Who could they be?"

Gil added a few more notes. "We know this spook likes to kill women," he said. "I'll look into it."

"And see if there's any correlation between these names and maybe a left-handed killer, Gilley. Also, maybe we should look into Brook Astor's history a little bit too."

"Anything else you want to add to my list?" Gil said, and I could detect a note of irritation in his voice. I might've been pushing him a little hard with all this searching.

"You're right, honey. Sorry. Listen, while you're working to find out more about these other men, Heath and I can look into the house on Stoughton. It seems to be the key here. Something about that house connects all of these men."

"I already traced the owner," Gil said. "It's a dead end."

"Ray?"

"No. Ray seems to be just the manager. The house is in a trust called the LSRLA Trust. What that stands for or who the members of it are is the real mystery."

"Is there any way to find that out?" I asked.

Gil shrugged. "Not one I can come up with online. You'll need the help of an investigator with a little more know-how about these things."

I sat up straight. "I may know exactly the kind of investigator who could help us find that out," I said. When they both looked at me quizzically, I said, "Kendra Knight. She seems like a top-notch reporter. I'm pretty sure she's already digging for the history on that house. Maybe she came up with something that will help us."

Gil and Heath both eyed me like I'd just said something crazy. "You sure?"

"Yes. And there's another call that I'm going to make, but I'm on the fence about telling you two about it because knowing what I'm about to do could get you guys in trouble."

Gil immediately put his fingers in his ears. "I don't want to know! I don't want to know!"

Heath took Gil by the arm and pulled him up and out of the way as he scooted down the couch to sit next to me. "You're thinking of calling Sable," he said flatly.

"We have to, don't you think? Luke's lawyer needs to know about the other names in the closet before he gets blindsided by the 'Lethal Luke' signature, which the police are sure to find sooner or later, especially if the murder weapon is still missing. And his lawyer may even be able to use it as reasonable doubt."

Heath nodded. "Okay. But, Em, tread carefully, okay? You put your own freedom at risk every time you talk to him."

"Well, don't do it on the phone," Gil said, his fingers still stuck in his ears. "The police could be tapping his cell."

I scowled at him. "Aren't you a tiny bit paranoid?"

Gil took one finger out to point to his computer. "You forget that I hack into people's conversations and thoughts and stuff on a regular basis."

"Good point. Okay, I'll have him paged at the hospital and ask to meet in a public place." I then eyed Heath with trepidation. "Would you mind if I went alone?"

"Yes," he said, but he was smiling. "But go alone anyway. I want to look into Ray's background a little bit."

"The landlord?" I asked.

"Yeah. I wonder if he knows about the evil in that house. I can understand that he may be just the manager and not the owner, but he's gotta know something or be connected to someone."

I tapped my chin. "You think he could be a relative or something?"

Heath grinned. "Don't know. That's why I want to look."

I rolled my eyes. "Got it."

"I'll also call Kendra and set up a meeting," he promised.

"Okay," I said, heading toward the door. "I shouldn't be long."

"If you are, then Heath will start getting the wrong idea," Gil called wickedly.

Oh, if only looks could kill . . .

Chapter 10

After struggling to find a parking space and finally settling for the nursing home across the street, I hustled into the hospital anxious to meet with my ex. I'd checked my rearview mirror constantly, hoping that I wasn't being tailed, and couldn't find any sign of anybody following me, but it made me nervous to take such a risk.

Still, I knew it was the right thing to do. I met Steven in the hospital cafeteria. I asked to see him alone, but he brought Courtney, and it felt super awkward because I knew he was firmly establishing his loyalty and commitment to her even though the display wasn't necessary — my heart belonged to Heath. I tried to hide my irritation and impatience with the unspoken message, but it was tough. "There's something you should know," I said, trying to get right to the point. "Actually, there're two things you should know, but if I tell them to you, then I put myself at risk, so I'm a bit hesitant to speak about it because of that." I watched Steven and Courtney absorb that, and then my ex cupped his fiancée's hand and leaned just a touch closer to her. "That's why I wanted to meet you alone, Steven," I said, the ice in my voice surfacing despite my best efforts.

"I understand," he said, perhaps a bit defensively.

I squared my shoulders and decided to quit quibbling and just say what I had to say. "I don't believe Luke is a murderer."

"Of course he's not," Courtney said, and I could see how much she loved her brother as her eyes watered. "He could never do anything so horrible."

I pressed on. "A few days ago, I went to the crime scene and felt around in the ether for some impressions. I wasn't able to connect with Brook's spirit, but I did get a pretty good feel for how the murder took place. I'm convinced someone other than Luke murdered Brook Astor."

"Did you see the killer?" Steven asked me, his eyes searching my face for any hint that I might be able to give him a name that would help clear Luke.

"No. I didn't see the killer. But I felt him, or rather, I felt the ether which absorbed the attack. The killer was right-handed."

Steven blinked. "Why is that important?"

"Luke is left-handed," Courtney whispered.

"Yes, but there's a little bit of a wrinkle here. Luke is left-handed, and so is the spook that got inside his head."

Steven and Courtney adopted identical expressions of confusion. "I don't understand," Steven said.

I shifted in my seat, trying to find a way to tell them as little as possible while revealing the parts they'd need to take to Luke's lawyer. "Heath and I are still working on Luke's behalf, even though we can't formally claim that we are. We've managed to track down another man with a connection to Luke's old rental house who's currently serving time in a prison up in New Hampshire. His name is Guy Walker and he murdered a girl named Amy Montgomery in the mid-seventies. Amy was stabbed repeatedly and she died just six doors down from you, Courtney."

Steven's fiancée covered her mouth with her hand.

"Walker got life in prison, but the freaky thing is that he used to live in the same house where Luke claims the shadow started haunting him, and Walker is also haunted by this same spook."

"How do you know?" Steven asked.

I grimaced. "Because we met Walker and saw it first-hand. We got it on film too, but it isn't anything that could be introduced as evidence in a court of law."

Steven rubbed his temples. He looked very stressed and even more fatigued. "How does that help clear Luke?"

"Well, it doesn't except that when Walker was taken over by this spook, he switched from being right-handed to left-handed. That means that if the spook had inhabited Luke's body and forced him to murder Brook Astor, then there would've been no need to switch to a right-handed approach. So, my current working theory is that this spook tried to get Luke to do something, but he was too strong-willed to be completely taken over, and while Luke was battling to get back into his right mind, someone else entirely murdered Brook, and Luke was just in the wrong place at the wrong time."

"His lawyer told me that Luke doesn't remember anything before waking up on the ground next to Brook," Courtney whispered so softly that I barely heard her.

"I was afraid it was something like that," I told her. "He tried to revive her, didn't he?"

She nodded vigorously. "He knows CPR, but she was already gone. He's terrified that he's responsible."

"I'm sure he's scared, but I really think someone else committed this crime."

"Which means there's a violent killer on the loose," Steven said.

"Yes, and I'm not sure right now if there's any connection to Brook's murder and this spook, but something is telling me that there is. I'll just have to dig deeper."

"What else can you tell us?" Steven asked.

I cleared my throat. "This next part has to do with the house Luke rented. Guy Walker lived there in the seventies, and something else that's even creepier—Dan Foster once called that place home too."

Steven and Courtney both looked taken aback. "Dan Foster?" Courtney said. "The man on the news who murdered that Sullivan woman?"

I nodded. "The very same. And I'm inclined to believe that that can't be a coincidence. Heath and I have been to the house, and while we couldn't sense any evil ghost haunting it, we did discover something that could be useful to Luke's lawyer. He'll need to go to the rental house and look in the bedroom closet. Tell him to make sure the light is on, and if I were him, I wouldn't waste another minute. I'd get over to that house before the police do."

"What's in the closet?" Courtney asked as I stood up and looked around, suddenly nervous about being spotted talking to Steven and Courtney.

"Go along with him and you'll see. In the meantime, know that we're still working on helping Luke."

"What else should we do?" Steven asked, reaching out to put a hand on my arm before I turned away.

I looked down at his hand and offered him a small smile. "Keep the lawyer from looking at me and my crew as the masterminds behind the crime, Steven. He'll want to point the finger at me, Heath, and maybe even Gil. You're paying his bill. Tell him we're off-limits. Hopefully what's in the closet will help that argument, and as we get more info, we'll pass it on to you to pass to him."

"I'll tell him," Steven promised, releasing me.

I left them with a slight wave and hustled out of there.

Heath texted me as I was getting back into my car. He'd made a date to meet with Kendra at the Starbucks just down from the hospital. I smirked when I read the text. I'd been gone a good hour and a half, and he was probably getting anxious thinking that I was meeting with Steven alone. I got back out of the car and decided to hoof it down to the coffee shop. As I was walking away from the car, however, something really eerie happened. I swore I saw a shadow out of the corner of my eye. Now, I often see shadows like this, quick little flutters of black at the edge of my peripheral vision, and often these are just the regular grounded spirits who're trying to get my attention because I seem to give off the vibe that I can hear them. I usually ignore them because there're just so many spooks in and around Boston. Seriously, tons and tons, and I'm only one girl and how much time do I have to try to cross each one over? Unless they're in pain or anguished, I typically keep walking.

But this was different. This was a flash of shadow and a cold shiver that ran up my spine. Immediately I knew this was no ordinary grounded spirit. In fact, deep in my gut I knew what the shadow was and it frightened me that the spook from the prison had somehow found me here.

I stopped and looked around warily, but saw nothing out of the ordinary. Still, I could feel something in the ether. Something menacing, lurking somewhere close, but not close enough for me to identify where it might be coming from. Mentally I called out to my spirit guide—Sam Whitefeather, who also happens to be Heath's grandfather—and asked for his protection.

Start walking, I felt Sam say. *Don't look back, just get going.*

I did as I was told, breaking into a trot and keeping it up all the way to Starbucks. Once I stopped, I checked the ether and couldn't feel that dark presence anymore, so I thought maybe Sam had intervened nicely. All the same I couldn't hold back the shudder that traveled along my shoulders.

I found Heath waiting in the coffee shop with a tall latte for me and a regular coffee for him. I hugged him gratefully and may have squeezed a bit enthusiastically because he said, "Hey, you okay, Em?"

I held on a little longer and replied, "Yeah. Just glad to see you and even more glad that we're together."

Heath chuckled. "Hanging out with your ex wasn't the dream date you expected, huh?"

I smiled and stepped back. "It was a working meeting," I said, tugging on his shirt. "Strictly business."

"Uh-huh. And how did this strictly business meeting go?"

"Well, Courtney was there—"

"The fiancée came? That's a mood killer."

"And I kept it pretty brief, but I think they understand that we're trying to help. I gave them the info to share with Luke's attorney, and also I told them about my impressions of a right-handed killer. Did you have any luck with the landlord?"

"I actually talked to him on the phone. He wasn't exactly forthcoming. He told me he'd been managing that house for about a year or so, but he wouldn't tell me who owns it. In fact, the more I pressed, the more he clammed up. He also shrugged off the idea that the place could be haunted. He laughed when I asked him about that. Other than that, I didn't get much on him. Gil's right. There's nothing online about Ray, although I did manage to find out his last name is Eades. The only other weird thing is that he lives about two blocks over from Courtney's place. According to the background check I ran on him through that program Gil designed, Eades has lived there for the past twenty years. How he came to manage the house on Stoughton Street I have no idea."

I sighed. "Damn. All we're getting here are dead ends."

Heath nodded, but then his eyes shifted over my shoulder and I turned to see Kendra come into the shop and look around. I waved to her and she juggled her bag, her phone, and what looked like a ream of paper over to us. Sitting down with a whoosh, she blushed slightly and said, "Sorry I'm late. It's been a crazy morning."

"Can I get you a coffee?" Heath asked.

Kendra's blush deepened. "That's okay," she said, unloading her stuff onto the table while also swinging her purse around. "I can get it."

Heath stood up. "You have your hands full, Kendra. Let me get you a cup of coffee."

She started to protest, then must've thought better of it because she said, "That would be really nice, thank you. I'll take a tall coffee of the day with room for cream, please."

Heath headed off to get her beverage and I thought I should wait until she got herself settled to say anything, but she beat me to the punch. "I was super surprised to get your call. Well, your boyfriend's call. Oh, wait. He is your boyfriend, right?"

"He is," I said.

"But you also dated Dr. Steven Sable, correct?" Kendra asked, all sweetness and smiles. "I found an article about you two from a couple of years ago. Sable's now engaged to the sister of Luke Decker, right? Dr. Courtney Decker, if I'm not mistaken."

Kendra subtly placed her phone in the middle of the table and I saw that it was recording our conversation. Without saying a word, I reached for the phone and handed it to her. "None of this is on the record, Kendra. None of it."

Kendra blinked rapidly. "Why not?"

"Because that's the deal for right now. We have information to share, but we're not willing to go on the record about it, so either turn that thing off or Heath and I are out of here."

"So, I can't do a story on you . . . *ever*?"

"Nope."

Kendra's charm disappeared in a flash. "I think you're wrong," she said. "I can do a story about you without your permission, M.J. I just can't quote you. But I'm pretty sure I have enough even without your cooperation to do an amazing story on you. I've been digging around and I've learned some things. I'd rather have your cooperation, but even without it, I'm still going to air your story."

Heath came back to the table and he picked up on the change in mood really quick. "What's happened?"

I looked up at him. "Kendra's playing hardball."

The corner of Heath's mouth quirked as he set down her coffee. "What'd you expect?"

I focused again on Kendra. "Maybe that she'd cut me a break."

To her credit, Kendra appeared a little chagrined. "Sorry, guys. It's my job."

I sighed. "Fine. Then how about we work out a deal?"

"What kind of a deal?"

"We're investigating the murder of Brook Astor and

maybe even a few others. I think we'll end up getting to the bottom of it soon. So, how about we share information with you as we get it, and you protect us as your source, and after this all blows over, you interview me and get an exclusive."

Kendra sipped her coffee and eyed me over the rim. "What's in this for you?"

I decided to be straight with her. "We could use someone with your investigative talents to help us figure out exactly what's going on here. Heath and I have identified a spook that's been taking over the minds of the men who live in that house on Stoughton. This thing is pure evil and it's either convincing them to commit murder or influencing the dark violent nature they already have within them."

Kendra choked on her coffee. "Hold on," she said when she recovered herself. "You mean to tell me you think there's some sort of possession story happening here?"

"Yes," Heath and I said together.

Kendra looked at us like she was waiting for the punch line, but neither of us even cracked a smile. "Guys," she said. "Come on. You can't be serious!"

"We can and we are," I told her. "Kendra, you yourself found the connection to two murderers and one suspected murderer all having a previous residence at that house on Stoughton Street. Do you think that's just a coincidence?"

"Well . . . no . . . but . . . really? I mean, come on, this isn't Hollywood. If I start writing about a case of possession and haunted houses, do you know what my producer is gonna say?"

"Great story?" Heath said, just to give her a hard time.

"No," she told him, a flash of anger in her eye. "He's

gonna say, 'Kendra, here's a box. Fill it with your stuff and good luck getting another reporting gig in this market.'"

"Then I don't know what to tell you, Kendra. Heath and I have seen this spook firsthand. We've seen it take over Guy Walker, in fact, and if you'd been there and seen what we'd seen, you'd be a believer too."

Kendra frowned at me like I was starting to really irritate her.

"You saw what M.J.'s capable of," Heath said, trying to convince her. "You even have it on film, right?"

Kendra pointed to him. "That's what I wanted M.J. to talk about. I wanted her to tell me how she knew about things that weren't reported in the news or introduced as evidence in the case against Dan Foster."

I cocked an eyebrow at her. "I interacted with Bethany's ghost. How else would I have gotten that info?"

Kendra inhaled deeply and let out a long low sigh. "If I go on the air and report that ghosts and spirits are real, I'll be the laughingstock of the news world. Don't you get it? I *have* to play the skeptic here."

I shrugged. "You don't *have* to play anything, Kendra. You can simply present the evidence objectively and let the general public come to its own conclusions."

Heath set his elbows on the table and leaned forward. "All we're asking is for you to keep an open mind while the three of us investigate this."

Kendra tapped her index finger on her coffee cup as she considered our proposal. "Fine," she said. "But once this wraps up, I get an exclusive interview with you, M.J. On the record, On air."

I struck out my hand. "Deal."

We shook on it and got down to business. I showed Kendra a photo of the interior of the closet in the house on Stoughton Street and her eyes widened. "What is that?" she asked, grabbing for my phone.

"It's the closet in the master bedroom of the rental house where Luke, Dan Foster, and Guy Walker all lived at some time or another."

"Who wrote these names on the wall?"

"We assume Dan and Guy did," Heath said. "We're not sure about Luke. And his attorney would prevent us from asking him about it."

Kendra made several notes on her notepad. "Who're these other guys?" she asked. "Killer Ken, Sy the Slayer, and Butcher Bill."

"Don't know," I said. "That's what we'd like your help in finding out. Basically, that house on Stoughton is a big fat mystery. We've learned that it's held in a trust, but who the members of that trust are, we can't tell, and we don't know how to go about finding out. The landlord, Ray Eades, has only been managing that house for the past couple of years, and he claims that he doesn't know anything about it being haunted, but I'm willing to bet that the owner might. We need to find out the name of the owner of that house and talk to him or her."

Kendra's gaze lifted up from my phone, and I could see the eagerness in her eyes. She had an even hotter story than she'd first realized, and she knew it. "Have you tried public records?" she asked us. "You could research the address and come up with a list of owners going all the way back to when the house was built. Most of that section of Boston was built in the twenties and thirties, and that house looks to be about that old. If you dig, you might be able to come up with the name of the owner who held the title right before the trust was enacted. That's probably going to be a relative of the person or persons who currently hold the trust. From there you can do a little more digging and see if the last name crops up online in connection with that address."

"Wow," I said to her. "Impressive that you'd know that."

Kendra shrugged, but a grin spread to her lips. "They teach you a few things in reporting school," she kidded. "Anyway, an afternoon down at the public records department should yield a result or two."

"I can tell you've spent some time down there. Maybe you could take the lead on that search?" Heath said, dropping a not so subtle hint.

Kendra laughed lightly. "So, I'm supposed to do all the grunt work, huh?"

"We'll help," I promised, even though digging through old records was the last thing I wanted to do.

Kendra jotted a few more notes to herself. Then she looked back up at us and I could tell she was already on to the next topic. "So, tenants of this house like to write their names on the walls of this closet with a creepy tagline. And some of them then go on to commit murder. That's the seed of a story, but not something my producer is going to green-light automatically."

"We don't know that only some of them go on to commit murder," I said.

"What's that mean?" she asked.

"Until we can identify who this Butcher Bill, Killer Ken, and Sy Slayer are, we have no idea what crimes they may have committed."

Kendra's brow furrowed. "I only found three criminal names connected to that house. Luke Decker, Guy Walker, and Dan Foster."

"That doesn't mean other murders didn't take place with a connection to that house," I reasoned. "Only that there may or may not be any public record of other criminals. In other words, either these other four were never caught, or they moved on to other residences and no connection was ever publicly traced back to what happened in that house."

Kendra toyed with her pen. "Okay, I'm gonna play devil's advocate here and ask, what do *you* think happens inside that house?"

I turned to Heath. "Let's show her the video."

Heath pulled out Gilley's iPad and angled it so Kendra could see. He then hit PLAY and our interview with Guy Walker began. She gasped a couple of times and when the video ended, she sat back in her chair, her complexion a little less rosy. "That was freaky!"

"Now you know why we're staying on the case."

But Kendra was still clearly thinking about the video. "Did you catch that creepy shadow behind Walker?" she asked. "I mean, it's like it went right into him and then he becomes a different person! And what was up with that voice?"

I cocked my head. "What voice?"

"Didn't you hear it? His voice changed. I swear it went down an octave or two."

I hadn't noticed, but when I turned to Heath, he was nodding. "Whatever happens to turn these guys into monsters, it starts in that house."

"But you were in there," Kendra said. "You had to be in order to take that photo of the closet. Didn't you get some sort of vibe or something with your psychic sense?"

"That's the truly creepy thing," I told her. "We could both pick up on the sort of residual presence of something evil in that house, but whatever it is, it wasn't there when we visited."

"Where'd it go?"

"Well," I said, choosing my words carefully, "I think that whatever this spook is, it doesn't haunt a specific location for long. I think it prefers to haunt people. Men in particular. And it's relentless. It wears these guys down until they're vulnerable to its evil influence, and then it gets inside their minds and maybe it even coaxes them to commit murder."

Kendra laughed, but I could see that she was starting to get rattled by what she'd seen on the video and our insistence that this stuff was real. "This is all so far-fetched and unbelievable," she said, but her voice lacked conviction. "How can an evil spirit actually take over someone's mind? Don't we all have free will?"

"You'd hope so," Heath said. "But, Kendra, I've felt a little of this thing, and it sort of sneaks up on you. Luke told us that while he lived in that house, he'd have night-mares so intense that he stopped sleeping. That lowered his defenses and allowed this spook access to his thoughts."

"So you think he did it?" she asked him. "You think he really did kill Brook Astor?"

"No," I said quickly. "We don't."

"You mean, this spook made him do it," she said.

"No," I repeated. "I don't think Luke did anything but try to save Brook. I think someone else murdered her and he came across her as she lay dying and tried to re-vive her. But she was already gone and he panicked and ran home."

Kendra looked puzzled. "But I thought you guys were making a case for 'the devil made me do it'?"

"It's complicated," I said. "But suffice it to say that at this moment we're convinced Luke didn't murder Brook."

"What's your theory on Dan Foster and Guy Walker? Think someone else committed those murders and they've been wrongly convicted?"

I shook my head. "Guy Walker is an evil man," I said. "You can see it in his eyes. I think he was only encouraged by this spook. He would've killed someone either way. And I know Dan Foster killed Bethany Sullivan because I saw the murder through Bethany's eyes."

Kendra nodded. "Yeah, that freaky thing you did out at the park. You really connected to her ghost?"

"It's what I do."

"I'm still on the fence about whether or not to believe you."

"As is your right," I said. I wasn't irked that she didn't believe. She'd be slow to come around, which was fine. Some people just took longer to convince.

"The question is, was Dan influenced by this spook, as you call it, or did he really just want to kill his ex-girlfriend?"

I shifted in my chair, eager to ask her my next favor. "I don't know. And I have no way of finding out. But you could."

"*I* could?"

"Yes. There's no way I'll get in to see Dan Foster. I have no credentials and no connection to him. But you do. As a news reporter, you could request an interview and talk to him about this spook."

Kendra laughed like I'd just said the funniest thing. "M.J., Dan Foster's attorney isn't going to let *any* reporter close to him until after the sentencing phase is over, and that won't be for another three months."

"Don't go through his attorney," I suggested. We needed to hear Dan's side of the story, because he could hold a clue about the origins of this spook. "Send a message to him directly, Kendra. I'll even tell you what to say. If this spook did get inside his head, then I think he'll want to talk to someone who understands the nightmare it must've been for him."

Kendra tapped her pen on the notepad. "Fine," she said. "But if he bites, you're coming with me."

"How're you gonna pull that off?" I asked. I had no press credentials and I doubted I'd be allowed to see Foster without them.

"I've got a press pass you can use. I'll take you in as my producer."

"Okay," I said, feeling both excited and nervous about the prospect of meeting Dan Foster after what Bethany's ghost had shown me. And that's when I had a thought and closed my eyes, trying to recall the moment when Bethany had been inside my head, showing me her murder. She'd seen Dan coming toward her, and she'd felt a tiny moment of relief to see him after being spooked by those disembodied footsteps out in the park, but then she'd seen the murderous intent in his eyes and the knife in his hands. . . .

"Em?" Heath said, and I felt his hand on my arm.

I opened my eyes. "Kendra, do you happen to know if Dan Foster is right-handed or left?"

She eyed me curiously. "Right-handed or left? No. I don't know which hand is his dominant. Why?"

The image in my mind of Dan coming toward Bethany was crystal clear; he'd been holding the knife with his left hand. It kept replaying in my mind too—as if Bethany's spirit was helping the image cement firmly in my memory. Instead of answering Kendra, I asked another question. "Do you happen to have any footage of Foster in court? Any footage where we might be able to see him write something?"

Kendra's brow furrowed. "Not with me, but I'm pretty sure we'll have something like that back at the station. Why?"

"I'm positive that Foster killed Bethany with his left hand. And if he's normally right-handed, then I think this spook really did take him over at the time of the murder."

Heath, who'd been fiddling with his iPad, said, "You're right, Em. He's right-handed." He swiveled the screen around so that I could see the footage he'd pulled up from the Web of Foster bent over a legal pad, scribbling with his right hand during his trial.

"How does that help us?" Kendra asked after she too had looked at the footage.

"We can offer that up as an excuse to interview him. Tell him that we know it wasn't really him that murdered Bethany and we think we can prove it."

"How can we prove it?" Kendra asked.

"I don't know. Maybe say something like, based on the forensic evidence, we can tell that the man who murdered Bethany was left-handed."

Kendra cocked her head at me again. "That's actually somewhat true," she said. "According to the coroner's report, several of Bethany's injuries occurred on the right side of her body, appearing to come from a left-handed assailant." When Heath and I both stared at her in surprise, she added, "I've been covering this murder trial for four months. I know it like the back of my hand."

"Ah, well, let's put some of that in the e-mail to Foster, then," I said.

But Kendra held up her hand and said, "That's not all of it, though, M.J. The coroner also reported that there was an odd anomaly to the wounds on Bethany's body. While several of the initial thrusts of the knife to Bethany's body were made with Dan's left hand, it appears that at some point during the attack, he switched hands and made several more using his right hand and the final wound, which was a slash to Bethany's throat, appeared to be made from left to right at an upward angle, clearly the mark of a right-handed killer."

"Huh," I said. That stumped me a little, but then I thought about what a bad man Guy Walker was, even without the spook's influence. Like attracts like, so maybe Dan Foster was no exception. "Maybe at the start this spook took over Dan's mind and got him to begin stabbing Bethany," I said. "But maybe it let go of his mind toward the end, and he dealt the final blow."

Kendra nodded. "In court, the coroner explained the anomaly by suggesting that during the attack the knife became slippery and that's why Foster switched hands. It sort of took apart the defense's claim that Foster had been sleepwalking at the time of Bethany's murder and wasn't conscious enough to realize what he was doing. Foster's lawyer said he'd taken an over-the-counter sleeping pill that'd put him into a sleepwalking state and he hadn't remembered anything about the murder, but I think the jury thought the fact that Foster had switched hands during the attack suggested he was far more conscious than he claimed to be."

What Kendra revealed about the coroner's report stunned me a little. I didn't believe there'd been any sleeping pill, but I did think the shadow spook had gotten into his head and maybe at some point the knife had become slippery. . . . But then, maybe Foster at that moment had actually come back into his own mind and he wanted to make sure he finished off his ex-girlfriend. I had no sense of Foster; I didn't know if he was a bad man or a good guy, so I couldn't really judge him until after we interviewed him, *if* we got that lucky.

To that end, I advised Kendra a little further about the e-mail she'd send to Foster. "Leave out the part about the throat slashing and switching hands," I said. "Just put in there that you think someone else with a connection to the Stoughton Street house might have murdered her. They may have even framed Foster for the crime. Tell him you poked around in the closet and uncovered several other names of suspected murderers."

"Basically use the defense we were planning to use for Luke with Foster to get access to him?" Heath said.

"Yes. I bet you anything he'll be surprised that you're working that angle, Kendra, and he'll see a ray of hope that maybe you can get him a lighter sentence or that something you dig up might get his conviction overturned."

"But Bethany's ghost said he still did it, right?" Kendra asked me. And I almost smiled at the fact that she was a self-proclaimed skeptic except when it came to my impressions from Bethany.

"Hell yeah, he did. But to what extent he was in control at the time of the murder is the question. And that's what we need to figure out by interviewing him."

Kendra was nodding. "I'm with you. Okay, I'll do my best to reach out to him, but even with that argument it's a long shot."

"That's okay. All we've got at this point are long shots."

We wrapped up with Kendra, agreeing to meet her down at the records office the next morning at ten thirty; then we headed back to the condo. Gilley wasn't at his usual spot on my couch, which I was actually grateful for. I wanted to spend some quality time with my honey.

And Heath and I were just settling into some of that quality time when the door opened and in walked Gil. "Good Lord, you two! Give it a rest already! You're like bunnies. In fact, you put bunnies to shame."

I sat up and pulled my shirt down, feeling a blush touch my cheeks. "Don't you knock?" I snapped.

"You ask me that every single time I walk in that door," Gil said. "It should be obvious by now that I neither knock nor apologize for it."

Heath shifted to the far end of the couch and grabbed a throw pillow, placing it discreetly in his lap. "I saw that," Gil quipped.

I turned to Heath. "Remind me to get a chain lock for that door."

"Oh, I will," he said.

Gil trotted in and sat on the chair opposite us, a wicked grin on his face.

"What'd you find out?" I asked, knowing that look.

"Something soooooo juicy," he said. "SO juicy!"

"A break in the case?" I asked hopefully. Man, we really needed a break in this case.

"No," Gil said, waving his hand like that was yesterday's concern. "Guess who's engaged."

I blinked. "Who's . . . what?"

Gil cupped his hands around his mouth. *"Engaged!"* he said, so bubbly with excitement he practically shouted the word.

I shook my head. What the hell was he talking about? "One of the Kardashians again?" I tried. The sooner Gil told us, the sooner I could get him to focus back on the case.

Gilley giggled delightedly. "No! Well, yes. Maybe. Conflicting tabloid stories at the moment, but we should know in a week or two if that rumor about a bun in the oven is true and—"

"Gil!" I said. Was he seriously focusing on Hollywood gossip instead of working this case?

"Right," he said, waving his hand again. "Not the point. Anyway, you're *wrong*! That's not who I want you to guess. So guess again."

"Do I have to?"

"Yes!" Gil giggled, squeezing his shoulders up around his neck. He looked ready to burst with excitement.

And then it hit me, and my jaw dropped. "Ohmigod . . . ," I gasped, sitting forward. "No way!"

Gil nodded vigorously. "Way!"

"But it's so soon!"

"I know, right? It's crazy!"

"How? When?"

"This morning! It just happened!"

I leaped to my feet, so excited that I could hardly stand it. Gil jumped up too and we hugged each other as we jumped up and down and laughed.

"Could someone please fill me in on who got engaged?" Heath said.

"Duh!" I told him, grinning ear to ear. "Gil and Michel!"

At the same moment Gilley said, "M.J.'s daddy and his new girlfriend!"

There was a pregnant pause and then I turned to Gil and yelled, *"WHAT?"*

Gil yelled back, *"WHAT?"*

And in the background Heath's laughter filled the ensuing silence. "Oh, man!" he said, in between guffaws. "You two . . ."

"What the hell do you mean, Daddy's engaged?" I was being mighty shriekish, but the situation simply called for a little howler monkey.

"I thought you knew who I was talking about!"

"NO!" (Howler monkey times eleventy.)

Gil put a finger in one ear. "I didn't need that eardrum, but thanks, M.J."

I let go of Gil, whom I realized I was still hugging, and went to sit down on the couch. "*How* could he be engaged? He just *met* this woman, right?"

When Gil didn't answer, I looked up at him. He shrugged and came to sit down next to me. Taking up my hand, he said, "Your mama died twenty years ago, M.J. It's about time your daddy moved on, don't you think?"

I shook my head. As long as I'd known Daddy, he'd never shown even a hint of interest in any other woman.

He simply sulked and worked. Those were the two constants from him that I could always count on, sulking and working. Six days a week that man headed to the office and conducted his business. It'd made him a wealthy man, but also a cold and emotionally distant one. Someone I couldn't connect with and, quite frankly, hadn't wanted to. But Daddy engaged was a new twist. Somehow it made him more human and I felt that part of my heart that loved him because he was my daddy surface and spread through me with more than a little melancholy. "He didn't even call me," I whispered, my eyes misting.

"Sugar," Gil said, squeezing my hand. "You never gave him your new cell number, remember? He had to call Mama to ask her to have you call him, and when she asked why, he had to break down and tell her his news."

I stared at Gil. "Is that how you found out?"

He nodded. "Mama says she's met this Christine Bigelow, and she likes her, and you know Mama always tells the truth about people."

I did know that. One of the wonderful things about Mrs. Gillespie was her honesty and plainspoken nature. "Did she pass on my number?"

Gil shook his head. "She wanted to protect you and she knew that if your daddy called you up in the middle of the afternoon to tell you he's engaged, that would throw you. So she told me to tell you and let you decide if you want to talk to him or not."

I turned my gaze to the floor. The weight of having to talk to my father and pretend to be happy for him settled firmly around my already overburdened shoulders. How could I talk to him about his happy news when my own life was currently in chaos?

"Did you want to call him, Em?" Heath asked.

I shook my head. I didn't. At least not right now. I

needed time to process this and figure out how I felt about it. "Not yet," I said. "After we resolve this case."

Gil's face fell into a frown and I could tell he was disappointed by my answer. "I can't, Gil," I told him. "It's just been too long and too hard for me to forget it all in one day."

His expression softened and he wrapped both hands around mine. "Okay, darlin'," he said. "Okay. I'll tell Mama to let your daddy know you'll call him in a week or two, and he'll understand."

I wiped my eyes. "No, he won't, but it's the best I can manage."

Gil rubbed my back and Heath got up to walk around the ottoman and extend me his hand. "Come on," he said. "You look like you could use a drink and something to eat."

On the way to our favorite neighborhood pub, O'Neil's, which was only a few blocks' walk, I had a chance to ask Gil about any research he might've dug up. "I'm drawing blanks," he confessed. "I can't figure out whose names are attached to that trust. I think it's gonna take a public records search."

"We heard the same thing from Kendra," I said. "She's gonna head down to the public records office tomorrow and do some research."

Gilley looked relieved. "Good. One less thing on my plate."

"Actually . . . ," I said.

Gil cut me a look. "What'd you do?"

"I may have suggested you'd go with her and help." Of course I was fibbing slightly. I'd told Kendra that Heath and I would help, but I wanted to go down to that public records office like I wanted a hole in my head, and offering up Gilley for the job seemed like a tidy solution.

Gil, however, was not at all pleased. He glared hard at me.

I smiled sweetly back at him.

His glare intensified.

So did my smile.

"You owe me," he said.

"We'll buy you dinner," I suggested.

"That'd be nice, for starters. But I'm gonna want more. Lots more."

At that moment Gilley's cell rang and after looking at the display, he sang, "Hey, sugar, how'd the shoot go?"

Gil babbled on with Michel for a block before I caught him saying, "Yes, I told her. . . . Not well, just like I said . . . I am being nice! . . . I swear I am! . . . Well, I can either be sensitive or I can be nice—take your pick. . . . ANYway, the thing that you're gonna love is that when I told her to guess who was engaged, she guessed you and me! Isn't that hilarious?"

I turned my head and discreetly rolled my eyes so Heath could see. He hid a grin and cleared his throat.

"Well, I think it's funny," Gil said. "Why? Because . . . I mean . . . you and me, Micha . . . engaged? Now, *that's* hilarious!"

I hooked my arm through Heath's and picked up my pace. "We'll need to move on ahead," I whispered.

"Why?" he whispered back. "That was just getting good."

"No. No, it wasn't. It's about to get ugly. Trust me."

Heath and I moved on ahead, and sure enough, fifteen seconds later we heard Gilley turn a little howler monkey too.

Heath and I walked even faster and reached the pub, slipping inside quickly. One glance over my shoulder as we stepped through the door showed Gilley standing in the middle of the sidewalk, yelling into his phone. He and Michel didn't often fight, but when they did, well, the queen in each of them came out and heads started rolling.

Gil came into the pub about the time that our drinks arrived. I'd ordered Gil his usual Manhattan and he shot it back in less than a New York minute. He didn't even sit down; he simply lifted the glass and threw it back. "He. Is. *Impossible!*"

"What looks good to you tonight, Em?" Heath asked, completely ignoring the hissy fit Gil was throwing.

"I mean, all I said was that I thought the idea of the two of us engaged was funny!"

"They have a great vegetarian lasagna here," I said.

"I *didn't* say that we weren't good together!" Gil spat.

"Yeah, that does look good," Heath said.

"And I *didn't* say I wanted to break up!"

"Or, the veggie burger is another way to go . . . ," I mused.

"God! He's such a child!"

"But the Caesar salad looks good too," I said.

Gil sat down with a loud humph and I held up a finger to catch the waitress's attention. She nodded and brought over the second Manhattan I'd ordered for Gil. Setting it down in front of him, she made haste to leave again, probably sensing the waves of frustration, anger, and hurt wafting off my BFF.

He sputtered and growled and grumbled through his second Manhattan, which went down a little less quickly before he settled into a really good pout. Then it turned into a pity party. Then it turned into a few sniffles and one or two sobs. Heath and I weathered the full spectrum and ate our meal in relative silence. Gil didn't eat much, but he made up for it by drinking like a fish. He switched from the Manhattans to something stronger (for Gil), appletinis, and I was a touch frustrated because I'd hoped he could do a little more work for us after we ate. Now he'd be good for nothing but bed.

After dinner we walked home with Gilley sort of slung between us. Right as we got to Gilley's door, his cell rang. He looked at the display and muttered incoherently, lifting his phone as if he was ready to throw it to the ground.

I grabbed it quickly and answered the call. "Hey, Michel, it's M.J."

There was a sniffle, then, "Where's Gilley?"

"He's right here, but he's not feeling so well right now. Can he talk to you tomorrow?"

Gil mumbled something else and leaned heavily against the door as he fiddled with the key.

"What's wrong with him?" Michel asked, concern in his voice.

"I bought him dinner and drinks," I confessed. "And he may have had a few too many of the latter."

Gil finally got his key into the lock and turned the knob with a triumphant, "Ha!" Unfortunately, he forgot to take his weight off the door as he turned the knob and he fell face-first into his kitchen. There was a loud whump, then, "Owwwwww!"

"Sorry, Michel," I said quickly. "Gotta go. I'll get Gil to call you tomorrow and you two can make up, okay?"

"Is he all right?" Michel asked as Heath stepped over Gilley's legs to help him.

"He'll be fine. He just tripped. The fall might've even knocked some sense into him."

"Okay," Michel said, but I could tell he was really regretting the fight he'd had with Gil.

"Hey," I said to him. "For the record, I didn't think it was at all funny that you two might've gotten engaged. I thought it was perfect. You guys make a really great couple. And I know Gil thinks so too, in spite of the ass he's being tonight—he really is crazy about you."

I heard Michel sniffle on the other end of the line. "Thanks, M.J. I hope he's okay. I'll talk to him tomorrow."

"Good man," I said, relieved that this was just a small spat between them. Michel had been a wonderful influence on Gilley, and I wanted them to stay together.

Heath and I helped Gil to bed, and by that, I mean we pretty much carried him all the way to the bedroom, hovered him over the bed, and let go before making a hasty retreat.

Chapter 11

The next morning Gil was on my couch again looking hungover and moody.

Perfect.

"Hey, bud," I said, keeping to the far side of the room just in case. "How ya doin' this morning?"

Gilley's narrowed eyes became slits. "Would you please explain how *this* happened?" As he turned his head a little more to the side, I saw the bruise by his right temple.

I decided to take the fifth. "Oooo, that looks like it hurt. How'd you do that?"

"You don't know?"

I widened my eyes and shrugged my shoulders. "No, honey love, I surely don't."

"You're a liar, Mary Jane Holliday. Every time you tell a lie, your Southern drawl comes out."

"Fine. You drank too much and got intimate with your kitchen floor."

Gil rubbed his temple. "Was that so hard?"

"No. But when you get drunk and hurt yourself, you usually blame me."

"It's usually your fault."

"Riiiiight. Is there coffee?"

Gil thumbed over his shoulder toward the kitchen and I headed there for some much needed joe. "Where's Heath?" Gil called while I was pouring a cup.

"He went for a run."

"You didn't go with him?"

"I was too tired," I said, coming back into the living room. Doc was already up and nibbling on a bird toy. After moving over to his cage to give him a kiss, I switched my attention back to Gil, who was typing on the computer. "What'cha doin'?"

"I'm researching Mr. Eades," Gil replied.

My brain was still a little foggy from just getting up, and I drew a blank on the name.

"The landlord on the Stoughton Street house," Gil said before I could even ask.

I moved over to sit next to Gil. "What'd you find?"

Gil sighed. "Nothing but his age and home address. The guy doesn't have an online footprint, which makes figuring out who he is and what he's about difficult. Everybody needs to get digital. It makes my job so much easier."

I quickly told him about Heath's conversation with Eades and Gil glared at me. "You'd think he'd tell me that before I spent an hour looking for dirt on the man."

"You know what we need to do?" I said, going for an enthusiastic tone.

"What?"

"Send you down to the public records office with Kendra. Have you fish around and see about coming up with a name attached to that trust. I really want to talk to the owner."

Gil leveled a suspicious look at me. "And while I'm down in the bowels of paperwork hell, what're *you* going to be doing?"

"Uh . . . running down more leads."

"What leads?"

I tried to think quickly, but Gil's question had thrown me and I was having a hard time coming up with something. "Heath has a list," I said.

"Really?" Gil said . . . maybe a wee bit too enthusiastically. "Show me this list of amazing leads you two will be *so* busy running down!"

"Like I said, Heath has it."

"He took it with him on his run, huh?"

"He takes it everywhere he goes."

"How stupid do you think I am?"

"That feels like a trap."

Gil slurped his coffee and turned back to his computer. "Best get dressed, sugar. We've got a long day ahead of us in the bowels of paperwork hell."

Heath still wasn't back from his run by the time we were ready to roll, so I left him a note (that begged him to come find and save me from the bowels of paperwork hell), and we headed downtown to meet Kendra. Gil parked the van in one of the parking garages and we found Kendra on the steps of the building texting on her phone.

"Kendra!" I called.

She jumped a little and looked up. I waved and she waved back. I introduced Gil and Kendra thrust out her hand, a glint of interest in her eye. "Hi," she said. "Nice to meet you. M.J. didn't tell me you were such a cutie."

Gil blushed and I wondered if Kendra was one of those rare individuals that didn't recognize a gay man even if he came packaged in a pink feather boa. "Aww," he said. "Stop it! And by that, I mean, go on, please."

The two laughed and she winked at me; she was definitely interested in Gil. Oh, this ought to be good.

We headed in and took the elevator down two floors to some basement level, then followed behind Kendra along a dark corridor into a room at the end that was filled with volumes of large record books, most of which looked very old.

There was a woman at a wooden desk who appeared to be as old as the oldest, dust-covered volume, and she croaked for us to sign in. We did and then Kendra waved at the volumes. "These are all the property records. First we have to look up the legal description . . ." Kendra's voice trailed off as she headed toward a stack of books to the far right.

I looked at Gilley and crossed my eyes; he giggled and crossed his too. We let Kendra take the lead and soon the both of us were standing dumbly next to her while she flipped pages in a huge volume. At that moment my phone bleeped. It was a text from Heath.

I'm outside in the car with the motor running if you want to attempt an escape.

I tucked my phone back in my pocket and turned to the withered woman at the desk. "Which way is the ladies' room?"

She croaked out a response and I excused myself, promising to be right back. The minute I was out the door, I ran for the elevator. Pressing the button, I tapped my foot anxiously until the doors opened. I rode it up to the main floor and walked quickly out of the building, finding Heath just down the street, double-parked and staring at his phone—probably waiting for me to text him back. I dashed to the car and got inside. "Go!" I yelled, and he hit the gas.

We zipped away and no sooner had we rounded the corner than Gilley called my phone. "Hello?" I said.

"You ditched me, didn't you?"

"Not at all, honey. I'm in the ladies' room." I motioned for Heath to drive faster.

"I can hear sounds of traffic in the background, M.J."

"There's a window open in the ladies' room."

"We're belowground."

"I went to the one upstairs." A car honked right next to us and I sent the driver a dirty look.

"When are you gonna give up the ruse?"

I sighed. "Probably now. We're far enough away that you can't catch us."

"Yes, but I know where you live." With that, he hung up.

I put my phone away. "Gil says hi."

Heath chuckled. "He'll get even, you know."

"I'll worry about that later. For now I'm just glad to be out of that dungeon. That was gonna be a hell of a boring morning."

"Yeah, well, I actually have a good reason for springing you."

I eyed him with interest. "What's that?"

Heath turned to me and bounced his eyebrows. "I have a lead."

"You do?"

He nodded. "I took the car and parked it downtown. Then I went for a run down Stoughton Street and talked to one of the neighbors."

"You did?"

"Yep."

"That was really smart, honey. I didn't even think of that."

"That's why you keep me around, Em. I'm good for a few things."

I laughed. "Oh, honey, you are good for more than just a few things." It was my turn to bounce my eyebrows.

"Anyway, the guy who lives next door said that the

house has seen quite a few tenants over the years. For the most part, the renters keep to themselves, but he became friendly with one guy who lived there about three years ago. A guy named Ken Chamblis."

I gasped. "Killer Ken!"

Heath nodded. "The neighbor, Brad Rowe, says that Ken was a little weird, but they got along, and they used to hang out and share a beer every once in a while down at the pub at the corner of Stoughton and Knox."

I consulted my internal map of the area. "That's about three blocks away from the rental house, right?"

"Four. And get this: Brad says that Ken moved out shortly after one of the waitresses from the bar was found murdered in the alley behind the pub."

My eyes widened. "Do you think . . . ?"

Heath shrugged. "Pretty suspicious coincidence, don't you think?"

"Did you research the murder?"

"I didn't have a chance. I had kind of a long run back to the car, and by the time I got to the condo you weren't there, so I had to shower and see if I could coax you out of the records room."

"Ha! Didn't take much, did it?"

Heath reached over and squeezed my knee. "Didn't figure it would, babe."

"So what do you want to do?"

"I think we should start with the pub and see if anybody who used to work there during the time of the murder remembers Ken and this waitress. It's just about eleven thirty anyway. How about I buy you an early lunch?"

"You're just full of good ideas," I said.

We parked in the small lot at the front of the pub— Sheedy's Place—and headed inside. The bar was dark and dingy—as if it'd never seen a decent scrubbing. We took a seat at the bar and Heath ordered beers for the both of us. The bartender was a woman who had the practiced and precise movements of someone who'd been at the job awhile. Heath asked for menus and also asked politely for her name. "Tracy," she said. "Just let me know when you're ready to order."

There wasn't much on the menu for vegetarians, so I ordered a simple side salad and a basket of fries and Heath had the fried fish sandwich. I let him take the lead, as I'd noticed Tracy's eyes widen a little at the sight of him. I understood completely. Heath was a beautiful guy.

"So, Tracy, a buddy of mine who comes here says there was a waitress who was murdered here a couple of years ago. Is that true?"

Tracy, who'd been tapping at her computer screen, paused and turned to Heath. "You mean Gracie? Yeah, it was really freaky what happened to her."

"Was she really murdered?" Heath asked.

She gave him an odd look and said, "Why you want to know about that?"

Heath grinned at her in that way that could make women swoon. Pointing to me, then back to himself, he said, "We're documentary filmmakers, looking for a new topic. My buddy mentioned the murder that happened here, and it sounded interesting. But he didn't know any details. He told us to come here and talk to someone who might've been here that night."

Tracy cocked her head at him. "I was here that night."

Heath's grin widened and he held his fingers up to form a square. "You know, I thought you might've been. And I gotta say, you have a face for the camera. If we do this project, I'll definitely want to interview you."

Tracy's face brightened. "Really?"

"Really," Heath said. "So, what's the story?"

Tracy moved away from the computer and over to a

cutting board, where she began slicing lemons. "No one really knows exactly. I mean, it was just another Tuesday night and kinda slow. Gracie, me, and Sarah—another waitress—were working and Sarah really wanted to go home early, but it wasn't Gracie's night to close. Anyway, Sarah—who's this total drama queen—finally wore Gracie down and talked her into closing, but Gracie wanted one more smoke before Sarah left, so she heads out back 'cause that's the only place we were allowed to smoke back then, and after about twenty or twenty-five minutes, she's still not back. We usually only get ten minutes for our breaks, and I thought Gracie was pushing it a little because she was pissed at Sarah, but still, close to a half hour seemed kinda rude. So Sarah asks me to cover for her while she heads off to find Gracie and drag her ass back in here, and about a minute later we all hear screaming. Everybody ran out to see what the hell happened, and Sarah's standing in the alley, screaming bloody murder. She's hysterical and she's pointing at some garbage bags stacked up next to the Dumpster. Nobody knew what the hell was going on until Trevor—our dishwasher—pulled one of the garbage bags aside and there's Gracie—eyes wide open, this really creepy expression frozen on her face . . . like a grimace or something, and she's covered in blood. Her throat had been slashed, man. Deep."

"That must've been awful," I said, feeling bad for Tracy that she'd had to witness that.

"I threw up," she admitted softly. "And so did Kyle, our manager. Seeing that . . . it still gives me nightmares." Tracy shuddered and her eyes watered. I felt even worse that we were dredging this up for her.

"Sorry I brought it up," Heath said. "I didn't mean to upset you."

Tracy shrugged, and forced a smile. I could tell she

didn't want him to feel bad. "Hey, what're you gonna do?" She then held up a finger and moved into the kitchen, returning a moment later with our food.

"Did they ever catch who did it?" I asked as she set the meal down in front of us.

Tracy shook her head. "The police investigated for a couple of weeks, and they thought maybe her ex might've done it, but I guess he had this really good alibi."

"What was that?" Heath asked.

"He was locked up that night for a DUI."

"Alibis don't get better than that," I said.

Tracy nodded. "Nope."

"Were there any other suspects?" I asked casually. "Like maybe one of the patrons?"

Tracy shook her head. "The police asked us that, and sure, there're always a couple of customers who have a little too much to drink and get obnoxious, but nobody any of us thought could be capable of that."

Heath squinted at Tracy. "You sure?" he asked. "Nobody before or after Gracie's murder sort of give you the creeps?"

Tracy squinted back at him. "Naw," she said, but then she seemed to catch herself. Lowering her voice, she said, "Well, there is this one guy, but I think he might just be crazy. Sometimes, that is. Other times he's almost okay. It's weird. I think when he's on his meds, he's okay, but there are days when I don't exactly want him to stay until closing, you know?"

Heath looked around the bar as if trying to scope out whom she might be talking about. "Is he here now?"

She shook her head. "No. But he comes in usually around lunchtime."

"What's his name?" I asked.

"Ken."

"Ken?" I said.

"Yeah. I don't know his last name. But he's weird."

"Weird how?" Heath pressed.

Tracy seemed to think about it for a minute. "It's hard to say. Like, he used to be almost normal but not quite, you know? Like, he wouldn't say much, but he'd watch people like he suspected them in some way. It's hard to explain, but he had an edge to him. A mean edge. He was someone you just knew you didn't want to piss off, 'cause he'd find a way to get even and the punishment would be way more intense than the crime. Anyway, he used to come in with another guy ... Brian ... no ... Brad, I think. Brad was super nice, and he seemed to chill Ken out when Ken started to get ticked off about something or at someone. Ken was here almost every Tuesday and Thursday night, and his buddy Brad joined him usually on Thursdays, but right after Gracie was murdered, both of them stopped coming in. That wasn't unusual—the murder sent a lot of our regulars packing. I saw Brad once by himself about a month after the murder, but he said that his wife was about to have a baby and he didn't think he'd be able to come in again after the kid was born."

"What about Ken?" I asked.

Tracy shrugged. "After Gracie died, I didn't see Ken again for, like, six months. The next time he came back in was just after Christmas and what was so weird was the guy was covered in crosses."

My forkful of salad paused on its way to my mouth. "Covered in crosses?"

Tracy waved her hand over her chest. "Yeah. He was wearing like ten crucifixes and had a couple more pinned to his coat. I didn't know if he'd gotten super religious or what, and I didn't ask. I just pretended to be really happy to see him. Anyway, he sorta sat down and ordered a beer, and he'd completely changed. Like I said, Ken used to have an edge to him, but when he started showing up again, it was like that edge was sharper. Meaner. Darker." Tracy shrugged a second time and she seemed at a loss as to how to completely convey what Ken was like now. "He creeps me out and all the crosses and the fact that he barely talks anymore sort of makes me want to keep my distance from him, but it's hard to get away when you're stuck behind a bar, you know?"

"Has he ever threatened you?" I asked. I had a feeling the crucifixes were to ward off Sy the Slayer, but I wanted to be sure.

Tracy shook her head. "No," she said, but I could tell she had more to say. "I mean, not in a way that would make me want to call the police, but every once in a while I'll be working, you know, in the weeds a little and the bar will be packed and all of the sudden the hair on the back of my neck will stand up on end and I'll feel goose bumps on my arms, and I don't know—it's like there's a change in the atmosphere, and I'll stop and look around and Ken will be looking at me like he wants nothing more than to do really bad things to me. I can't explain it other than—"

Tracy stopped midsentence and her gaze traveled to the door.

"What?" Heath and I both whispered to her.

"Speak of the devil," she said.

We turned slightly and looked behind us, spying a man in his mid to late thirties with dirty blond hair, unshaven, a little unkempt, and his own gaze firmly on the floor. He started to shuffle our way and Heath and I both turned our attention back to our lunch. Ken took a seat at the bar and Tracy greeted him warmly, but I could detect the false note in her voice.

Ken muttered something unintelligible and I eyed him discreetly. He took off his coat and I could see half a dozen necklaces wrapped around his neck; each had a crucifix dangling from the chain. He crossed himself as the beer he'd obviously ordered was set in front of him. "Your usual, Ken?" Tracy asked him.

He grunted but didn't look at her. Then I noticed he had started muttering under his breath, and although I couldn't quite catch what he was saying, I swore it sounded like the Lord's Prayer.

Tracy turned and put her back to Ken as she made a face for us like, "See? He's a freak!" We nodded subtly.

Heath and I continued to eat in silence, both of us sneaking glances at Ken here and there. As we were wrapping up our lunch, Ken's burger and fries arrived and he finally lifted his chin to mutter a thanks to Tracy. As he did so, however, something really odd happened. I'd been watching Ken subtly, taking in the way he fiddled with his crucifixes and noting that he was clearly right-handed, but as he finished thanking Tracy, something in his expression changed. It was almost exactly what Heath and I had experienced with Guy Walker. In an instant he became someone else; even his voice changed as he said Tracy's name.

She hid it well, but even she seemed startled and somewhat alarmed. She backed up and headed straight for the kitchen, and as she passed by us, I could see the goose pimples lining her arms.

Ken lifted the burger and did something else really odd. He sniffed it. The burger was dripping with juices—I could tell it was quite rare—and the way he sniffed at it was revolting to me.

Ken then snickered and put down the burger. Turning to me, he looked me dead in the eyes. "Hello, Mary."

I heard Heath's breath catch and felt his hand immediately go to the small of my back.

Ken then took his left index finger and swirled it in the juices from the burger on his plate. Lifting it then to put it in his mouth, he made an *Mmmm* sound and I felt my stomach muscles clench.

Heath stood up, reached into his back pocket, and pulled out his wallet. Taking out a twenty and a ten, he laid it down on the bar and grabbed my elbow. "Let's go."

"Leaving so soon, Mary?" Ken said. "And here I thought we could have a playdate together."

I took Heath's hand and let him pull me quickly toward the door.

"Maybe next time, then," Ken called, and he followed that with a wicked laugh that sent my skin crawling.

Once we were outside, I said, "We can't leave Tracy to deal with that!"

Heath hesitated, looking back toward the bar door, and I could tell he was really torn. That spook had tried to get inside his head down on Comm Avenue, and I wondered if it might try again. It was dangerous to let him get too close to the spook. And it was clearly dangerous to let me get too close to Ken. We had no magnets with us. We were completely vulnerable.

Heath solved the problem by taking out his phone and punching the screen. "Hi, I'm outside Sheedy's Place on Knox Avenue and I think I see smoke coming out of the roof and it smells like something electrical might be burning. I don't know if there's a fire up there, but maybe somebody should check it out?"

With that, Heath hung up and grabbed my hand again and we were rushing toward the car. Once inside we hunkered down and waited as a series of sirens began to sound in the distance. They got closer and closer and within another minute there were two fire trucks parked outside the bar. The patrons and staff came out soon after, and Heath and I watched Tracy hover safely with the other employees as Ken, back in his coat with his head down and crossing himself, ambled down the street without a backward glance.

Heath and I then got out of the car and approached the small group of employees. We motioned to Tracy and she pushed her way over to us. "Listen," Heath said, handing over his business card to her. "I want you to stay away from Ken. Tell your manager that he skipped out on his bill or something, but make him persona non grata from now on, okay?"

She took his card and appeared a little confused. "I don't know that I can do that."

"You can, Tracy," I told her. "And you will. He's dangerous in more ways than you know. You have to stay away from him."

Tracy licked her lips. "Yeah, okay. He really is creepy."

"And no leaving the bar without an escort either," Heath said, putting a hand on her shoulder. "If you get scared, or stuck in that place alone at night, you call me on the number on the card. That's my cell. I always answer, no matter what time, day or night."

Tracy smiled up at him, a look of wonder in her eyes. "Wow," she said. "You're so nice."

"I have my moments," he said, grinning back. "Just stay safe, okay?"

"You don't think Ken actually wants to hurt me, do you?"

"I don't know what that guy wants to do, Tracy, which is why you need to be really careful from now on, okay?"

"Should I call the police?"

"Not unless he tries something or gets upset that he's not allowed in the bar anymore. If he says or does anything that's threatening, you get a restraining order, okay?"

She nodded. "Okay. Thanks, you guys."

We left Tracy about the time the firemen had cleared the building. We avoided eye contact with them, and hoped the guilty looks on our faces didn't give us away. Still, it was the only way to make sure that Tracy was safe from the likes of Sy the Slayer.

Heath and I then walked down the block to the next street and turned left, keeping a careful eye out as we went. We got to the alley behind the bar and peered warily into it.

It smelled of stale beer and garbage. Not exactly inviting. Heath and I proceeded into the alley, and I flipped on my sixth sense, "feeling" out the energy of the place. I also knew that Heath did the same.

We walked slowly and cautiously, constantly looking behind us to make sure Ken hadn't come into the alley, but for the most part we were alone. We got to the door that we suspected was for Sheedy's, and Heath tried the handle. It was locked. Good.

Then I looked at him with a silent question. "I don't feel her," he said.

"Let's head down a little further."

We walked another few yards to the large Dumpster—which I assumed had been the crime scene for Gracie's murder—and poked around the area, but there was nothing left in the ether to feel out. The area was sort of dense with the comings and goings of people cutting through the alley, from the bar, from other shops, the garbage trucks, etc., etc. It was impossible to cut through all that "noise" to get to Gracie's murder, and neither of us could sense her ghost, so it was likely that she'd already crossed over.

Mentally I tried to reach out to her spirit, but I got nothing. I could tell Heath also tried, but it was radio silence.

At last we gave up and headed back to the car.

"Now what?" I asked Heath as he started up the engine.

He shook his head, clearly frustrated. "Did you see how Ken switched hands?" he asked me. "He was right-handed up until the spook took him over."

"I did notice that. Which means he could be a suspect for Brook's murder. If he's been under the spook's influence for this long, maybe he's turned into a killer who doesn't need a spook to do his dirty work."

"The guy is definitely whacked," Heath said. "And what the hell was he mumbling?"

"I don't know for sure, but I think it was the Lord's Prayer. I think Ken is super freaked-out by Sy the Slayer getting into his head and he's doing whatever he can to keep him out. What's scary is that it seems to be the case that once this spook has ahold of you, he doesn't seem to want to let go. I'm caught between feeling sorry for these guys and wondering if they were already bad men who would've murdered anyway."

"Tracy did say Ken had an edge to him even before Gracie was murdered," Heath said, staring out the window moodily.

My phone rang at that moment and it made me jump. I answered it and heard Kendra say, "Guess what!"

"You found out who owns the house on Stoughton Street?" I asked hopefully.

"No," she said, her voice still excited. "Dan Foster has agreed to an interview. We go in tomorrow morning at ten."

"Great," I said, but there was no enthusiasm behind the sentiment. "Swing by my place and pick me up?"

"Sure. I just dropped Gilley off at his condo and he said he lives one floor below you, so I know where it is. By the way, Gilley is supercute."

Kendra had already changed tracks, but I was still contemplating the interview with Dan Foster. I knew the spook was going to make an appearance, and Kendra had no idea what she was in for.

Kendra chatted at me about Gilley for another minute or two before promising to pick me up the next morning between nine and nine thirty and I hung up.

"Trouble?" Heath asked when I tucked my phone away.

"Isn't there always?"

Chapter 12

Kendra arrived at my door promptly at nine. Gilley was in my kitchen, conspicuously hanging around, pretending to want coffee. This was after an entire late afternoon the day before where he'd complained and complained about how clueless Kendra was not to spot the obvious and how she'd practically hung all over him. "Girl has no gaydar . . . at all. It got embarrassing!"

And yet, I'd learned that after I ducked out on them, the pair had soon grown bored researching the Stoughton house and opted for a quick bite at a nearby restaurant that had turned into several hours of lively conversation, giggles, and appletinis. I wondered if Gilley realized that he'd just been on a date with a girl.

So, when Kendra arrived with her cleavage pushed up, a fresh coat of lipstick, and boots with heels high enough for her to wobble on, I knew that Gil had a problem.

Still, he flirted and she flirted back for ten minutes before she boldly wrapped her arm around his middle and said, "I think you and I should go out. How about Saturday night?"

To which Gilley immediately stiffened and said, "Uh . . . Kendra, you should know something about me."

"Uh-oh," she said, but still in that playful flirtatious voice. "Sounds serious."

"It is."

"What is it?"

"I'm engaged."

I leveled a look at Gil. The little bastard. Why he didn't just tell her he was gay was beyond me, but maybe he was thinking of letting her down easy.

"You're engaged?" she said, immediately letting go of him. "For real?"

Gil nodded solemnly, and then his phone rang. "There's my fiancé," he said.

"What's her name?" Kendra asked, her hands finding her hips.

"Michel."

Well, at least that part wasn't a complete lie.

Kendra harrumphed and glared at Gil while he took the call with an exuberant, "Hey, sugar, you're up early!"

I waved at her and motioned for the door and we left a red-faced Gil to talk to his "fiancé."

"Men are such pigs," Kendra said as we got in the car.

"Some of them can be," I said. "But some are really wonderful."

"You referring to your boyfriend?"

"I am. He's pretty great."

"Yeah, well hold on to him, M.J., because all the ones I meet are either born liars or gay."

Little did Kendra know she'd just flirted with both.

"Oh!" she said suddenly. "I almost forgot. Look what one of my assistants found!"

Kendra handed over her smartphone and I looked at

the display. It was a photo of a group of what looked like hospital staff and other people in business attire. Behind the group was a sign that read WINSTON SENIOR CENTER ELDER CARE FUND, and as I squinted at the faces, one stood out.

"That's Luke," I said, pointing to his image.

"Yep. Guess who he's standing next to."

I looked and saw Luke's sister, Courtney, standing to his left. "That's his sister, Dr. Decker," I said. I searched the group for Steven's face, but didn't see him.

"Look to Luke's right," Kendra said.

I did and there was a woman with long wavy brown hair and a tremendous smile. She looked both relieved and excited. "I don't know her."

"You should," Kendra said.

"Why should I?"

"Because that's Brook Astor."

I gasped and felt a sense of dread settle into my midsection. Luke had his arm wrapped around her waist. They were definitely friendly.

"She worked at the hospital a couple of years ago. She was the fund-raising coordinator for the hospital and the elder care center across the street."

"When did she quit?" I asked, still staring at the photo.

"Not long after that picture was taken. At that time, her ex was a resident at the hospital and, according to my source, a nurse who was friends with Brook, the split was hard on her—she learned that her ex had cheated on her, and she hadn't seen it coming. The nurse also said that, for a short period of time, Brook and Luke hung out together."

My eyes widened. "Hung out how exactly?"

Kendra shrugged. "Don't really know for sure, but the rumors suggest that they were more than just friends. The nurse suspected something was up, and she was shocked by it because Luke's about ten years younger than Brook. She thought Brook might've been leaning on Luke to get her through the divorce. She said she thought maybe he didn't take their split so well."

I sighed and handed Kendra back her cell. This was looking worse and worse for Luke, and I had to question my theory that he wasn't a murderer all over again.

I told Kendra a little about what'd happened with Heath and me at the bar the day before. She was riveted, but I could also see some of the skepticism in her eyes. "So, was this Ken Chamblis ever listed as a suspect in the investigation?"

I shrugged. "Don't know. Heath and I couldn't find out much online. I was hoping maybe you had a source at the police station that could look into it."

"Oh, I do and I will."

"Also," I said, "if you can possibly ask your source whether or not there's any indication in the autopsy report of a right-handed or left-handed killer in Gracie's murder, I'd appreciate it."

"Which hand was Ken's dominant?"

"Right, until the spook took him over—then he became a left-hander."

"That is so freaky!"

I then tried to prepare her for the same possibility happening to Dan Foster during our interview. "Which reminds me," she said, completely unfazed by the thought of Foster becoming possessed by an evil spirit. "You'll have to hold the camera during the interview. I was going to bring Mike, my camera guy, but we're only allowed two people in at a time."

Kendra then fished around in the small pocket next to her seat and brought up a sheet of paper. "These are the questions I'm going to ask. Can you take a look and let me know if I've left anything out?"

I took the paper and peered at the list of questions. I was shocked by how terrible they were. Kendra was obviously interested in poking the bear, because most of her questions were meant to bait Foster into admitting he'd killed Bethany Sullivan—something he'd steadfastly refused to do throughout his trial. There were a few token questions at the end where Kendra was humoring me by asking Foster if he felt possessed by an evil spirit at the time of the murder, or if he often heard the voice of a ghost telling him to do bad things. It was a joke. And it ticked me off.

"Kendra," I said evenly. "If this is what you plan to ask Foster, then I'm not going with you and you can pull over right now and let me out."

She turned her attention away from the traffic to stare at me. "You can't be serious."

"I'm dead serious."

"M.J.," she said, curling her hands tightly around the steering wheel, "I went through a lot of trouble to set up this interview. Something *you* asked me to do."

"Yes, I wanted your help getting in to see Foster, but if you're gonna treat this as an opportunity to get his confession on camera and turn my investigation into a joke, then I want no part of it."

"I didn't say it was a joke!" she yelled.

I lifted the interview sheet. "Mr. Foster, do you often hear the voices of evil spirits urging you to kill innocent women?"

Kendra's face reddened. "I thought it'd be in line with what you were after."

I shook my head. "We'll never get to that question because either your first, second, or third question is gonna make him stand up and walk out of the interview." Kendra glared at me, but I wasn't backing down. This little chat with Foster was too important. "Kendra, you're putting him on the defensive, and the reason he granted us the interview is because we let him know we believed there was another force at work here. We have to go in there making him believe we're there to help him. This is not the time to hit him with some gotcha journalism."

With narrowed eyes, Kendra shifted her gaze away from me and focused on driving in silence for the next few minutes. At last she grudgingly muttered, "Fine, M.J. We'll play it your way. Tell me what you want me to ask him and I'll ask."

But I didn't trust her. I suspected the reporter in her was just a little too ingrained and I was really starting to doubt this whole plan. "I should do the talking," I said.

She laughed. "You're kidding, right?"

"No."

"M.J.," she said, using as level a tone as I'd used earlier, "I asked you along as a courtesy. I could've taken Mike in with me and left you behind."

"You think this'll be fun for me?" I shot back. "Kendra, you have *no* idea what we're up against. I know you don't quite believe any of this is real, but I'm here to tell you that it is, and we are playing with forces that are incredibly dangerous. If you start underestimating the potential danger involved in exposing yourself to Dan Foster and by extension the evil spirit who may be taking over his mind, then you expose yourself to a danger you will be completely unprepared to handle."

She rolled her eyes. "Foster's behind glass," she said. "There's no way he can hurt me."

"Ken Chamblis is still out there," I replied. "And maybe there're others, Kendra. That closet had seven names and we've only accounted for five of them. And that still doesn't answer the question of who the right-handed killer of Brook Astor is."

Kendra lifted her phone with the fund-raising photo

and waved it at me. "Obviously Luke's the guilty one," she snapped. "I mean, come on, how much proof do you need?"

"It wasn't Luke," I said firmly. I wasn't one hundred percent convinced, but Brook was stabbed by a right-handed killer, and Luke was a left-hander. Even if Sy the Slayer had taken over Luke's mind at the time of the murder, he wouldn't have switched Luke over to using his right hand, because Sy was also a lefty. I knew that was a threadbare thing to cling to, but I just couldn't believe that Luke had committed that murder.

"This is my story," Kendra said, and I could tell we were close to the point where she would grant my wish not to go with her to the interview, and pull over to let me out.

"I'm not trying to take the story away from you," I replied, and then I had an idea. "Hey, you know what? Maybe there's a way we can work together on this and still have it appear as if you're asking the questions. I know that sometimes when a reporter is interviewing someone, there's a sort of dub over of the reporter's questions if the sound quality isn't so great or the lighting is bad. What if I ask the questions, we get Dan to answer on camera, and then, later, we can dub you in asking the same questions?"

Kendra seemed to think that over. "Yeah," she said at last. "That could work."

"Cool," I said, relief in my voice. But then I felt a moment of panic when I realized that I'd have to carry the entire interview with Foster. I had no idea who was gonna show up for the interview—whether we'd get Dan for the whole time, or if Sy would even make an appearance. And I wasn't even sure I *wanted* Sy to show up. He scared the hell out of me, but I knew I also had to convince Kendra of his existence if she was going to take us seriously and continue to help us with the investigation.

In the few minutes that remained, I tried to mentally prepare for either scenario with Foster and felt the sudden presence of Sam Whitefeather—my spirit guide—step close to my energy. I relaxed a little, knowing he was extending me what protection he could from the other side.

Kendra and I had to show our IDs and press passes to be allowed into the back lot where the county lockup was. As Foster hadn't been sentenced yet, he was still being held by Suffolk County. He'd be transferred to a state pen as soon as his sentence came down.

We went through more ID checks and a similar process to the one Heath and I had faced a few days before when we'd gone to see Guy Walker; then we were escorted into a fairly large concrete-block room. What alarmed me was that there was no glass separating us from the prisoner. There was simply a table with two chairs on one side and one chair on the other. We'd be face-to-face with Foster, and I could see Kendra fidget nervously with the camera while we waited. She hadn't expected this setup either.

We sat in silence for maybe fifteen minutes before the far door opened and in shuffled Dan Foster. He wore handcuffs and leg shackles and a loop of chain around his middle. A guard escorted him in and kept one hand on Foster's back as he made his way slowly over to the table.

Foster kept his eyes down, not, I suspected, because he was ashamed, but because he was trying not to trip. The leg shackles only allowed him to take very small steps, and I will admit that I felt not an ounce of sympathy for him because if Sy the Slayer came in at any time, those shackles could be the difference between life and death for Kendra and me.

Foster took his seat and put his hands up on the table.

The chain from his waist made a loud clatter against the table before he finally settled into a fairly comfortable position.

Bethany's killer looked us over and I let him without saying a word. I could sense Kendra wanted me to say something to get the party started, but I had to be slow and careful here. At last Foster sat back and seemed to stare at us expectantly.

"Hello, Mr. Foster," I said softly. I wanted to keep my voice as level and calm as I could.

"You the reporter?" he asked, looking from me to Kendra, who was holding a small camera and recording the interview.

"I am today," I said.

He cocked his head quizzically, but I didn't elaborate. Instead I said, "As we said in our e-mail, we're here to talk to you about the house on Stoughton Street."

Foster's eyes narrowed with suspicion, but it was odd, because I could almost detect some contempt there too. I studied him closely. His nose was crooked and it'd obviously been broken more than once, and there was something about the set of his jaw that made me think that might've been broken too. His knuckles were thick the way a boxer's were, and when I looked into his eyes, I knew he was no innocent. There was an edge to him—probably the exact same kind of edge that Tracy had described belonging to Ken Chamblis.

"That house is a bad place," I told him, attempting to gain his trust. "It's a place where decent guys begin to have nightmares, and if you stay there long enough, you start to lose sleep, and you get the feeling that even when you're away from the house, something from there is following you."

Foster leaned forward, his gaze locked on mine. I had his full attention.

"Something lives in that house," I said next. "Something evil."

Subconsciously I saw Foster nod his head slightly.

I raised my hands and hovered them close to my temples. "And that evil starts to get inside your mind. It starts to take over your thoughts. It turns people . . ." I let my voice trail off and watched Foster carefully. He didn't even blink. It was like he couldn't believe I knew what'd happened inside that house. That someone was believing in his long-held secret.

"It turned Dan Foster into Deadly Dan. Am I right?"

The unexpected happened, something neither Kendra nor I could have foreseen. Dan Foster began to laugh. He shook his head and said, "You have no idea what you're playing with, little girl," he said so softly I almost didn't hear him. Then he looked up at me again and added, "You're playing with the devil himself and if you're not careful, he'll come to your house next."

I felt a chill go right through me. There was something so foreboding about what he'd just said, and I tried to shrug it off as Foster simply wanting to scare us, but it was hard to continue to look him in the eye.

I decided to carry on with the interview. If Foster was this cocky, maybe he'd reveal something about the origins of Sy the Slayer. "When was the last time you saw the shadowman?" I asked boldly.

Foster laughed again like he thought my questions were ridiculous—like I was a child asking why the sky was blue. "The shadowman?" he said, and I knew he was about to toy with me. "I see lots of shadows, lady. One came to my cell two days ago and told me he'd found a new playmate. Said her name's Mary. I don't know who she is, or where she is, but she'll be dead before the month is out. You wait. It'll happen."

My pulse quickened and my breath caught. I knew

then that Foster was saying Sy visited him regularly and Sy was referring to me. What I didn't know was whether Foster knew that I was Mary. I had to work very hard to continue to sit there calmly and not bolt out the door with the intention of booking the next flight out of Dodge. I could also see Kendra turn the camera toward me, and I knew she was as stunned as I was because I'd told her that I'd introduced myself to Guy Walker as Mary. And that Ken Chamblis had turned to me at the bar and called me Mary.

"Do you know who's going to do the deed?" I asked Dan.

He shook his head. "No," he said. "Won't be me, though," he said, holding up his chains with a wicked grin. "The shadowman, he's got somebody on the outside. I always knew there were others like me."

I lifted my cell phone and tapped the photo app to show him the closet from Stoughton Street. Foster leaned forward a little to look and that wicked smile spread. "That Luke name is new," he said, squinting. "Maybe he's the guy for the deed. Maybe he's the one that murdered my sweet Bethany. I loved her, you know," he added, and I didn't believe him for a second. "I would never hurt my sweet Beth."

I put the phone down into my lap as much to take the image away from Foster as to hide the fact that my hands had started shaking. I knew without a doubt that Dan had been present for at least a portion of Bethany's murder. He'd been present of mind when he cut her throat. I knew it as certain as I knew anything. Still, Foster seemed to be having fun toying with me and that was good for gathering more information. "Did you know any of the other men the shadow used?" I asked.

"Nah," Foster said casually, and I could sense he was

lying. What I didn't know was how many of the other men he'd met.

"I have a theory about who the shadowman is," I said, lifting the phone again to point to the photo. "I think he's the first name in this closet. Sy the Slayer."

Dan leaned forward, but it was a bit more like a lunge and he said, "If you're not careful, he'll answer when you call his name."

Kendra and I both sat back a little and the guard leaned forward and put a hand on Foster's shoulder. It was a warning and Foster immediately sat back. "Sorry," he said, but given the sick grin he wore, he obviously wasn't.

Still, he was answering all my questions, so I decided to press on. "It's okay," I said. "Do you have any idea where the shadowman might've come from?"

Foster shook his head. "Nope."

That reply seemed genuine. And then I decided to gauge his reaction to a running theory I had. "Do you think he might have a connection to the house's landlord?"

"Lester?"

I blinked. "Who?"

"The landlord. Lester Atkins. I only met him once when I signed the lease a couple of years ago. Nice old geezer. Don't know if he's connected to the shadowman or not, lady."

"Actually, I was thinking of Ray Eades."

"Don't know him," Foster said, and he was starting to look bored.

"Ah," I said, wondering if we'd just hit pay dirt on the owner of the house. I made a mental note to get Gilley to look into a Lester Atkins for later and then tried to think of more questions to ask before I lost his attention completely, but at that moment a sudden and bitter chill came over the room. And it was a chill I was all too familiar with. Foster seemed to be aware of it at the same moment I was, because he sat up straight and his eyes moved from side to side. "Shit," he whispered. "Here's Johnny . . ."

All of a sudden something dark seemed to appear right behind him and then it was gone. And so was Dan Foster. His body was still in front of us, but his entire expression had changed into one I recognized. Instinctively I sat as far back in my chair as I could. "Hello, Mary," Foster said. "I was hoping you'd come see me again."

Next to me, I heard Kendra's sharp intake of air.

Foster turned to her as if seeing her for the first time. "And you've brought a friend," he said. "How nice. A double date."

"Sy!" I said loudly to get his attention off Kendra. He seemed far too interested in her. "Who are you and where did you come from?"

Sy kept his eyes on Kendra, as if he knew it was bothering me. It was clearly bothering her, because she scooted her chair back a bit. "Where did I come from? I came from Sheedy's. Didn't you see me there?" he taunted, finally pulling his gaze away from Kendra to stare at me. "I saw you, Mary, didn't I?"

"What other eyes have you been looking through, Sy?" I asked.

Foster leaned back in his chair and laughed evilly. "Through a few special eyes, Mary. Through Dan's, and Bill's, and Mike's, and Ken's, and Guy's, and Luke's. Such willing eyes all of them. They lust for it as much as I do. As much as I lust for you, Mary." Foster licked his lips seductively and it was all I could do to hold still in my chair and not bolt out of there.

And then, Foster's gaze lifted above my right shoulder and he said, "Who's the old Indian?"

For a brief moment I didn't know what he was talking about, but then I realized he must be talking about Sam. "He's here to protect me from the likes of you," I told him, bolstered by the knowledge that Sam was right behind me.

Foster wiped his lips with his fingers. "Oh, yeah?" he said, and I could hear the challenge in his voice. "Maybe I ought to see how safe you feel around that other Indian, Mary. Maybe I'll go visit with him now...."

I jumped to my feet, my fists balled and anger coursing through me. "You leave him alone, Sy!" I yelled, but it was already too late. Dan Foster blinked and I knew I was looking at him again.

"He'll get to him before you can," he rasped as if hosting Sy the Slayer had taken all of his energy.

I didn't even wait long enough to comment. I grabbed Kendra and ran for the door.

To say that I urged Kendra to get us home as quickly as possible is to suggest that Gilley can get a little pitchy when he goes all howler monkey. We arrived at my condo and I sprinted from the car even before it'd come to a full stop. I'd called Heath over and over from the prison and from the car, but he hadn't answered, and neither had Gilley when, in desperation, I'd called him. I didn't know what was happening, but I feared the worst.

Skipping the elevator, I took the stairs two at a time, rounding the landing of Gilley's floor just as he was coming out. "Oh, hey," he said, holding up his phone. "I was just about to call you back. Sorry I didn't pick up, I was on the phone with Micha."

I ignored him and kept going, pushing my aching muscles to climb the stairs faster. I could hear Gil call after me, but I didn't have time to explain. Before I'd reached the landing, I called out to Heath, and I didn't care which neighbors I might be disturbing. "Heath!" I shouted. *"Heath!"* I got to my floor and my rubbery legs barely kept up as I forced them to sprint to the door. I pounded on it with one fist while reaching into my messenger bag for my keys. *"Heath!"*

At last the door was pulled open and my sweetheart stood there. The sight of him, though, made me catch my breath. He stared at me with such intensity that for a moment I felt terrified that Sy had managed to worm his way into Heath's mind. But then he reached out and took me into his arms and pulled me close. "Em," he said with a tremendous sigh of relief. "He's been after me for the past twenty minutes!"

"Call up your grandfather!" I told him, panting hard but trying to hold on to him as tightly as I could manage. I knew he was under assault and it was my worst fear to lose him to this evil spirit.

"Call up Whitefeather!" I said next. Whitefeather was another ancestor of Heath's. A very powerful warrior and spirit who'd helped us once when we'd needed him most.

I leaned back and cupped Heath's face between my hands. "Call out to Whitefeather!" I insisted. Intuitively I felt that was the answer and at the same time I also opened up my own sixth sense. The energy around Heath was intense, but as I begged him to call upon his ancestor, there was a shift. It was subtle at first, and then it expanded, growing larger, calmer, more protective. In my mind's eye I could see the brave warrior Whitefeather, standing behind Heath—the two nearly identical in appearance even down to that gorgeous white stripe of hair at the temple. And then, the energy shifted even more and the tension in Heath's eyes relaxed. "It's gone," he said.

I sagged against him, squeezing him tight again. "Thank God!" And then I thought about the fright I'd had, knowing Sy was trying to get into his mind. "Why didn't you answer your phone?"

Heath's body shifted and I saw him reach for his phone in his back pocket. "Huh," he said. "It's dead. Sorry. I didn't know you were trying to call me or I would've picked up."

From behind us I could hear Gilley coming up the stairs. I ignored him and leaned back to plant a kiss on my boyfriend's lips, so happy to have him fully back and not under attack by Sy the Slayer anymore.

And then I heard Gilley say, "Hello, Mary."

Chapter 13

Heath and I both stiffened. I was afraid to turn around. "Hey!" I heard Kendra call from the stairwell. "Is everybody okay?"

I risked taking a peek over my shoulder and saw Gilley, his gaze turning away from Heath and me as he looked toward Kendra slowly climbing those stairs. "Kendra!" I yelled, twisting around. "Go back to your car!"

But she kept climbing and stopped just a few stairs away from Gilley. "Oh, hey," she said to him. "How's your fiancée?"

"My fiancée?" he repeated. "I only have eyes for you, Kendra." The way Gilley said her name made me shudder. It was Gilley's voice, but with more rasp, and the inflections were all wrong. Gone was that slight Southern lilt he had when he spoke, and there was a definite South Boston accent now present in his speech. Also, he reached up with his left hand to scratch at his chin.

"What's with you?" she asked him, coming up the next few stairs.

I rushed forward and grabbed Gilley by the arm. Pulling hard, I twirled him around and pushed him straight toward my condo. "Go home, Kendra!" I shouted, continuing to push Gilley as hard as I could.

"M.J.!" I heard her call out, but I still slammed the door behind us.

Heath had read my mind and he was already approaching Gilley with one of the magnetic vests. "Oh, Mary," Gilley said, reaching down to grab my wrist in a viselike grip. "Don't play with me. You know how this will end."

I winced because Gilley's grip became tighter and tighter, and just as I was about to cry out, Heath wrapped the vest around him.

Gil's hand immediately relaxed and he swayed a little, but then he blinked and it was my best friend again. "Where's the fire?" he asked.

I was shaking so much with adrenaline and fear that my eyes misted. "You okay?" I asked him, cupping his face just as I'd done to Heath.

"Of course I'm okay," he said. "What's with you? And why'd you race up here like the place was on fire?"

I dropped my hands to hug him fiercely. "Would someone please tell me what the hell's going on?" he snapped.

I hugged him tighter. With Whitefeather's help, Heath could fend off Sy. But Gil was a completely different matter. He was already vulnerable to spooks, and now that Sy had been inside his mind, the access door would always be open and Gilley would always be vulnerable. My mind raced with the possibilities of Gilley ending up like Luke, and it was in that moment that I fully understood Courtney's fierce loyalty to her brother and her fear that she was losing him.

"Em," Heath said softly.

I let go of Gilley, who looked both perplexed and frustrated because he knew we weren't telling him something. "Do me a favor," I said to him. "Until I say otherwise, wear this vest."

Gil looked down and shifted under the weight of the vest. "When did I put this on?"

"Just wear it, Gil," I said sternly.

"It's hot," he complained. "And why're you insisting I wear this?"

I decided to go with a half-truth. "Sy the Slayer paid a visit to Heath. I'm worried that because the spooks like you, you might also be a target."

Gilley's hand flew to his mouth. "He was *here*?"

"Sort of," Heath said. "I managed to fend him off, but, Gil, I think it's best if while you and I are in the same building, you wear that."

Gilley reached down and began buttoning the vest. "I'm going back downstairs," he announced. "I'll turn up the air and live in this thing, but, guys, we gotta figure out how to shut this spook down, okay? My honey is coming home in four days and I can't greet him at the door wearing this!"

I thought of something else then, that mental note I'd made to myself at the prison. "Gil, can you research one more name for me?"

Gil dropped his chin and looked up at me in that "Are you kidding me?" way.

"Just one more name, I promise."

"Who is it this time?"

"A guy named Lester Atkins."

"Why?"

"Just do a search and see if he comes up as a possible murder suspect in any unsolved murder cases. In fact, do a broad search of him and see what you can come up with."

"Lester Atkins. Sounds made up."

I sighed. I wanted Gilley to leave and have a project so that Heath and I could talk about what to do. "Please, Gil?"

"Fine, but you owe me," he said.

"Yes, yes. I owe you. I'll just leave everything to you in my will, okay?"

Gil rolled his eyes, but he turned on his heel and left, so I breathed a sigh of relief.

"That's bad," Heath said the minute the door closed behind Gilley.

"Really bad," I agreed. "What do we do?"

"We have to find the source, Em. Now, more than ever, we have to find out who Sy the Slayer is and where he's hidden his portal."

I nodded. "Let's go over what we know," I said. And then I told him all about the interview with Dan Foster.

"It's obvious to me that Foster had a mean streak in him before he started renting that house on Stoughton," I said once I'd filled him in. "And I'm convinced that he was present in his own mind at least in part when Bethany was murdered. He didn't look even slightly remorseful about it either."

Heath walked over to my laptop and typed in something. He then swiveled it around to show me the screen. "A lot of the evidence used at Foster's trial is available online. I found this after you guys left this morning."

I moved over to the couch and pulled the laptop close. "Bethany had a restraining order out on him," I said. "That confirms my suspicion."

"Yep. And she'd reported him to the police six months earlier during their breakup because he'd gotten physical with her. He cracked one of her ribs and gave her a black eye."

"Bastard."

Heath nodded. "Before that, she told several friends that she was scared to break it off with him because he had a temper and he'd gotten physical with her while they were together."

"So, Sy just helped him do what he was probably going to do all along," I said.

"That's what I think."

I rubbed my temples and tried to put some order to my own thoughts. "What I don't understand is how Luke fits into all this. The men who rented that house that we've managed to track down all had an edge to them, Heath. They're not good men, and likely weren't good men before they rented that house. And I don't know where that leaves us."

"Where that leaves us? Regarding what, Em?"

"Luke. I know we only met him twice, but he just doesn't seem the type, you know? But I have to admit that Kendra showed me a new piece of evidence this morning that's starting to shake my faith in him." I then told him about the photo Kendra had shown me of Brook.

"So Luke *knew* her?"

"Apparently. She worked at the hospital as some fund-raising coordinator or something and they met there."

"What was the fund-raiser?"

"I don't know. Some old people's home or something. The point is that Luke and Brook knew each other and were even spotted hanging out together. There were rumors that their relationship was romantic, but as far as I can tell, that's only a rumor."

"So we're still back at square one," Heath said with a sigh. "Killer Ken is on the loose, and we also think he got away with at least one murder. Sy the Slayer could have other accomplices roaming the city, and he has it out for you, too."

I didn't tell Heath about Sy telling me that I was going to die by one of his accomplices' hands; I thought it best to keep that mum for the moment. But then something else jumped into my mind and I dug through my messenger bag for my phone. Pulling it up, I dialed Kendra's number, but either she wouldn't pick up or she wasn't near it, because I got her voice mail. "Kendra, it's me. Please call me. I owe you a big explanation, I know, and I'm sorry for slamming the door in your face. I swear there's a good reason, though, so call me back, okay?"

"Think she's mad?" Heath asked as I set the phone down in the middle of the ottoman.

"Oh, I'm sure she's mad. It's just a question of how soon she'll cool off enough to let me explain. I also want to tell her to take some extra safety precautions. Sy was pretty interested in her when he took over Foster's body at the jailhouse."

Heath's expression became concerned. "Do you think she'll listen to you about being cautious?"

I shrugged. "Maybe. She seemed pretty freaked-out when Foster morphed into Sy. I think it'll be enough to convince her to be careful."

We both stared at my phone for a moment and I knew Heath was willing it to ring just like I was. Finally I picked the phone back up and texted her, requesting she call me back right away. We spent another few minutes staring at the phone again, but Kendra didn't call back and I growled with irritation. I had a feeling she was purposely ignoring me. "How long do you think she'll stay mad at you?" Heath asked.

I shrugged. "Dunno. Maybe an hour. Kendra's pretty headstrong and I got my way a whole lot today. She may take the rest of the morning to get back to me." I then picked up the phone a third time and texted Kendra a longer message, telling her that after our interview with

Foster, I thought it a really good idea if she was careful and took some precautions for her own safety. I hoped that even if she was too irritated to talk to me, my cautionary message would at least sink in.

"What do we do now?" Heath asked after I showed him the message I'd sent her.

I frowned at the phone one more time, irritated that Kendra seemed to be playing games and wouldn't call me back. I felt anxious and overwhelmed and frustrated. This was such a difficult and complicated case that I desperately wanted to take a break from it. Permanently. But I couldn't because Sy had found a way into Gilley's mind, and that would have me sticking with it until I locked that evil son of a bitch into his portal if I had to chase him through hell to do it. "How about we get some index cards and spend a little time figuring out what we know, and what we don't know?"

"How are we gonna know what we don't know?" Heath said with a playful grin as he wrapped an arm around me.

"Oh, trust me, that pile of index cards is gonna be the biggest pile."

Heath and I spent the next two hours laying out the case on three-by-five index cards while Doc serenaded us with bits of songs Gilley had taught him. All the songs had altered lyrics and were inappropriate for audiences under eighteen.

Still, there was something kind of hilarious about a little gray bird singing, "I'm too sexy for my feathers, I'm too sexy for my feathers, I'm too *sexy*."

"So, on the list of things we know," I said once we'd laid out all the cards, "is that Guy Walker killed Amy Montgomery in nineteen seventy-five. He's currently in prison and unable to do Sy's dirty work. Then," I added, picking up the next card, which had required a bit of

Internet searching to fill out completely, "we have Killer Ken, aka Ken Chamblis. Based on the fact that Sy obviously gets inside Ken's head, and the fact that, like the other girls, Gracie's throat was slashed, we're fairly convinced Ken was responsible for killing Gracie Stewart in the alley behind Sheedy's Place on April tenth, twenty ten. What he's been up to since then is a mystery, but he's no longer living at the Stoughton house. He's also right-handed, so he *could* be a suspect in Brook Astor's murder."

"He's definitely still under Sy's influence," Heath said. "And Sheedy's is a hike from Comm Avenue, but who knows what Ken's got for transportation?"

"Right," I said, tapping my finger against my lips while I thought of another question we hadn't asked. "We need to know where Ken lives. See if maybe his residence is closer to Comm Ave these days."

Heath moved over to the computer and began to click the keys. "According to Switchboard.com, Ken has several different addresses. Not sure which one is his current address, but he definitely once lived on Stoughton Street."

"Any of those addresses bring him close to Comm Ave?"

"Two," Heath said, writing them down. "One is about three miles south, and the other is two and a half miles northwest."

"Within walking distance of Brook's murder scene."

"Looks like it."

I sighed and fished around for the next card on the floor. "After Ken, we've got Dan Foster, who killed Bethany Sullivan in the park across from her apartment—"

"That's about ten miles from the Stoughton Street house," Heath interrupted. We'd come up with that little tidbit, thanks to Google Maps.

"Yes, but his car was found not far from the murder scene and, according to the evidence posted online you found an hour ago, Dan's steering wheel had traces of blood on it, and the tank was empty. He obviously murdered Bethany and tried to drive away, but he ran out of gas—which is why the cops found him wandering the streets not long after discovering Bethany's body.

"Anyway, the only thing that's really relevant to us right now is that Dan was in prison and he couldn't have murdered Brook. Which leaves two names on our list that we have yet to identify. Butcher Bill and Murdering Mike. Oh, and Sy the Slayer."

Heath squatted next to me to peer over my shoulder. "We're missing some years," he said.

"Hmm?"

"Well, if Sy was already dead when Guy Walker was available to be possessed, and he was running loose in nineteen seventy-five, then Sy must've been killing people before 'seventy-five."

"Yeah, but the question is, how many years before? This psycho could be from the eighteen hundreds for all we know."

"I don't think so," Heath said. "I think evil spooks like him don't lie low for long before they start looking for ways to entertain themselves."

"You're thinking Sy could've been alive in the sixties or even early seventies?"

"It's possible."

I scribbled a note on the index card and went back to the other two. "We need to find out who Butcher Bill and Murdering Mike are." I then reached for my phone and called Gilley. "How ya doin'?" I asked, still worried about him.

Gilley yawned. "I'm fine now that I've had a little nap. What's up?"

I felt my temper flare. "What's up? What's *up*? Are you for real, Gil?"

"What?" he asked innocently.

"We're trying to solve this case and you're *napping*?"

"I'm up now," Gil said, a note of irritation in his voice.

"Did you do any research on Lester?"

Gil yawned again. "I found two men in the U. S. with that name. Neither of them lives or has lived in Massachusetts."

"Crap," I said.

"Is that all?"

"No. You owe me other stuff."

"Like what?"

I felt my temper flare again. I just knew Gil was trying to be difficult, but because I was mad, I couldn't immediately think of what I'd assigned to him, so my brain went right to the names on the two cards I held in my hand. "Heath and I think that Butcher Bill and Murdering Mike might've been active between the years nineteen seventy-six and roughly two thousand nine or ten."

"Oh, that'll be a snap to look up," Gil said drily.

"Just see if there were any women murdered between those dates who might've had similar MOs to all the other victims. See if there were any girls stabbed on the streets late at night by unidentified suspects. Or even known suspects. Or even convicted criminals."

"You don't ask for much, do you?"

I sighed, trying to find a common theme between all the murders, and then I had one. "Gil, in all the murders that we know Sy the Slayer had a hand, the murder weapon was never found. Not even in Bethany's case, which is weird because Dan Foster was arrested only an hour after her murder and he still had blood on his clothes and hands."

"Luke didn't come home with a knife either," Gil pointed out.

"Yeah, but I'm still not convinced he did it. Anyway, plug that into the search."

I'd been staring at the list of killers from the closet and, getting an idea, switched my gaze over to the index cards of all the murdered women. "You know, the victims might also be a link. All the women were white, but I think they might've ranged in hair color." I'd seen a photo of Bethany, who was blond, and Brook, who had brown hair. "Still the ages aren't too far apart. Brook was the oldest at thirty, but all the others were in their late teens or somewhere in their twenties. And maybe there's something about their build—see if the known victims were all around the same height and weight."

I could hear Gilley scribbling down some notes and I was happy he seemed to finally be taking this seriously.

"Okay," he said. "That it?"

"For now."

"Good. Can you get me something to eat?"

"Are you kidding?"

"No. Remember? You owe me."

I sighed heavily to let him know he was pushing it with me, but I also had to admit that he sort of had a point. "Fine. What is it you'd like, your royal highmaintenance?"

Gil gave me his order and I took Heath's lunch order too and he said he was going out for quick run while I was picking up lunch. I was glad because I didn't want him to be alone in the condo, where I couldn't get to him quickly if I needed to. About the time I was pulling up to the deli, I realized I'd left my phone behind in my messenger bag. I'd only grabbed my wallet on my way out.

I had to suffer through what felt like a long wait while

my order was prepared—there's nothing worse than realizing you've left behind your electronic tether.

At last I had the order and raced home. I breathed a sigh of relief when I passed Heath on his way back to the condo and I had to marvel at the beauty of the man as he ran. Heath has an amazing stride. He moves so lithely, so effortlessly, he's like a gazelle. It's amazing to watch. I waited for him in the parking lot and he glided in and smiled when he spotted me. "You were really flying," I said as he slowed to a stop. The turkey wasn't even breathing hard.

Heath checked his watch. "It's a perfect day," he said. "I always run better when it's cool."

I took a peek at his time. "A six-twenty pace?" I said. "Whoa!"

He wound an arm around my shoulders. "I was having fun."

"I'm totally slowing you down," I said. "No more running together."

Heath made a derisive noise. "The only thing better than really opening up on a day like today is running with you, babe."

That made me feel all warm and googley inside.

We checked in with Gilley on our way upstairs, and after handing him his lunch, he said, "Who do you love?"

"You apparently," I replied, reading his expression well.

"Yes. Yes, you do!"

"What'd you find?"

"Not what. Who. I found Butcher Bill."

"Get out!"

"Before or after I tell you about Billy Boy?" Gil said, rocking back on his heels.

"After. Spill it, Gillespie."

"Well," Gil said, dragging it out even longer. "I believe Bill the Butcher is actually Bill Radcliff, who was convicted of murdering two women, Heidi and Paula Kennedy, sisters who shared a house on Stoughton Street just a half block down from the rental house."

"When was this?" I asked, interrupting Gil.

"The girls were murdered in late June nineteen eighty-two. Bill had a fixation with one of the girls and they went out a couple of times. By all accounts he turned into a stalker and one night he caught Heidi out at night walking home from the train station. He followed her nearly to her door before stabbing her, and while he was in the middle of the attack, her little sister, Paula, came running out of the house to stop him and he stabbed her too.

"She lingered in a coma for a few days afterward, and they thought she'd pull through, but she developed an infection and died in the hospital after telling the police who the attacker was."

"Where's Radcliff now?" Heath asked.

"Don't know," Gil said.

I eyed Gil sharply. "Wait. I thought you said he'd been convicted of the girls' murders?"

"He was," Gil said. "He spent twenty-five years in the state pen and was released two years ago. I was able to confirm through the newspaper article that he lived in the house on Stoughton at the time of the murder, but there's nothing other than his prison address since then. I also can't find a record of him online, but that doesn't mean much. He would've been behind bars during the tech revolution, so I doubt he has a smartphone."

"So how do we find him?"

"We could try to find out through his parole officer, but those guys don't usually give out that kind of info without a damn good reason."

"I'd say Brook Astor's murder is a damn good reason," Heath said.

Gil made a face. "Try convincing his parole officer that Bill had a hand in a murder where another guy's currently awaiting trial. A guy who was found covered in the victim's blood, hiding in the upstairs bedroom of a house just down the street from the murder scene moments after the killing."

I sighed. "See what you can find out, Gil, okay?"

"Oh, you know it," he said. "Right after I eat."

"Of course," I said, and couldn't hide a slight grin. I was willing to cut him a little slack because he had helped us come up with another viable suspect for Brook's murder. Then I thought of something else. "Did you maybe get any other details about him or the murder, Gil? Like, was the murder weapon found? Or if he was maybe right-handed?"

"Don't know about the right-handed or left-handed characteristic, but I was able to learn that the murder weapon was never found. At least from what I read in the article, it was never recovered."

"Well, that takes care of number five. What about number six on our list of mystery killers: Murdering Mike?"

"So far, he's a complete mystery. Of course, if you look at the photo of the closet, his name is low and close to Sy's, so maybe that means something."

"Like what?" Heath asked while Gil moved to the kitchen to get some plates for our meal.

"Well, it could mean that the closet is somewhat chronological. If you look closely, you'll see that Sy's name is the lowest, then Mike's, then Guy's, then Bill's, Dan's, and Ken's, then Luke's."

"Ken killed Gracie before Dan killed Bethany," Heath said.

"Yeah, I know, it's not perfect, but maybe those two got a little confused when they wrote their names in the closet. It looks a little like a tree, though, when you just look at the image. I think that maybe Mike may be one of our older killers."

"Okay," I said. "Run with that theory and see what you can come up with. If you're right, then you'll want to look for someone maybe in the sixties or even earlier. And if that's the case, then maybe we can rule him out due to age."

Gil nibbled on a potato chip. "I wish I could find this Lester Atkins," he said. "Or who that freaking house belongs to."

"What did you guys find out about it?" I asked, remembering that Gil and Kendra had been left to that task when I'd bolted the day before.

"Not much."

"How much is not much?" I pressed, because Gil was looking guilty.

"We blew off the search right after you left and went to find food and drink."

I sighed. "Well, I'd appreciate it if you called Kendra and gave the search another go." As that came out of my mouth, I remembered that I still hadn't heard from her. Reflexively I patted my rear pocket. Then I remembered that I'd left my cell upstairs in my messenger bag. I excused myself and headed up to retrieve it. There was a message from Kendra. I tapped the voice mail as I hurried back down the stairs. "Hey, M.J., listen, I'm always careful when I'm working this kind of a story, and you can explain all you want about this morning, but first I think I've figured out the link between this Sy the Slayer and the Stoughton Street house. I've got a deadline to make and some other stuff to run down first, though, so plan to meet me in the parking lot of the nursing home across from the hospital a little later. I'll call you after three with the time and I'll fill you in when we meet up."

I walked back into Gilley's place and told the guys about Kendra's message. "Does that mean I don't have to call her and go back to that dungeon?" Gil asked.

"Dunno, Gil. Depends on what she tells me this afternoon." I then heard a beep and looked at my phone. "Dammit," I said as an image of the battery popped up with a red stripe across the bottom.

"What?" Heath asked.

"My phone's out of juice. Gil, you got a charger nearby?"

"On the counter," he said. "You can take mine off," he added. "I'll put it back on later."

I put my phone on the charger and stared at it a little frustrated. There wasn't any other lead we could track down before I talked to Kendra, and I really wanted to go for a run to work off some of my anxiety, but I didn't want to leave the condo without a phone. "Gil?"

"Yeah?"

"Can I borrow your phone while I go for a run?"

Gilley narrowed his eyes at me. "No way, M.J. If memory serves me, I believe you're on your fourth phone in less than a year and they're crazy expensive. You have a habit of destroying your gizmos and I need that phone. Besides, my charge was pretty much out too, and as I just plugged it in when you went upstairs to get yours, I don't think there's enough battery for you to use it."

"What's with all our phones not holding charges?" I said.

"Can probably blame it on Sy," Heath said, before he pulled his own phone out of his pocket and handed it to me. "Here," he said. "Take it."

"You sure?"

"Yeah," he said. "I'm gonna stay here and keep an eye on things." He motioned subtly with his chin to Gil, and I understood. Gil was likely to get tired of wearing his vest at some point and Heath wanted to be nearby should Sy show up unexpectedly.

"Maybe I shouldn't go," I said.

"Oh, you should go," Heath said. "Besides, there's not much we can do on this case until you hear back from Kendra. Go for a run. It'll do a lot to settle you."

I leaned forward and kissed him. "Thanks, sweetie."

Gilley yawned loudly as he sat back and gave a pat to his full belly. "Y'all do your thing. I'm gonna get in another nap."

I waved to them and headed out.

The run was just what I needed and I went a little longer than I'd planned. Heath was right. It was the perfect day for a good long run. When I got back to the condo, I snuck into Gilley's place and saw him sleeping comfortably on the couch, his vest draped over him like a blanket. I tiptoed over to my phone and took it off the charger, plugged in his, then headed upstairs, where I found Heath on the computer typing away. "How was your run?" he asked absently.

"Really good. You were right. It's a gorgeous day."

Heath didn't say anything else and I walked over to peer over his shoulder. "What'cha doing?"

"I'm digging into Murdering Mike. Gilley showed me how to get into this database where I could fish around for anything that might look like it could fit."

"He taught you how to do his dirty work, huh?"

"He's a talented hacker," Heath said. "And I'm a quick learner."

"Any luck?"

Heath sighed; sitting back, he swept a long lock of hair out of his eyes. "Nothing yet. I've been going year by year, and I'm almost done with the sixties. Although, there was a string of murders that went unsolved close to that neighborhood, but the women were all strangled."

I shook my head. "In every other case the women were stabbed and/or their throats were slashed," I said. "Doesn't fit that Sy would get the men he possessed to change methods."

"My thinking too."

"The thing that puzzles me is this elusive murder weapon. I mean, has anyone done any kind of comparison to the wounds of the other murders? I know it sounds crazy, but what if, in each case, it was the same murder weapon?"

Heath's brow furrowed. "You think?"

I shrugged. "It could be," I said. "I mean, how else is it that in every single case the knife used just vanishes? What if the knife originally belonged to Sy, and he has the men use it to murder these women and then he has them stash it in a familiar place to him so that the next killer can find it?"

"The only familiar place it could be would be the house on Stoughton," Heath said, and I could see an idea sparking in his eyes. "You up for a road trip over to that house to snoop around again?"

I checked my watch. It was almost three. Kendra was going to call me soon to tell me what time to meet up, but I could certainly go with Heath and root around with him. "Okay, but if Kendra calls, we may have to go meet her."

"Sure."

"And we're both wearing vests," I told him.

"Okay," he said. I knew I'd get no argument there.

"What about Gil?"

"I checked on him fifteen minutes ago and he was sleeping like a baby under the vest. I think as long as he's covered in magnets, he'll be okay."

"Good," I said. "Let me take a really quick shower and we'll go."

Heath and I were in the car and headed to Stoughton Street just ten minutes later. When we got there, it was pretty obvious that the police had already had a run through the place. The front door was smeared with fingerprint dust and when we cupped our hands and peered through the glass window, we could see that much of the home had been emptied.

Heath stood back and looked at me. "How's your radar for finding stuff?"

"Not great. Yours?"

"Not bad."

I waved a hand at him, "After you, then."

Heath stood back from the house and stared down at the ground. My own feelers could sense him flipping on his radar and searching the area for anything that might point to a murder weapon. He then lifted his chin and said, "This way."

I followed him around back to the bedroom window. Heath walked right up to it and pulled up on the sill. It lifted with a bit of a creak. "You're going in there?" I asked anxiously. Not only was it breaking and entering, but I was worried about Sy the Slayer making another attempt to get into Heath's head. Even though he had his vest on, I still worried that he might be vulnerable.

"Yeah, I'm going in," he said. "You coming?"

I bit my lip. I was normally a straight-as-an-arrow kind of girl, and breaking the law wasn't something I was ever comfortable with. But this was a special circumstance. "I guess," I muttered, moving over to the window.

Heath went in first and I followed. The room felt brighter and then I realized why—it'd been freshly painted.

As if we were both thinking the same thing, Heath and I moved to the closet and he opened it up. The interior gleamed with a fresh coat of white paint. "Shit," he said.

"Do you think Eades knew the police were likely to visit?" I asked.

"If he's in the loop about what goes on here, then, yeah, probably."

"Do you think he has the murder weapon?" I asked next. "Or could he be the right-handed guy we're looking for?"

Heath shook his head. "Don't know, Em. He was a little gruff when we met him, but I don't know that I got a killer vibe off him."

"Me either," I said with another sigh. I turned away from the closet and walked around the small bedroom. All Luke's stuff had been removed, but the place still had a stifling quality to it.

"Where else should we look?" I said.

Heath didn't answer, so I turned around only to find him still staring at the closet. "Heath?"

My sweetie bent down and ran his hand across the carpeted floor. I moved to peer over his shoulder. "What is it?" I asked.

"There's something under here," he said, and I realized he still had his radar turned on and was feeling out the place for any evidence left behind.

I bent down too and waited for him to figure out what he was picking up on. At last he reached into the far left corner and tugged on the edge of the carpet. It came up easily. "Would ya lookit that?" Heath whispered.

Under the carpet was a thin plank of wood that didn't belong with the other planks. Heath fiddled with the edge of it to get it to lift up and there we saw a narrow well, the perfect place to hide a knife. Heath got out his cell and clicked it on to shine some light into the well. It was empty except for a few smudged rusty-looking spots along the side and at the bottom of the well.

I sucked in a breath. "Is that blood?"

"I'd lay odds that it is," Heath said.

"So that's where the murder weapon for at least one, if not all, of the murders has been hiding."

"Yep."

I put a hand on Heath's shoulder. "Does your radar sense that it might still be here?"

"No," Heath said. "I'm thinking this empty well was what I was supposed to find."

I felt a cold shiver snake up my spine. "We find that knife, we find our killer."

Heath replaced the thin plank of wood and pressed the carpet back into place. "What're your thoughts about telling the police about it?"

I wavered with indecision. "I don't know. I mean, maybe they already found it?"

"Maybe, but I doubt it, Em. I think they poked around in the closet, saw that it was empty, and moved on."

"So what do you think? Should we call and tell them about that hiding spot? And the names on the back of the closet? And if we do, how do we tell them we know about it?"

Heath stood up and closed the door. "Let's not call them yet," he said. "It could make things even worse for Luke. For now let's lie low and wait for Kendra to call."

I looked down at my watch. It was almost four. "I wish she'd call already."

"She probably got tied up with something. Come on, let's head back to your place and chill out until we hear from her."

We drove back to the condo in relative silence, both of us tense after being in the Stoughton Street house.

When we entered my condo, I found Gilley on my

couch with Doc on his shoulder. "Hey, baby!" Doc called, adding a wolf whistle.

I couldn't help but smile. Doc had this little birdie voice that was most similar to my voice at the age of eleven when he'd first come into my life. Sometimes he could imitate Gilley's deeper voice and sometimes he used my adult voice, but for most new words he learned, he kept it in that sweet upper octave.

"Your phone's been ringing off the hook," Gil said moodily.

My brow furrowed and I took the cell out of my back pocket. "No, it hasn't."

Gil lifted the cell next to him high in the air. "Yes, it has. You took my phone and left me yours."

I felt a jolt of alarm and clicked the phone in my hand to turn it on. Sure enough Michel's photo greeted me. It was Gilley's wallpaper. "Son of a bitch!" I yelled, stomping over to the couch. "I took the phone off the charger!"

"Which was my phone," Gil said without a hint of apology. "I unplugged yours after it was charged and put mine on."

"How the hell was I supposed to know that?" I snapped, grabbing the phone out of his hand and throwing his on the couch. I was so mad because I knew I'd likely missed Kendra's call. "And why the hell didn't you answer my phone when it rang and call me on yours if you knew I had it?"

"You had yours locked," Gilley snapped back. "Jeez, M.J., it's not my friggin' fault!"

I knew I owed him an apology, but I was too wound up and anxious. I quickly unlocked my screen and saw that I had two voice mails from Kendra. I motioned for Heath to follow me out the door and listened to the first voice mail as we raced down the stairs. "Hey, M.J., it's Kendra. I'm finally free. Let's meet at four o'clock. The parking lot of the nursing home right across from the hospital. Man, do I have a great lead to tell you about!"

The voice mail ended and I swore several more times as Heath and I raced to the car. "She wanted to meet at four!" I growled as we got in, and Heath squealed the tires as he backed out of the space. "Damn Gilley!"

"It's only quarter past," Heath said. "We can be there in fifteen minutes."

I called Kendra to tell her that we were on our way, but I got her voice mail. "Son of a . . . ," I muttered while I waited to leave her a message. Finally it clicked over and I said, "Kendra, it's M.J. I'm so sorry. Gilley had my phone and I didn't realize you'd called. We're on our way. We should be there by four thirty. Please call me if that's an issue."

I hung up and laid my head back against the seat rest, so frustrated that I'd missed her call. "Hey," Heath said, reaching out to squeeze my hand. "It'll be okay, Em."

I sucked in a deep breath and let it out nice and slow, trying to calm my nerves. Then I tapped the phone screen again and clicked on Kendra's next voice mail. "Hey, M.J., not sure if you're getting my messages. I'm gonna send you an e-mail just in case. Hope something gets through. Okay, call me back if you can."

I switched from the voice mail over to e-mail and read Kendra's message, which was essentially the same as what she'd already told me on the voice mail. "Leave it to her to be cryptic about this big lead of hers," I muttered.

"Try calling her again," Heath suggested.

I did and the line picked up, but I didn't hear anyone say anything. "Hello?" I said. "Kendra?"

Something odd sounded in the background. It was a sort of wet gurgle. "Kendra?" I repeated, pulling the phone away to check the contact ID and make sure I'd dialed right. "Hello? Hello?"

I closed my eyes, trying to listen. It was the oddest thing—I could hear a sort of liquid bubbling, but not much else. Maybe some traffic in the background, but nothing intelligible. "Kendra?" I said loudly. "Can you hear me?"

"What's going on?" Heath said.

I gripped the phone tightly. Alarm bells were starting to go off in my head, and I just *knew* Kendra was in trouble. *"Kendra!"*

With two beeps the phone disconnected.

I dialed right back and waited with mounting panic as the phone just rang and rang, then finally went to voice mail. "Kendra! It's M.J. If you're in trouble, just hit the callback button!" I hung up the line and crossed my fingers. No calls came in. "She's in trouble!" I said, turning to Heath.

"We're almost there." His knuckles were white on the steering wheel.

"How far?" I asked even as I turned my head right and left to see where we were.

"A few blocks," he told me.

My knees bounced with anxiety. Should I call the police? Would we get to Kendra quicker? Was she even in the place she said to meet us? Maybe she was somewhere else and in trouble.

Heath pushed the accelerator and darted around other cars as he zoomed down the street. I had to grip the handle over my door to hold on while he made a very sharp right turn. The car jolted as it hit an uneven elevation and Heath screeched to a halt in the first available parking space. We jumped out of the car and looked frantically around. "That's her car!" I yelled, pointing to the silver Honda across the parking lot. "Kendra!" I shouted, darting toward her car.

Heath came up right next to me and we ran stride for

stride to the car. As we got within a few yards, however, I saw a smudge of bright red against the car door. "Oh, God!" I gasped, knowing it was blood.

Heath reached out and grabbed my arm, halting me. "Wait!" he said, looking around. "Just wait, Em!"

I pulled against his grip. "It's hers!" I said, close to panic. "She's hurt!"

Heath was looking all around and he moved with me to the car. He peered inside the vehicle and shook his head; then he looked to the right and left sides of it and shook his head again. "Where?" he said. "She's not here, Em. . . ."

"Kendra!" I shouted. Some people coming out of the nursing home looked over at me, but I ignored them. *"Kendra!"*

"Call her," Heath said suddenly, pointing to my phone, which was still gripped tightly in my hand.

With shaking fingers I dialed and waited with a pounding heart for the line to pick up. It started ringing on my end and I took it away from my ear. Listening close, I thought I heard something coming from a few cars away.

Heath heard it too, because he took me by the elbow and we edged down the line of cars, the ringing getting louder before it cut off. I lifted my phone to my ear again and heard Kendra's voice message. I ended the call and redialed. The ringing started up again and we followed it down two more cars, but didn't see Kendra. And then I saw another smudge of blood along the side of a white SUV. "There!" I said, and darted forward.

Heath still had hold of my elbow and he checked me. "Together," he whispered. We crept along the cars to the other end and looked around. No sign of Kendra. "Call it one more time," he said.

I redialed, praying we weren't too late. We heard ringing again and it sounded like it was coming from right under our feet. I sank down low and looked under the SUV. There was Kendra, eyes open and staring at me as she lay in a pool of blood that was growing bigger by the second. I couldn't help it, I screamed and reached for her hand. It was still warm. "Kendra!" I cried just as Heath shouted for someone to come help us.

"Kendra!" I yelled again, willing those staring eyes to blink, to move, to not look so vacant. A sob bubbled up in my throat. *"Kendra!"*

And then, like a miracle she gasped just enough to let me know she was still clinging to life.

I got down on my belly and wiggled under the car. Behind me I could hear Heath continue his shouts for someone to get a doctor. "Oh, Kendra," I said softly when I managed to wiggle close enough to her to put a hand on the side of her head. If she died here, I didn't want to her to die alone. "I'm here, honey," I said. "I'm here. Help is coming. You just have to hang on a few more seconds, okay? Just hang on, Kendra. Just hang on!"

Her mouth opened and another bubble of noise came out. I realized her throat had been cut and wondered how she was still alive. And then her hand moved and I could see that the effort was costing her. I put my hand down toward hers and in her palm I felt her phone. I was about to close my hand over hers to reassure her when she pushed the phone into my palm and pulled it away again. And then her eyes closed.

"Kendra!" I said sternly. "Kendra, you listen to me! You hang on, okay? You hang on!"

But those lids didn't open again and I couldn't tell if her chest had stopped its feeble rise and fall. And then there were what sounded like a dozen footfalls all around the car. Heath called my name and I knew it was his hand on my calf. I knew I needed to back away from

Kendra and let the medical staff do their thing, but my brain was still reeling from the fact that Kendra might've just died right in front of me.

"Em!" Heath said more firmly as other people wriggling under the SUV came into view. "Come on, Em, come on out and let them help her."

I nodded, even though no one was looking at me—all eyes were on Kendra. On my elbows I backed out from under the SUV, and once I was clear, Heath lifted me into his arms and held me gently as I sobbed and sobbed.

Chapter 14

By some miracle, Kendra pulled through long enough to make it to surgery. Heath and I sat in the waiting room for hours while they worked on her, first in the ER, then in surgery. It was touch and go there for a long time, but we were told that she'd made it through the surgery and was now in a medically induced coma up in ICU. She was listed as critical, and a kind nurse told us that if Kendra was to make it out of the woods, the next forty-eight hours would be the toughest for her.

Kendra's producer and several people from the station came to the hospital to both see about her and cover the story. One of the anchors actually asked us if he could interview us. Heath gave him such a dirty look that the guy sort of scuttled away and avoided eye contact after that.

The police of course were also called to the scene, and Heath and I were put into a small conference room to wait for our *favorite* investigator, Detective Souter. I sat numbly while we waited, not able to get that blank stare on Kendra's face out of my mind. She'd looked so helpless. And of course I blamed myself. She'd been waiting for us, and if I'd just checked the phone I'd carried with me to Stoughton Street, I would've realized that it was Gilley's and we would've gone right back to retrieve my cell.

Which reminded me that I had Kendra's cell phone. I rooted around in my messenger bag, where I'd put it while we waited for Kendra to be taken into the hospital. I was going to have to hand it over to Souter, I knew. I cringed when I realized the phone was slightly sticky, and smudged with Kendra's blood. As I freed it from the bag, I accidentally turned the cell on. Kendra didn't have her screen locked by a security code, and more because I was nervous and fidgety than anything else, I swiped the arrow to unlock the screen. Up came a photo I recognized. It was the one of Luke and Brook Astor at the fund-raiser. I realized Kendra must have been looking at it when she was attacked. Why?

"What's up?" Heath asked me just as approaching footfalls and mumbled voices alerted us that someone was coming.

Almost without thinking, I turned Kendra's phone all the way off, then tucked it into the folds of my shirt.

I'm "gifted" in the cleavage department, so I was pretty confident Kendra's cell wasn't sticking out or noticeable. Just to be sure, I zipped up my bubble vest. No sooner had I done that than the door opened and Souter came in.

Heath and I endured a two-hour interview with the detective. We were honest about much of what we'd been up to. I told her that we were investigating Brook Astor's murder on our own, as we didn't believe her theory that Luke had killed Brook, and that Kendra had come into the mix just a few days earlier, helping us research the history of the Stoughton house.

She was very interested in the connection between

that house and several other murders, and she seemed particularly intrigued by the photo I showed her of the closet before it'd been painted.

"When was this taken?" she asked me.

"A couple of days ago."

"And you didn't call to tell me about it?"

"You didn't seem too keen to believe anything I said the last time we got together."

Souter eyed me with agitation and suspicion, but I was used to that look from her. "Going back to this afternoon, you say you got a voice mail from Kendra that she was here and waiting for you at four o'clock, and when you got here, you found blood on her car but no sign of her?"

I explained for the third time how we'd followed the sound of her telephone to where she was hidden under the SUV. "I think she might've crawled under there," I said. "To hide from her attacker."

"Can I see your phone?" she asked.

I handed my phone to her. She checked all the incoming and outgoing calls and even listened to Kendra's voice mail. I then saw her look me up and down and I realized she was probably checking me for blood splatter. I knew there was no blood on my clothes, as when I'd wiggled under the car, I'd been careful to avoid the pool of blood leaking out of poor Kendra.

"So where's Kendra's phone?" Souter asked next, almost as if she could smell it on me.

I furrowed my brow and hoped I looked confused. "Don't you guys have it?"

"No," she said. "I already checked and it wasn't on her person or in her purse."

"Weird."

"Did you see her phone when you found her under the car?"

I scratched my head. "I don't remember." Turning to Heath, I said, "Did you see it?"

"I was trying to get help," he said. "I barely saw anything other than all that blood."

Souter tapped her finger against the tabletop; I figured she didn't believe either of us. "Mind if I look inside your messenger bag, Miss Holliday?"

I made a motion for her to go ahead and she rummaged through the contents, which weren't much more than a hairbrush, some notes on our investigation, some protein bars, and a bottled water.

Souter set the messenger bag aside and said, "Mind emptying your pockets for me?"

She said it to both Heath and me, and with an exasperated sigh I stood up and turned out all my pockets. "If you ask for a strip search next, I'm calling my attorney," I told her.

She smiled, but it wasn't nicely. "You two keep turning up at the scene of violent attacks. What else would you have me do?"

"Believe us when we tell you that there's a connection between all these murders," I said, pulling up the top page of my notes from the stack of things she'd gotten out of my messenger bag. "I'm telling you, all these murders are connected and there's an unidentified man out there who's responsible for Brook Astor's murder."

"Yeah," she said, pretending to humor me. "And he's right-handed."

I felt my temper flare and the memory of Kendra lying under that SUV flashed through my mind as vividly as if I were looking at her there and then, and I realized that she'd been lying on her back but twisted a little to the left. The wound on her neck had been deepest on the left side, which was why there was so much blood leaking out of her. I recalled she'd even had her left hand pressed up against the wound. With a jolt I realized Kendra had also been attacked by a right-handed person. "It was the same guy," I said breathlessly.

"Same guy what?" Souter asked.

"The same man who attacked Brook Astor also attacked Kendra. Her neck wound was on the left side of her throat. He was a righty."

"Unless he cut her from the front," Souter said.

I looked at her like she had to be kidding. "Check it out, would you?" I snapped.

Souter didn't say anything and that's when I stood up and started to gather my stuff. "I think we're done here, unless you want me to call Mack and have him come down to tell you himself that Heath and I won't be answering any more questions."

Souter closed her notebook and stood up too. "Don't leave town," she said, and walked out the door first.

Hours later, after we'd learned that Kendra was in ICU, we went home, and after checking on Gilley to make sure he was still wearing his vest, Heath and I both collapsed into bed, our own vests resting across our feet.

I slept fitfully, plagued by nightmares about Kendra under that car, her life slipping away, so it was no surprise when I finally gave up and got up before dawn had even broken. I was restless with worry over Kendra and the fact that I felt no closer to putting all these discordant dots together. I moved out to the living room and eyed the note cards still laid out on the rug.

Kendra's phone was on the ottoman, where I'd guiltily set it the night before. I hadn't had the courage to turn it on again because I'd been worried the police would be able to track it.

But it was now four thirty in the morning and even Souter had to be asleep. Closing the door so as not to disturb Heath, I turned on Kendra's phone. Swiping the arrow, I eyed the home screen with all of Kendra's apps. I went right to her photos and pulled up the photo she'd had open at the time of her attack.

Luke smiled brightly out at me and so did Brook Astor. What was it about this photo that had sparked further curiosity from Kendra?

And then I realized something that made me gasp. I'd been calling Kendra from the car, and I knew she'd picked up the line at least once. That gurgling sound was her trying to tell me she was in trouble. It could have been immediately after her throat was cut. And the reason the sequence of events was critical was that if Kendra had been looking at this photo at the time she took my call, then the screen would have switched over to her contacts app, and when I swiped to unlock her phone, this photo wouldn't have come up. That meant that Kendra had purposely pulled the picture up about the time we looked under the car for her.

But why?

Was it an accident?

Was she feebly trying to answer her phone and she'd simply hit this photo randomly?

I considered that and then I remembered something else. When I'd reached out to hold her hand, weak as she was, she'd pushed her phone into my palm.

This photo on her screen was no accident. Kendra wanted me to see it. It held a clue she wanted me to see.

But what was in the photo that Kendra wanted me to pick out?

Or who?

I searched the faces, all of them seemingly happy and full of fun. And then I noticed two things that I hadn't before. One was that, almost out of view of the camera, there was a figure slightly out of focus who looked remarkably like Raymond Eades. He seemed to be pushing a wheelchair toward one of the tables, and I could see him only in profile, so I wasn't positive it was him, but it looked enough like him to send a round of warning bells through my head.

The second thing I noticed was that the fund-raiser itself was for the Winston Senior Center. Which I now knew was the name of the nursing home across the street from the hospital.

"No way!" I whispered, finally making the connection. If Ray Eades was connected to the senior center, then that had to be the lead Kendra wanted to show me when she asked me to meet her there.

Just to be sure, I fished out my phone from my messenger bag and tapped my way to my voice mails, rooting around for the first message Kendra had left me the day before. "Hey, M.J. Listen, I'm always careful when I'm working this kind of a story, and you can explain all you want about this morning, but first I think I've figured out the link between this Sy the Slayer and the Stoughton Street house. . . ."

And that was it. She'd found a link between Sy the Slayer and the Stoughton Street house, and I had to believe Ray Eades was the link. He was the property manager for the Stoughton House, but how did he connect to Sy the Slayer? And what did the Winston Senior Center have to do with any of this other than maybe a place where Eades hung out? Gilley's research showed that Eades lived a couple of blocks away from Courtney's house on Comm Ave, so I didn't think he lived at the center. He was pretty spry and maybe not quite old enough to be a resident there. So what was it that Kendra wanted me to see?

I paced the floor of the living room for almost two hours, going over and over the case in my head and wondering what specifically Kendra could have found. Finally I crept into the bedroom, grabbed some jeans, a sweater, and my vest, and tiptoed out. I left Heath a note just in case he woke up, but I figured he'd sleep at least a few more hours undisturbed.

I made my way by car over to the nursing home and avoided the spot where Kendra had been lying before I chose a slot that allowed me to see the front doors. I didn't know what time the center opened, so I called it up on my phone and saw that it opened at eight. I had about forty-five minutes to kill, so I went in search of coffee and waited in line for nearly that long to get my cup of joe.

I parked back in the same spot at the center and watched the clock until about five after eight; then I approached the front door cautiously. I was nervous and jumpy and couldn't seem to settle down.

The automatic doors opened with a whoosh and I proceeded forward, looking around, feeling very exposed. There didn't seem to be many people about, but to my right was a desk where an elderly woman with curly white hair and a name tag that read DAISY sat. "Good morning," she said cheerily. "Who are you here to see?"

I bit my lip and took a chance. "The last name is Eades," I said, thinking that maybe Raymond visited the center because he had a relative here.

The woman's cheery smile broadened. "You mean Raymond? Oh, he won't be here for another half hour, but Mr. Akers is in the living room and I'm sure he'd love some company until Raymond arrives."

Mr. Akers? I thought. Who the heck was that? "Oh, that sounds nice. I'd love to visit with him. Which way is the living room?"

The woman pointed back down the hall and instructed me to take the hallway past the main entrance all the way to the end and turn right. The living room would be on my left.

I thanked her and turned away. I was still without much of a plan and hoped that one clue would lead to another until I could figure this whole thing out.

Following the woman's instructions, I managed to locate the living room. There were a surprising number of residents hanging out, playing cards, watching television, or simply staring out the window.

I eyed them with nervous apprehension. I had no idea who Mr. Akers was, so I surveyed the room, taking note of each face ... and then my gaze traveled to one man in a wheelchair and my own legs almost gave out from underneath me. Sitting in the corner all by himself was none other than the man who'd attacked me in my out-of-body experience almost a week before.

At that moment the old man lifted his chin and our eyes met. I swear my heart nearly hammered its way right out of my chest as he stared at me and then he broke into a grin and lifted his hand to wave at me.

I thought about turning tail and running, but then I realized there wasn't one hint of malice in those eyes. In fact, he looked so tickled to have caught me staring at him, and then he waved me over.

I hesitated and he put his hand on his own heart as if he'd die if I didn't come over to see him. Slowly and cautiously I stepped into the living room. There were loads of people and staff about. If this guy tried anything, I'd have help at the ready. When I got close enough, he said, "Hey, cutie. Who're you looking for?"

"I'm not sure," I said, because I really wasn't anymore.

He cocked his head curiously and put his gnarled hand back over his heart. "Well then, can I pretend you're here to see me? Lester Akers at your service, milady."

My eyes widened. "Lester *Akers*?" I repeated.

"Yes," he said with a chuckle. "You've heard of me?"

I shook my head, but I knew he'd already caught the hint of recognition. "You didn't by any chance used to live in a house on Stoughton Street, did you?"

Lester's brow furrowed and his eyes became guarded. "That's my rental," he said. "It belonged to my brother; then it fell to me."

"Oh," I said, trying to invent a cover for myself. "I used to live on Stoughton Street and you looked familiar. I was Brad Rowe's girlfriend for a while."

"Well, I used to putter around that place when tenants moved out. That was before I started driving wheelchairs," Lester said, his smile still intact.

"What happened?" I asked before I realized that might be a little nosy.

"Cancer," he said. "Spread to my legs a year ago. Now it's in my back."

"Oh, I'm so sorry," I told him. I'd had no idea he was so feeble.

Lester waved a hand as if it were no big deal. "What're you gonna do?" he said with a shrug.

I nodded and tried to offer him an encouraging smile. It felt tight and not very genuine. I didn't know where else to go with our conversation.

As it happened, I didn't have to. Lester lifted his chin again and said, "Ah, here comes my buddy. He manages the house now. Maybe you've seen him around too."

I stiffened, knowing that Raymond Eades was approaching. Thinking quickly, I pulled my cell from my back pocket and said, "Oh, I'm so sorry, but this is a call I have to take." I then put the phone to my ear and pretended to start a conversation while turning away from Lester and keeping my back to Raymond. I had no idea if he'd recognize me, but I decided not to risk it.

Carefully I navigated the room, always keeping Lester and Raymond at my back, and made it safely out of there. I then walked a little farther down the corridor and wondered what to do next. I decided to take a chance and walk back past the door and take a quick peek inside. That's when I caught Raymond wheeling Lester toward the French doors, which appeared to lead out to a patio with lots of tables and chairs.

I walked back into the room and crossed over to the doors. There were even more residents out on the patio and I saw a small table with only two chairs that was partially hidden by a half wall, and luck was on my side because Raymond had wheeled Lester over to a table on the other side of the half wall, and the two men were facing away from me.

Ducking quickly out the door, I edged over to the table and took a seat. Pretending to fiddle with my phone, I eavesdropped in on their conversation. ". . . nothing I can't take care of, Lester. Just a little fingerprint dust. The thing I can't figure out is, who went in there and painted the place and cleaned it up? I tell you it's the damnedest thing. One day the place is a mess—I mean, I was getting ready to clear all that junk out—and I came back three days later and it's clean as a whistle and freshly painted."

"That house has always been strange," Lester said. "I keep thinking maybe we shouldn't keep renting it out."

Eades made a dismissive sound. "You need the money if you're gonna stay here, Les. You can't make the rent on this place without the rent on that one."

Lester was quiet for a moment; then he said, "I hear you, but it seems like over the years that house has attracted more than its fair share of trouble. Remember that killer Guy Walker? I couldn't believe I'd rented the place to a man so evil. And before him there was Bill Radcliff. He killed those two young sisters. Terrible man."

"And now we've had two more like that with Luke and Dan. I'd say it was the neighborhood, but none of the other houses has had that kind of trouble. I was hoping that raising the rent would solve the issue of bringing in the wrong kind of people, but it didn't work with Luke Decker, so now I don't know what we should do."

"Burn it," I heard Lester say, but he said it so softly I almost didn't catch it.

Raymond also didn't quite catch it. "What's that?" he said.

Lester sighed. "Ray, I want you to promise me something," Lester said.

"Anything, Les. You know that."

Akers lowered his voice and I had to strain to hear. "After I'm gone, I want you to burn that house to the ground. The wiring's old, and it wouldn't take much to get it to overload. You're an electrician. You know how to make it look like an accident, right?"

Ray made a sound like he was incredulous and I peeked up over the half wall to see him staring wide-eyed at his friend. "Les . . ."

"Promise me, Raymond. Promise me."

Before Ray could say anything more, however, they were suddenly interrupted by another male voice. "Mr. Akers, Nurse Killjoy says that she found your medications under your pillow this morning."

"Hey, Doc," Akers said. "Nice day out, don't you think?"

"Lester," the doctor said sternly. I took another peek over the half wall at the handsome doctor in scrubs staring down at Lester. Still, there was a little grin on his face, and I suspected this was a game the two men played often.

"That stuff makes me tired," Lester complained.

"It'd make you less tired if you took it on a regular basis and allowed your system to adjust to it."

"I don't like it."

"Don't much care, Lester," the doc said, and held out his closed hand. I suspected the meds in question were in the doc's hand.

"You think they're so great, you take 'em," Lester said. He was turning into a bit of a child about it.

"Les," Raymond said. "You gotta take your meds."

"We could let the cancer continue to attack your bones unchecked," the doc said. "But you complain so much about the pain in your back that I think you might prefer being a little tired to curled up in the fetal position from the pain."

"You play dirty," Lester said.

"It's my job to keep you alive and in as little pain as possible, buddy," the doctor said kindly, still holding out his hand.

Lester finally held out his own hand, palm up. "How about I promise to take them at lunch?"

"How about you take them now while I'm watching?"

"How long I know you, Doc?" Lester said, still bargaining.

"Too long," the doctor said with a chuckle. "And talking about me when I was a young Doogie Howser who barely knew his way around a medical ward won't get you out of taking these meds right now."

Over a speaker attached to one of the corners of the building, a voice said, "Dr. Fitzstephens, Dr. Danghame, Dr. Lucas, and Dr. Morgan to the conference room, please."

"Ooo," Lester said with a chuckle. "That's you, Mickey. Better get going if you're gonna make that presentation. I hear that pretty drug rep from Pfizer brought the good doughnuts and coffee."

The handsome doctor folded his arms across his chest. "Take the pills, Les," he said.

Lester sighed dramatically and popped the pills into his mouth. The doc then unfolded his arms and reached into his lab coat pocket; pulling out a bottled water, he handed it to Les. "Drink it down," he said. "You'll need to hydrate with those."

Lester grumbled something else but drank the water. The doc then asked Lester to open his mouth and lift up his tongue. Even though I couldn't see Les's face, I'm assuming he cooperated because the doctor then nodded and said, "I'll tell Kirsten she has an admirer out here. Maybe she'll come out after the show and bring you a doughnut."

"Maybe pigs will fly," Lester said, and he and Raymond chuckled.

The doctor joined in and then waved his good-byes. "I hate those damn pills," Lester complained after the doc had gone.

"If they keep you from being in pain, I say they're worth it," Raymond told him.

"I'm always in pain anyway and on those pills I lose track of stuff," Lester said next. "You know I gotta keep alert."

"Yeah, yeah," his friend said. "That's not pills, Les. That's old age."

"Bah," Lester said. "I say let the cancer take its toll. I got no love for this place now that I can't walk."

"You'd leave me?" Raymond said playfully.

"To be with my Rosie? In a heartbeat."

Under my nose I smelled a small waft of sweet perfume and had the sense that the spirit of the woman named Rosie was tapping me on the shoulder.

"God rest Rosie," Raymond said. "Worst thing I ever did was introduce the two of you. I could've had her if I'd kept her from meeting you."

Lester scoffed. "Like that woulda stopped us. One look and we knew, Ray. All it took was that one look."

"You still catch yourself signing?" Ray asked.

Lester held up his hands and made several motions that were clearly sign language.

Ray signed something back and the two men laughed.

"Sometimes, when I dream, I swear I can still hear her voice," Lester said. "It's been sixty years since she was able to say a word and I can still hear the sound of it in my head. She had such a pretty voice. Such a shame she lost it."

"Ahh," Ray said, waving his hand dismissively. "She got on just fine without it."

The two men talked on and the whole time the gentle spirit of the woman I knew was Rose stood next to me, as if listening in too. Gradually I detected a slight slur come into Lester's speech, and then his head began to droop. "Yep," Ray said, getting to his feet. "Those drugs are starting to take their effect. Let's get you back to your room for a nice nap and I'll be by later this afternoon for a game of cards."

I shifted in my chair away from Ray as he maneuvered Les out from the table and back toward the French doors. I felt Rose's energy hover around me for a little longer and I had the sense that she was asking me to go talk to Lester again on her behalf, but I wasn't willing to do that. There were too many questions still at play here and I had to get home and wake Gilley up in order to ask those questions, because I suspected that Kendra had discovered Lester here at the center, but what his link to Sy the Slayer was I still wasn't absolutely sure. I had my suspicions, but I wasn't positive.

After waiting for about five minutes to make sure Ray and Lester weren't around, I got up and headed back through the living room, keeping my eyes on the floor as I walked down the corridor back to the front entrance. The automatic doors opened and I trotted to my car, feeling anxious until I was safely behind the wheel. As I started the engine, however, something really weird happened. I put the car into drive—I'd pulled forward through one space into the other so I was facing out of it, which gave me a clear view of the center—and as I was about to take my foot off the brake, I saw a shadow slide across the white stucco and slink its way through the glass doors.

It happened so quickly that I almost didn't think it was real. But then the seed of an idea began to form in my mind and I truly hoped I was wrong. With renewed determination, I headed home.

I found Heath snoring softly, his hand sweetly extended toward my side of the bed, as if, even in sleep, he wanted to be reassured of my presence. I moved to his side and kissed his cheek. The faintest hint of a smile spread to his lips, but then he fell back into snoring softly again and I left him alone.

Tiptoeing out of the room, I made my way down to Gilley's place and knocked. There was no answer, so I used the key Gil had given me years ago when we'd first bought our respective condos, and let myself in. There was an eerie quiet about the place and I hesitated for a few seconds in the kitchen before moving deeper into the condo. I didn't know if Gil had kept his vest close all night and the memory of seeing that shadow move across the face of the nursing home was still fresh in my mind. "Gil?" I called softly. I felt a little guilty about waking him up, but what I needed to know wouldn't wait. "Gil?"

I heard rustling in the bedroom and headed in that direction. "Gilley?" I called again, knocking on his bedroom door. "Honey, I need your help. Are you up?"

The door was abruptly opened and Gil stood there, disheveled and quite unhappy to see me. "Don't you sleep?"

"It's nine thirty," I said, lifting my wrist to show him my watch.

"Oh," he said, looking surprised as he tipped forward to look at the time. "Well, then . . . come back in an hour." With that, he shut the door in my face.

I sighed impatiently and tried the handle. Before I could even get my hand on it, though, I heard the click of the lock. "Gil," I said sternly as I knocked a few times just to let him know I wasn't going away. "Come on! I think I found the lead that Kendra was trying to tell me about yesterday."

"In an hour!"

"It can't wait that long!"

There was no answer, so I began knocking again and didn't let up. Just about the time I was convinced there were bruises forming on my knuckles, Gil unlocked the door and pulled it open, only to glare hard at me. "You are *such* a pain in the ass—you know that, M.J.?"

"I love you too, Gilley."

He shook his head and rolled his eyes, but he didn't try to shut the door in my face again. Instead he moved past me, heading toward the kitchen. He stopped in front of the counter and snapped, "You didn't even get the coffee started?"

"Sorry!" I said, moving quickly to get that going. Gil was much easier to handle fully caffeinated. Once I had the coffee brewing, I said, "Want to hear what I found out?"

Gil sat moodily on one of the barstools at the kitchen counter and watched me through puffy, narrowed eyes. "No."

I ignored that and told him everything that'd happened at the nursing home. Just like I'd hoped, the coffee and the events of that morning had their effect and he started to show some interest. "So, you think Lester Akers has something to do with Sy the Slayer."

"Yes, but I'm not sure what. Still, he is the spitting image of the man who attacked me in my out-of-body experience from the other day, even if the guy I met today in the nursing home seemed genuinely charming and sincere. I can't figure out what the actual connection is, but while you're researching Lester Akers, I'm going to make a call and try to put another piece of this puzzle into place."

Gil nodded and shuffled off the barstool. Moving over to the couch, he pulled his laptop close and got to work.

Meanwhile I dug out my cell and called Courtney. "Hello?" she asked, and I could tell that she'd seen the caller ID and was surprised to hear from me.

"Courtney?"

"Yes, M.J., what can I do for you?"

"I have a question for you and I need a straight answer. It's critical that you be honest with me, okay?"

"I've been honest with you," she said sharply.

"I'm not doubting that, but this question isn't something I think you'll want to confess the answer to, because you're going to want to protect your brother, but you *have* to be honest with me, okay?"

"What's the question?" she asked, and I couldn't tell if she was willing to tell me the truth.

"Did your brother have a relationship with Brook Astor?"

There was no answer for so long that I had to call out to Courtney again. "I'm here," she said. "M.J., I'm not sure that I can answer that."

"Listen," I said, "I *have* to know, Courtney. Please."

I heard her let out a breath and then she said, "Yes.

Luke met Brook when they both worked on the senior center foundation's fund-raiser. Luke worked there briefly a year and a half ago. At the time, Brook was going through a divorce and my brother was a shoulder she felt she could lean on. To him she was older and more sophisticated than the girls he was used to seeing. He fell for her. Hard. But I know my brother, and I know he would *never* hurt Brook. He adored her—even after she broke his heart, he talked about what a good influence she'd been in his life. He wasn't angry. He was grateful."

"I believe you," I told her. She was defending someone I was now convinced was innocent. I simply knew that the same person who'd attacked Brook had also attacked Kendra, but how that person was connected back to Sy the Slayer was something I was still trying to work out. "Listen, I'm close to solving this thing, so don't lose hope, okay?"

"You're close to . . . ? You mean you're still investigating? Even after what happened to that poor reporter last night?"

"You know about Kendra?" I asked in return.

"Yes, of course, I was a surgical consult. She lost a considerable amount of blood and we were worried about her brain function. I saw you and Heath in the waiting room last night—in fact, I was the one that had the nurse tell you how Kendra was doing. Normally that information is strictly reserved for family."

I almost didn't know what to say. "Thanks, Courtney," I said. "I really appreciate it."

"Would you like to be updated about her condition?"

"I would," I said. "If it's not going to get you in trouble."

"It won't. But please be careful and discreet with any information I give you about her condition."

I promised I would be and got off the phone. "Hey,"

Gil said as I stood there, thinking through the puzzle pieces and trying to put them into place. "I've got something for you."

I moved over to sit next to him. "Tell me."

"Lester *Akers*, not Atkins as Foster mispronounced it, is seventy-eight years old, widowed, and his last known residence was Seven-five-seven-three Comm Ave."

I gasped. "That's the building next door to Courtney's!"

"Yep. He lived there for over fifty years."

"Tell me what else," I said, feeling my heartbeat tick up and knowing Gil had more to share.

"Lester was a twin. His identical twin brother was killed in a hunting accident in nineteen sixty-eight. Guess what his twin brother's name was."

"Sy Akers."

"Yep. Or, more correctly, Sylvester Roger Akers. And get this: When Lester and Sylvester were in their early thirties—this was in 'sixty-six—there was a small string of unsolved murders in that part of town. Three women over the course of a year were found brutally stabbed to death, and the last victim had her throat slashed."

I put a hand to my mouth. "No way . . ."

"Way. And wanna know what else?" I nodded eagerly. "Sylvester Akers was questioned by police, but his brother, Lester, offered up an alibi."

"Oh . . . my . . . God . . ."

"It gets even better," Gil said. "Or worse, depending on how you look at it. About six months after the last woman was found murdered, Lester's fiancée was brutally attacked by a knife-wielding unidentified assailant. The victim—"

"Rose," I said.

"Rose*mary*," Gil corrected, and my breath caught again. Sy seemed particularly fascinated by my name whenever he came through any of the men he possessed.

"Tell me about the attack on her," I said.

"According to the *Boston Globe*, which reported the incident, Rosemary was walking over to Lester's place on Comm Ave when she was grabbed from behind and her throat was slit. She barely survived, but her vocal cords were cut, leaving her mute for the rest of her life."

I closed my eyes and felt a well of sadness for her and, quite frankly, for Lester when I thought back to how sweetly he described the last time he'd heard her voice and how he'd learned to sign, just for her.

"Was she able to identify her attacker?" I asked, already guessing at the accident.

"No. The news report said that she had no memory of that night or her attacker. Police strongly suspected it was the same man who'd killed the other three women, but Rose wasn't stabbed, so they couldn't be sure. And then there were never any more murders like that in the area, so the trail ran cold."

"Tell me about the hunting accident," I said next, remembering what Gil had said about the way Sy had died.

"There's nothing much to tell," Gil said. "During deer season, Akers was upstate when he was shot about a hundred yards away from his hunting shack. The police concluded that it was likely another hunter who probably didn't know he'd shot a man, not a deer. They never found the shooter."

I had another theory entirely, but I didn't voice it out loud. "Is that all of it?" I asked.

"Nope, there's one more little tidbit that I think you'd be interested to know. Sy's obituary states that at the time of his death he lived in the home his parents had left the brothers, which was on Stoughton Street."

"The parents set up the trust," I said, and recalling the

name, I added, "The LSRLA Trust. Lester and Sylvester are the first two initials."

"The parents were Roger and Louise Akers," Gil said, shifting windows on the computer screen to show me his notes from Sy's obit. "So the acronym must stand for the Lester, Sylvester, Roger, Louise Akers Trust."

I had almost all of the pieces. Almost. I knew I had to go back to the nursing home.

Standing up, I said, "Okay, I gotta run another errand. You stay here and keep that vest on."

"I need a shower," Gil said, giving himself a cursory sniff.

I turned away, anxious to get back to the nursing home. "Then drape the vest over your shower door," I called over my shoulder. "I mean it, Gilley. Keep that thing close."

"It's annoying!" he yelled back.

I paused at the door. "It's only for another day or two," I said to him. "I promise."

With that, I headed upstairs and found Heath just getting up. "Hey, pretty woman," he said when he saw me. "Feel like a run?"

"No. And you need to get dressed and come with me." I moved into the room and pulled open the dresser drawer, tossing a pair of jeans and a shirt at him.

"Can I wake up first?" he asked.

"No," I said, pulling open the curtains to let in the light. "Come on, babe, we've got to go!"

"Where's the fire?"

"I'll explain in the car."

Heath drove and when I got to the part about how I'd already been to the senior center once that morning, he nearly pulled over to lecture me about the stupid risk I'd taken. "You should've woken me up," he said.

I apologized and kept telling him about everything

that'd happened. Gradually his anger at me subsided, especially when I told him about Lester's twin brother, Sy, and how Lester's fiancée and future wife had been attacked by a knife-wielding assailant who was never identified or caught.

"What do you make of the hunting accident?" Heath asked.

"I find it highly suspicious," I told him. "And that's why I want to get back down to the senior center. I want to talk to Lester."

"Okay, but no more of this going it alone—you hear?"

I rolled my eyes. "Fine. Then no more sleeping in for you."

Heath reached out and squeezed my hand. "I'm being serious."

"I know, and I'm sorry. You're right. I should've woken you."

We got to the center and asked to see Lester at the desk with the same cheery elderly woman still behind it. "I'll call his room," Daisy said.

After a few seconds she put the phone down and said. "I'm afraid Mr. Akers isn't answering. Sometimes he has trouble staying awake in the afternoons, and he'll sleep right through to dinner. You're welcome to come back this evening and try again, or tomorrow morning. He tends to be at his most alert in the mornings."

I drummed my fingers on the countertop. "Thank you," I said. "We'll be back."

Heath and I left the center and went back to the condo, where I spent much of the rest of the day pacing the floor and muttering to myself. Heath tried to coax me into going for a run, but I was too distracted. I was missing something, I just knew it. Something vital, and it felt like it should have been right in front of me, but I couldn't put my finger on it.

And then, like a little bubble finally breaking the surface, a thought came to me and I raced to make a call. "Courtney?" I said when she answered.

"Did you find out something?" she asked by way of hello.

"Maybe. Listen, I need to know how your brother came across the house on Stoughton Street."

"What do you mean?"

"I mean, how was it that he rented that particular house?" The thing that'd been bugging me was that it simply felt like too much of a coincidence that Luke—whose sister lived right next door to the house Lester Akers had lived in for fifty years—would rent the very house across town that was once the residence of his evil twin brother.

"I think he just saw it on Craigslist," she said.

"Is there any way you can check for me?" I pressed.

"I can try," she said. "But, M.J., I have to be careful, because Luke's attorney has already warned Steven and me that our phone calls with Luke are all recorded by the county and our conversations can be used against Luke in court."

I paced back and forth several steps. This was risky, but I felt so strongly that it was a crucial question. "I understand, but please, Courtney, I swear I wouldn't ask if it wasn't vital. I'm so close to figuring out who killed Brook and attacked Kendra. I need to know."

"Okay," she said, but she hardly sounded happy about it.

"Can I ask how Kendra's doing?" I said next.

"She's still alive, which is a good thing. Still critical too, but we got her through the night, which is a tremendous victory."

"Is there any way to get us in to see her?" I asked, knowing that was probably impossible, but I was still struggling with some serious guilt about not being there for her in time to prevent the attack the day before.

"Oh, no, I'm sorry. Not only is that against hospital policy, but they've stationed a guard outside her door, and nobody but immediate family is allowed to visit her."

"They've stationed a guard?" I repeated.

"Yes, that's typical in cases where there's been an attack on someone's life—especially this close to the hospital. She really was lucky she was right next door at the senior center."

And there it was—that elusive thread tugging at me again. Kendra had been at the senior center for a reason, and I assumed that reason was to interview Lester . . . but the odd thing that I couldn't quite figure out was that, in the photo from Kendra's phone, Lester's face wasn't visible, and Raymond Eades's face was only partially visible. Had Kendra really recognized Ray? Had she been following him around all day and discovered he was a friend to Lester? *Why* had Kendra been so ready to meet me at the senior center and *what* had she wanted me to work out from the photo?

And then I had another idea and begged off the line with Courtney. I then called the TV station where Kendra worked and asked to be put through to her producer. "Campbell," a man barked into the line when he picked it up.

"Uh, hello, Mr. Campbell, this is M. J. Holliday calling—"

"M. J. Holliday?" he repeated. "*The* M. J. Holliday? The person who saved my reporter's life yesterday?"

I blushed. "Uh, I don't know about that, sir, but my boyfriend and I were the ones who found her after she'd been attacked."

"You calling to get an update on her condition?" he asked me.

"No, sir. I mean, I've got a source who tells me that she's still critical, but she's made it through the first night, so that's a positive sign."

"Yeah, that's all we know too. So what can I do for you?"

"I was on my way to meet Kendra when she was attacked, and she had a lead on this Brook Astor investigation that she wanted to talk to me about, but she never got a chance to tell me about it. I'm wondering if she talked to you or any of your staff about what she might've discovered."

"She didn't talk to me about anything new, but that's pretty common with Kendra. She doesn't bring me something until it's solid. You might want to check with her assistant, though. Chandler's usually in the loop on this stuff. She should know something."

"Chandler?" I asked, moving over to the pen and paper I kept in the kitchen to write the name down. "How do I reach her?"

"I'll patch you through. I think she's out right now, but she's pretty good about returning voice mails. Hold on a sec and I'll send you over."

Kendra's producer clicked off the line before I could ask for Chandler's direct number. A moment later I was listening to a voice recording of Chandler Wilcox, who sounded all of sixteen years old. I was sure she was older than that, but probably not by much.

At the sound of the beep I said, "Chandler, this is M. J. Holliday. I was working on an investigation with Kendra Knight and supposed to meet with Kendra when she was attacked yesterday afternoon. I know she had discovered something she wanted to tell me about, but she never got the chance. I'm wondering if you might know what lead Kendra had discovered that she might've wanted to share with me. If you could please return my

call as soon as possible, I would very much appreciate it."
I then left my number, repeating it twice, and hung up.

Heath came back from his run at that moment and he
swept me up into his arms. "You're sweaty," I said, and I
couldn't help the small giggle that came out when he
twirled me around.

"I'm horny," he said, dipping down to nibble at my
neck.

"Oh, you're always horny," I said, pretending to push
him away.

He then pulled his head back and in an instant his
expression changed. "Hello, Mary," he said, and I froze.
Heath blinked and instantly let go of me. Backing away,
he put his hands to his head and said in a strained voice,
"Run!"

"Heath!" I cried out, reaching for him.

"Get out!" he yelled, backing farther away from me.
"Em, just get the hell outta here right now, okay?"

"Call Whitefeather!"

Heath's voice became even more strained. *"I am!"*

I was trembling and I didn't know what to do. Heath
backed farther away from me, and I could see he was
trying hard not to look at me. "Where's the vest?"

"Bedroom," I said, taking a step in that direction.

"No!" he said. "Just get out of here until I can get this
thing out of my head!"

I fought back the tears of fear and frustration that were
forming at the corners of my eyes and finally grabbed my
messenger bag, my cell, and flew out of the condo.

I made it down the steps and to Gilley's door. I
knocked hard and tried the knob, but it was locked. "Gilley!" I called desperately. I didn't know what to do to
help Heath. Sy's appearance had happened so unexpectedly, and I was terrified that Heath seemed to be struggling mightily against the evil spirit.

The door opened as I pounded on it and Gilley stood there with a wicked look on his face. He wasn't wearing his vest, but he was holding a very sharp knife. "Hello, Mary," he said. "I was wondering when you'd come by for our date. . . ."

As if in slow motion I saw the knife start to arc up toward me and I leaped back, taking several blind steps backward. *"Heath!"* I screamed as I tripped and went falling down the stairs. I rolled down several steps, feeling every hard bump, until I could stop myself. Twisting myself around, I saw Gilley on the landing, still holding that knife and looking like he was getting ready to come after me.

"HEATH!"

Up the stairs I heard a door open. "Em?!"

"He's got Gilley!" I shouted, scrambling to my feet and heading down several more stairs.

"Run!" I heard Heath shout. "Em, *run!*"

I didn't wait around for him to yell it again. I turned tail and got the hell out of there.

Chapter 15

I didn't stay at the condo. Instead I got in my car and drove like a bat out of hell, gripping the steering wheel and bawling my eyes out. I reached for the phone several times to call the police, but each time I stopped myself. What was I going to say? That my best friend was possessed by an evil spirit that also was making an attempt to possess my boyfriend and both of them were trying to kill me?

It was all so crazy I could hardly believe it myself. I did finally call Heath, but it went straight to voice mail, and I wondered if Sy had drained the battery again. I tried Gilley's line next, and got the same thing. "Dammit!" I yelled, striking the steering wheel with my palm. Knowing I might be a bit of a road hazard, I pulled over and tried to collect myself. There was no one I could call and nothing I could do until either Heath or Gilley called me.

Except . . .

I wiped my eyes and wondered if I had the courage to

face Lester alone. After a little debate with myself, I decided I did have the courage and drove straight to the senior center. I found Daisy again and she called down to Lester's room. He was up and agreed to have a visitor, and then Daisy gave me directions. "He's got one of the best rooms with a garden view," she said. "It's the end unit all the way down corridor B on the right-hand side. Here's a map. It'll help."

I took the map and referred to it several times as I navigated the maze of hallways on the way to Lester's room. I found him groggy but sitting up in bed, watching TV. "The lovely lass from this morning," he said when he spotted me. "Hello, young lady. To what do I owe the pleasure of your company?"

I closed the door and moved to his bedside. "Mr. Akers, my name is M. J. Holliday, and I'm investigating a murder. A woman named Brook Astor was viciously attacked a week ago outside her apartment on Commonwealth Avenue."

I watched Lester's face very closely, and as I suspected, it registered first confusion, then great shock and sadness. "Brook?" he said. "You mean, Brook Astor from the fund-raiser?"

"Yes."

"Oh, no," he said. "Oh, that's terrible."

"Mr. Akers, I want to talk to you about your brother."

Lester's expression immediately darkened and became wary. "My brother?" he said. "My brother's been dead for over forty years, M.J."

"Yes, but Sy the Slayer has been hard at work, hasn't he?"

Lester's face drained of color and his mouth fell open. "How do you know about him?"

"Because he's been taking over the minds of various men throughout the years, Mr. Akers. He's been haunting them day and night, but mostly at night. He's been coaxing their mean streaks, their anger, and maybe even their psychosis, and he's been encouraging them to kill. He's also had them all use the same weapon to carry out their evil deeds."

"No," Akers said, shaking his head vehemently. "No, I've got him under control."

My brow shot up. "*You* have him under control?"

Akers seemed to understand he'd said something incriminating. "I . . . I . . . I mean . . ."

"You mean you *know* your brother's ghost is around?"

Lester shut his mouth and stared at me for a long moment, defiant. I met his gaze and mine didn't waver. At last I saw the defiance fade, quickly replaced by guilt. "Sy showed up in my dreams after his death," he admitted at last.

I narrowed my eyes at him. Time to drop another bomb. "You mean, he showed up in your dreams after *you* took care of him out in the woods, right?"

Lester's eyes widened and his mouth pressed into a thin line. I could see I'd hit on the truth. "Sy was never quite right in the head," he began softly. "My earliest memories are full of his cruelty to me, to our pets, to other childhood friends. He had a fascination with blood. He liked the smell of it, the taste of it. It was like an addiction to him. He seemed to thirst for it, and it scared our parents to the point that they wouldn't let Sy out of their sight. My dad would take him hunting, hoping to satisfy Sy's sick need, but it only seemed to excite my brother even more, and eventually Dad stopped taking him. Then he nearly killed me in a fight we had when I was seventeen and my parents told me it was best if I moved out. So I did, and they were stuck with him.

"The stress of dealing with Sy's psychosis took its toll on my parents. My dad had a heart attack when he was only forty-five, and Mom got cancer only five years later. During the last year of her life, girls in our neighborhood started dying. Mom and I both suspected Sy, and when he was brought in by police for questioning, he named me as his alibi. Mom was in the hospital, on her death-bed, and she begged me to cover for him, so like a fool I did.

"After we buried her, I told Sy that I would never cover for him again, and if he tried to hurt another girl, I'd personally turn him in."

Lester's voice broke at that moment and he had to look away. I gave him a little time, then said, "What happened when you threatened to do that, Mr. Akers?"

Lester cleared his throat and turned back to me. "He tried to kill my fiancée, Rosie," he whispered, and he looked so pained that my heart went out to him. "She knew all about Sy, and what my mother had asked me to do for him. I tried to keep her a secret from him, but he learned about her soon enough. She would go to the hospital to look in on Mom, and she told me that she and Sy met one afternoon. Sy had been so charming, and I knew she wondered if all my stories about him were true, but she trusted me, and the next time she saw him at my mother's bedside, she avoided him. Then, as if he knew she was trying to avoid him, he started showing up at the flower shop where she worked, and once or twice he tried to pretend he was me, but Rosie knew better. She told me it was in his eyes and the fact that he always called her Mary instead of Rosie or Rosemary. Then he started bumping into her at the market, or at the library, and I began to really worry about his interest in her. I worked long hours—I was a train conductor back then—and I couldn't always be around to protect Rosie, so, before I even had the money for a decent ring, I popped the question and told her I wanted to get married right away.

"Back then you couldn't live together unless you were married, and moving her into my new house was the only way I knew to protect her. Then, one night a week before our wedding, Rosie was on her way over to my place to drop off a dinner she'd made special for me when Sy came up behind her and slit her throat. A man walking his dog saw the attack, but not the face of the man who tried to murder Rose. He got to her and helped keep her alive until an ambulance came, and I've thanked God every day since for that man—otherwise I know Sy would've made sure to finish the deed.

"Still, after I got to the hospital, I wasn't a hundred percent sure it was Sy, and Rosie mouthed 'No' when the police asked her if she'd seen who attacked her, but the minute they left, she reached for a pen and paper and wrote down Sy's name to show me. Then she tore it up into tiny pieces. She knew it'd be awful for me if there was a trial. I'd have to admit that I'd lied about Sy's alibi, and I bore the exact face of a killer, which would've been plastered across every newspaper in Boston. Rosie trusted me to protect her from any further harm. She knew I'd take care of it."

I nodded. "And *you* knew that he'd attack her again, or someone else, unless something was done."

Lester seemed to hesitate and I could feel him begin to retreat away from me, as if he was realizing he'd already said too much. I had to hear more, so I decided to use everything in my arsenal to coax the truth out of him. "Mr. Akers," I said, "I think you should know that I'm a spirit medium. I can connect with souls that have moved across to the other side."

Lester's eyes shone with interest. "You are?" he asked. "I believe in stuff like that, M.J."

"Good. Because next to me is your wife, Rosemary." I opened up my energy fully to Lester's deceased wife and she filled my mind with something that looked like a gesture. I felt compelled to take my right hand and tap my chest, then cross both my arms and point to Lester. And then I repeated the first part of the gesture, tapped my chin, and pointed again to him.

Lester's eyes misted. "You know sign?"

"No," I said. "That was from Rose. What does it mean?"

Lester mimicked my gesture, but his was more pronounced. "I love you," he said as he made the first movements. "I miss you," he said for the second set.

"She's here," I told him. "She says to thank you for burying her in that blue dress. It wasn't her favorite, but she knew it was yours, and it was important to you to see her one last time in it."

Lester made a noise that was a half-sob, half-choking sound and he pushed his fist up to his mouth. He then started to sign in earnest, but there were no words to accompany the gestures. "I don't understand sign," I said. "I'm sorry. I have no idea what you said."

"Can Rosie see me?" he asked.

"She can."

"Then she knows what I said," he told me, wiping his eyes.

"Do you trust me enough now to tell me what happened to your brother?"

Lester took several deep breaths and stared at his lap for a long time. At last he said, "He liked to hunt on weekends. I knew his habits. I also knew what I had to do."

"Where's the knife?" I asked. I suspected he had it.

"The one he used against her? I don't know. I searched his hunting shack and never found it. I looked all over the house for it too, but I couldn't find it there either. It was his favorite hunting knife. Dad gave it to him when Sy turned sixteen. It was the same knife he used on me when we got into it that time before my folks told me I had to leave. I know Dad tried to take it away from Sy, but he told me he couldn't find it. The bastard had hidden it good. I know it's the one he used on Rosie and the other girls. There was something evil in Sy. Something demonic."

"I believe it," I told him. "Tell me when his ghost started showing up."

Lester shook his head and stared at the blanket across his legs. He looked so much frailer than when I'd met him that morning. "It was a few years after Rosie and me got married," he said. "She spent weeks in the hospital after the attack recovering, and she and I had to learn how to sign, but we never brought up the subject of my brother again after I showed her the article in the paper about Sy's hunting accident. Rosie had simply nodded and squeezed my hand, and I admit I never loved her more than in that moment. We married a few days before she was released—the hospital pastor did the honors. Rosie came home to my house and we adjusted to our new life together and it was wonderful for several years. We tried to have kids, but it never worked out for us, which was okay because we still had each other."

Lester's eyes misted and he wiped them with his sleeve. I was moved by the love he carried for his deceased wife and subtly I felt her energy come stand next to me again, but I didn't want to distract Lester, so I waited for him to continue. "Anyway, I thought our life together was perfect until one night I woke up and I couldn't move. What was even stranger was that I was lying in the middle of the living room of my parents' house. And then out of the kitchen walked Sy with that hunting knife in his hand and a terrible look in his eye.

"I couldn't make any sense of it, because everything about the dream felt so real, except I was totally paralyzed and my dead brother was about to stab me. And then Sy put his foot on my chest, just to show me that I was no match for him, and then he stabbed me, right in the abdomen. I felt the knife. I felt the searing pain of it and I felt myself bleeding to death, and then I blacked out."

I was a little stunned by Lester's story. It was very similar to the OBE I'd had, and with a shudder I wondered, if Heath hadn't shown up and rescued me, would I have been stabbed too?

"When I came to, I was back in my bed, but in agony. Rosie got me to the doctor, and I had a severe kidney infection that no one could figure out the source of. And for years I was plagued by them, and then, about six years ago, they found cancer in my left kidney, which then spread to my bones. I know it sounds crazy, but I'm convinced Sy was the cause of it."

I nodded to let Les know that I thought so too. His brother was a powerfully evil force, capable of causing great harm, so it seemed plausible to me that he'd been responsible for the poison that put a tumor into Lester's kidney.

"Anyway, Sy kept coming into my dreams, not every night, but often enough that I'd lose sleep. I told Rosie what was happening and she got me sleeping pills, but they didn't work and then the dreams got worse. Soon Sy was coming into the room with a poor girl in his grip and he'd stab her right in front of me, then slit her throat. It was terrible, and I started avoiding going to bed. I'd get up and pace the room, trying to stay awake until I was so tired that I'd fall asleep and not dream, but I was also so sleep deprived that I started making mistakes at work.

"One day when I almost took my train down the wrong set of tracks, which would've been a disaster, Rosie put her foot down and told me we had to do something. She said she'd been doing some research and she found this spiritualist—he was an Indian medicine man or something—and he said he could help me. With no other option I gave in and decided to go see him. At his house he brought me to this tepee-looking thing and sat me down in the middle of it. Then he gave me some sort of potion and he told me he'd sit with me while the potion took effect. Then, the craziest thing happened: I was back inside my parents' house, and Sy was there too, but this time I wasn't paralyzed. Sy came at both of us, and me and the medicine man fought Sy to the ground. Then the medicine man told Sy that he'd given me a powerful potion, and that I was now Sy's master. He'd never again bring me to that place and paralyze me. I was free to fight him, and the medicine man made sure to let Sy know I was stronger because I was connected to the world of the living. He also told Sy that he would join me whenever I came to that place and help keep Sy in check."

"And what happened?" I asked, because I knew that Lester hadn't been able to stop his evil brother from haunting others and influencing their thoughts.

"Well, it worked for about a year. Every time I found myself in my parents' living room, I was joined by the medicine man and we fought Sy to the ground each time. But then one day, when I was back in the hospital with another kidney infection, I woke up to find myself alone with Sy—there was no sign of the medicine man. My brother and I fought one-on-one, but I was so tired from the infection, and Sy won. He laughed when he'd beaten me and said that from now on the odds were even. I learned a few days later that the medicine man who'd helped me was killed in a car accident.

"Over the years I've had many fights with my brother. I've won most of them, but there're times when I've been sick with a kidney infection or something else and I've lost the battle and it's those times that I feel him get away from me."

"Did you or Ray know he was haunting the men who rented the house on Stoughton Street?" I asked next.

Lester's face fell and he stared again at the blanket. "Ray doesn't know a thing about it, and I didn't at first either," he said. "I just thought that house might be attracting bad men. It didn't dawn on me that Sy was behind it until Dan Foster's trial. And then Ray told me a few days ago that the last tenant had been arrested for murder, and I started to think that maybe we should just let that house stand vacant. He's over there, M.J. My brother has found a way to get loose from me and he's over there now."

"He's been very active lately," I said, and then I stepped away from Lester and opened up my sixth sense to really look at him. What I saw astonished me.

The ether all around Lester vibrated in a way that I was used to seeing in haunted houses, but usually that type of vibration was visible to my eye only in a central location like a wall, or a stairwell, or a small patch of ground.

What I realized was that Lester Akers was the portal his brother was using to come and go from one realm to another. What that medicine man had intended to do, I couldn't say, but what he had actually done was turn Lester into the portal for his brother. I had never in all my years of ghostbusting even heard of such a thing, but it explained how Sy the Slayer was able to move about so freely. If his portal was tied not to a house but to a living being, then he could draw energy from his brother and go where he pleased.

I then let my eyes travel to Lester's crippled form, and I realized that the infections and the cancer that had spread unchecked to the man's bones were probably a result of all that energy being slowly drained away from him by his brother.

"You're the key," I said to Lester. "Or rather, you're the doorway."

"I'm the what?" he asked, and there was a hint of fear in his voice.

"Your brother has gone from being imprisoned by you to using you as his portal, Mr. Akers. As long as you're alive and in a weakened condition, he can use you to come and go as he pleases." I went on to explain what a portal was, and what I thought the medicine man had done in creating a portal for Sy that was bound by Lester's body. "I can't tell you how unusual that is, Mr. Akers. I've not only never heard of a person acting as a portal before today—I never even thought it was possible."

Lester's shoulders sagged. "I'm so tired," he said. "I've been trying to keep him contained for thirty years, and I'm so very tired."

I reached out and squeezed his hand. "I can't imagine." The truth was, though, that I had no idea how to shut down a human portal. The only thing I could think of was to take off my vest and hand it over to him. "Lester, until I figure this whole thing out, do me one favor. Keep this near you at all times. Wear it if you can, okay?"

He took the vest and his arm dipped with the weight of it. "What's in here?" he asked, feeling the bubbles.

"Magnets. They should help keep that portal under control until I figure out what to do."

"What do you usually do with portals?" Lester asked curiously.

I grinned sideways and reached into my messenger bag, pulling out several magnetic stakes that I had taken out of my car just in case there was trouble with Lester. I put them in a line on the bed so he could see. "Usually we drive a few of these babies right into them. But in your case, how about we find another, less invasive way to handle this?"

Lester chuckled and picked up one of the stakes to examine it. He then tapped it against the base of his lamp and it stuck tight. He took it off the lamp and hovered it over his chest. "I'm a little like a vampire, huh? You need to drive a stake through my heart to keep the bad stuff from hurting people."

I shook my head and touched the vest now resting on his legs. "The vest will work just fine for now until I can try to come up with something else. Like I said, it's important for you to keep that close."

Lester handed me back the stake and saluted. "Yes ma'am. I'll keep it close, but come up with something soon, okay?"

My phone rang at that moment and I glanced at the ID, hoping it was Heath. It was. "I will, Mr. Akers, but would you please excuse me for one second, I have to take this call."

Lester waved at me to go ahead and I moved to the hallway to answer the phone. Hello?" I said. "Heath?"

"It's all clear," he told me. "I had to hold Gilley down for the past half hour. He fought me tooth and nail and I couldn't even let go long enough to get a vest on him, but about three minutes ago Sy gave up or just left. I'm not sure which."

I glanced behind me toward Lester's door. I wondered if putting the vest on Lester had been enough to yank Sy away from Gilley. I hoped so. "I'm on my way back," I told him.

"Where are you?" he asked.

"Uh . . . ," I said, thinking there was no way I was going to let him know I'd gone back to the senior center on my own. At least not until I got home. "I'm at the coffee shop. Can I bring you back something?"

"Sure," Heath said. "But stop off on your way home and get something stronger to put in it. I could use a drink after my wrestling match with Gil."

I laughed, so relieved that he sounded like himself again. "I'll be home in a little bit. Stay safe until then, okay?"

"I've got my vest on," Heath said, which reminded me about Mr. Akers back in the room. "But get home soon. I'm gonna worry about you until we catch this guy."

"I'm on my way," I promised. After hanging up with Heath, I went back into Lester's room and said, "I'm so sorry, but I've got to go. I'll come back a little later and check on you, okay?"

"Can you come back around eight?" he asked as I began to gather up the spikes still lined up on his bed. "No one comes by between eight and ten, and a man gets lonely."

I tucked the spikes into my messenger bag and gave him a thumbs-up. "I'll be here," I promised. Lester smiled but it wasn't the carefree smile he'd graced me with that morning. It was forced and I could tell he was still anxious about what I'd told him, about being a portal for his brother.

"Try not to worry, Mr. Akers," I told him, squeezing his hand. "I swear to you that my associates and I won't rest until we come up with a plan to deal with your brother's ghost."

"Thank you, M.J.," he said, squeezing my hand in return. "You're very kind."

I left Akers and headed out into the hallway, my mind a whirl of thoughts. I had no idea how to deal with a human portal, and I was worried that there might be no good long-term solution. What's more, I still didn't know who might've killed Brook and attacked Kendra.

As I was trying to navigate the hallways to the exit, my phone went off again. "Hello?"

"M.J.?" said a high squeaky voice. "This is Chandler Wilcox. Kendra's assistant?"

"Oh, Chandler, thank you so much for returning my call," I said. "And I'm so sorry about Kendra."

Chandler's voice cracked a little as she thanked me, but she pulled herself together and got to the heart of the matter. "I went through all of Kendra's notes, and the last thing she had me research was Brook Astor's legal name."

My brow furrowed. "Her legal name?" I said.

"Yes. She wanted to know if Astor was Brook's married last name, or her maiden name."

"That's weird," I said, at last coming out of the maze to the automatic doors of the front entrance. "Which one was it?"

"It was her maiden name. She changed it from Lucas back to Astor right after her divorce."

"Huh," I said. "I wonder why that was important."

"There's nothing else in the notes," Chandler said. "But I know she had me pull up all the research I could find on Brook yesterday afternoon. She wanted me to try and get a copy of the divorce decree too, but I got pulled in another direction by one of the other reporters, so I didn't have time to get to it, and Kendra said she'd handle it. The last time we talked, she was headed down to the public records department to hunt that down."

I stopped dead in my tracks. I'd been listening to Chandler, but something else had been tickling my thoughts. Something that was tugging on my mind so much that I felt I needed to pay attention to it. And then, I realized what it was, and I nearly dropped the phone as all the rest of the pieces hovered above their respective slots, ready to be cemented into place. "Chandler!" I said sharply, shaking with excitement.

"What?" she asked, alarmed.

"You said that Brook's married name was Lucas? Was that by any chance Mickey or Mike Lucas?"

"Yes. Dr. Mike Lucas."

"Oh, my God!" I said, leaning against my car. "I need you to do me one more favor, Chandler. I need you to see if you can locate a previous address for Dr. Lucas, see if he once lived on Stoughton Street—"

"He did," Chandler said. "Kendra asked for me to verify that for her yesterday."

I was trembling so much now that I almost couldn't manage to swing my messenger bag around to get into it and dig for Kendra's phone. At last I had my hand on it and pulled it up; clicking it on, I swiped to unlock it and there was the photo she'd been trying to show me. I searched the faces and spotted Dr. Mike Lucas in the back row, wearing a forced smile and glancing sideways at his ex-wife and Luke Decker, their arms around each other's waists.

I had one more call to make to completely cement my theory and I ended the call with Chandler and dialed Courtney's number. "Pick up!" I whispered as it rang. "Come on, Courtney, pick up!"

She did on what must've been the final ring. "I was just about to call you," she said. "I was on the other line with Luke, asking him where he'd learned about the rental house on Stoughton Street."

"What'd he say?" I asked.

"He said that someone wrote down the address and left it for him on his desk one day. He told me the note simply said that the anonymous person heard that he was trying to find a place to rent, and that the house was cheap and close to campus. He said he didn't even think about it until I asked."

I knew all too well who'd left that note. And I could clearly picture Dr. Lucas standing in front of Lester, holding out his right hand, which held those pills that made Lester so tired and weak and vulnerable to his brother's comings and goings.

And then I was grabbed from behind and yanked roughly backward into a choke hold. "Hello, you little bitch," Dr. Lucas whispered at the same moment I felt the tip of something sharp go into the side of my neck.

I made the only sound I could—a squeak of terror. I clutched the arm holding me and clawed at it, but the choke hold only intensified and I couldn't breathe. Little dots of light began to color my vision and I was lifted off the ground and carried several feet away from my car. With mounting panic I realized Lucas was carrying me toward the large fence that enclosed the Dumpster. Once we were around the other side of it, no one would see us.

I kicked and clawed for all I was worth, but the edges of my vision began to go dark. I was losing consciousness and nothing I did even slowed Lucas down. But then I remembered something I'd seen on TV a few years earlier. An expert in self-defense had suggested that if you were put into a choke hold, the best thing to do was to let your body go completely limp. This would force the attacker to bend forward, and put him off his center of gravity. From there, you could pivot and kick back against the extended leg of the attacker.

How all that made its way into my brain, I'll never know, but I did exactly as the instructor had suggested. Allowing my body to go completely limp went against every instinct I had, but I forced myself to do it, and it actually worked. Lucas bent forward, and the second he was bent almost double, I shifted my weight to one leg and kicked back as hard as I could with the other. I heard a loud snap and Lucas screamed in my ear. He let go of me quick and I tumbled out of his arms to the ground.

In turn, he fell too, and reached for his knee, holding it and howling with pain. I didn't wait around for him to get up again. Instead I scrambled to my feet, darted forward, and kicked him right in the face, also as hard as I could. I was mad enough to kill him in fact.

There was another sound that is best not described, but let's just say I was pretty sure I either broke or dislocated his jaw, and probably broke his nose to boot. The blow knocked the sense right out of him. He didn't pass out, but he looked close to fainting, so I staggered away from him to run for the door of the senior center, screaming bloody murder the whole way.

A considerable amount of chaos followed. Lucas was in no shape to do much but try to crawl away from the scene. He didn't get very far, and a large knife was found lying near where I'd drop-kicked his ass. A knife that had dried blood on it. When Souter showed up, she pulled me into a vacant room at the senior center and eyed me critically as I sat in the chair, trembling from head to toe. After eyeing me up and down, she said, "You look pretty shook-up, Holliday. You okay?"

I actually let out a small laugh. It was so absurd. This woman had been such a hard-ass and on my case for over a week, and I was shivering so much that my teeth were rattling while I pressed a small piece of gauze to my neck where the knife had nicked me. Souter's sudden concern was ridiculous. "I'll live, Detective."

She seemed to get it and her next move was unexpected. She got up, told me to sit tight, and ducked out the door. A few moments later she was back with two steaming coffees. Handing one to me, she said, "How 'bout those Bruins?"

I shook my head ruefully and sipped at the coffee. "I like them for the Cup," I said, laughing a little again.

"Yeah. Me too. They're wicked good." Souter added a wink and then she made a little more small talk, about the weather and such. At last the coffee and her relaxed attitude took effect and I stopped shivering. "You ready to tell me what happened?"

I nodded and got on with it. I told her everything, holding nothing back, not even my conversation with Lester Akers. I didn't care if she thought I was crazy, I knew I wasn't.

To her credit she listened to all of it without interruption except to have me elaborate on a point or two while she took detailed notes. When I was done, she leaned back in her chair, moved her reading glasses off her nose, and said, "So, let me get this straight: This Sylvester Akers possesses these men and gets them to commit murder?"

I shook my head. I'd seen too much of the real nature of the men listed in the closet to think that's what was going on. "No, but he does help draw out the psychotic nature of men already predisposed to violence. At best, I think he encourages them to act on their homicidal thoughts, and during the act of murder I think Sy is very much present, hence all the wounds made by a left-handed attacker. Sy enjoys the bloodlust and jumps into their minds to share the experience." And then I remembered Gilley standing in front of me in the doorway of his condo wielding a knife, and I knew that Sy had been getting stronger as his brother's condition worsened, and he was starting to influence the minds of innocent men too, like Luke and Gilley. I kept that part to myself, however, because I knew that Souter wasn't likely to understand.

Souter looked back at her notes. "Still," she said skeptically. "Seven homicidal men all living at some time in one house? That seems a little far-fetched, don't you think?"

I shook my head again. "Not to me. It's my experience that positive energy attracts positive energy, and negative energy attracts negative energy. I believe the men in question were drawn to that house by some inexplicable force they couldn't quite name. Once they were there, they became angrier, more withdrawn, and their thoughts grew darker and eventually turned to murder. But I also want to point out that, for the record, it's not seven homicidal men we're talking about—it's six, including Sy Akers. I believe that Murdering Mike and Lethal Luke were one and the same."

"Mike Lucas," she said.

"Yes."

She sighed and looked at her notes again. "We ran a quick background check on the good doctor and know what we found?"

"Another body?" I guessed. I knew deep in my bones that Lucas had killed before.

"Yeah. He had a girlfriend as a med student who was found stabbed to death in her apartment. Supposedly the doc found her and tried to revive her, before calling nine-one-one. She lived in a rough part of town with a dope dealer for a neighbor and he was a straight-A student, so nobody looked too closely at him as a suspect."

"Where was he living at the time?" I asked.

She tapped her finger on the table. "Stoughton Street."

"That's what I thought."

"In light of all this we're going to open that case back up. And now it looks like I'm going to relook at him for Brook Astor's murder, along with reopening the Gracie Stewart murder too."

"Ken Chamblis is someone you'll want to interview

for her murder. Talk to the bartender at Sheedy's—her name is Tracy. I don't know where Chamblis lives, but I'll bet you can track him down."

"Oh, we will," Souter said, making a few more notes.

"As for Brook Astor, I'm telling you, Dr. Lucas did it," I said. "And he tried to frame Luke Decker for it. He knew Luke and his wife had had an affair during their divorce."

"Yeah, we heard about that too, but he wasn't the father of her baby; that we know for sure."

"Do you think it was Dr. Lucas's?"

Souter shrugged, but then she shook her head. "I don't think so. One of the day nurses we interviewed said that Brook came to the hospital shortly before she was murdered to confirm her pregnancy. She'd confided to the nurse that she was dating somebody new—a guy who lived in L.A.—and it was getting pretty serious. Brook was thinking about moving out there to be with him, and we were able to eliminate the new boyfriend as a suspect. We thought that'd point to Decker as the killer more firmly, but then we couldn't figure out how he might know about her pregnancy until we learned that any of the hospital staff could easily access Brook's medical files. I figured maybe Dr. Decker had poked around where she didn't belong and had passed on the info to her little brother, but that theory always bothered me because Luke and Brook had split up a full year before. And I couldn't see Dr. Decker risking her medical license to pass on the news of the pregnancy to Luke. I mean, she's a smart lady. Why would she want to stir up trouble?"

"She didn't," I said. "It was Dr. Lucas who accessed the medical records. I think he found out she'd been to the clinic, started looking into her medical records, and discovered the pregnancy. Maybe he even knew about the guy in L.A. I bet he killed her because she'd had the nerve to leave him when she discovered he was cheating on her, and not even a year later she's having another man's child. He's the type to want to get revenge for something like that, and I'll bet he thought it was a pretty clever idea to frame Decker for her murder while he was at it."

Souter nodded, but I could tell she'd wait until after she had a chance to interview Lucas to confirm our suspicion.

"The thing I don't know," I said, "is what was Brook doing on Comm Avenue in the middle of the night?"

"She got a series of phone calls on her cell from an unidentified number," Souter told me. "It came from a burner phone and we were pretty sure it was the murderer luring her there. I wanted to make it stick that the calls were all made by Decker, but the first two calls came into her cell while you had Decker under surveillance. We confirmed the time stamp on your end, and in the video Decker's sleeping like a baby while Brook's phone is ringing with whoever was calling her on the burner phone."

"Lucas," I said. "He called her and somehow got her to go there."

"What I can't figure out," Souter said, "is how did Lucas know Decker was going to leave his sister's place that night so that he could frame him for murder?"

"It was Sy," I said. "This spook forms intimate relationships with the men he possesses. They share thoughts and ideas and I'll bet you that Dr. Lucas and Sy the Slayer had this all planned out for a long time. Our team was the wrinkle in their plan, though. And then I believe that Kendra made the connection between Dr. Lucas and his former residence on Stoughton Street and maybe she even discovered the murdered ex-girlfriend and put it all together. What she didn't know was that Dr. Lucas was probably keeping tabs on us, knowing we were close to figuring it all out. He kept Lester drugged so that he could take full advantage of Sy and maybe he found Kendra all alone in the parking lot and had the perfect opportunity to silence her."

Souter inhaled deeply and let it out in a sigh. "I hope that girl pulls through," she said.

"I have faith," I said, because I did.

Souter smiled. "Faith is good. All right, Holliday. I've kept you long enough. Your boyfriend and your partner are outside in the hallway pacing a groove in the floor. I'll let you go, but if you think of anything else you want to tell me, you call."

"I will," I promised.

Souter held the door open for me, and before I even knew what was happening, I was pulled forward and wrapped up in my boyfriend's arms. "Thank God, thank God, thank God," Heath whispered over and over as he carried me several steps down the hall.

"Hey, babe," I said, hugging him back just as tight. "I'm okay," I told him before he could even ask.

Heath didn't say anything; he just held me for a long time and I was so moved by his concern that I felt tears sting my eyes. "I swear I'm okay," I repeated.

Heath sighed into my neck. "Don't ever scare me like that again," he whispered.

"Deal."

Heath then set me down and kissed me lightly. I stepped back and was turning away when Gilley barreled into me and hugged me so fiercely that I couldn't breathe. He also made an attempt to lift me off my feet, but he only managed to stumble a few steps with me. "Gil," I squeaked. "I'm okay. Please ease up."

He released me and stepped back and I was so

touched to see that he was actually sobbing. *"You scared the hell out of us!"* he shrieked.

I winced but reached out to wipe at his cheeks. "I'm sorry. It wasn't on purpose."

"Don't do it again!"

I held up a hand, taking a vow. "I promise."

And then another figure stepped forward and I realized it was Steven, his face a mask of concern. "Are you hurt?" he asked me, lifting my chin to look at my neck.

"I'm fine."

He took my pulse and then stared deeply into my eyes and I realized how much he actually still cared about me. I felt a flush hit my cheeks and I was glad Heath was standing behind me and couldn't see my face. And then Steven seemed to catch himself and his expression became more clinical. "We were worried."

His fiancée then stepped forward and took up my hand. "I heard it all through the phone," she confessed. "I recognized Mike's voice, and everything clicked into place."

"Courtney was the one who called in the attack," Gilley said. "That's why the police got here so quick."

"And she called us," Heath said, with a note of gratitude.

"Well, it all turned out okay," I insisted, feeling suddenly exhausted. I glanced at a nearby clock. It was only ten after eight, but I was ready to go home and get into bed. I eyed the skeptical faces all around me and I tried to push a reassuring smile onto my lips. "Really, guys, everything is fine now."

But it wasn't.

No sooner were those words out of my mouth than the sounds of screaming erupted nearby as a nurse came running down the hallway. Souter, who'd been talking to a few other detectives just down from us, whirled around and the whole group was off in a flash. A chill ran up my spine and Heath grabbed my hand and our little group rushed after the detectives.

We were stopped by a male nurse in the hallway who warned us not to get close. "It's pretty bad," he said.

"What happened?" I asked anxiously. I couldn't be sure but I thought the commotion was coming from Lester's room.

"One of our residents fell just as the nurse was coming to give him his meds," he said. "He impaled himself with some sort of spike, and I think he's dead."

My jaw dropped and I reached around for my messenger bag. Digging through it, I counted the spikes in the bottom of the bag. I'd pulled seven from the car. There were only six in my bag. I hadn't even thought to count them when I'd come back in from the hallway after talking to Heath. And Lester's words about being like a vampire who needed a stake driven through his heart to stop the evil came back to me, and I knew—I just *knew*—what he'd done.

I turned away and pulled at Heath's hand. He followed me and I walked all the way outside to the back terrace before sinking to the pavement and dissolving into a puddle of tears. I'd never felt so guilty in all of my life.

Later we learned that Lester had left a note behind. It read simply,

It ends with me. Please bury me in this vest. It was given to me by a friend who refused to judge me, even though she knew all my sins.

Chapter 16

I met Steven at one of our favorite lunch spots. I'd told Heath that I had a hair appointment, which was true — I did have one, but not for an hour. I felt a little guilty about lying to him, but I knew it would only bug him if I told him the truth about this meeting with my ex.

Steven was five minutes late, but when he showed up, he looked more handsome than I'd ever remembered and my breath caught at the sight of him. What was surprising was that I wasn't moved by melancholy for what could have been, but joy at seeing someone I'd once loved deeply so happy. He radiated with it and it made him a stunning picture of a man.

After kissing me on the cheek, he sat down and said, "You're not coming to the wedding."

I smiled. "No. I could offer you a legitimate excuse, but I think we should be honest with each other, don't you?"

"We should," he said.

"I think it's a bad idea because as much as I know you love Courtney, and I love Heath, there's still a spark between us and I still care about you."

Steven looked at me for a long moment without commenting. Then he took my hand and kissed it before placing it over his heart. "There will always be a little bit of you in here," he said.

I nodded. "The same is true for me."

"You and Heath seem very happy together."

"We are."

"He takes good care of you?"

"The best."

"Then I'm happy for you."

"Me too."

"And . . . ," Steven said, his voice trailing off as if he was searching for the right words, "I don't know that I ever thanked you, M.J. For helping us with Luke. He's much better now and he's already reapplied for the fall semester."

"I'm so glad," I said. There'd been no signs of Sy the Slayer after Lester's death. "Did you hear about Dr. Lucas?"

"Yes, it's all over the hospital. He took the deal."

Lucas had made a full confession after the DA had offered him forty years with a chance for parole in 2044. It was a crap deal if you asked me, so little to pay for such an evil man, but the alternative had been millions of dollars of the state's money spent on a court trial and probably a similar sentence. Ken Chamblis had also been arrested for the murder of Gracie Stewart, which I gave Detective Souter huge props for.

"Did you hear about the old house?" Steven asked me.

"Gilley told me he saw it on the news. Burned to the ground in an electrical fire."

Steven nodded. "Good riddance."

"Good riddance is right," I agreed. "And how's Kendra's recovery?"

"She's making excellent progress," Steven said. "Courtney checked on her this morning and she'll be released next week and back on the air in no time."

I smiled again. "Good. Or maybe not so good. I owe her an interview."

"Yes, so I hear. And I also hear you're doing readings again?"

"I am, but only for the next week. Then Heath, Gilley, and I are heading down to Valdosta."

Steven's brow lifted. "You're going home?"

"My daddy is getting married."

Steven grinned. "Wedding bells are all around you," he said. "Maybe you and Heath should take a turn."

That made me laugh. "Oh, I think Gilley and his boyfriend, Michel, will beat us to that punch. I've never seen Gil so head over heels."

"Good for him. But I still say you and Heath should tie the knot. You're good for each other. And if you get married, I promise not to come to your wedding either."

I shook my head ruefully, but I was grinning ear to ear. We then ate lunch and laughed and talked like old times and it was really good. And then Steven paid the bill and held out his hand to me as I got up. "When you get back, let's keep in touch," he said.

I nodded, but it was the first time I'd been dishonest with him since meeting him there. "Let's."

As I looked at him, I could see reflected in Steven's eyes he knew that we wouldn't.

He then hugged me tight and kissed the top of my head and I felt tears touch the corners of my eyes. "I won't ever forget you, M.J.," he said.

"And I won't ever forget you."

With that, he stepped back, squeezed my hand one last time, and was gone. It was the last time I ever saw him, but it was a sweet ending all the same.

Read ahead for a sneak peek at the next
Ghost Hunter Mystery,

NO GHOULS ALLOWED

Coming in January 2015 from Obsidian.

"*This* is where you grew up?" my boyfriend, Heath, asked me as our van came to a stop.

I stared up at the large plantation home of my childhood and tried to see it through Heath's eyes. The stately six-bedroom, five-bath home sat atop a large hill, which I used to roll down when I was little. I had found such joy in rolling down that hill. And the grand, ancient sixty-foot oak tree that dominated the far right side of the yard, where I'd had a swing that I used to ride for hours. And the long wraparound porch, where I'd spent lazy summer days cuddled up with a good book and glass after glass of pink lemonade.

Of course, all of that was before my mother had died. Before all the joy went right out of my life and right out of that house.

Looking up at the dark redbrick manor with black shutters and a gleaming white porch, I could see that not much had changed about the house in thirty years. It still looked as grand, charming, and pristine as ever, but inside I could feel the ghosts that haunted the old Southern home. Literally.

"Are we there yet?" Gil yawned from the backseat. Gilley is my BFF. He's been my best friend for more than twenty years, so he knows my history well.

"We're here," Heath said, arching his back and stretching. It'd been a long drive from Boston to the southern Georgia city of Valdosta. "I didn't know this place was gonna be so . . . big."

Gil sat up and leaned forward. "M.J. didn't tell you?" he asked, like I wasn't in the van. "Her daddy's a very wealthy man."

I scowled. Gil made it sound like that was something to be proud of. But since my mother's death twenty-three years ago now, Daddy had always put his work before me, so I hardly thought it a positive thing. Plus, he'd never once offered to help me out in all those years Gil and I had struggled to make ends meet in Boston.

"Yeah, he'd have to be rich to afford this place," Heath said. My gaze shifted to him. He looked intimidated, and I thought I knew why. Heath came from far humbler—but perhaps more honorable—circumstances.

"Hey," I said, reaching for his hand. "It's his money, not mine."

Heath tore his eyes away from the house. "Yeah, but, Em, I mean . . . look at this place."

"It's just a house," I said, leaning in to give him a quick peck before getting out of the van.

As we exited the van, the front porch door opened and out stepped Daddy. My breath caught in surprise at the sight of him. I barely recognized the man standing there.

My father had always been a tall and imposing figure. Well over six feet tall, he'd been a big barrel of a man who'd gone prematurely gray, then silver, and whose countenance had always appeared to be tired and over-worked. The man on the porch, whom I hadn't seen in several years, was still tall and imposing, but he'd trimmed down by at least forty pounds—pounds that he'd always carried around his middle and that he really had needed to lose. His hair was also darker, but it suited him and made him look ten years younger, and his face, normally set in a deep frown, was actually lifted into an expression I'd never seen him wear. The man actually looked happy.

"You okay?" Heath whispered and I realized he'd come right up next to me and taken my hand.

"Yeah," I said, shaking my head a little. "He just looks—"

"Amazing," Gil said on the other side of me. "Lord, M.J., is that really Montgomery Holliday?

"Hey there, Mary Jane," my father called from the porch with a wave. "I was expectin' you a little later. Y'all must've made good time."

"Hey, Daddy," I replied as we headed up the walk toward the stairs. "We did make good time."

My father nodded and adopted something halfway between a grimace and a smile, but I couldn't really fault the man for it. If you don't ever smile even once in twenty years, I expect you'd be out of practice.

The porch door opened again and out stepped a lovely-looking woman perhaps in her late fifties or early sixties. She had a regal quality about her, with short-cropped and perfectly coiffed blond hair, bright blue eyes, and a trim figure. Her smile was brilliant and con-tagious, and she clapped her hands at the sight of us. "Ooo!" she exclaimed. "Monty, is this your daughter?"

I had climbed the steps and now stood in front of Daddy and the woman who must be his new fiancée,

Christine Bigelow. "This is her, dear," Daddy said, stepping forward to open up his arms to me.

For a moment, I just stood there, confused. Daddy hadn't hugged me since the day my mother died. In fact, that was perhaps the last day he'd ever touched me tenderly, so this open display of affection was throwing me a little, and I didn't know how to react.

Next to me I heard Gil clear his throat, then push me with his hand a little, and I sort of took two awkward steps forward. Daddy hugged me with three neat pats on the back before letting go. He continued to wear that strange half-smile, half-grimace too.

And then I was wrapped up in another hug from Christine. She squeezed me tight and added another "Ooo!" Then she stepped back and held me at arm's length. "Mary Jane, I have heard so many wonderful things about you! Your father simply raves about how smart and amazing his little girl is!"

"You have?" I said. "He does?" I wasn't trying to be a snot. I was actually really surprised that Daddy would say anything even remotely kind on my behalf. He'd spent decades letting everyone else know what a disappointment I was to him.

"Well, of course!" she said, and then her bright eyes turned to the two men at my side. "Now, don't tell me. Let me guess," she said to them. Pointing to Heath, she said, "You must be Heath Whitefeather, Mary Jane's boyfriend, and you," she said next, pointing to Gil, "must be Gilley Gillespie, Mary Jane's best friend. Am I right?"

"What gave it away?" Gil said, and I wanted to roll my eyes. Gilley was actually wearing mascara and blush today, along with blue nail polish. He loved flaunting his flamboyant side in my conservative Southern Baptist father's face.

"Your mama described her handsome son to a T,"

Christine told him slyly. The tactic worked: Gil blushed and I knew she'd just claimed another ally.

"It's very nice to meet you, ma'am," Heath said, extending his hand to her.

Christine laughed lightly and shook her head, stepping forward to hug Heath. "Oh, none of that formal stuff for family, Heath!" she said.

I hate to admit it, but the lovely warmth and charm of the woman had an effect on me. I liked her. A lot. And I couldn't understand what she'd first seen in my father, but looking at the dramatic change in him, I had to be grateful because it was a world of difference.

Once she'd had her fill of hugs, Christine took up my arm and Gilley's and said, "Now! Let's all step inside and have ourselves a proper lunch, shall we?"

We were all set to follow her and Daddy inside when a pickup truck came barreling up the drive at an alarming speed, honking its horn to get our attention. Daddy's posture and countenance changed in a second, and he edged forward to the top step, ready to handle whatever was to come next.

Heath moved over to stand next to Daddy, and I could tell that my father approved of the move and perhaps even of Heath at that moment. The truck came to a stop and out jumped a man in jeans, a plaid shirt, a stained cowboy hat, and work boots. "Mrs. Bigelow!" he called urgently.

"Clay," my father said, his voice full of the authority that used to send me scurrying.

Clay removed his hat and nodded to my father. He looked out of breath. "Mr. Holliday, sorry to trouble you, but we've had another situation at the work site."

Daddy moved down two steps toward Clay, and Heath followed him. Next to me, Christine stood rigid, biting her lip as if she knew the news was bad.

"It's another accident," Clay said.

"What happened?" Daddy demanded.

"The scaffolding in the ballroom gave way, sir. Two of my men were sent to the hospital."

"Oh, no!" Christine exclaimed. "Clay, are they badly injured?"

Clay clenched and unclenched his hat. "Not real bad, ma'am, but bad enough. Boone's got a busted ankle, and Darryl might have a broken arm."

Christine's posture relaxed a fraction. "Oh, that's dreadful," she said. "But I'm so grateful it wasn't worse! Monty, after lunch we should go straight to the hospital to see the men. And of course I'll cover their medical expenses."

"Now just hold on here," my father interjected. "Clay, that scaffolding is your responsibility. If it wasn't properly put together, Christine ain't gonna be responsible for no medical expenses."

It was Clay's turn to stiffen. "Mr. Holliday, sir, that scaffolding was put together right. Why, I checked it myself this morning. Just like I checked all the other equipment and rigging that's somehow managed to come apart, or blow up, or fail on us and cause nothing but accidents at this job site. It ain't us, sir."

"Well, then, who's responsible?" Daddy snapped.

Clay fiddled with his hat and looked at the ground. "It's like I told you last time, Mrs. Bigelow," he said, avoiding my father's sharp gaze. "We think your place is cursed, and, ma'am, I truly am sorry, but I'm pulling my crew."

"You're what?" Daddy roared loud enough for Clay to jump.

But the foreman wasn't backing down. Donning his hat, he looked directly at Christine and said, "I'm real sorry, ma'am. But that estate has somethin' bad creeping through those halls. I've tried to tell you that I don't think it's a good idea to keep messin' with it, and maybe you'd best cut your losses too, before you or someone you love gets hurt same as my men. Anyway, we're leaving. I just wanted to come tell y'all in person."

With that, he turned and headed back to his truck, even though Daddy called after him to come back and talk about it.

As Clay's pickup drove away, I turned to Christine. She looked stricken.

I knew from the gossip mill that Daddy's new fiancée—a wealthy widow from Florida—was also new to our small city. She'd purchased the estate of what had once been a prominent family here, the Porters of Valdosta, only six months earlier. She'd hired Daddy to represent her during the purchase, and Gilley's mama suggested that the two of them had taken to each other immediately. That Christine had managed to transform my old curmudgeonly father into a more youthful and happy man in such a short time was a true testament to her character, I thought.

And I also felt better knowing that it didn't appear she was after Daddy for his money. If she had enough cash to purchase and renovate the Porter estate, then she was well-off indeed.

The Porters had made their money through tobacco, but as smoking declined beginning in the nineteen eighties, so had the family fortune. Through mismanagement and family greed, much of the Porter's once-vast fortune had been squandered, and most of the family had fled Valdosta in shame.

A few members still lived in and around the area, but the estate, which the family had been trying to unload for decades, had become a huge tax burden. It too had fallen on hard times as it'd been all but abandoned since the early 2000s. The word was that Christine had picked it up for a song, but it needed so much in renovations that no one thought it a bargain.

"That's the third contractor to quit on us in as many months, Monty," Christine said, her voice holding a slight note of panic.

Daddy turned and came back up the steps, reaching out for her hand, which was still looped with mine. "Now, now, Christy, don't you worry. We'll find another, better contractor."

I could see that Christine's eyes were beginning to water, and she blinked rapidly to fight the tears. "But what if he's right?" she whispered. "Monty, what if there really is something in that old place causing all those accidents?"

Daddy adopted a patient look, but I could see he didn't believe a word of it. That didn't surprise me—even though I'd shown him enough evidence through the years to convince mostly anybody, Daddy never admitted that he believed in ghosts.

"Bah," he said. "Christy, Clay's just covering his tracks, is all! He's trying to avoid getting sued by his workers, honey. I'll bet money he didn't check that scaffolding, and it's his fault it fell down."

"We could check it out," Heath said suddenly. "M.J. and I could go over there and tell you for sure if there's a spook haunting the place."

My eyes cut to him and I shook my head subtly. But he was focused on Christine, who was obviously distressed. I knew he wanted to help, but he didn't know my father.

And just as I suspected, I saw Daddy's own eyes cut to Heath and his lips press together in a disapproving scowl.

But Christine had already stepped forward and

reached for Heath's hands. "Oh, would you?" she cried desperately. "I'd be most grateful, Heath." Turning to me, she added, "Most grateful to both of you!"

I stood there dumbstruck, not really believing what'd just happened. One minute we were headed in for a nice get-to-know-you lunch, and the next minute Heath was committing us to a ghostbust on our vacation. Which of course was my luck.

"It'd be our pleasure," Heath assured her, nodding his head and smiling encouragingly at me.

"Of—of course," I stammered as Christine hugged first Heath, then me and showered us with thank-yous.

Daddy cleared his throat, his irritation lessening but still simmering below the surface. "Well, now that's settled, maybe we can all go in now and enjoy our lunch."

As we filed into the house after Daddy, Gilley sidled up next to me wearing a mocking grin. He was enjoying this a little too much.

"Shut it," I hissed at him.

Gil adopted an injured expression. "I didn't say a word!"

I glared at him. "Oh, but you will."

"Well," Gil replied, "that's a given, sugar. That's a given."

ALSO AVAILABLE FROM
NEW YORK TIMES BESTSELLING AUTHOR
VICTORIA LAURIE

WHAT A GHOUL WANTS
A Ghost Hunter Mystery

M. J. Holliday has the unusual ability to talk to the dead. But when it comes to a vengeful ghost and a mysterious drowning, this time she may be in over her head....

AVAILABLE IN THE SERIES
What's a Ghoul to Do?
Demons Are a Ghoul's Best Friend
Ghouls Just Haunt to Have Fun
Ghouls Gone Wild
Ghouls, Ghouls, Ghouls
Ghoul Interrupted

Available wherever books are sold or
at penguin.com

ALSO AVAILABLE FROM
NEW YORK TIMES BESTSELLING AUTHOR

VICTORIA LAURIE

The Psychic Eye Mysteries

Abby Cooper is a psychic intuitive.
And trying to help the police solve crimes
seems like a good enough idea—but it
might land her in more trouble than even
she can see coming.

AVAILABLE IN THE SERIES

Available wherever books are sold or at
penguin.com

OM0014